The House
By The Sea

The House By The Sea

Anna Macklan

PIATKUS

Author's Note

In writing *The House By The Sea*, the author found the following works particularly helpful in providing background information on Ireland and Argentina, and on the events and historical figures of the period.

KEE, Robert — The Green Flag. 3 vols. Penguin, 1989

BOYLE, Andrew — The Riddle of Erskine Childers. Hutchinson, 1977

HAVERTY, Anne — Countess Markievica: An Independent Life.

CUNNINGHAME Graham, R.B. — Tales of the Horsemen. (From the Horses of the Conquest). Canongate, 1981

HUDSON, W.H. — Long Ago and Far Away. Dent, 1918. Reprinted, 1962

SCOBIE, James R. — Argentina: A City and a Nation. OUP. 2nd ed., 1971

First published in Great Britain in 1996 by
Judy Piatkus (Publishers) Ltd of
5 Windmill Street, London W1

The moral right of the author has been asserted

A catalogue record for this book is available from the British Library

ISBN 0-7499-0348-1

Set in 11/12pt Times by
Action Typesetting Ltd, Gloucester
Printed and bound in Great Britain by
Bookcraft (Bath) Ltd

Wintour Family Tree

- Richard Wintour b 1791 d 1860 m Maria Powell b 1803 d 1853
  - John b 1827 d 1892 m Ernestine Wills d 1891
    - John b 1861 d 1868
    - Matthew b 1863 d 1868
    - **Charlotte** b 1867 m. 1. Dudley Sarn 2. Rolf von Eberbach 3. Bill Paget
    - **Alice** b 1865 d 1920 m Richard
      - **Victor** b 1886 m Evelina Stonefield **(Evie)**
        - Richard **(Rickie)** b 1913
        - Claire b 1919
      - John **(Jack)** b 1887 d 1914
      - Beatrice Ernestine **(Tina)** b 1889 m **George Coxe**
      - **Melissa** b 1894 m Timothy Leifson
        - Timothy b 1922
  - Matthew b 1830 d 1895 m Constance Reynolds d 1899
    - Richard b 1862 d 1894 --- Mena Donovan d 1892
      - **Julio** (adopted by Lucio Castillo) b 1892 m **Sofia Almedo**
        - Francisco b 1917
        - Rosa b 1922
    - **Hester** b 1864 m **Daniel Molloy** d 1919
      - **Paul** b 1887
      - **Caitlin** b 1890
    - Marianne b 1866 m Everard Lister
      - Frederick b 1887 d 1917
      - Cicely b 1889
  - Beatrice b 1835 d 1890 m Enriques Sentos d 1883

Part 1

1907–1908

Chapter One

The August day, Victor Wintour's twenty-first birthday, was fading. As the sea lapped round the jetty at Carron and crawled up the sliver of beach, lights were appearing at the big house on the cliff at the end of the village. The Wintours were dressing for the celebrations. Not since 1848 had an heir to Belcarron reached his coming-of-age; in 1907, the family thought it had something to celebrate. What their Irish tenants thought was another matter, but they had danced and fiddled the night before, they had drunk Mr Victor's health and their own until the dawn streaked the sky. Now they were waiting to see the guests arrive for the ball.

A grand affair it was to be, with a marquee set up in the grounds and hired waiters and glasses coming all the way from Cork. Before the ball there was to be a dinner for the family and special guests, but that was to be at the house. No one envied Maisie, the cook, or Bridie and Peg, the maids, who would be running round in the heat of the kitchens, the poor things.

In her room overlooking the bay, Victor's mother, Alice, sat before her mirror fastening at her neck the Wintour pearls. She wore a gown of blue silk trimmed at the sleeves and on the train with lace and, in her still dark hair, Aunt Beatrice's diamond pin. For her age, which was forty-two, she looked well. A little heavier, perhaps, a little more dependent on good lacing than in her youth, but the years had been kind, she was still beautiful. Looking away from her reflection, Alice drew a pair of long kid gloves slowly over her fingers. Though willing to take every care with her appearance, beauty was not important to her now.

Belcarron was important. Until her time there had always been a son to inherit the land Cromwell had given her English ancestors, to run the estate from the house by the sea. But Alice's two young brothers lay in the churchyard. On the death of their father, John Wintour, Alice and her sister Charlotte had inherited Belcarron.

The present house was a square, white Georgian residence, built to replace an earlier house destroyed by fire. Alice had been born and spent her life there, apart from the years in the Argentine with her husband Richard. Richard was also her cousin. If Aunt Beatrice had not left him her *estancia*, John Wintour would have made him his heir, and Alice would rather have shared with Richard than Charlotte. Charlotte had done things Alice would never forgive and though it had taken almost every penny she could raise, she had bought her sister out. Now Charlotte was abroad, no one knew where, Richard was dead, and Alice was running Belcarron as she had run it very well for thirteen long, lonely years.

Time was passing; she should go, see that Victor was ready to greet his guests. Yet she lingered, taking a last look at Richard's photograph by her bed, at her mother's portrait of Mena, painted long ago when Mena had been a housemaid at Belcarron. Two faces from the past, two people locked in her heart. Straightening her shoulders, putting on her public face, Alice took her candle and opened the door.

Tina and Melissa, her daughters, came hurrying through the shadows to greet her, followed by their cousin Cecily.

'Mama, how beautiful you look in that blue!' cried Melissa, who at thirteen was being allowed to stay up for dinner as a special treat. 'Oh, why must I always wear this dreary white?'

'She's only saying that to make you say she looks beautiful too,' Tina said with a laugh. 'You know our Melissa!'

As Melissa shook back her yellow hair, which was tied with a blue velvet ribbon to match her sash, Alice smiled and said they all looked beautiful. They were so radiant, so buoyed with excitement, it seemed the truth, although only Melissa had inherited the Wintour good looks, and as they laughed and blushed, Alice's heart warmed to their happiness. She asked if they had seen Victor, and Tina told her he was still dressing. 'Loading himself with his new watch, new cuff links, cravat pin and cigar case – it must be lovely to be twenty-one!'

'I'd much rather be seventeen,' cried Melissa. 'Twenty-one – doesn't that seem rather old?'

As the girls, still laughing, held their skirts and ran down the stairs to the hall, Alice made her way to Victor's room, which had been her parents' and was one of the largest in the house. It should have been her own, but she preferred the room she had used as a girl and it seemed right for Victor to have the larger one. Whatever was best usually turned out to be Victor's.

He was standing at his mirror, brushing his blond hair with his new silver-backed brushes, a present from Richard's sister Hester in America, while the candlelight gleamed on the gold cuff links given him by Richard's second sister, Marianne. At the sight of him, so tall, so fair, so like his father, Alice felt a familiar stab of disappointment. So like, yet not like. Victor was not another Richard, she knew she should not expect it. She did not expect it of Jack, who was also tall and fair and had the Wintour nose, but dear Jack was his uncle Matthew all over again and in nature Victor was like no one at all.

It was only when he stood up from a chair in the shadows that Alice saw Jack too was in the room. With an indulgent smile, she noted that his tailcoat was already rumpled and his white tie a travesty, whereas Victor, as usual, looked as though he had stepped out of a bandbox.

'Good evening, Mother,' said Victor, giving her one of his casual smiles that always made her feel she was somehow excluded from his interest. 'Have you come to chivy me?'

'You know we mustn't keep dinner waiting, Victor.'

'I came to tell him that very thing,' said Jack.

'You mean, to get me to do your tie,' Victor retorted. 'For pity's sake, Mother, do it for him, or he'll disgrace us all.'

Alice, smiling, reached up and redid Jack's tie, straightening the fit of his coat and brushing off specks. 'There you are, Jack. Down you go! We really mustn't linger.'

Jack kissed her cheek. 'Thanks, Mother. I don't know what I'd do without you.'

'Why, one of these days you will find yourself a wife and she will take care of you, as your aunt Constance used to take care of Uncle Matthew.'

'No matchmaking,' Victor said firmly. 'We're not ready for wedding bells yet.'

'Of course not, Victor, you're both far too young!'

'Yes, so don't go pushing those Morry girls.'

'The Morry girls?' Alice exclaimed. 'They're children, Victor, younger than Melissa!'

'Which will make them just right for us in a few years' time, and I have the feeling you and Cavan Morry are already making plans. Thing is, we're not ready for the supreme sacrifice, are we, Jack?'

'Oh, stow it,' Jack replied uncomfortably. 'Uncle Cavan's been a good friend to us.'

'Indeed he has,' Alice flashed. 'Try to be more generous, Victor. This is your special day, remember.'

'You mustn't mind my little joke, Mother.' Victor smoothly took her arm. 'Of course, the Morry girls are sweet and Cavan's a brick. I know what he means to you.'

'Let's go down,' she said quietly and, as Victor opened the door for her, wondered why she had thought he was like no one at all. There were times when he reminded her all too clearly of Charlotte.

Chapter Two

It was Victor's stated opinion that the guest list for the dinner party couldn't have been more boring. All those old cousins and family friends – was a fellow to be yawned out of life because he had reached the age of twenty-one? After a steely look from his mother, however, and a reminder that his own friends would be coming to the ball, he had accepted with good grace and done his duty nobly. In reply to Cavan Morry's birthday toast, he surprised everyone with an excellent speech, thanking his mother and family for all they had been to him and the guests for their generosity, promising that they and Ireland would always be in his thoughts, especially in Argentina, where he was due to take up his share of his inheritance.

'Well done, old chap,' Jack whispered, as he sat down to applause, and Alice smiled at him with tears in her eyes.

'You're so right, Victor, we shall think of Ireland always.'

Edwardian Ireland was very different from the Ireland of Alice's youth. Since the death of Charles Parnell, the movement for Home Rule seemed to have gone into decline. 'Fallen asleep,' as one old campaigner put it, 'while the Sinn Feiners and Gaelic Leaguers make play.' The name Sinn Fein still meant very little but the Gaelic League was one of many societies trying to make Ireland look to its past, to find a character that had nothing to do with politics. W. B. Yeats and other writers were bringing back Ireland's old heroes in poetry and plays; people didn't need such heroes as Parnell any more, which might have pleased the landowners if they had not had other worries. The Land Purchase Act, designed to help tenants buy their own land, was to them the most sinister writing on the wall.

'Mark my words,' Bernard Mountain, Cavan's brother-in-law, growled over his coffee after dinner, 'when the tenants have been helped to buy all our land, there'll be no estates left. Just the big houses and nothing more, you'll see.'

Into the chill that followed this remark, Lionel Pearce, Alice's lawyer, murmured, 'I said it would come. Don't you remember, Mrs Wintour? When you first took over Belcarron? I said then that land-purchase schemes would change everything.'

'Because the terms are so generous!' Cavan cried. 'Tenants don't have to wait to buy land, they don't have to save, they are given the most handsome loans. But what is money to us without land? I know some owners are very willing to sell, but as I see it, this act is taking away what has been ours for centuries.'

'Should it have been?' asked Jack, but Tina knocked his arm so that he spilled his coffee.

Kitty Mountain called, 'No politics, please, this is a special occasion. Think of Victor.'

'Victor's the lucky one,' Bernard retorted. 'Isn't he going out to the Argentine, where landowners have the sense not to let the tenants own any land at all?'

'I believe people are calling it Argentina now,' Victor drawled, 'but what's in a name? It's a republic, it makes its own rules, and as far as I can see, the *estancieros* can do as they please. Which is why I believe it is the place for me. Now – should we all be moving to the marquee?'

Everyone declared the ball to be an immense success, the band excellent, the sprung floor of the marquee perfect. Even Jack, who was no dancer, managed a few waltzes, and Victor, doing his duty again, danced with everyone he was supposed to partner. But the most affecting moment for the older spectators came at the beginning of the evening, when Victor opened the ball with his mother and it was as though Richard Wintour lived again.

'Oh, poor Richard!' Marianne wailed into her handkerchief. 'Oh, I can't bear it, I really can't! It's too sad.'

Everard Lister, her clergyman husband, sitting next to her on a small gilt chair, said it was indeed.

'But you don't remember seeing them dance together as I do. Oh, heavens, that wonderful Fitzmirran ball we all went to! I can see them now, Richard and Alice, he so tall, just like Victor, and his hair so golden, and she so lovely, in pink, as I remember, yes, I'm sure it was rose pink...'

Marianne's red-rimmed eyes followed the graceful figures of Alice and Victor as they dipped and bowed and circled the floor alone, until gradually other couples joined them and Everard asked Marianne if she would like to dance. But she was deep in reminiscence, reminding him that it was at the Fitzmirran ball that Richard had proposed to Charlotte, only she had turned him down for Dudley Sarn and what a disaster that marriage had been, had it not?

'I never knew Richard had proposed to Charlotte before Alice,' Everard murmured, getting a word in at last, but Marianne gave a little scream of disbelief. Of course he knew! Everyone knew! Charlotte had seen to that, but it was the same night Hester had run away to Dublin with Uncle John's groom and no one could think of anything else at the time.

'I should think not,' Everard said with a shudder. 'How your sister could ever have taken up with a Catholic and a Fenian, I can't imagine.'

'And one who skipped bail and ran away from the law!'

'He did come back to face it, my dear, we must give him credit for that.'

'And they let him off! Said it was too long ago, all the witnesses were dead, or some such nonsense.'

'At least that makes it better for Hester. There is not the burden of disgrace she would have had to carry.'

'Which she should have carried,' Marianne snapped, colouring. 'Oh, but I wouldn't be her for a kingdom, money or no money! Nor Alice, come to that, though she has money too. You know she got half the *estancia* when Richard was murdered, and the other half went to the children? Now, in this country it would all have gone to Victor.'

'He's already heir to Belcarron, I don't think he need complain.'

'No, indeed.' Marianne's eyes were raking the dancers for

her daughter. 'Has he danced with Cecily yet, have you noticed?'

'Can't say I have, but shall we essay a waltz ourselves?'

Sedately taking the floor, they passed Tina whirling by in the arms of George Coxe, Mavis Morry's cheerful English cousin. He was a successful doctor in Westminster, but as he smiled down into his partner's face, he looked no more than a boy. Marianne whispered incredulously, 'Why, I do believe that young Dr Coxe is paying court to Tina!'

'Is that so surprising? Tina is attractive enough, and only eighteen.'

'Oh, yes, youth counts for a lot, of course, but Tina is not the beauty of the family and Alice says she's never been interested in admirers. She is said to like young men as friends.'

'I may be an unworldly clergyman, but I know how much truth there can ever be in that!'

'But Tina is very serious-minded, Alice says, and wants to do something worth while in her life. I do hope,' Marianne added with a sudden frown, 'that she is not going to turn out like Hester!'

'May I take you for some lemonade, Miss Wintour?' George Coxe asked, as the waltz came to an end. 'Or do you have someone waiting to dance with you?'

'Who knows?' Tina threw her dance card into her evening bag. 'I'd much rather have lemonade, anyway. Come on, let's go over to the house. We can sit on the stairs.'

'People are sitting on the stairs?' George asked, allowing himself to be pulled out of the marquee and across the grounds, where the Chinese lanterns in the trees swung in the night air.

'Of course. Means you can get away from all the eyes, if you understand me.' As they seated themselves on the elegant staircase, not too close to other couples, Tina added, 'I do wish you wouldn't call me Miss Wintour, you know. And I don't want to call you Dr Coxe – makes you sound too old.'

He flushed and hastily drank some lemonade. 'By your standards, I am old.'

'Why, how old are you, then?'

'I'd rather not say.'

'Twenty-nine? Thirty? Thirty-nine?'

'I'm thirty-six. And you're eighteen. You see, I'm twice your age.'

'Well, you won't always be,' she said reasonably. 'When I'm twenty-five, you won't be fifty. Look, you mustn't worry about your age. Everyone says you're very young to be such a brilliant physician and it's much more important to have achieved that, isn't it, than be a spotty boy straight out of school?'

'Oh, Miss Tina, you're so refreshing! May I ask you something? When I return to London, may I write to you?'

Her eyes showed her pleasure. 'You haven't forgotten I'm going away?'

His face fell. 'I didn't know. I thought only your brothers were to go to Argentina.'

'They're going to Argentina, I'm going to New York.'

'New York!'

'Yes, my cousins asked me long ago if I'd like to visit when I left school and Mama said I might. It's so exciting, you see, because I'll be making the trip by myself – well, except for Miss Wynne, my old governess. She's going out to a new post, so she'll sail with me, but it won't be the same as going with family, will it?'

'Certainly won't,' George agreed gravely. 'And are these cousins the Molloys I've heard about? The ones who run the bookshops?'

'It's Cousin Hester who runs the bookshops. Her husband Daniel – he was groom here once, you know – is an American Congressman.'

'Congressman!' George shook his head admiringly. 'You know, that's amazing. That's the sort of thing that really gives me hope.'

'Hope?'

'For the future. A future where Englishmen will not see Irishmen as ignorant Paddies incapable of running their own country.'

Tina raised her eyebrows. 'You're in favour of Home Rule, then?'

'Does that shock you?'

'No, but I dare say it shocks the Morrys.'

'Ah, we don't talk politics. But it's only since I've been

coming over to visit that I've seen the situation for myself. I may be an Englishman, but I can't accept it.'

'You mean England running Ireland?'

'I mean people who have nothing to do with Ireland running Ireland. Would you want Dublin running England?'

'The Wintours have been here for centuries, George. Do you say they have nothing to do with Ireland?'

Although his face had lit up at her use of his name, he nodded. 'I'm afraid I do say that. They came as conquerors, they are still conquerors. There will have to be change. I don't advocate violence –'

'Many Irishmen do.' Tina's manner had taken on a slight coolness which George did not miss. When he tried to maintain that the situation bred violence, that it was only to be expected in some cases, she shook her head. Her cousin Hester was passionately in favour of Irish independence, but never through violence. When Daniel Molloy had threatened violence to Belcarron years before, it had nearly broken Hester's heart. Terrible things had happened then. Aunt Charlotte's husband had been accidentally killed. Daniel had been charged with causing an affray and broken bail to run to America. 'So you see,' Tina finished, 'that's how the Molloys come to be where they are – through violence.'

'In their case, though, they have done well, haven't they?'

'Yes, it doesn't seem fair.'

'But it proves my point. Away from the situation at home, the Irish find themselves, they show what they can do.' George suddenly took Tina's hand. 'Let's not talk any more about other people,' he said urgently. 'Won't you give me your New York address, so I can write to you?'

Her coolness forgotten, Tina smiled radiantly. 'I'll give it to you now!' she cried.

It was the small hours before the carriages and the hired waiters had departed and Bernard Mountain's motor had coughed its way home to Schull. Alice and the family, with the Morrys and George Coxe, who were overnight guests, gathered in the hall for last drinks and candles, still the only form of upstairs lighting at Belcarron. The next morning the marquee would be taken down and packing begin for the Wintours' travels abroad.

Marianne asked about Melissa, who had already gone to bed. How would she manage with all the family away?

Alice replied, with a smile, that of course Melissa considered herself very ill used, but it was better she should not miss time from her boarding school and she would be spending Christmas with Mavis and Cavan, who were second parents to her, anyway.

'We're really looking forward to having her,' Mavis put in, and Alice gave her a grateful smile. 'Jack and I will soon be home,' she finished. 'I can't spend too long away from Belcarron and Jack must return to Oxford. It's bad enough Victor's not taking his degree, I don't want Jack to do the same.'

'As though I'd need a degree as an *estanciero*!' Victor exclaimed, setting down his glass.

Cavan Morry raised his eyebrows. 'You plan to be one, Victor?'

'Part of one, you might say. I only hold a small share in the *estancia*.'

'And I may come out and claim my bit,' Tina said with a laugh, but Victor did not smile.

'There is no question of your having to claim anything, Tina. Mother takes half and the rest of us share the other half equally. That is Argentine law.'

'Seems a good idea,' observed Freddie Lister, Marianne's tall, raw-boned son. 'Why don't we adopt it here?'

'Why indeed?' asked Jack.

'Younger sons have a hard time here, I suppose,' George remarked. 'But of course the estates are kept intact.'

'Exactly,' Victor snapped, 'and in my view that should happen in Argentina too. Now may I light candles for the ladies?'

One by one, people drifted upstairs, calling their goodnights, and poor Bridie was still waiting. Alice told her to go to bed too, she and Mr Victor would see to the lamps downstairs and lock up.

'I might in fact just fall asleep on my feet,' said Victor, as Bridie gratefully made off.

Alice kissed his cheek. 'It's been a good day, hasn't it?' she whispered.

'A splendid day. All thanks to you.'

'If only your father could have –' She stopped. After an awkward moment, Victor briefly touched her hand.

Their duties done, she watched him ascend the stairs, his yellow head drooping, his fingers already unloosening his white tie. Did she expect too much of him? It was natural he should want to see the land that was their second home, should want to do new things, meet new people. There was no doubt he found Belcarron dull.

But Jack does not, she thought. Jack is like me, he is only happy here.

But Jack would never inherit Belcarron, that was the pity of it.

Slowly, she climbed the stairs, the last of all the party to move through the quiet house to her bed.

Chapter Three

Alice found returning to the Argentine as painful as the opening of an old wound. She had been back only twice since Richard's death and would have liked never to go again, but Victor had reached his majority, there were formalities, she was needed. So, Buenos Aires must be faced again and this time the *estancia*, which would be worse. Not only must she meet its special memories, she must also meet Julio, Richard's son.

He was fifteen. She had not seen him since he was a baby, not since Paola, Lucio's wife, now dead, had taken pleasure in telling her that Richard was his father and had asked Lucio to adopt him. There had been bitterness, of course, for Julio's mother, who had died in childbirth, was Mena, Alice's maid and dear friend. But the bitterness had passed. Julio had become the son Lucio had always wanted. Probably he never saw, as Alice saw when she was shown Julio's photographs, that he was a perfect Wintour. Dark, not blond, but in every other respect as much Richard's son as Victor or Jack, who would be meeting him for the first time. At the thought of that meeting, Alice was filled with nervous dread. The secret she had kept for so long could not be kept for much longer.

As their ship moved slowly through the yellow waters of the Plata, Alice, concealing her fears from her sons, talked of the old days. This great, wide river they were negotiating was very shallow where it reached the port of Buenos Aires. In the past, ships had not been able to dock and passengers had had to complete the journey in small boats or even on the backs of strong men. Things would be easier today. Land had been reclaimed, there was a new waterfront, there was continual dredging. These changes, at least, were for the better.

'You mean some changes are not?' asked Jack, screwing up his eyes at the skyline of Buenos Aires which was coming into view through hazy, shimmering light.

'We shall have to wait and see,' Alice replied. 'Lucio tells me great things are being done. It would be absurd, of course, to expect the Argentine to stand still.'

Although their own memories of it were patchy, Victor and Jack knew something of the country they were approaching. They knew its history had been turbulent and that peace had been achieved only about the time their parents had arrived on honeymoon in 1885, to help Great-Aunt Beatrice run her *estancia*.

How on earth had Great-Aunt Beatrice ended up in Argentina? they once asked. They were told she had always been wild, had gone looking for adventure and found it on board ship for South America, where she met Enriques Sentos. His family were criollos, descendants of the first Spanish colonists of Argentina, who raised cattle on the pampas and spent their leisure in Buenos Aires. After he and Beatrice married, they travelled the country from the warm north to the cold south, and Beatrice adored it all, the mountains and the plains, the gauchos and wild horses, even being chased at times by hostile Indians. There was colour and excitement and danger in Argentine life and always had been, from the days of Spanish rule when the country was part of a vast viceroyalty, to independence and beyond. In fact, when everything settled down and there was peace and prosperity, Beatrice said she found it dull.

'But she didn't really object to the boom times,' Alice told her sons, with a smile. 'She always admitted, money could be exciting too.'

Those were Victor's sentiments. 'The way I see it,' he said now, taking off his hat to wipe his brow in the humid air, 'we should be damned – I mean, *very* – grateful to Great-Aunt Beatrice for leaving us the *estancia*. I know it's brought problems and there weren't always boom times –'

'Indeed there were not,' Alice returned quickly. 'There were bad times as well as good.'

'But you weathered them and whatever happens, people always seem to want Argentine beef, don't they?'

'That's true, of course. I've never said we should not be grateful.'

'And the way things are going at Belcarron, we'd have been in a sorry state without the cash from here, shouldn't we?'

'Mother knows that, Victor,' said Jack, 'don't rub it in.'

'We should be going below,' Alice told them, after a pause. 'We'll be coming into port soon.'

Fighting a way through the port of Buenos Aires was exhilarating or exhausting, depending on one's point of view, thought Alice, who was herself wearied by the noise and smells, the crowds and livestock, but who could see the interest on the faces of Victor and Jack. They made arrangements for their steamer trunks to be sent direct to the Avenida Lila, then hired an open carriage so that they might see something of the city before arriving at the old Sentos house.

'Lucio was right about the changes,' Alice remarked, as they drove through the capital and saw on every side splendid new parks and boulevards, new buildings going up and old buildings coming down. 'At least they seem to have left the colonial architecture alone.' She pointed out the great Catholic cathedral and the old viceregal and government buildings.

'I find it all very fine,' Victor commented, his eyes shining.

'Maybe, but to me too much is strange.' Alice put up her parasol. 'And how warm it is! At home, we should have been having the autumn gales by now. I never did like the seasons being so different here.'

'You are surely not missing the gales, Mother? This city is magnificent, I'm very impressed. It's my sort of place, I can tell.'

'Are you impressed, Jack?' Alice asked.

He pulled a little at his golden moustache. 'Too soon to say. It's certainly very fine, what we've seen, but it has a strange sort of character, hasn't it? Sort of mixed.'

'Cosmopolitan is the word,' Victor told him, 'and it's what I like. Anything that matters, I imagine you'd find it here.'

'So the *porteños* think,' Alice replied. 'To them, the Argentine *is* Buenos Aires.'

'It certainly has more motors than I've seen anywhere else,' Victor declared. 'I know we can't use them on the pampas, but I vote we get one for the city. What do you say, Jack?'

As Jack replied that he was all in favour, Alice shook her head.

'What is this fascination with motorcars? I really can't understand it.'

'Tina can. If we get one at home, she plans to learn to drive.'

'Tina . . .' Alice gave a long sigh. 'Oh, I do miss her! And Melissa. It's going to be so long till we see them again.'

'I'm sure the time will pass quickly,' Jack said comfortingly. He peered under Alice's parasol at her face, white with fatigue. 'Have you seen enough, Mother? Shall we find the house now?'

'Oh, please.' She lay back, gratefully. 'Tell the man to drive to the Avenida Lila.'

The old Spanish-style house in a quiet, unfashionable part of the city had not changed. Here was the door in the wall, the same clanging bell one had to ring to gain admittance, the lemon trees in the courtyard, the glass front door, open. And here was Vittoria, Beatrice's cook, who had taken over as housekeeper on Carlotta's retirement, waiting ecstatically to greet them.

Tall and strong and still dark-haired, she folded Alice in her arms, and then, at the sight of the handsome, golden sons, reborn Don Ricardos, wept a few happy tears. Some years before, her prayers to the Virgin for a husband had been answered in the shape of a widower, Jorge, who did not mind that she had no dowry and was glad to take over old Francisco's duties, driving a hired carriage when the family was there, acting as caretaker when they were not. Now he carried their hand luggage through the scented, shuttered rooms, followed by Vittoria, shouting instructions to her maids, while Alice moved silently out to the patio. This was the time she dreaded, when she must look out over the river and feel the presence of Richard and Aunt Beatrice, but know herself alone.

'All right, Mother?' Jack asked quietly.

She looked up, smiling, and pressed the hand he had laid on her shoulder. I should not think myself alone, she chided herself, not now.

'How much do you remember of this house?' she asked at dinner.

Very little, it appeared. It was the *estancia* that had remained in their minds.

'Especially the day of the *pampero*,' said Victor. 'I thought then we were all going to die, I thought the wind would just blow us all away, along with the dead birds.' He glanced at Jack and smiled. 'I don't suppose you remember much of that, Jack, you were under your bed most of the time. The same as when the gauchos killed a cow. My word, how you used to howl!'

'I don't apologise,' Jack said shortly. 'Anyone who didn't mind the way the gauchos slaughtered animals would need to be pretty callous.'

'The gauchos are a dying breed themselves now.'

'They'll still be killing things.'

'And you'll still be under your bed?' Victor smiled. 'Seems it's just as well I'm staying on, not you.'

'I'll leave you boys,' Alice murmured, rising. 'I'm so tired, I think I'll go straight up to bed. Don't be late, we have a lot to do tomorrow. First the bank, then the lawyer's.'

'I suppose I'll be signing papers all day?' asked Victor, as he and Jack got politely to their feet. 'It's quite something, coming of age.'

'Yes.' Alice hesitated. 'First, I'd like to go to Papa's grave.'

'Of course.' The brothers kissed their mother goodnight and, when she had left them, sat down again and lit cigars. Jack drank some port and sent the bottle to Victor.

'You're right,' he remarked, 'this country is magnificent, but I'm glad I'm not the one who's staying.'

'You'd rather be at Belcarron, I suppose?'

'You know I would.'

'Haven't forgotten I'm the heir?'

'How could I? You remind me every other day.' Jack studied his cigar. 'But if you plan to set yourself up as an *estanciero*, I don't quite see how you are to run Belcarron as well.'

'Mother will live for years yet. In the meantime, I believe I can have a good life in Argentina. As I said, it's my sort of place.'

'And you, of course, won't mind the way the gauchos kill cattle.'

'Dear old soft-hearted Jack!' Victor leaned across and patted Jack's arm. 'Haven't changed, have you? I used to wonder sometimes how you got through school.'

'Never took the trouble to find out, did you?'

'I was a year ahead, old man.'

'Makes me laugh, you know, that Mother thinks you looked after me.'

'Why should I have looked after you? No one looked after me.'

'You've never in your life needed looking after. Your great strength, isn't it?'

'And why you envy me, I suppose?'

'I don't envy you, Victor.' Jack stood up. 'That's something you'll never understand.'

The following morning, Alice, wearing a lilac dress and a large white hat, visited her aunt's grave in the cemetery of Santa Teresa. Beatrice had been buried near her husband Enriques, and Victor and Jack stood with bowed heads as Alice placed flowers and said a prayer. Not far away, Mena and her young husband lay together under a single stone, and Alice laid flowers there too and read aloud the inscription.

'"Sacred to the memory of Liam Flynn. Also, Philomena Mary, beloved wife of the above. 1869–1892." Only fifteen years ago ... Sometimes, it seems much longer ago than that.'

Richard's grave was in the Protestant section of the cemetery and was well cared for by Vittoria and by Lucio, when he came to Buenos Aires. Alice placed her flowers, then stood back, staring down at her husband's carved name. It never seemed to her that this grave had much to do with the man she had known and loved. Richard didn't belong under that stone, he should not have had to lie there, missing all the years, the long, long years they should have had together. Time was supposed to be a healer, as it passed, but whenever Alice came back to the Argentine, she felt time had stood still.

She turned to look at Victor and saw that his face was impassive. While Jack's eyes were filled with tears, there was no sign of emotion from his brother, no sign at all that he cared. Richard had been his father too, he had adored his first-born. Why should his son not weep?

'Why do you never, ever, show your feelings?' she whispered furiously, 'Why does nothing ever seem to matter to you?'

Victor raised his fair eyebrows in surprise. 'You think I have no feelings, Mother?'

'I say you don't show them!'

'Men are trained from birth not to show them, aren't they?'

'Jack shows them!'

'Wouldn't do for us all to be like Jack.'

'Why not, Victor, why not?'

'Mother, we can't all be the same,' Jack said uncomfortably. 'And Papa did die a very long time ago.'

Alice's eyes flashed, her lip trembled; then she turned aside, staring down at the flowers she had placed on Richard's grave. 'You are right, of course,' she said in a low voice. 'Your father has been dead for many years, I shouldn't expect you boys to mourn as I do.'

'You know what they say, Mother,' Victor murmured, 'life is for the living.'

'For your sakes, I have tried to remember that.'

'And you've done well.' Jack took her arm. 'No one could have done better for us than you. It's only natural, coming back here, you should feel things all over again. We understand.'

As Alice moved away, Victor muttered, 'All the same, she's like Queen Victoria, isn't she? Always mourning, always putting Papa on a pedestal. It's not possible for us to feel the same.'

'She could have married again any number of times and never has,' Jack remarked. 'I've always thought Papa must have been a very fine man for Mother to miss him so.'

'Oh, I dare say you're right,' Victor agreed, carelessly. 'Trouble is, it's damned hard to live up to the Albert Memorial, isn't it?'

*

That afternoon, Jorge drove them to the new premises of the Stonefield Bank near the Plaza de Mayo in the heart of BA. Here they were to meet Arthur Stonefield, who had taken over the bank and their affairs when his father had died two years before, much to Alice's sorrow. Edward Stonefield had been something of a father figure to the young Wintours in the old days, an urbane, good-looking man whose courtly manners had charmed and whose counsel Alice knew she would miss. By contrast his wife, Venetia, now also dead, had been shallow and cold with a pale withering stare her son had inherited. Though Arthur was always polite, Alice could not like him.

He greeted them now with some cordiality, ushering them into his fine new office, showing them to seats, taking his own behind his vast desk. Over the years, he had changed very little, still retaining a boyish slightness of figure and a head of soft fair hair that made him seem younger than his forty years. His eyes, however, were no warmer than Alice remembered and his mouth still drooped in peevish lines. She would have given a great deal to see his father sitting in his chair.

When she complimented him on his new premises, he gave a gratified smile and said they were pleased with the move. 'Had to be made, of course, our old place was shovelled away. You'll have seen all the new construction going on?'

'Yes, indeed. I hardly recognised the city.'

'All part of a big plan. The government wants BA to become the showplace of South America. A second Paris, you might say.'

'As long as the past is not altogether forgotten.' Alice gave a smile.

'Of course, of course, the colonial heritage must be preserved. It's just that a city such as this needs good hotels now, and theatres and fine shopping areas. You'll see, Mrs Wintour, everything will soon be looking splendid.'

'And from what I've heard a man may not walk down the Plaza without a coat,' Jack remarked. 'That should cut out the undesirables. I mean the poor, of course.'

Arthur fixed him with a cold stare. 'This city cares a great deal for the poor, Mr Jack, but one would not expect them to go shopping in the Florida, any more than in Bond Street in

London, or the Champs Elysées in Paris. I'm sure you understand me?'

'Perfectly. If you are building a new Buenos Aires, why should it be different from any other city designed for the rich?'

'Jack,' Victor rapped, 'I don't think Mr Stonefield wishes to hear your radical views at the moment.'

'Oh, I understand Mr Jack's views,' Arthur said quickly, 'and I want to make it clear I'm as anxious as anyone else to help the less affluent. Here in BA, we have the excellent barrio system, neighbourhoods where people can live and go to work, send their children to school, have everything they need –'

'And keep out of the way of the rich?' Jack asked lightly.

Arthur rose and pressed a bell. 'Mrs Wintour,' he asked, with a stiff little bow, 'may I offer you some of my Earl Grey tea? I have it sent out specially.'

After tea had been served, the papers that would end the bank's trusteeship of Victor's holdings were produced. Jack, bored by the formalities, wandered away to look out of the window at the banana trees shading the street outside, and sighed. Yes, everything was going to look spendid here and BA was a fine city, but not for him. As he remembered the white house overlooking the sea back home, he felt a sudden pang of homesickness.

'It will be your turn for all this next year, Mr Jack,' Arthur Stonefield called to him. 'I hope you are not against a little profit-making? The *estancia* is doing well.'

'I'm glad to hear it,' Jack said shortly. 'Why should I be against profit-making? All I can say is that profits should be used rightly.'

'Very commendable,' Victor commented, with a smile. 'Let's see what you do then, Jack, with your quarterly cheques.'

Arthur, after an awkward pause during which Jack and Victor glared at each other, asked when they planned to leave for the *estancia*. The day after tomorrow, Alice told him.

'So soon? I'm sorry. My wife and I were hoping you'd all come to dinner.' Arthur turned to Victor. 'But we'll make it some other time and if you're staying on, Mr Wintour, you must let us show you round. We have everything in BA, you know, from polo to play-acting, and every sort of club. I'll see you're put down for the English Club without delay.'

'You're very kind,' Victor responded. 'I shall look forward to seeing you when we return.'

'Perhaps you would care to visit us on the *estancia*?' Alice asked, a little hesitantly. 'With Mrs Stonefield and your daughter, of course? Our manager has arranged a fiesta to celebrate Victor's coming of age, you will know the sort of thing – an *asado*, gaucho races ...'

'Why, we should be delighted, Mrs Wintour! You are most gracious.'

'The ladies will not mind the ride from San Vicente? The road is still not suitable for carriages.'

'No, indeed, we visit the country regularly; everyone does these days.' Arthur smiled from Victor to Jack. 'You will enjoy your first *asado*, I promise you. No one roasts beef like the gauchos!'

'I'll send you a card, Mr Stonefield,' Alice promised and rose. 'But now we really must take our leave. We still have to visit the lawyer's.'

'You know that Alberto is head of the firm since his father's retirement? I'm sure you will find him as efficient as his father.' Arthur's smile grew a little bleak. 'We sons, you know, try to live up to our fathers' reputations. It's not always easy.'

Alice lowered her eyes in some confusion, but the banker appeared to notice nothing and politely escorted her and her sons to their waiting carriage.

As soon as they were on their way, Alice turned a furious stare on Jack.

'I'm sorry,' he said at once, 'did I embarrass you?'

'You embarrassed Mr Stonefield. What possessed you to talk in that way to him?'

'Sounded like a dashed Bolshevik,' Victor put in. 'Lord knows what he thought of you.'

'I don't care what he thought of me,' Jack returned sharply. 'He annoyed me. Smug fellows of his sort always annoy me.'

'Is this our saintly Jack talking?' asked Victor. 'What's got into him?'

'Mother, you know you don't like him yourself,' said Jack.

‘Perhaps not, but I give him credit for what he does.’ Alice turned to Victor. ‘All the same, I shouldn’t think he’d make a very interesting companion for you, Victor. He’s far too old for you.’

‘True, but I shall need some introductions and he’s the man to make them. By the way, how old is his daughter?’

‘She’s only a child, no more than fourteen. Surely, Victor, you’re not intending to spend all your time with the Stonefields in BA? Your inheritance is the *estancia*.’

‘Part inheritance,’ said Victor.

Two days later, the formalities of Victor’s ownership completed, they left for the Estancia Sentos.

Chapter Four

They were to be met at San Vicente by Lucio with the horses they would need to complete their journey. Would Julio be with him? Alice's heart was thudding against her ribs as she scanned the faces of the few people who had come to meet the train. There was no platform, for San Vicente, like most townships of the pampas, was too small to have a station. As Alice remembered it, there had been some private houses, a church, a doctor's office and the *pulpería*, the inn which doubled as local store. The years seemed to have added very little more.

Victor gave Alice his hand as she picked her way through a little crowd of barefoot children, her skirts trailing in the dust, while Jack saw to their boxes, which were to be carried by ox cart.

'I can't think what has happened to Lucio,' Alice said worriedly, then gave a sigh of relief as she saw the manager hurrying towards them, bareheaded, his hands outstretched, the same good Lucio, thinner, older, but handsome still.

'Doña Alicia!' His hands closed over hers as he apologised for his lateness; it had taken him longer than expected to ride over with the peons and horses, but now all was well. The horses were waiting at the *pulpería* and a room had been arranged where Doña Alicia could change into her riding habit. Ah, but how well she was looking! The same as ever, *por cierto*, quite untouched by time!

'You too, Lucio, you're the same.'

'No, no.' He put his hand to his head. 'See the grey? Since my Paola go, I am –' he shrugged – 'my age.'

'You must meet my sons,' she said gently.

As she presented the yellow-haired young men, straight and tall in riding clothes, Lucio caught his breath. 'No, no, is not possible! Is Don Ricardo again, is two Don Ricardos – so like, so like . . .'

'They are like,' Alice agreed. She swallowed, took a deep breath. 'But Lucio – your own son – is not Julio with you?'

'Julio?' A great smile spread over Lucio's face. He turned his dust-stained hat in his fingers. 'Is at the *estancia*, Doña Alicia. I say to him, come; he say, is shy, you understand?'

'Of course, he is only a boy.'

'Fifteen years old, but tall!' Lucio raised his hand high to demonstrate.

Jack smiled indulgently, and Victor grinned. 'We're very much looking forward to meeting him,' Jack told Lucio.

'Also your daughters,' Alice said quickly. 'How are they, Lucio?'

'Ah, two are married, Anna and Carlotta, I have only Isabella at home. She wait to see you now, with Julio.'

'I'll – I'll go and change.' Alice, keeping her face averted, hurried across to the *pulpería*.

There was no hope, she was sure of it. As she changed into her riding habit in the back room provided, her fingers fumbling over buttons and hooks, Alice tried to face the situation. In a few short hours, her sons would know all that she had kept from them over the years. How stupid she had been not to have told them before! When they were younger, they might have understood less and cared less. Whatever their feelings, as they grew up, there would have been no shock. Instead, she had set their father on a pedestal. Now he was about to topple from it.

As she studied herself in her little mirror, Alice remembered Lucio's words, 'I am my age.' She pinched her cheeks to try to bring back colour, and thought, How pale I am! I too look my age today and the boys will wonder why. When they see Julio, they will understand. Could there be any chance at all they would accept? She shook her head. They would not be able to accept. She had never forgotten her own feelings when Richard had suggested that Mena might be John Wintour's child. Even though Mena was someone very dear, the idea that her father might have betrayed her mother in such a way had shocked and appalled Alice at the time. The truth of it had never been known and she had learned to put it from her mind, but the truth of Julio's birth was something that could not be denied. When her sons discovered it, they would never forgive Richard; they would probably never forgive her, for concealing it from them for so long.

They rode for some time in silence, Lucio leading the way, the peons bringing up the rear, and the Wintours managing as best they could with their unfamiliar criollo horses. The road, no better than a cattle trail, was just as Alice remembered it, although the changes elsewhere were clear enough. Once there had been only cattle on this land, with wild horses galloping in the distance; the vast tracts of grass had seemed like a great sea, rolling away beyond sight. Now there were crops and wire fencing, tenant farmers working in the fields, who looked up and waved as the little party rode by. The pampas wasn't a sea any more. There were no wire fences in the sea.

Jack moved to ride next to Alice. 'Mother, I was wondering, why haven't we changed the name of the *estancia*?'

'Changed the name?' she repeated, rousing herself from her thoughts.

'Well, it's still called the Estancia Sentos, but there hasn't been a Sentos there in years. Shouldn't it be the Estancia Wintour now?'

'I don't know about that.' Alice looked ahead down the straight, never ending track. 'People here don't find our name easy. It was always the Estancia Sentos to your father and me, I suppose we just never thought of changing it.'

'I bet Victor will want to change it.'

'Perhaps, but I feel we should wait until everyone can have a say.'

'Even Melissa? We'll have to wait some time, then.'

'Just as well. In my view there have already been too many changes.'

'Is anything wrong?' Jack asked, trying to see her face behind her veil.

'No, why should there be?' She jerked round in her saddle to look at him. 'Why do you ask me that?'

'I only thought you looked worried.'

‘Only about keeping on this horse,’ she answered, trying to laugh. ‘I’m out of practice riding Argentine style.’

‘I was never in practice, I’m already as stiff as a board.’

Sensing that his questions were unwelcome, Jack allowed his horse to fall back. He knew his mother was worried because he always knew when things were not right for her, but if she wouldn’t tell him what was wrong, how was he to help? Tina would have known what to do, but Tina was far away. Jack wished suddenly that she were not.

He was beginning to feel more confident in his handling of his horse, able to look around now at this land which was new, yet not new, for memories were stirring. He must have travelled this route by ox cart in the old days, holding Mena’s hand as they bumped slowly over the ruts, must have stared up at the clear sky and watched the birds circling, must have wailed and complained, asking when they would be *there* ... His mother had told him all about those journeys and Victor said he remembered them, but for Jack they were only fragmented pictures floating in his mind, he could not put them together.

What he saw now was impressive. Alice might say that the pampas was no longer what it had been; there was still plenty of it, anyway. Compared with Ireland, the sheer vastness was breathtaking. Even more astonishing was the fact that he owned a part of it. He, who had no share at all in the little fields he loved back home! It was another strange fact, and a bitter one, that as one of his mother’s tenants he might have had more chance of owning Belcarron land than as Jack Wintour, younger son.

Suddenly Alice, ahead, gave a cry. ‘There’s the house! Do you see it? Victor, Jack, do you see it?’

‘I can see poplars,’ Victor called.

‘Yes, the poplars round the plantation. You always see those first when you ride from San Vicente.’ Alice was trembling as she fixed her gaze on the dark silhouettes of the trees in the blue distance, the poplars, the willows, shade trees planted by the Sentos family so many years before when the *estancia* house was new. There were orchards, too, though it wasn’t possible to see the peach trees yet and they were too late, of course, for the blossom that hung in great pink clouds in August. Urging on her horse, Alice could just make out the roof of the house itself. She cried back to her sons, 'Quickly! Let's get on, let's get there!'

'Doña Alicia, take care!' Lucio shouted as she passed him, galloping. 'Remember Don Enriques!'

Enriques Sentos, Beatrice's husband, had been killed in a riding accident on the pampas and Alice herself had often quoted his death as a warning to Richard not to take risks. Now she was heedless of Lucio's caution. Her old home was waiting, filled with ghosts, holding a new ghost she knew she must face and wanted to face, so that she might accept whatever lay ahead. In spite of Lucio's anguished cries, she was the first to arrive at the house where the tall, dark-haired boy stood waiting.

He came forward and stood looking up at her as she looked down from her horse at him. Behind her, the men had halted, as though to watch this meeting.

'Doña Alicia?' the boy asked.

'Julio?' she whispered, filled with the bittersweet pain of recognition. The photographs had not lied, this was Richard's son. The shape of the head, the straight nose, the finely moulded mouth, even the way he held himself, one hand raised to push back the thick, black hair that was all he appeared to have inherited from his mother. For a moment, Alice allowed herself the deep pleasure of seeing in him her own Richard, but as she took the hand he extended and dismounted with his help, apprehension seized her again and she turned away her head.

The peons led away the horses as Lucio came hurrying forward, calling to his son to come to be presented to Doña Alicia's sons. Alice, because she had no choice, painfully raised her eyes.

'*Buenos días*, Julio,' Victor said with an easy smile.

'*Buenos días*,' Jack echoed and put out his hand.

As Julio murmured something in return, Alice stood rigidly still. Was it possible they had seen nothing? She could not believe it. There he stood, a reflection of themselves, and their eyes were passing over him as if he had indeed been Lucio's son. Then it came to her. That was what they expected to see, so that was what they saw. Julio Castillo, a long-legged boy with dark hair whose father adored him – what could he have to do with them? She did not know whether to laugh or cry.

'Speak to him in English,' Lucio was urging her sons. 'Julio will answer, he speak very good English. I teach him myself, then he go to school, very good school, is run by the fathers at San Marcos. He have holiday now in your honour, but then he go back, he work hard, I wish him to go to university. Please, speak to him!'

'*Papá*!' Julio murmured, flushing scarlet, but suddenly no one was looking at him any more. A girl in a simple print dress, her rich, dark hair coiled on her neck, had appeared at the open front door.

'My Isabella,' Lucio said softly.

At fifteen, she was the same age as Julio, but whereas he was still a boy, she was already a woman, attractive, provocative, her body under the thin dress quite mature. It was no surprise to Alice that her sons appeared unable to take their eyes off her.

'Come meet Doña Alica,' Lucio whispered in Spanish, and Isabella obediently bowed and touched Alice's hand, but as she raised her lustrous dark eyes, what Alice read in their depths chilled her heart. This was Paola again, Paola as she used to be – and liking Alice no better.

'You are tired, Doña Alicia?' Lucio asked with concern. 'You wish Isabella take you to your room?'

'*Gracias*, no,' Alice answered, though she was in fact bone tired. 'First I should like to see –' She looked into Lucio's face and saw that he understood her.

'I show you,' he told her quietly, and led the way through the passageways of the house to Richard's old study. 'Is not much change, Doña Alicia, is never use.'

She looked round the small room, at the desk, the leather chair, the window someone had opened. This was where Richard had sat that last night, working on the codicil to his will, making provision through Lucio for Julio. This was where the two witnesses had joined him to sign their names, before one had left and the other, Antonio Sentos, had put his thin-bladed knife into Richard's body, taking away his life's blood – and her own, or so it had often seemed over the years. Even now, so many years later, she felt drained, only partly alive.

'*Gracias*,' she said to Lucio, and turned away.

In the room she had once shared with Richard, she washed, changed into a loose wrapper and lay on her bed. She found herself suddenly longing for Tina, of all her children the only one she could lean on, for though Jack was her comfort, Tina was her support. Why ever had she allowed her to go to America? Why had she not insisted Tina came to the Argentine? Because Tina had wanted so much to do something on her own on leaving school and Alice had not wanted to stand in her way. It was right she should have the chance to spread her wings a little, meet Hester and Hester's children, see New York and Washington. It was right, too, that Alice herself should learn to let go. But as she moved her head restlessly on her pillow, Alice remembered Isabella. Tina, by now enjoying herself in New York, would have no idea of the new apprehension that had taken over Alice on looking into a girl's dark eyes.

Chapter Five

Alice was right: Tina was enjoying herself. The city of New York fascinated her. So did her cousins, particularly Caitlin. There was also the feeling that here for the first time she was free. Free from close family, free from schoolmistresses, free from the burden of keeping Mama happy. Victor, of course, did not trouble himself to share that burden and Melissa was too young, but for Tina and Jack, trying to make up to their mother for their father's death was a continual aim in life. They did not mind, they accepted gladly, but now that she had temporarily set the burden down, Tina knew she was relieved.

Although resentful at first of Meg Wynne's company on the voyage out, she had rapidly become grateful for it. Everyone else on board ship appeared to have someone and to have been alone then might have taxed even Tina's nerve. As it was, she and her ex-governess got on well, far better than in the old days when they had battled it out over textbooks. After leaving Belcarron, Miss Wynne had taught in a London girls' school and was looking forward now to a new post in Westchester. She had changed very little, was still fair-haired and strong-jawed, still direct, and also still unmarried. By choice, she explained; her career meant more to her than home and family. No doubt Tina found that strange? Not at all, Tina told her, she wasn't sure she wanted to marry herself. There was surely more to life than ordering meals and checking laundry lists?

'Some people want children,' Miss Wynne observed.

'Oh, I dare say I might want a family one day,' Tina replied, 'but first I'd like to do something for myself.'

'I can understand that. After all, you still have the whole

world to see.' Miss Wynne smiled. 'New York will be a good place for you to begin.'

As the SS *Coronation* sailed past the Statue of Liberty and brought her into one of the greatest ports in the world, Tina excitedly agreed. When Miss Wynne, ever cautious, pressed her card into her hand and told her she must be sure to get in touch, should she feel homesick, Tina stared at her in astonishment.

'It's very kind of you, Miss Wynne, but really I shall be far too interested to feel homesick.'

'It's just that you are to be on your own, away from your family –'

'I'm not going to be on my own, Miss Wynne, I shall have my cousins.'

'But you don't know your cousins, do you?' asked Miss Wynne.

It was true she had not seen them since she was a child, yet as soon as Hester and her children had swept Tina back to their spacious apartment on the Upper West Side, Tina felt she had known them all her life. She would not be telephoning Miss Wynne; she felt completely at home.

In fact, the Molloys had two homes, the New York apartment and a small rented house in Washington, used when Daniel was attending Congress. Although based in New York when Tina arrived, he was so involved with his newspaper and his fund raising for the Irish that she rarely saw him, which secretly suited her very well. Cousin Hester, whose sweetness and intelligence shone from a face scarcely lined, liked to say that Daniel had mellowed over the years, but when he turned his hard stare on Tina, she felt she was sitting on a powder keg. Here was a man who had once threatened to destroy Belcarron and looked as if he still might. As she was whirled through the kaleidoscope of New York's sights, she was relieved to think that Belcarron was so very far away. From him.

It was Paul and Caitlin who mainly acted as Tina's guides, for Hester was busy with her bookshops. Paul, now twenty and at Columbia University, was handsome in the Wintour way, with the yellow hair and fine features of Victor and Jack, whereas Caitlin was all Molloy, too close to Daniel for Tina's comfort, but very pretty and also strong. She was a year younger than Tina but seemed older; it was always she who chose where they should go.

'Is there any place I haven't seen?' Tina asked at one point, having been shown Fifth Avenue and Central Park, the Flat Iron skyscraper, the Pulitzer skyscraper, the elevated railway and the underground railway, the shops, theatres and museums, Coney Island and she didn't know how much else besides.

'Why, you'd need to stay here for ever to see everything,' Paul told her. 'How about it?'

'I don't think I'd mind!'

One humid afternoon, they came back early from a gallery, weary from the crowded streets, and collapsed in Hester's shaded drawing room, drinking the iced coffee brought in by the Irish maid.

'How I wish we had an icebox at home!' Tina sighed. 'This is such an amazing city, isn't it?'

'Because we have iceboxes?' asked Paul, laughing. They all felt pleasantly at ease, just the three of them, for Hester was at her head office and Daniel at his paper.

'Oh, come, you know what I mean,' Tina murmured.

'You're liking it here, then?'

'I've never had such a wonderful time.'

'In spite of Papa?' asked Caitlin. She was lying on the sofa, her boots undone, her hands folded behind her dark, curly head, her eyes, which could be as fierce as her father's, bright with interest.

Tina hesitated. 'It is disconcerting when he looks at me sometimes,' she admitted. 'I know he's seeing the wicked Protestant Ascendancy in person. But what can I do? I can't change my background.'

'Would you,' asked Caitlin, 'if you could?'

There was silence in the airless room. Tina looked from Caitlin to Paul. It didn't seem to her that the question could be serious.

'Why ever should I? I'm not ashamed of being a Wintour of Belcarron.'

'I guess not.' Caitlin stood up. 'You've been raised to be

proud of that, no one can blame you.'

'Blame?' Tina's strong chin came forward. 'Now, look, there's no question of blame here. Your family may have different ideas from mine; it doesn't mean mine are wrong.'

'We rather think they are,' said Paul gently.

'Well, you've been raised, as you put it, to think that, haven't you? But there's no right or wrong about the matter.'

'If you think about it, you'll see there is,' Caitlin replied.

'If I think about it? Of course I think about it. Everyone I know thinks about the Irish question.'

'And do they think it right a foreign country should rule another? Do you?'

Under her cousin's challenging gaze, Tina felt suddenly like an animal at bay, and at the same time angry that she should be made to feel so.

'You can't call England a foreign country, Caitlin. It's part of the British Isles, so is Ireland. So are Scotland and Wales.'

'Let's not talk about Scotland or Wales. Ireland is a country in its own right, never mind the geography. How do you think the English would feel governed from Dublin?'

Tina opened her mouth, then closed it, remembering George Coxe. He had made that point and made it again in the letters she had been receiving. Now here was Caitlin putting it too and Paul waiting, ready to join in. For the first time since her arrival, Tina felt a stranger. She stood up and asked if they would excuse her, she would like to rest in her room for a while.

Paul at once leaped to his feet and opened the door for her. 'I'm so sorry, we've upset you, haven't we? It's unforgivable, when you're a guest in our home. Caitlin, please apologise to Tina.'

'Don't be silly, there's nothing to apologise for. You have your views, I have mine, let's just agree to differ.'

'Can't do that,' Caitlin murmured, putting her hand on Tina's arm. 'This is too important to put aside; to us it's the most important thing in the world. Listen, will you let me lend you some books? On Irish history?'

'It's very kind of you, Caitlin, but I don't think I need any history lessons.'

'Really? How many people died in the famines, then?'

'Oh, for heaven's sake!' Tina pulled herself free from Caitlin's hand. 'Are my people to be blamed for the failure of the potato crop as well as everything else?'

'Nearly a million people died. If they had been in England, would they still have died?'

'You're saying the English let the Irish die?'

'No, they simply didn't know what was really happening. Because Ireland is another country, not part of England.' Caitlin's eyes shone. 'Proves my point, doesn't it? Ireland should have self-government.'

'Proves it to you, perhaps,' Tina retorted, 'but you see what you want to see. Will you excuse me?'

In her bedroom, a pleasant room with watercolours of Ireland on its pale walls, Tina took a chair and gave herself up to homesickness. Miss Wynne had been right after all, and she, Tina, should have listened to her. Perhaps she could still get in touch with her? It would be so comforting to talk to someone who knew her family were not monsters, that they cared about Ireland, that Ireland was their country, too. All these people – Caitlin and Paul, George Coxe and Daniel, even Cousin Hester – would like to see Ireland taken away from the Wintours and those like them, whose home it had been for centuries. Why? What purpose would it serve? There would be no magic wand waved over the Irish because they cut themselves off from the English, and Tina refused to believe it was what most Irish people wanted. Caitlin and Paul wanted it because their father had taught them to want it, Daniel because he was a hothead and a troublemaker, Hester because she loved Daniel. As for George Coxe – Tina bit her lip. She couldn't think why George Coxe should want it.

A soft tap on her door made her jump up, straighten her skirts and push back her hair. It was Caitlin who came in, looking very sweet, a chastened expression on her pretty face, a bundle of books in her arms.

'I'm so sorry to disturb you if you're resting, but I just thought you might like to look at these. If you have time, you know.'

Tina said, graciously, she had not been disturbed and, if Caitlin really wanted it, would look at the books.

'Oh, good!' Caitlin immediately closed the door, set down the books on Tina's side table, and pulled forward a chair for herself.

'Shouldn't we be getting ready for dinner?' asked Tina.

'No, not yet, there's plenty of time. Mother's not even back yet and I guess Papa won't come back at all. He was going to a meeting of Clan-na-Gael – that's the Irish-American Republican association, you know.'

'Is it?' Tina's mouth tightened grimly.

Caitlin gave a charming smile. 'It's so funny, Tina, but this is all a bit like the time Mother first got to know Papa. She used to lend him books when he worked in the stable at Belcarron.'

'But he converted Cousin Hester, not the other way round.'

'And you think I'm out to convert you? So I am.' Caitlin leaned forward, suddenly earnest. 'Oh, Tina, I know I'm right about you. You're like Mother; once the truth is shown to you, you'll always accept it. It's the way you are, I can tell.'

'You're not the first who's tried to convert me,' Tina said in a low voice, 'but he didn't succeed and neither will you.'

'Oh? Who's that, then? Do I know him?'

'He's an Englishman, a doctor, he visits friends of ours at Castle Morry.'

'He's the one who writes the letters?'

Tina stared. 'How do you know that?'

'It wasn't difficult. He puts his name on the envelope: Dr George Coxe. I've seen them on the hall table. Why, Tina, you're blushing!'

'No, I'm not. There's nothing romantic between us, we're just friends.'

'Oh, come, I've heard that before!' Caitlin said with a laugh, and Tina thought, She's not really interested in the idea of a love affair, she's just trying to keep me happy so that I'll listen to her.

Aloud, she said again there was nothing between herself and George, it wasn't likely there would be, she was no beauty, after all.

'Why, Tina, that's a terrible thing to say about yourself!' cried Caitlin.

'Is it? Well, you don't know what it's like to be the only

plain one in a family where everyone else is handsome.'

'Looks don't matter, really they don't.'

'Maybe not for men, but they do for women.'

'Well, they shouldn't. That's another thing I'd fight for, if I had the time.'

'Women's right to be plain?'

'Women's right to work. If women had jobs, they wouldn't need to use their looks to marry for a living.'

'I'm not sure I want to marry. I don't know what I want to do.'

'I know what you can do. You can work for Ireland with me!'

'Oh, Caitlin, can't you ever come off your soapbox?'

'No, I'm serious. If you're looking for a cause, there's one right here. Listen, next year I leave school and go to college –'

'College?' cried Tina. 'You're really going to college? Oh, I'd give my soul to go to Oxford!'

'I'm going to college to please Mother, but then I'm going to train as a nurse and I'm going to learn to shoot.'

'To shoot?' Tina caught her breath. 'Whatever for?'

'Because it may be useful.' Caitlin's consciously applied charm had quite evaporated. As she stood at the door, one hand on the knob, her face was blank of all emotion. 'We shall not necessarily get what we want by peaceful means.'

'And you're asking me to join you? I could never agree to violence, Caitlin. Violence is always wrong.'

'So Mother says, but if the cause is just, it is right to fight, even the Church says that. But it may never come to it anyway. All I want is to be ready for the fight if there is one.' Caitlin's smile returned. 'Promise me you'll read the books, Tina.'

Although she said she would, Tina's face remained troubled, and she could not return her cousin's smile.

Chapter Six

As Hester poured coffee at breakfast next morning, she turned concerned eyes on Tina's empty place. 'Where's Tina?' she asked. 'It's not like her to be late.'

'Especially when there are hot cakes,' said Paul.

Daniel Molloy raised his greying brows but said nothing as Hester told Caitlin to go and call Tina, she might be unwell.

'It's all right, Mother, I hear her coming. She's probably just overslept.'

Tina, wearing a pretty, sprigged shirtwaister and dark-blue skirt, came in swiftly and took her place at table with a brief good morning. She was rather pale.

'Are you all right, my dear?' Hester asked kindly, as Paul passed the hot cakes.

'Quite well, thank you, Cousin Hester.'

'You look tired. Did you not sleep?'

Tina's gaze slid to Caitlin and away. 'I was reading rather late.'

'Oh, Tina, you haven't strained your eyes? It's never a good thing to read by artificial light, you know.'

'They say electric light's as good as day,' Paul remarked. 'Everyone's going over to it.'

'Gas is good enough for me,' Daniel growled. His Irish brogue had never changed over the years. 'There are better things to spend money on than trying to replace the sun.' He stood up, saying he must get on, and, having kissed Hester's cheek, nodded to the others round the table and went out.

As usual, the atmosphere lightened with his departure. Hester poured more coffee; Paul sprawled back in his chair and buried himself in the *New York Times*; Caitlin fixed a bright gaze on Tina but said nothing. It was only when Hester had left and the breakfast things had been cleared that she said softly, 'Tina, did you really stay up reading my books?'

'I did.'

'So, what do you think?'

Tina stood up, kicked back her skirts and walked slowly to the window. She said nothing.

'Has it been a shock?' asked Paul quietly, as he came to stand beside her. 'I mean, finding out?'

Tina folded her arms and stared down at the traffic below.

'We understand how you're feeling,' Caitlin murmured, also moving to stand near Tina.

'And how would you know how I am feeling?' asked Tina.

'Well, because of Mother. She had to face what you're facing. It's not easy to accept that your own people are oppressors.'

'How do I know those histories are true?' Tina cried fiercely. 'They only show one side of things.'

'Tina, it's all documented,' Paul told her, 'the domination, the Penal Laws, the evictions, the famines –'

'I've already said we were not responsible for the failure of the potatoes!'

As Caitlin was about to make a passionate reply, Paul suddenly pushed both girls towards the door. 'Come on, it's a lovely day, let's not waste it arguing indoors. I vote we all go walking in Central Park, what do you say?'

'I say it's a good idea,' Tina answered, with some relief.

'Go get your hats, then, girls, and we'll take the streetcar. One of these days, you know, I'm going to have myself an automobile.'

'Now you sound like Victor,' Tina told him, finding a smile.

Central Park, like most things in New York, seemed larger than life.

'Here's 840 acres of open space in a city where land's so scarce they have to build in the sky – who says New York has no heart?' asked Paul.

Together, they paced the long paths, looking at the strolling New Yorkers, the children and nursemaids, the backdrop of tall buildings rising on the skyline, the beautiful trees. Tina remarked on the late-summer warmth and Caitlin said she would not be able to picture the place in winter, when the temperature dropped lower than any she would have known in Ireland and there would be drifts of snow and skating on the lake for weeks on end.

'At least you keep your houses warm. I sometimes think there are more gales inside Belcarron than out, in the winter.'

'Belcarron.' Paul steered them towards a bench under trees. 'I'd love to see it again. Tell me, Tina, do you ever see your aunt Charlotte?'

'Aunt Charlotte?' She looked at him in surprise. 'Why, no, I don't believe she's been back to Belcarron for years. No one sees Aunt Charlotte.'

'You don't know what's happened to her?'

'It's said she's in Germany, married to some kind of baron. Why do you ask?'

'He once fell in love with her hat,' Caitlin said, with a laugh, 'so Mother tells it.'

'No, I fell in love with her,' Paul corrected, 'but you have to remember I was only three at the time.'

'How forward of you to be in love with anyone,' Tina said lightly, 'especially when everyone at home thinks you're destined for the priesthood!'

'Never in this world,' he retorted, colouring. 'Who says that? I've never had the slightest vocation.'

'Your own aunt used to say you'd end up a cardinal, so your mother told mine.'

'Aunt Theresa!' Caitlin burst into laughter. 'Oh, what a joke! She'd be so disappointed if she knew Paul falls in love with someone different every week and is only going to run Molloy's Books when he finishes college.'

Tina's foot traced patterns in the dust. 'At least he'll have a career, which is more than I'll ever have.'

Caitlin snatched up Tina's hand. 'I've told you what you can do, Tina. You can work for Ireland. Now that you know the truth.'

Tina shook her hand free. 'Why me? Why do you keep asking *me*?'

'Because you're strong and a lady and because you're from the other side. It all counts, you see – the more people with your background support us, the more the English will see the cause is just.' Caitlin's eyes were shining, her lips trembling;

she looked ready to leap to her feet and lead a march of protest there and then. Tina, though, turned to Paul.

'What do you think, Paul? Are you with Caitlin? Do you think the cause is just?'

'Paul always sees both sides,' Caitlin put in quickly. 'Don't go by Paul.'

'The Irish are not saints, there's been violence on their side as well as the English,' Paul said mildly, 'but I don't say there are two sides to the Irish question, no, that's not true.'

'But you don't justify violence?' Tina pressed.

'No, I don't. That's where Caitlin and I part company.'

'We may get what we want without violence. Let's not discuss that now.' Caitlin's blue gaze held Tina's with frightening intensity. 'The point is, Tina, now that you know the facts, are you on our side?'

'I need more time.'

'No, you don't. Once you're shown the truth, you'll believe. I told you, that's the way you are.'

Tina set her chin. 'It's no good trying to bully me, Caitlin. I'll make up my own mind.'

Caitlin sat back on the bench, her face darkening; then she shrugged and smiled. 'All right, I agree, that's fair. You should make up your own mind.'

'Just as long as you agree with her in the end,' Paul said with a grin. 'No, seriously, Tina, we do understand how difficult this is for you, having to face the facts.'

'The facts of the suffering?' asked Caitlin. 'Or that one's family caused it?'

'The Wintours never caused suffering!' Tina cried. 'That I don't have to believe!'

'One's class, then,' Caitlin amended coolly. 'That's where it hurts, doesn't it?'

'Your class too, remember. You're half Anglo-Irish.'

Caitlin stared. 'I'm Irish-American. That's all that counts.'

Late that evening, Tina wrote two long letters. One to her mother, continuing her list of all she had seen and done; the other to George Coxe, dealing with very different matters. As she bent over the paper, the pen moving rapidly in her hand, her blue eyes softly glowing, she looked almost beautiful.

Chapter Seven

As New York's autumn moved into winter and Tina began to think of going home, summer had already come to the pampas. Early December was hot and dry, the grass yellowing on the plain, the thistles huge but light, ready to burst and float on the still air. Alice said these were the days when one longed for Irish rain and Irish green and Jack agreed, but Victor argued the other way. How often at home did they long for the sun? They should make the most of it, now they had it.

Both Victor and Jack had taken to riding the pampas every day. Sometimes with the gauchos to *rodeo*, the cattle round-up, smaller and less dramatic than in their father's day; sometimes with Lucio or Julio to see the sheep or the crops, or the land set aside for the alfalfa to feed the prize beef cattle. At the end of the day, Victor was always ready for a session with the gauchos, either practising their style of horse racing – he had already decided to enter himself in the races at his own fiesta – or riding with them to San Vicente to drink brandy and water in the *pulpería* and listen to their songs. Occasionally, Jack would go too, but more often he would stay behind to talk to Julio, who had become a favourite of his – and to keep a lookout for Isabella.

She was far too elusive. Julio was always around but his sister seemed to stay in the house Lucio had built for his family at the back of the orchards. When Jack casually mentioned this to Alice, she gave him a sharp look and said that young Argentine girls were not expected to mix with young men. Naturally, her father would wish Isabella to stay in her own home where, no doubt, she had her tasks to perform.

'Julio seems free to do as he wants,' Jack observed.

'That's the way of the world. I'm afraid boys always have more freedom than girls. Haven't you heard Tina on the subject?'

'I happen to think she's right to complain.'

'So do I, but there are good reasons for protecting girls, Jack, as you very well know.'

'Surely Isabella doesn't need protecting from us, Mother? We are sort of family, after all.'

'You think you are part of Lucio's family?'

'Well, I do sometimes feel like an older brother to Julio.'

'And also to Isabella?' Alice asked, after a pause.

She did not miss her son's quick flush; she only hoped he had not noticed her own.

Quite elaborate plans had been made for Victor's fiesta. As well as the Stonefields from BA, guests from neighbouring *estancias* had been invited for a programme of gaucho races and ring games, followed by a grand *asado* when an ox would be roasted in hot coals. There would be local songs and guitar playing, dancing and toasting; no one would expect to get to bed before dawn.

Surely this would be his chance to be with Isabella, thought Jack, but he had no great hopes. Lucio would escort her everywhere, or else Margarita or Vittoria would act as chaperone; she might as well be fastened to them with a ball and chain. It was unbearable to think he could never get close to her, when she drew him so strongly he would have broken any barrier to reach her. But he could scarcely break down her father's encircling arm, or Vittoria's.

He was in love as he had never been before, so completely consumed by his feeling for her, he would have married Isabella tomorrow if that were possible. It wasn't, of course. She wasn't even of age and would she want him, anyway? He didn't know, he was driven mad by not knowing, and always at the back of his mind there was the thought of Victor. He had seen the way Victor looked at Isabella on the rare occasions she appeared, he knew what those looks meant and the knowledge brought sweat to his brow. Yet Victor was no fool. Even if he had the opportunity, he would not risk the consequences of seducing the daughter of Lucio Castillo. He would leave Isabella alone.

The Stonefields were to arrive the day before the fiesta, bringing with them Arthur's married sister, over on a visit from England. Alice had instructed Victor to meet their train at San Vicente and though he had groaned over it, he could find no way to refuse. When Jack said he would go riding with Julio, Victor told him he was a lucky devil. Now he, Victor, was damned if he knew what to say to the Stonefields.

'Why, I thought you were quite happy getting to know Arthur Stonefield,' Jack countered.

'Yes, but there are three females tagging along and I shall have to find them horses and be polite and it will all be an uncommon bore.'

'It's your party, must do your duty, old man.' Jack laughed and, as Victor rode off fuming, took pleasure in for once scoring over his brother. A day on the pampas was much to be preferred to escort duty with the banker and his family.

'Julio!' he called, '*vámonos*!'

There was a humidity in the air that made the land shimmer and would make ideal conditions for a mirage, Julio told Jack when they had been riding some time. 'You think, you know, you see water, but you ride and ride and is no water, only mirage.'

Jack, wiping his brow, said all this talk of water had made him thirsty. In the next shade they found he would stop for a drink.

'I gather thistles, I make fire for *mate*,' said Julio, who had all the gaucho skills, and when they found trees for shade, soon had his kettle singing. 'Is good, Don Juan?' he asked, passing Jack the gourd of tea made from dried ilex leaves.

'It's very good, but I wish you wouldn't call me Don Juan, it's not my name. Jack will do.'

'Don Yaques?' Julio asked, doubtfully.

'Not Don, just Jack.' As Julio still hesitated, Jack made him try to pronounce his name the English way. 'That's right, you're getting it. There's no need to use the Don, we're friends, aren't we?'

'I do as you wish, but I think this no please my father. With him is always Doña Alicia, Don Victor –'

'With me, it's Jack.'

Handing the gourd back to Julio, Jack put his hands behind his head and looked up at the sky through the dark leaves of the *ombú* trees. He thought of his father, lying as he did now, watching the plovers, perhaps drinking *mate* tea with Lucio as Jack had drunk it with Julio, and for a moment the shadowy figure of Don Ricardo became real to him, more real than at Belcarron. For some reason he never liked to think of his father at Belcarron. There were sadnesses attached to him there which Jack believed had nothing to do with his death, mysteries no one explained, which perhaps should not be explained. It was better to think of him here, on the pampas he had loved.

Feeling Julio's eyes on him, Jack sat up and smiled. Julio smiled back, fanning himself with his hat while the dappled light caught his glossy black hair.

'Jack, will you do something for me?' asked Julio.

'Of course. What is it?'

'Will you tell me of my mother? I mean my real mother?'

Jack brushed bits of grass from his shirt. 'Has your father not told you about her?'

'Lucio is no my father, Jack. Is very good. And Paola, she very good to me, my wonderful mother always, but no my real mother. Lucio, he tell me, my mother is Irish maid who work for Doña Alicia. I think maybe you know her.'

'Her name was Mena, but I'm sorry, Julio, I don't really remember her. She died when I was very young.'

'But maybe you think of some little thing to tell me.' Julio leaned forwards, his fine, dark-lashed eyes fixed on Jack's. 'I have no picture, you understand, no picture here –' he tapped his brow – 'in my mind.'

'My mother has a portrait of Mena. I've seen it, at home in Ireland. It was painted by my grandmother.'

'Tell me, please, how she look?'

'Very pretty. Very Irish. Dark hair, like yours, and blue eyes. A sweet smile.'

Julio nodded. 'I wish I might see that portrait. Maybe one day I go to Ireland, then I see.'

'You plan to go to Ireland, Julio?'

'*Cómo no*! Of course, I wish to see my country.'

'Yet you are Lucio's adopted son. Argentina is your country, isn't it?'

'*Si, si*, I live nowhere else. But where a man come from is very important. I know nothing of my father, all I have is my mother. One day I see her country, is right.'

'And your mother would have been happy for you to see her home. I'd like you to see mine, too, Julio. It's called Belcarron.'

'Is the big house? Yes, I know.'

'You'd be very welcome to stay there, very welcome indeed.'

'*Gracias*, but I think –' Julio lowered his eyes – 'I think I no stay at Belcarron.'

'We'll talk about it when you come.' Jack yawned and stretched and said perhaps they should be making a move.

Julio said there was something else he would like to ask, something he would like explained. Jack and his family came from Ireland, yet were not Irish, how was that?

'We're what is called Anglo-Irish.'

'Is English, *si*?'

'Only in the way criollos here might be called Spanish.'

'They are conquerors of Ireland?'

'Originally, maybe. Now we think of ourselves as part of Ireland.'

'But England still rule you?' Julio shook his head. 'Now here, Jack, is not the same. We win independence long, long time ago, the criollos shake off Spain. Why you no wish this? Why you no shake off England?'

Jack laughed. 'Shake off England? We're part of England!'

'You just say now you are part of Ireland.'

'We are, we're both. Julio this is called the Irish question, I'm afraid you are never going to understand it. Let's go.'

'No, no, wait, Jack, I think it is wrong England rule my mother's country. Maybe is the Irish who should shake off England? How you think, Jack?'

'I think you're right, Julio.'

'Then you fight? You fight for my mother's country?'

'I don't know about that. There's no war at present.'

'Is only way for freedom, Jack, to fight.'

At Julio's earnest expression, Jack clapped him on the shoulder and said they'd discuss it later. Now, they should stamp out the embers of their fire, shouldn't they? It would never do to start a fire on the pampas at this time of year.

They were almost back at the *estancia* house before Jack brought out what was in his own mind. 'Julio,' he said, casually, 'about Isabella –'

'Isabella?' Julio repeated in surprise.

'We never seem to see her. Doesn't she ... doesn't she like us?'

'Of course, she like.' Julio grinned. 'She like Don Victor.'

Great black clouds seemed to obscure the sun as Jack bowed his head. 'She told you that? She said she liked my brother?'

'She like his looks, Jack. Is *hermoso, si*?'

'Handsome, yes, very.' Jack did not look up.

'You know, Jack, you are handsome,' Julio said softly. 'Is true.'

'Not as handsome as Victor, Julio.'

'I think, more. Because kind. My sister think so.'

'She thinks me kind?' Jack raised his head and laughed. 'Why is that never a compliment?'

'Please?'

'Nothing. Let's hurry, Julio. The visitors will have arrived from BA.'

'Jack, I tell my sister to come talk to you. I teach her my English. She know many, many words.'

'I think she'd rather talk to my brother.'

'No, no, to you. I tell her, Jack, I promise.'

Julio's eagerness to please was so obvious, Jack in his misery had to smile. 'Very well, Julio, you tell her. Now, let's get home.'

The *sala*, the parlour, was still much as Alice had known it as a bride, still furnished with Sentos furniture and Sentos rugs, but there were also Wintour pictures and photographs and the flowers Alice always arranged to make a room her own. On that humid afternoon when Jack and Julio arrived, it seemed to be full of women in pale dresses, Alice herself and the ladies of the Stonefield family who had already changed from their riding habits. There were men, too, Arthur, Victor and Lucio, though they seemed overshadowed by the height of the women's upswept hair, their enormous sleeves and curving silhouettes, this being a time when fashion was elaborate, even on a hot afternoon on the Argentine pampas.

Blanche Stonefield was in her late thirties, tall and heavy, with abundant copper-brown hair and hazel eyes. Lucinda Bury, Arthur's sister, was slighter and less colourful and Arthur's daughter, Evelina, was fourteen years old and thin as a beanpole. Neither Evie nor Lucinda could keep their eyes from wandering towards Victor, Evie because she had never in her life seen anyone so handsome, Lucinda because he reminded her so much of Richard Wintour, for whom she had once cherished a secret, youthful passion. At Jack's entrance, however, both turned their heads.

He stood in the doorway with Julio, flushed and dishevelled, his yellow hair wild, his hat tied at the back of his head, and when Julio made moves to go, firmly held his arm.

'We'll just stay a moment, Julio. Let's say hello, then go and change.'

'Do have tea,' Alice called, then froze.

Lucinda Bury was advancing, her eyes darting from Jack's face to Julio's, her clear voice exclaiming, 'Why, Mrs Wintour, I declare, I never knew you had *three* sons! Is this the youngest?' She put out her hand to Julio. 'He has your dark hair, but how like he is to his father. Heavens, they're all Richard, aren't they? They're Richard all over again.'

Chapter Eight

'Is it true?' asked Victor quietly.

Alice made no reply. Jack sat staring at his hat.

They were alone in the *sala*, Lucio having hurried Julio away while Blanche, like some large, well-dressed shepherdess, drove her family before her, Arthur mumbling apologies, Evie bewildered, Lucinda crying, 'Lucio's son, do you say? *Lucio*'s? Dear God, what have I said?'

'Is it true?' asked Victor again, his colour heightening and mottling, as his father's had before him. When Alice still said nothing, he laughed. 'Of course it is, you have only to look at the fellow! In God's name, why didn't we see it for ourselves? We saw him every day –'

'You never looked at him,' Alice murmured.

'And you didn't need to look at him, did you? You knew he was Papa's bastard, you've always known, haven't you?'

'Don't speak to Mother like that,' Jack rapped, throwing his hat to the floor.

'Jack, all I want is the truth.'

'Whatever it is, Mother's not to blame.'

'Didn't she hold him up to us as an angel of virtue? All these years –' As Victor's voice suddenly cracked, Alice winced and put her hand to her eyes. 'I can't believe it of you,' he finished, after a moment or two. 'I can't believe it of you, or him.'

'Victor, I'm sorry, I only wanted to protect you.'

'No, you wanted to protect Papa.'

'That was natural, wasn't it? Sons should look up to their fathers.'

'Yes, but to make him out so wonderful, to keep it up, year after year, and all the time there was this fellow here we were all going to meet. Did you never think what it would be like for us, when we found out?'

'Finding out isn't important,' said Jack, rising and beginning to pace the floor. 'What matters is that Papa betrayed us all. That's what I can't forgive.'

'It wasn't the way you think, he never meant it to happen!' cried Alice. 'When you're older, you'll understand. Mistakes are made, someone pays, that's always been the way.'

'Mena paid,' Jack said shortly. 'She died.'

'Your father paid, too; he was devastated.'

'Was he?' Victor's smile was derisive. 'Why did you send him away from Belcarron, Mother?'

Alice stood up. 'I am not going to discuss your father any more, Victor. You have the truth now about Julio and I'm sorry it had to come out as it did, I should have prepared you for it.' She turned aside, a little unsteadily. 'We must just learn to live with it. There is nothing else to do.'

'You've already learned to live with it,' Jack muttered.

'Not with your knowing it.'

'You realise you'll have to tell Tina?'

Alice, on her way to the door, stopped and turned a look of horror on Jack.

'This isn't going to go away, Mother. Tina will meet Julio one day, she'll have to know, so will Melissa.'

'Melissa!'

'When she's older,' Jack said hurriedly. 'We're all family, aren't we? The girls must know what we know.'

'Oh, it's all so humiliating, isn't it?' Victor cried suddenly, as Alice sank into a chair. 'I don't mean that there's a bastard in the family, that's nothing unusual, I suppose – it's the way we were made to look such damned fools. That idiot woman taking Julio for our brother –'

'He is our brother,' Jack cut in, 'half-brother, anyway. You can't deny it, Victor.'

'Exactly. That's what sticks in my throat. That Papa put us in this terrible position and Mother let him do it!'

'How can you be so insensitive?' Alice cried, leaping to her feet. 'I've tried to explain to you how it happened –'

'No, you haven't explained,' Victor retorted, 'you haven't explained anything. All we can see is that Papa took what he wanted and didn't give a damn for the consequences. Fellows do that all the time – we're not asked to admire them.'

'Your father was not one of your varsity friends, Victor. He was a fine man and an honourable one – yes, whatever you think, he was!'

'Then why did he betray you?' asked Jack passionately. 'You must see how it looks, Mother.'

She was silent, pacing to and fro before them. 'Yes, I can see,' she said at last, clasping her hands hard, 'and at first I didn't understand any more than you did. I shall have to admit that I was very deeply hurt. But Mena called it a moment of madness and that is what it was. I was away in Ireland, your father and Mena had to stay behind. They were both depressed and lonely; Mena had lost her husband some time before, your father was missing all of us. There was no secret affair, nothing of that sort, just one moment of madness –' Alice's voice faltered – 'and their whole lives were changed.'

'And ours,' said Victor flatly.

'Of course, all our lives. But do you see now how it was?'

Jack bent his head, as though begging not to be spoken to; Victor shrugged. Alice's face slowly crimsoned in anger.

'I see you're both determined not to understand. Well, understand this. I won't have you speaking against your father, reviling his memory. I won't have you shutting him out of your lives. You will grant him the respect that is his, or you will leave this family. Is that understood?'

'Perfectly,' Victor replied, his blue gaze icy, his face still mottled raw. 'But just tell me please what we are to say to the Stonefields.'

'And to Julio,' added Jack.

Alice hesitated. 'We need say nothing to the Stonefields. They will not speak of this to us.'

'And Julio?'

'I will speak to Julio.' Alice glanced distractedly at her small gold watch. 'Now I must see Vittoria about dinner.'

Left alone, the brothers exchanged glances.

'So,' Victor said softly, 'Papa wasn't the Albert Memorial,

after all.' He laughed. 'In a way, you know, I don't mind what he did.'

'You gave a pretty good imitation of minding, then.'

'It's as I said, this kind of thing happens all the time. I don't suppose I should have thought twice about it, if Papa hadn't always been held up to us as such a saint.' Victor's brow darkened. 'Or if the boy hadn't been here, right under our noses. That's what I find so intolerable.'

'And how do you think he finds it?' Jack asked wryly. 'It's Julio who's come worst out of this, Victor – Julio and Mother. They've been hurt and they shouldn't have been.'

'So have we been hurt. In fact, the only person who got off scot-free was Papa. Mother can say what she likes, he did as he pleased and left other people to pick up the pieces.'

'Now he's in pieces,' Jack said slowly, 'his image, I mean. Everything he was to us has been shattered, hasn't it?'

'And a lot of other things besides.' Victor shook his head angrily. 'I envy you, Jack, going home. At least no one knows about this at Belcarron.'

'*I* know,' said Jack.

Somehow they endured dinner, although Lucio, who had been invited, sent a message asking to be excused, and the maids kept whispering among themselves and sending sidelong glances at Alice and her sons. Blanche and Arthur did very well, batting the conversation expertly between themselves, with the occasional comment from Alice, who could always be relied upon to do her duty as hostess, but Victor and Jack sat silent as stones and Lucinda and Evie scarcely raised their eyes. Afterwards, the visitors pleaded tiredness – 'Must keep ourselves fresh for Victor's big day tomorrow,' Arthur cried cheerfully – and went early to bed. Again the Wintours were left alone.

'My big day,' Victor repeated, lighting a cigar. He might have said more, had it not been for the warning flash from Alice's eyes.

'You don't want me to smoke?' he asked, deliberately choosing not to understand.

'I don't want you to say any more. And, yes, I'd prefer you to smoke outside.'

'Very well, I'll take a stroll.'

'Where?' asked Jack quickly.

'Anywhere. You want to come?'

For a crazy moment, Jack had pictured Victor strolling with Isabella, which was not likely tonight of all nights. At Victor's invitation, he breathed again and said he would probably go to bed early.

'Yes, you'll be tired,' Alice murmured, when Victor had left them. 'We're all tired.'

'I'm not, I just want to talk to you.'

'Oh, Jack, what is there to say? I know you think I have deceived you.'

'I know what you've been through, that's what I know. But we have to think of Julio.'

'Do you imagine I am not thinking of him?'

'His father gave him away,' Jack said slowly. 'How does a boy accept that?'

'It was for the best, Jack, really it was. Lucio wanted him, he was desperate for a son –'

'But Julio was Papa's son.'

'Not mine.' Alice looked away from Jack's direct gaze. 'Though I did once think of taking him.'

'Why didn't you, then?'

'It was after Mena died. I wanted to take him for her sake, but that was before I knew – before I knew the truth.'

'So he was given to Lucio.'

'Lucio had already offered to take him. Oh, don't look at me like that, Jack! We don't live in an ideal world. Bringing up Julio at Belcarron would have been impossible, it would have been like asking Mama to take Mena –'

As Alice halted, the blood rushing to her face, Jack sat back, staring at her. 'What are you saying?' he asked quietly. 'That Mena was my grandfather's child? My God! No wonder Victor says this sort of thing happens all the time!'

'Victor knows nothing of this, Jack!'

'Don't worry, I won't tell him. But how many more skeletons are there in the cupboard? How many more secrets have you been carrying all these years?'

Alice stood up. 'I think I'll go to bed, Jack. I can't talk any more tonight.'

Immediately, he put his arm around her shoulders. 'I'm sorry, Mother, I didn't mean to upset you, you've had enough torment, God knows. Hearing that about Grandfather, it was a bit of a shock, that's all.'

'I know, I know. I should say I'm sorry, too – springing so much on to you.'

'All I really wish is that we could have done the right thing by Julio.'

'You say we, but you mean me.' Alice gave a sob. 'I couldn't have done it, Jack, I couldn't have been reminded – all those years, think of it! And he has been happy with Lucio, I know he has.'

Jack's youthful face was stern. 'He's not happy now,' he replied.

Chapter Nine

Early on the morning of Victor's fiesta, Alice hurried through the dews of the orchard to the house Lucio had built some years before. She was sure he would be up, probably like her had not slept, and she could only pray that he had not already ridden out with the gauchos to *rodeo*. Between them, she and Lucio had made terrible mistakes; they could only help each other to face the consequences.

The cottage was looking charming in the still weak sunlight, its painted shutters thrown wide, the nasturtiums climbing its walls slowly opening their flowers, but Alice had no eyes for it. To Isabella, who answered her knock, she gave an anxious smile and asked if she might see her father. The girl said he was having *mate* tea.

'I promise I won't keep him, but I must speak to him. Please.'

Isabella shrugged. She was not so pretty that morning, Alice thought. Her hair was scraped back unbecomingly, her face seemed heavy. After a long dark stare, she unwillingly stepped back and motioned Alice to come in.

Lucio was sitting on his patio, staring into space. At Alice's entrance, he rose and bowed, but her heart smote her as he took her hand, he looked so worn. When Alice had refused his offer of tea and Isabella had noisily left them, they stood for some time looking into each other's tired eyes.

'I never meant this to happen,' Alice said, moving at last to a chair near Lucio's. 'I never meant to hurt Julio. You know that, don't you?'

'I blame myself, Doña Alicia. I should have told him

myself.' Lucio spoke in Spanish, as though to use English then would have been an effort beyond him.

'I should have told my sons,' said Alice.

'No, no, Doña Alicia, how could a lady speak of such a matter? It would not have been right.'

'Ah, you make me feel better, Lucio, but you see it has all come out anyway and my sons blame me. At least, Victor does.'

'And Julio, he blames me. Now he knows his father gave him away, he forgets he was happy. He says I should have told him the truth.'

'He should remember all you've been to him!' Alice cried. 'You are his true father, Lucio, you brought him up, loved and cared for him –'

'Only because his real father did not want him. That is what he sees. That breaks his heart.'

'My husband did not forget Julio, you know,' Alice said, her voice trembling. 'Have you told Julio of the provision made for him?'

'Yes, yes, he knows about the money. But money is not love, Doña Alicia. Julio knows he never had Don Ricardo's love.'

'Where is he?' she asked, after they had been silent for a while. 'May I speak to him?'

'He is walking in the trees. He does not wish to talk.'

'He may talk to Jack, they've become very close. I'll ask Jack to go to him.'

'You may try, Doña Alicia, but your son is a Wintour. I do not think Julio will wish to talk to a Wintour. I am sorry.'

They were silent again, going over in their minds where they had failed, taking what comfort they could from the fact that they were not alone.

Jack had not waited to be asked to talk to Julio. He had already spent some time looking for him in the orchards and the outbuildings, and had finally found him in the screen of trees the Sentos family had planted which was by now almost a wood. Jack remembered this wood from his childhood; it had been one of his favourite places and he was not surprised Julio had gone there for solace. I should have tried here first, thought Jack.

Julio was leaning against an acacia tree. He was dressed in gaucho clothes, wide *bombachas*, colourful shirt and a leather belt studded in silver; his feet were bare. As Jack approached through the grass that was filled with tiny white flowers, he gave no sign.

'Julio?' Jack whispered. 'I've been looking for you. May we talk?'

Julio looked at him but said nothing.

'I know you're feeling upset, you've had a shock, but I want to help. We're friends, aren't we? You'll let me help?'

'Yesterday, we are friends. Not today.'

Jack ran his handkerchief across his brow. 'Julio, you're not being fair. What you discovered about – about my father – has nothing to do with me.'

'Is true. Nothing to do with me is to do with you.'

'Don't twist my words, Julio. You know what I mean. I'm still your friend. I'm more – I'm your brother, and I want you to know that I'm proud to be that; I'm glad you're my brother. I hope you'll say you want to be mine.'

'No, I no want to be your brother. I am not your brother. Your father was Don Ricardo. Mine is Señor Lucio Castillo. How can I be your brother? *Adiós*.'

With a mock bow, Julio turned and walked lightly away, his bare feet making no sound in the grass, the sunlight striking through the trees catching the silver at his belt.

As families in crisis do when they have to, the Wintours put on a good face for their guests, smiling and bowing, shaking the hands of the brightly dressed crowd filling the plantation. Alice, exquisitely dressed in striped grey silk, drew admiring murmurs wherever she went, followed by her two handsome sons, but Jack, wretched enough over Julio, was made even more so by his failure to get near Isabella. She was looking beautiful, he thought, in a white dress and straw hat with red ribbons, but, as he had feared, went nowhere without an escort. Now it was Vittoria, now haggard Lucio – Jack was in despair. Then a move was made to the paddock where the races were to be held and it occurred to him that now might be his chance, the chaperones' attention might be on the horses, not Isabella. His hopes rose.

The gauchos had put on their best *bombachas* for this fiesta day and anything silver they possessed, such as buckles, studs or knives, but not their special-occasion boots; for the races and the *sortija*, they went barefoot.

Victor, though he had tried it, had elected not to take part in the *sortija*, which involved riding at full gallop towards rings slung on a rope between posts, inserting a stick and carrying off the rings. 'All a damned sight more difficult than it looks,' he told Jack. 'I'll stick to the races.'

'Without your boots?' asked Jack, and Victor snorted. Was he crazy? What gentleman rode without boots?

'What gentleman rides in a gauchos' two-horse race?'

'Look, I'm the *estanciero*, I'll show the gauchos they're not the only ones who can ride, boots or no boots!'

'Well, I don't promise to bet on you,' said Jack.

Betting on the races was all-important. The gauchos cared nothing for money as such, their wants, apart from a good horse, being few; winning was what counted to them, winning the race, winning the bet, and their obsession was infectious. On race days, everyone, from *estanciero* to *mestizo*, put on a bet.

The *sortija* over, the competitors mounted for the first race and proceeded to circle round and round, eyeing each other, while some of their companions stationed themselves as judges at the far end of the course and the rest prepared to cheer.

Arthur Stonefield turned to his sister. 'Must seem funny to you, Lucinda, seeing this sort of thing again. Not exactly Ascot, eh?'

Lucinda, though expensively dressed and even a little powdered, looked far from well as she tried to smile. The fact that she had blundered into revealing the Wintours' secret had kept her awake most of the night and had taken her back to her youth when Richard Wintour, the unattainable, had given her her first longings for love. She had known nothing of sex in those days, nothing of what Richard had wanted from that boy's mother. If she had known, how gladly would she have given it! Far more gladly than to her own husband, whose lovemaking had never taken the place of her dreams. It had been years before she had forgotten Richard and the anguish of his death. Now she had opened up not only his secret but also her own wound and the pain was bad. How did Alice bear it? she wondered, watching Alice's small, slim figure standing next to Blanche. Even the comfort of her handsome sons must be lost to her, now that there was Richard's other son darkening her life like a cloud on the horizon.

As the race seemed at last about to start, young Evie gave a cry of excitement, but when Lucinda turned to look at her, she saw that Evie's gaze was fixed, not on the riders, but on Victor Wintour who was waiting his turn. Poor child, she thought, correctly reading Evie's expression, may she have better luck than I had.

The start had been a false one. '*Vamos!*' one rider had cried and leaped away, but the other had walked his horse backwards, as the watchers groaned, until the first had to return and then the circling began again.

'How they enjoy this ritual!' Blanche exclaimed. 'I always wonder if it will go on all night.,'

'Seems like it,' Alice replied, 'but this time I think they're off.'

It was true. Both horsemen were away, riding down the course so close together there was no room to put a pin between them, each one trying to edge the other off, striking with bare feet at the sides of the horses, at the drumming heels, while the watching gauchos roared and the judges waved. Suddenly, it seemed, one had won.

'These races are over so quickly, I can't think why they bother to race at all,' Evie remarked. 'When does Victor ride?'

'Victor?' her father repeated, raising his eyebrows. 'I was not aware you were on first-name terms with Mr Wintour, Evie.'

'Oh, come, Arthur, you sound like Mama in the old days,' Lucinda told him. 'Young people are much more casual now.'

'Not in BA,' he replied, but it seemed to Evie, studying his face closely, that he was not altogether displeased.

'I believe Victor races next,' Lucinda whispered, smiling, and Evie, relieved she could now legitimately watch him, smiled back.

Victor's opponent, sharp-eyed and sullen-mouthed, was savagely bringing his nervous piebald to order when Victor, now mounted on a small chestnut, positioned himself at the starting point. He looked extraordinarily handsome, sitting erect in his saddle, not moulded into it, gaucho-style, his yellow head high. And to the politely concealed derision of the onlookers, yes, he was wearing boots.

'Carlos!' the men shouted, as the sullen gaucho paced his mount to and fro; then a surprised silence fell. Another rider had appeared, one they knew but whose turn it was not. The rider was Julio.

Alice, catching a painful breath, was suddenly aware of Lucio at her side and Jack's face, very pale, opposite her in the crowd. 'Lucio, what is Julio doing?' she asked quickly. 'He is not due to ride yet, is he?'

'He wish to ride against Don Victor,' Lucio answered, his eyes cast down. 'I cannot say why, Doña Alicia.'

'Will the other man let him?'

'I think so, yes. See, he give way.'

But as Carlos, shrugging, rode to the sidelines, allowing Julio to take his position at the start, it was plain that Victor was angry. Although he said nothing, the stiffening of his shoulders and the gathering of his brows might have daunted Julio at any other time. Not now. His Wintour features had never looked more arrogant, as his eyes went over Victor and came to rest on his boots. Then he smiled. And the mottled colour rose to Victor's face and stayed there, as the starter waved his scarf and the race began.

'*Vamos!*' cried Julio, and made to move away. Victor went with him, then Julio drew back. As the gauchos laughed approval, Victor's hand tightened on his whip but he kept his control, circling as Julio circled.

'The ritual again, you see,' sighed Blanche, then, glancing at Alice's strained white face, was silent. Lucio had given Alice his arm, but she had turned away, searching for Jack. He was no longer where he had been in the crowd, but her eyes found him standing next to a girl in a white dress and a hat with red ribbons. So Vittoria had permitted him time with Isabella? Isabella's eyes, however, were only for the riders in the race.

It was Victor's turn to pretend to start and as he forced Julio to come back to him, the gauchos cheered and threw up their hats. Don Victor was good, already he knew a trick or two, he would make a fine *estanciero*.

'*Vamos!*' Julio howled suddenly.

'*Vamos!*' Victor echoed, and both shot away together, this time in earnest.

'They're off!' cried Arthur Stonefield, as Evie fiercely clasped her hands. 'By God, that boy can ride! He's sticking to Victor like glue. I think he's trying to unseat him.'

'It's Victor who has the boots,' Lucinda drawled, 'why doesn't he try to use them?'

'Too late, young Julio is drawing away.'

It was true, Julio was in the lead, riding low against the wind, his head down against his horse's neck. Victor, scarlet in the face, made frantic efforts to catch up, digging in his booted heels, using his whip, straining his last breath, it seemed, not to be beaten. It was no use. Julio, to the applause of the gauchos, slipped from his horse at the winning point. As Victor reached him, Julio looked up at him and smiled again.

'You bastard!' Victor whispered, leaning low to say the words into Julio's face. 'I'll get even with you.'

'*Un millón de gracias*, Don Victor,' Julio answered. 'Try.' Bowing, he turned away.

'Your brother has won?' Jack asked Isabella, whose profile was all he had seen. When she turned her large eyes on him, he felt his heart lurch.

'You no see?'

'I was watching you.'

'Don Victor is your brother. You no watch him?'

'I wanted Julio to win. You, too, of course?'

'Julio? No.' She gave a radiant smile. 'I wish Don Victor to win.'

It did not matter that Lucio appeared and escorted his daughter away. Nothing, in fact, mattered at all. When Victor, still flushed, still with a hard, vindictive look in his eyes, came up and said he needed a drink, Jack led the way to the wine.

'Was that Isabella you were with?' asked Victor, as they stood together under the trees.

'You know it was.' Jack drained his glass. 'Don't get any ideas.'

'Ideas?'

'About geting back at Julio through her.'

'Good God, would I do that?'

'You might.'

'I'm not a fool, Jack. After what happened to Papa, I'm not likely to meddle with an Argentine.'

'Julio, as it happens, is not an Argentine.'

'He's been brought up as one. And I don't fancy a knife in my back, *gracias*. Isabella may be pretty, but she's not worth that.'

'You haven't the faintest idea what she's worth.'

'You've done wonderfully well,' Blanche told Alice, when the last guests had ridden home, when Victor's fiesta was at last over. 'Don't tell me it hasn't been a strain.'

'It's been a strain.'

'I'm so sorry, you know, about what Lucinda said, she'd rather have died –'

'It wasn't her fault. Please tell her not to worry.'

Blanche pressed Alice's hand. 'I expect what you'd really like now, my dear, is to get to your bed.'

No, thought Alice, rising to find Blanche a candle, what I'd really like would be to pack my box and sail for Belcarron. She took comfort in knowing that the passage was booked. She and Jack would be home before the spring.

Chapter Ten

Tina was also thinking of her return home, but her feelings were mixed. Of course she wanted to see Melissa agan, but Mama and Jack would not be back until the spring and, though it would be pleasant enough to spend Christmas with the Morrys, Castle Morry was not Belcarron. As for George Coxe, she had no idea when she would see him again and was beginning to regret some of the letters she had written him. Had she perhaps been a little too enthusiastic about her new interest in the Irish cause? Might he think she was just trying to win favour with him because that was his cause too? It wasn't true, her interest was genuine, and she wasn't trying to win favour because she wasn't sure she wanted that, wasn't sure of what she wanted at all. She was sure, though, that she was going to miss the Molloys, she was going to miss New York.

Her cousins had shown her so much – Washington, New England in the fall, the beautiful lakes and mountains of New York State – but what she had most enjoyed and would never forget was New York itself. Perhaps all great cities were as exciting, she didn't know, she had so little experience, but she could not believe any other city had as much to offer as New York.

'I feel a different person here,' she told Hester. 'I feel so much more alive than at home. Do you know what I mean?'

Hester, who had been spending more time with Tina since Caitlin had returned to school and Paul to college, gave a quiet smile. 'I do, of course. When we first came here, I felt the same.'

'Not now?'

'Not so much now. In the early days, it all seemed very different from anything we'd been used to, free and exhilarating. Even democratic.'

'Isn't it?' asked Tina, a little surprised.

'Yes, but less than I first thought. Oh, please don't misunderstand me, America is a wonderful country and New York is a wonderful city, and I shall always be grateful that Daniel has been happy here from the beginning. All I'm saying is that there are distinctions here, just as everywhere else. They may not be so apparent, but they are there.'

'I think I understand,' Tina said slowly. 'Cousin Daniel was accepted by the Irish community but not by certain other sections?'

Hester nodded without speaking.

'And you have not been accepted either?'

'As you say, by certain sections. Not only because I am Mrs Daniel Molloy, but because I run my bookshops.'

'But as Miss Hester Wintour you'd have been accepted, wouldn't you? In spite of your bookshops?'

'Perhaps, but I'd have been thought a little odd.' Hester gave a sudden smile which lit her tranquil features with youthful radiance. 'But, really, what does it matter? One can be perfectly happy in New York without appearing in the Social Register, as Daniel and I have found. We have our Irish and political friends, I have my literary circle, Paul and Caitlin know people everywhere.' Hester had been arranging flowers when Tina joined her. Now she picked up some white chrysanthemums and began to snap stems and strip leaves. 'I don't want to be critical of this country, which has given us so much. We could never have been as happy in Ireland.'

'And you've been happy here, haven't you?' Tina asked softly, her eyes on her cousin's nimble fingers. 'Do you want some water in that vase?'

'Please.' As Tina filled the vase from a large jug, Hester gave her a long, considering look. 'Does that surprise you?'

'No, no, of course not.'

'Of course it does. It surprises everyone.' Hester placed the vase on a side table and stood back to admire it. 'Beautiful, aren't they? Paul sent them.'

'Beautiful,' Tina agreed. 'It's just that your background and

Cousin Daniel's were so different. And there's always been so much prejudice ...'

'Yes.' Hester gave a long deep sigh. 'If I have any regrets it's that I upset my family at the time. Papa always understood, but my mother only accepted Daniel when Caitlin was born, and even your father, Tina, took a long time to forgive.'

'His own sister!' Tina cried hotly.

'My dear, that's why he couldn't understand.' Hester shrugged. 'I was a Wintour, you see ... But your mother stood by me, she was always for me and I'll never forget it. And things worked out well in the end. I knew I could be happy with Daniel and I have been happy. I knew he could do great things and he has done great things. We should never have doubted.'

'You've done great things, too, Cousin Hester. Look at your bookshops!' Tina shook her head. 'You don't know how much I envy you.'

'Envy me? For my bookshops?'

'For knowing what you want.'

'You mean, you don't?'

'That's it, I don't.'

Hester glanced at her watch. 'Why don't you come downtown with me this afternoon, Tina? To my office?'

Tina had already visited her cousin's bookshop and admired it, but had never seen the office from which Hester controlled her little empire. 'I'll get my hat,' she said, with alacrity.

The winter day was bitterly cold, with a stinging wind that Hester said would bring snow. It was a relief to reach the steam-heated offices at the rear of the busy bookshop, to be brought coffee and cookies, to take off their hats and jackets and put their chilled hands to their chilled faces and begin to thaw out.

'Caitlin told me about this kind of weather when I first arrived,' said Tina. 'It seems so long ago now.'

'When it's almost time for you to leave us. We shall miss you so much.'

'And I you.' Tina bit into a cookie. 'Oh, dear, I don't think I want to go.'

'Maybe you needn't.'

Tina's dark-blue eyes widened. 'Whatever do you mean?'

'I mean, you might like to stay. Make a career with me. I employ quite a number of people, you know.' Hester touched Tina's arm. 'Come, look here for a moment.'

From Hester's private office, it was possible to see through glass partitions into the larger office where her staff were busy invoicing, typewriting, working at ledgers, glancing from time to time through more glass partitions into the shop itself, where other assistants were serving customers. Tina noticed that many of the staff were women, all the same kind of quick, competent New Yorker she so much admired. She put a hand to her damp, dark hair and glanced enquiringly at Hester.

'Eventually, Paul will take over from me, running Molloy Books,' Hester told her. 'We've come a long way since I opened my first little shop in Dublin, called Irish Books for the Irish. As you know, we stock most types of book now – novels, biographies, textbooks, schoolbooks. I think my poor father, long gone, would have been proud. He gave me the money to start up, all those years ago.' Hester's smile was tender. 'But Mama never really approved. "A woman's place is in the home" was her motto, but I'm afraid I never learned it.'

'It's so wonderful, what you've done,' Tina whispered, 'but I could never be a part of it, really I couldn't.'

'Paul will need someone to help him. You have a good head on your shoulders, you could be the one.'

'Cousin Hester, you don't know me, or you'd never ask. I'm no reader, I know nothing of books.'

'You once told me your best subject at school was mathematics.'

'And science, what bits we were taught.'

'So, you're not literary. But bookshops don't need only literary people, Tina. Running them is like running any other business, you need common sense and a good head for figures, which you have.' Hester again touched Tina's arm. 'Please, Tina, think about it.'

From the windows fronting the street, Tina could see the first driving flakes of snow. She stared at them for some time, her mind working furiously. Hester, from her rolltop desk, watched the changing expressions of her face.

'You could be trained, you know,' Hester said quietly, 'there are business colleges that take women. Isn't a proper career what you want, Tina?'

'Yes, but –'

'But what?' Hester left her chair and came to stand beside Tina at the window. 'Is there someone at home?' she asked softly. 'The young man who writes the letters?'

'There's Mama,' said Tina.

'Ah.' Hester turned back to her desk and looked down at the papers waiting for her attention. 'So there is. But I hadn't forgotten her, Tina. Obviously you'd need her approval.'

'But I could never live so far away, Cousin Hester. You do see that, don't you?'

'Tina, I know your mother, she's my dearest friend as well as my cousin, and I know she'd never want you to sacrifice an opportunity for her. If there was something you wanted to do and it involved living away from her, she'd want you to do it.'

'But I should have to be very sure I wanted to do it.'

Hester gave a sigh. 'That's true, of course.'

'I'm terribly grateful for the suggestion, Cousin Hester, truly I am, and I'd like to give it some thought –'

'I hope you will, Tina.'

'But I was wondering, while I'm here –' Tina was apologetic – 'do you think I could look at some books about nursing? I've been meaning to ask you for ages, ever since Caitlin talked about it, but there's been so much happening . . .'

'Of course, my dear.' Hester gave no sign of disappointment. 'I'll show them to you now.'

Time passed. Hester worked her way through the letters requiring her signature, had several discussions with one of her accountants, returned to her desk and made some telephone calls, then, as the clock chimed five, looked up with a start. Good heavens! she thought. I've quite forgotten Tina.

She found her in a quiet corner of the shop, completely absorbed in a large textbook; at Hester's step, she looked up, her eyes alight.

'Tina, I'm so sorry, I've neglected you,' said Hester. 'Come, you must be dying for a cup of tea.'

'Oh, Cousin Hester, don't worry about tea,' Tina whispered.

'I've discovered what I want to do!'

Hester gave a wry smile. 'I don't suppose it's to help Paul run my book chain, is it?'

'I'm so sorry . . .' Tina scrambled to her feet, holding fast to her book. 'I really am, you know, it could have been wonderful. But do you think I might buy this book, Cousin Hester?'

'Of course you won't buy it, you shall have it as a present from me.'

'You're so kind, you're one of the kindest persons I've ever met.' Tina impulsively leaned forwards and kissed her cousin's cheek. 'Thank you.'

'Now let's go home and have some tea and you can tell me what you plan to do.' Hester glanced at the title of the book in Tina's hand. 'Although I think I can make a very good guess.'

'No,' said Tina, 'I think you'll be surprised.'

They went out together into the snow.

On Tina's last night in New York, Paul and Caitlin came home for the special dinner Hester had prepared. To Tina's astonishment, Daniel arrived too. He was to leave for Washington the following day, and she had never expected he would give her his time, but he did more, he gave her a Christmas present.

'Why, Cousin Daniel, I don't know what to say!' She looked down in some embarrassment at the small wrapped package he had slipped into her hand.

''Tis something to be reminding you of America,' he told her gruffly, 'an Indian necklace from one of the reservations.'

'Why, I'll treasure it!' cried Tina delightedly. 'I'll keep this and open it on Christmas Day and think about everyone here. Thank you, Cousin Daniel, thank you very much.'

His forbidding features relaxed, his hard gaze softened, and for the first time Tina saw in him the attraction that had drawn Hester to him so many years before. 'You've a good heart, Tina,' he murmured, 'and a good head. I'm thinking you'll go far.'

'There, you see, he's not so bad, is he?' Caitlin whispered, as her father moved away to help the maid bring in the celebratory champagne cup. 'Papa likes you, you know, Tina, even if you are a Wintour, and it's not just because you've seen the light on Ireland. You're his sort. Direct, no nonsense, honest.'

'Do go on,' Tina answered, laughing and blushing, 'this

kind of talk really suits me.'

'No, I mean it.' Caitlin fixed her with a solemn gaze. 'You're a good friend, Tina, you always will be. Whatever happens in the future, I know I'll be able to rely on you.'

'For what?' asked Tina, her laughter dying. 'I don't know when we'll even see each other in the future. I mean, if you're in America and I'm in Ireland.'

'You know I'm to be in Ireland too. It's all very well, Papa and Mother saying they can work for Ireland here, but all they can do is raise money. The real work has to be done over there, hasn't it? I'm sure you know what I'm talking about.'

Paul, catching Tina's troubled expression from across the room, came over and slipped his arm into hers. 'What's up, Tina? You're looking sad and that's not allowed tonight. You can cry tomorrow, but tonight we'll eat, drink and be merry, or Mother will know the reason why!'

'Paul, Tina and I were having a serious conversation,' Caitlin said irritably. 'This is our last chance before Tina sails.'

'Look, I'll keep in touch,' Tina murmured, 'and I'll do anything I can to help – short of violence.'

Caitlin's gaze flickered. 'Please, Tina, see how things go, keep an open mind, that's all I ask.'

'You're the one with the closed mind, Caitlin,' Paul told her. 'We're all in agreement about what has to be achieved, but there are right and wrong ways of going about it.'

'And my way is wrong, is it? Look, if we wait for a political solution, we'll wait for ever. You talk to Papa's friends, they'll tell you what's needed.'

'Have some champagne cup and cool down. We mustn't spoil Tina's last evening, you know.'

'My last evening ...' Tina shook her head. 'I never really thought it would come. You folks will come over and see me, won't you? If you don't promise to come to Belcarron, I shan't be able to leave.'

'I said I'd come to Ireland,' Caitlin replied. 'I never said anything about Belcarron.'

'She'll come, all right,' Paul said, pushing the two girls towards the maid with her tray of glasses. 'Don't worry, Tina, you won't be able to keep us away.'

*

It was hard, next day, making the goodbyes. The firm handshake from Daniel before he left for Washington was not too bad, but chatting on board ship and having to keep up a brave front before Mr and Mrs Warren Frobisher, friends of Hester's who were to 'look out' for Tina on the voyage, was a terrible ordeal. Though she wanted her cousins to stay, Tina also wanted them to go, so she might be on her own and shed a few tears in private. It was a relief when the crowd on deck began to thin and the call came, 'All ashore that's going ashore', and Paul said, 'We'd better go.'

'Oh, Paul!' Tina stretched up and kissed his cheek as he held her close, then turned and clung to Caitlin.

'Don't forget,' Caitlin whispered, her blue eyes stormy.

'Forget what?'

'Anything!'

They laughed and kissed, and then it was Hester's turn. Dear, calm, dark-eyed Hester.

'Oh, do come over soon!' cried Tina. 'Come and see Mama and all of us!'

'I'll bet we come for your wedding,' Paul said with a grin. 'No, seriously, I'll lay a dollar.'

'Tina has much better things to do than get married,' Caitlin declared.

Hester smiled and murmured, 'But she's not saying what.'

The Frobishers, who had been tactfully standing a little apart, moved nearer to Tina as her cousins swiftly kissed her again and hurried to leave the ship.

'Keep in touch!' cried Tina, wildly waving.

'And you!' they called.

'Goodbye, goodbye!' Tina turned aside, Jennie Frobisher's hand on her arm. 'And goodbye, New York,' she added quietly.

'Why am I crying?' she asked herself in her cabin, dabbing at her pink eyelids. 'I do want to see home again, and Mama and Jack when they come, and Melissa and the Morrys. I really shouldn't be crying.'

She knew in her heart, however, that this trip to America had been special; that however many times she came back in the years to come, there would never be another trip like this one. Now that it was ended, she was crying just for that.

It occurred to her, as she was laying out her dress for the first-night reception, that she had missed a name from the list of people she wanted to see. But would she see George Coxe anyway? Probably not, unless, perhaps, he came to Liverpool to meet her. Oh, what a foolish idea! Of course he wouldn't come to Liverpool. She couldn't think why she had ever thought of such a thing.

All the same, when the ship came in to Liverpool at the end of the long, dull voyage, and Tina saw only Cousin Everard waving, she felt quite absurdly disappointed.

Chapter Eleven

Castle Morry, inland from Clonakilty, was larger and grander than Belcarron and though at one time had been in a sorry state, was now in excellent repair, thanks to Mavis Morry's fortune. Tina found she was, after all, glad to see it again, and Melissa, of course, and Cavan and Mavis, and even the Morry children, who stood around with undisguised interest, waiting to see what presents she had brought. Melissa declared she couldn't wait to hear Tina's news and dragged her up to her room before she had even taken off her hat. 'Oh, Tina,' she wailed, 'I've been so lonely!'

'Poor Melissa, what about all your friends?' Tina, with her arm around her sister, stood at the square, sashed window, looking out at the familiar view. It was desolate enough on that December afternoon, with the light fading and the mist rising. Beyond the dark skeletons of the trees lay the blue-green fields, but no sea, of course. That was what one missed at Castle Morry, and tears suddenly stung Tina's eyes for Belcarron. She wished Mama had been back, and the boys. And George Coxe.

'You mean, at school?' asked Melissa. 'Oh, I suppose school wasn't any worse than it always is, but it's been dreadfully boring here. Hugh is so awful, always teasing and getting in the way, and Daisy and Moyra are so childish. They still play with dolls and don't care a bit what they wear. Oh, it's lovely to have you back, Tina!'

'As though I care what I wear!' Tina laughed and moved to begin her unpacking.

'Well, you're looking different somehow.' Melissa studied

her with a critical eye. 'I think you're prettier!'

'Thank you, I'm so glad to have your approval.'

'No, but you are. I wonder why?' Suddenly Melissa darted forward and snatched up a dress Tina had laid on the bed. 'Oh, that's lovely, that's really fine material. Did you get that in New York?'

'I did, I bought it ready-made at one of the stores. They have truly wonderful shops in New York, Melissa, you'd think you were in heaven.'

'Ready-made? You mean, it wasn't measured for you? How strange, how exciting!' Mesllisa's eyes shone. 'I'd love to go to a shop and look at dresses all set out, so that one could choose. New York sounds just my sort of place. Full of everything.'

'That's a very good description.' Tina gave a sigh of remembrance. 'You must certainly go there when you're older.'

'I don't want to go when I'm older, I want to go now. But, of course, Mama would never let me. Did you like Cousin Hester?'

'Yes, I did, I liked everyone, but I think I've had enough questions. Don't you want to see your present?'

When they were going down for tea, Melissa still in raptures over her new silk dress, Mavis, smiling, waved a telegram at them.

'Good news! George is arriving tomorrow!'

'George?' Tina repeated stupidly.

'My cousin, of course – George Coxe. He usually spends Christmas with Annette in Essex – that's his sister, you know – but he asked if he might come to us this year, I'm not sure why.'

'Why did I desert my sister in Essex?' George stared delightedly into Tina's face. 'Because I knew you were to be here.'

He had not long arrived; it was already dark and the lamps were lit in the drawing room, where everyone except George and Tina was dressing the Christmas tree. They sat at a distance, supposedly watching, actually only looking at each other, each feeling on the brink of something magical, as the tree in the corner began to take on its special radiance.

'I can't tell you what your letters meant to me,' George said in a low voice. 'I didn't embarrass you, did I? Writing so often? I mean, your cousins didn't mind?'

'Of course not. Cousin Hester would never interfere.'

'Yet she was taking the place of your mother over there, I didn't want to presume.'

'Heavens, what are letters? Why should anyone mind my getting letters?'

'You liked them, though? You were glad I wrote?'

'Very glad, I loved them.'

'Though you wouldn't have had much time to think of me, when you had so much to see and talk about.'

Tina said there had certainly been a lot to see, but they had talked mainly of Ireland. Caitlin and Paul were dedicated to the cause of Irish freedom, as she had told him in her letters.

'You also said Paul looked like your brothers. He's handsome, then?'

'Oh, very. And Caitlin's very pretty.'

'Caitlin's no threat, though.'

Tina laughed, feeling a strange, heady excitement fill her veins. 'You surely don't think of Paul as a threat?'

'I do. I regard him as a rival. You said he was handsome.'

'I said he was like my brothers.'

'But he's not your brother, he's your cousin. Cousins can marry cousins.'

'George, I promise you, I am not at all interested in Paul in the way you mean.'

George gave a long, satisfied sigh and looked across at Melissa, who was standing on a stepladder held by Cavan, trying to fix the star at the top of the Christmas tree. 'I wish there was somewhere where we could talk on our own,' he whispered.

'I don't suppose they'd notice if we went to the library.'

'You don't think so?'

'Why should they?'

Like two criminals, they crept furtively from the room and hurried across the hall to the library, where firelight shone on rows of unread, leather-bound books, but where no lamp had been lit.

'Should we light it?' asked Tina.

'No,' said George.

As he drew her gently into his arms, Tina thought, He is going to kiss me! It's happening, I'm going to be kissed! And then, foolishly, Wouldn't the girls at school be surprised?

They had often talked of what it would be like to be kissed by a man, and some had declared it would be shocking and others frightful, but Tina had never said what she thought, that it might be enjoyable, for it had always seemed likely to her that she would never be kissed at all. She was considered clever and not pretty and everyone knew it was the pretty girls who could look forward to love, while the clever, plain ones must simply hope. But here she was, about to be kissed and certain, as she waited for George's mouth to meet hers, that she was going to like it.

She was right. As soon as she felt his lips, soft and tentative at first, as though not sure of their welcome, then increasingly ardent, delight possessed her and she returned his kiss with a passion that surprised them both.

'Oh, Tina!' George whispered, releasing her at last. 'You know I love you, don't you? I love you and want to marry you.'

She should have cried, 'Oh, yes, and I love you and want to marry you too!' It was what she wanted, surely? What every girl wanted – to be kissed and loved and proposed to. Yet she said nothing.

'Tina, please, say something,' George was murmuring urgently. 'You don't know how I'm feeling!'

'George, dearest, I don't know what to say.'

He drew back as though stung. 'You mean, you don't love me? Why did you let me kiss you, then? Why did you kiss me back?'

'I do love you, George. I see now that I've loved you for a long time. All the time I was in America.'

'Then say you'll have me! I know I'm much older than you, but if we love each other, that needn't matter. We could share so much, you see, we could work for the same things. We'd be lovers and partners, Tina, we'd have everything!'

She pulled herself from his arms. 'George, please light the lamp.'

'Are you worried in case someone comes in? We can tell them we're engaged!'

'Please light the lamp,' she said again, and he did as she asked.

When light flooded the room, she turned to face him. 'George, please believe me, I do love you and I want to marry you, but we may have to wait. There's something I want to do first.'

'For God's sake, what?'

'Promise not to laugh, or think me a fool?'

'Just tell me what it is, Tina, please!'

'All right. I want to train as a doctor.'

George took a step backwards, his fair, cheerful features appearing so astonished, he might have been stunned by a physical blow.

'A doctor?' he repeated. 'A doctor, Tina?'

'You did promise not to laugh.'

'I'm not laughing.' He pushed his hair back from his brow and stared wildly into Tina's face. 'Tina, whatever gave you such an idea?'

'Caitlin and I had discussed taking up nursing. I read some medical textbooks. Then I knew I didn't want to nurse people, I wanted to cure them. Especially women, because so many doctors don't seem to pay much attention to the special problems women have.' Tina's eyes were bright as she looked into George's. 'I want to be like Elizabeth Garrett Anderson, a woman doctor, working for women. It's not so ridiculous, is it? Women are allowed to practise, you know.'

'My darling girl, have you any idea of what's involved? Of how long it takes?'

'Of course. I've gone into it all thoroughly. I know it won't be easy, but I believe I could do it.'

'You'd never stand it. You can't even imagine the kind of thing you'd have to do, the horrors you'd see ...'

'I'm strong,' she said simply, and George, his shoulders sagging, said no more.

'Will you help me?' she asked, snatching at his hands. 'I could come to London to train, you know, we could be near each other. It would be wonderful.'

'That's what you're offering, is it? Tina, I can't afford to wait, I haven't the time.'

'That's nonsense, George!'

'No, by the time you qualify, I'll be in my forties. I don't want to have to wait for marriage as long as that.'

'What are you saying? You won't wait for me? You'll give me up?' Tina drew back, her face stricken. 'I couldn't let you do that, George. I love you.'

'Yes, but you want things all ways, don't you?'

'Well, so do you. Don't you want marriage and a career?'

'It's different for men.'

'Yes, it always is, isn't it?' Tina's eyes flashed. 'But why should it be different? Tell me that.'

George groaned. 'You know why, Tina. Women have to have the children.'

'I've always thought there was more to life than bringing up children. One day, people will have to understand that.'

'I'm sure you're right. In the meantime – Tina, will you marry me?'

'If I may be a medical student as well.'

He gathered her into his arms. 'Darling, I don't see anyone stopping you.'

'Tina,' came Melissa's voice at the library door, 'whatever are you doing in there all this time? Don't you want to come and see the Christmas tree?'

Chapter Twelve

There were no Christmas trees at the Estancia Sentos, but Alice was making plans for some small festivity when she and Jack returned to BA. Victor would come too, but in the New Year they must say goodbye to him and Alice was rather worrying about that: not that there was any need, Victor was going from strength to strength as an *estanciero*, he probably wouldn't miss them at all.

Of more concern was Jack, with his white face, shadowed eyes and look of one who could not sleep. Poor boy, thought Alice, he was in love with the unattainable, but that happened to so many young people and must be endured like a fever until it passed. As it would. As soon as he was back home again, back at Oxford, he would forget Lucio's daughter, who in a year or two would marry someone far more suitable. All they must do was get through the days until it was time to leave.

At least Julio was no longer on the *estancia*. Lucio had sent him back to his boarding school in BA and since the day of Victor's fiesta, he had not been seen. Isabella, too, was keeping out of everyone's way, and Jack, who felt she must be avoiding him, was tortured by frustration as he hung around Lucio's house, hoping to see her come out, even to shake a cloth or something, but when she did she was careful never to look his way and he never had the courage to call her name.

Then one day, when he was least expecting it, he saw her away from the house. He had been lying in the orchard, watching little scarlet birds he didn't know, when in the distance he caught sight of a pink dress. He shot to his feet and raced through the trees to catch her before she disappeared, although he wasn't even sure she was real.

She was real.

'Isabella?' He managed to say her name.

She was smiling at him. Was it a mocking smile? Did she think him a fool? He stood there before her, racking his brains for the Spanish to say, 'Will you walk with me?' but not finding it, while she watched and waited and put her smooth hand to her black hair. Finally, he pointed down the trees and she seemed to understand.

'You wish I walk?' she asked.

And there they were, walking together. He couldn't believe it, he and Isabella, walking in the orchard! It was as though he were dreaming and would soon wake up and find himself alone. He knew he mustn't waste these moments which wouldn't last and might not come again, he must say now all that was in his heart, make her understand he loved her and wished to marry her, would wait for her as long as she liked, if only she would agree to take him. She might, he tried to tell himself. After all, he had things to offer. He was considered to be English and the Argentines admired the English, he had a share in the *estancia*, he could surely provide for her, could even make her Doña Isabella, which would surely please her?

'Isabella!' he cried, as all these thoughts gathered momentum in his head. Catching her hands, he made her swing round to face him. 'Isabella, you must forgive me if I speak to you, I know I should speak to your father –'

'*No entiendo*,' she said politely and freed her hands.

'You don't understand?' He stared at her, distractedly. How could she not understand? Wasn't it written all over him what he was trying to say?

'*Enamorado*!' he cried. 'I am in love with you! I wish to marry you!'

'Marry?'

'Yes, marry!' His hands, damp with sweat, wound themselves in hers, but with a deliberation that chilled his heart, Isabella again freed herself. Her eyes were like dark stones, quite without warmth.

'I no marry you,' she said flatly. 'Is not possible.'

'Why? Why isn't it possible? If you're worried about your

father, I shall speak to him today. I'll go now, ask for your hand in the proper way, then I'll wait for you as long as you like, until you're ready . . .'

He knew she was not understanding, was perhaps not even listening. All the time he was speaking, she was simply waiting until he stopped. When he did, she said, 'I am betrothed.'

'Betrothed?'

'*Si, prometida.*'

'But when? No one said, no one told us, your father would have surely said, wouldn't he? Isabella, please answer me!'

She shrugged, she said nothing.

'Ah, I understand,' Jack gasped, wiping his brow. 'You haven't told your father, have you? You're keeping it a secret. Why? Who has promised to marry you and not spoken to your father?' Already a great fear was working in Jack's mind. 'Tell me the name of the man, tell me!'

'Is Don Victor!' she cried with a triumphant smile.

Victor was in his room, stepping out of a hip bath, when Jack, without knocking, strode in and slammed the door shut.

'Here –' he tossed Victor a towel – 'dry yourself. I want to talk to you before I knock you down.'

'What in damnation is the matter?' asked Victor, laughing, as he began to towel himself. 'Have you completely lost your senses?'

'You know damned well what's the matter. You've been making love to Isabella, when you swore to me you'd leave her alone. A child of fifteen, and you've promised to marry her!' Jack was so clearly near to losing what command he had over himself, even Victor's coolness deserted him and he tried to calm his brother down.

'Look, old chap,' he began, but Jack's face flamed.

'Don't old-chap me!' he shouted. 'I can't bear to listen to you, it makes me sick to look at you. A beautiful, trusting girl like Isabella, and you have to add her to your trophies, don't you? You have to promise to marry her because that's the only way you could get her and now the poor child thinks she is betrothed. *Prometida*, she told me, *prometida* to you!'

'Sit down,' ordered Victor and, before Jack could resist, had pushed him into a chair, where he stood over him tall and powerful, his blue eyes like flint. 'I never promised to marry Isabella,' he said distinctly. 'I never made love to her.'

'Oh, don't lie,' Jack said wearily. 'Why should she say such things if they weren't true? It's pointless to deny them, everyone knows what you're like.'

'Oh? What am I like, then?'

'For God's sake, haven't you been with half the women of Oxford already?'

Victor seemed amused. 'Jack, I'm flattered. If that's my reputation, I'm afraid it's not deserved. But when I told you I wouldn't get involved with Isabella, it was just the truth. She's attractive, she's very mature for her age, but I wouldn't lay a finger on her, she's not worth the risk.'

With a sudden, violent movement, Jack pulled himself from the chair and sent Victor flying. 'I'm going to Lucio,' he got out, breathing hard. 'See if he believes you; I don't.'

'Wait!' shouted Victor, as Jack made for the door. 'Just first explain how you came to be talking on these intimate terms to Isabella. Have you been trying to make love to her yourself?' At the look on Jack's face, Victor laughed. 'I see you have. A child of fifteen, eh? Maybe you're the one who's been promising marriage?'

'You're right.' Jack came back into the room. 'I did promise her marriage. I asked her to marry me. Unlike you, I meant it.'

Victor's face changed. 'You promised to marry her?' he whispered. 'A girl like Isabella? What in hell do you think you were playing at? Did you think you could take her home to Belcarron? To pay calls on the county? Visit the tenants? Tell Maisie what to cook?'

'Why not? She could have learned what to do. Plenty of men marry foreign wives.'

'You'd have been laughed out of the county and she'd have been utterly miserable. It would be like trying to grow a passion flower on the clifftop. Oh, Jack, I knew you were crazy, but not as crazy as this.'

Jack's face was working, his lips trembling. 'Maybe we'd stay here, then. We could, I'd have the right.'

'You'd give up Belcarron for that little –'

As Victor searched for a word to describe Isabella, Jack didn't wait to hear it. His fist shot out and caught Victor on the mouth, jerking his head back, sending him reeling. 'Get dressed,' Jack said curtly. 'You're coming with me to Lucio's.'

'I'm damned if I will!' Victor cried and, shaking the blood from his mouth, knocked Jack to the floor, from where he was trying to rise when Alice appeared in the doorway.

She would not allow either of them to speak until Victor had dressed and she had bathed their cut lips and marched them to her own sitting room. 'Now,' she asked coldly, 'which of you is going to tell me what that was about? I've never been so ashamed of you in my life.'

Jack kept his eyes down, but Victor said thickly that Isabella had made a false accusation against him and he and Jack were fighting over it.

'Like a couple of cavemen? Haven't you both been educated to know better than that? What was this accusation?'

Jack looked up. 'Isabella told me that Victor had promised to marry her and they were betrothed.'

'Betrothed?' Alice drew in her breath. 'Oh, Victor!'

'Oh, Victor,' he mimicked, 'why should you immediately believe her rather than me, Mother? Whatever happens, it seems I am to blame. No one listens to me, no one believes me –'

'Of course I'm prepared to listen to you, Victor, and I want to believe you –'

'But you can't, because my name is Victor. I'm the one who's cold and hard, so I must be telling lies, is that it?'

'No, that is not it!' cried Alice, as the bitterness of his look went to her heart. 'I love you, I'd never blame you without cause. It's only that Isabella is so young, only a child –'

'Exactly what I said,' Jack put in, but Victor turned on him. 'Keep your mouth shut, Jack, you're the one who caused all this trouble in the first place.'

He swung back to Alice. 'Did you know he had proposed to Isabella himself, Mother? Planned to take her home to Belcarron, make her Mrs Jack Wintour? How does that sound to you?'

Alice went pale. 'Is this true, Jack? Did you ask Isabella to marry you?'

'Yes, I did. I told her I loved her, I told her I'd wait for her.

That was when she said she was already betrothed.' Jack shot a look of fury at his brother. 'To Victor.'

'Dear God, what are we to do?' whispered Alice.

At dinner, Alice felt ill; exhausted with the effort of controlling two blond strangers who were her sons, at present glowering at each other across the dark Spanish table. She had insisted they should behave as usual, have dinner like civilised people, not go rushing across to Lucio, upsetting him, frightening Isabella. Later, when they had thought about things, they could decide what to do. Perhaps Alice herself should talk to Isabella in the morning –

'No!' cried Jack. 'I can't wait until then!'

'Nor can I,' said Victor. 'I want my name cleared now.'

'Let's see how we feel when we've finished dinner,' Alice ruled firmly. 'This is a delicate situation and must be handled in a delicate fashion.'

'Very well, just don't expect me to eat anything,' Jack grunted.

But Victor, feeling his jaw, said he'd be damned if he'd be put off his dinner by other people's mischief-making.

'Victor!' Alice protested.

'Sorry, Mother.' Victor, looking far from apologetic, drank his wine.

When the meal was over, Alice took coffee, while her sons fretted and fumed. 'Do hurry,' Victor groaned. 'Isabella might be going to bed.'

'Everyone dines late here,' Alice returned. 'Isabella will not have gone to bed.'

Lights were still on in Lucio's cottage and Lucio himself was at the door, smoking a cigar, when they approached. Alice said at once they would not keep him long, there was something they had to discuss. At the tone in her voice, Lucio's smile faded and he showed them inside.

'Is Isabella at home?' Alice asked, as her sons stared down at the tiled floor of Lucio's parlour.

'Of course, Doña Alicia. You wish I call her?'

'Perhaps it would be better if I spoke to you first. You see, the fact is –' Alice put her handkerchief to her lips – 'there appears to have been some mistake.'

'Mistake?'

'Yes, it seems that Isabella thinks – has said – Don Victor wishes to marry her.'

Lucio stared in astonishment. 'Don Victor wishes to marry Isabella?'

'So she has said.'

Lucio swung round on Victor. 'You say this is a mistake, Don Victor? You say is no true?'

'I say it is not true because it isn't true. Please call your daughter, Lucio, so that I may speak to her myself.'

'Certainly, I call her,' Lucio replied slowly. 'I think she know already you are here.'

When Isabella entered, Jack thought he had never seen her looking so beautiful. She was wearing the same pink dress she had worn earlier in the orchard, but her black hair was loose on her shoulders, giving her an air of intimacy that made her seem even more desirable. Victor's eyes on her were, however, as cold as winter. If she noticed, she gave no sign of nerves; her own gaze was expressionless.

'Isabella,' Lucio said in English, 'you say that Don Victor wish to marry you. Is this true?'

'Is true, *Papá*, I swear it.'

The little room was very still. Lucio was staring at his daughter with a strange troubled expression, while Alice, the only one seated, felt for Jack's hand. Victor took a step forwards.

'Isabella, why are you lying?'

'I no lie.'

'How can you say that? You know I never asked you to marry me!'

'*Si, si*, many times.' Isabella, flinging back her hair, spoke in rapid Spanish.

'What does she say?' cried Victor.

Lucio translated. 'She say you make love to her, Don Victor.'

'It's not true, I never made love to her!' Victor's face had taken on a look of anguish. 'This is like a nightmare! Why is she doing this to me?'

'Why should she, Victor?' Alice asked.

Jack echoed, 'Yes, why should she?'

'I don't know, I tell you! Ask her, ask her now, for God's sake!'

'I no lie,' Isabella said again, and drawing at a chain around her neck, brought out a small silver ring. 'See, here is the ring you give me, Don Victor. Is my betrothal ring.'

As she held it out for them all to see, Lucio turned away, his face working, while Jack went white and Victor stood transfixed. Alice, however, rose and, moving closer, looked hard and long at the ring as it swung on the end of its chain held by Isabella. It was a cheap little ring, the sort a child might have, the sort Alice could not imagine Victor giving to any woman. She raised her eyes slowly to meet Isabella's. They were filled with dark triumph.

Why, she's lying, thought Alice. Lying to hurt us, as Paola hurt me. Paola's weapon had been the truth, but lies could hurt as much as truth, if they could not be disproved. It was Victor's word against Isabella's, but Alice had no doubt now which she should take. She went to Lucio.

'I'm sorry, Lucio, I was right when I said there had been a mistake. Don Victor is telling the truth, he is innocent of this charge. We must bid you goodnight.'

'Mother,' said Victor, taking her hand, his eyes on her face filled with a new, soft light, 'thank you.'

'*Papá*!' cried Isabella, running to her father and grasping his arm, '*Papá*!' She spoke furiously in Spanish, her eyes flashing, as Victor, releasing Alice's hand, strode to the door.

'Come on, Mother,' he called over his shoulder.

'Doña Alicia, what can I say?' cried Lucio. 'You say is no true, but my Isabella, she say is true, where is truth here? I swear my daughter tell no lie.'

'Lucio, let us talk in the morning.' Alice turned to Jack. 'Jack, we'll go back to the house.'

Jack stayed where he was. 'You're going to believe him, Mother? You're going to believe Victor? Why? Why should you believe him?'

'I can't explain now. It may have something to do with Isabella's mother.'

'Paola? You are blaming Paola for this?'

Alice lowered her voice. 'It's possible she may have talked against us, as a family. Then there has been the news about Julio, Isabella may be trying to – I don't know – repay us. Please, Jack, let's go back to the house and talk later.'

'No. I love Isabella and I want to marry her, I intend to speak to Lucio now.'

'Jack, I implore you, please stop, please think before you do this!'

'Will you excuse me?' Jack quietly put his mother aside and approached Lucio standing with his arm around Isabella's shoulders. Isabella was quiet now, but her face was a mask of anger, while Lucio seemed bemused.

'Señor Lucio, I have the honour to ask for your daughter's hand in marriage,' Jack said, with a formal bow. 'I love her and I will care for her all my life. She has refused me once, I hope she will take me now.'

'No, I will not!' cried Isabella. 'You are another Wintour to ask for me, dishonour me. I say, no, no, no! Go home, leave us. Go home to your Irlanda. We no wish you here.'

Chapter Thirteen

Two days later, Alice and her sons returned to Buenos Aires, where the peace of the Avenida Lila was like calm after storm. They all needed calm. Jack carried Isabella's rejection like an open wound; Victor was on edge; Alice had another grief: Lucio had told her he was leaving the *estancia*. It was not possible for him to work with Don Victor, she must see that, and no doubt Don Victor would not wish to work with him.

'Oh, Lucio,' she had mourned, 'oh, please reconsider. Think of Don Ricardo.'

'It will break my heart, Doña Alicia, but I cannot stay.'

'You still accuse my son? I promise you, he is not guilty of deceiving your daughter.'

'Doña Alicia, you are a mother, you believe your son, but I am a father and I believe my daughter. Is no way we have the truth, so is better I leave.'

'You know Victor is very inexperienced. How is he to manage without you, Lucio?'

'I find him very good man, no need to worry, Doña Alicia. Then I find a new place to work.'

'And Isabella?' Alice asked, after a pause.

'She stay with her sister in Rosario. Is young man there very fond. I think she marry him when she is of age.'

'I hope she will be very happy,' said Alice. She decided she would not tell Jack that piece of news until they were far away from the Argentine.

'Well, I for one am glad Lucio has decided to go,' Victor grunted. 'If he hadn't, I should have sacked him myself.'

'No, you would not,' Alice snapped. 'I own half the *estancia* and I say Lucio need never leave if he wants to stay.'

'Even after what his daughter tried to do to me?' cried Victor. 'I thought for once you were prepared to take my part.'

'Taking your part would not have meant losing Lucio. Anyway, this is all water under the bridge now.' Alice rose and straightened the skirt of her blue walking dress. 'I have ordered the carriage; who will go with me to the shops? It's almost Christmas and I've done nothing.'

'Christmas?' Jack repeated. 'How can you think of Christmas at a time like this?'

'Life goes on, Jack, isn't that what people are always saying to me?' Alice adjusted her hat. 'Victor, I believe you said you would come with me?'

'If you wish it.' He rose, his handsome face moody. 'Anything is better than staying here watching Jack feel sorry for himself.'

Jack, without answering, lit a cigarette and walked out to the patio, where he stood looking towards the river. When the door had banged on his mother and Victor, he flung himself into a wicker chair and gave himself up to misery. At first, he had really believed in Isabella; now, though, he wasn't sure. If Victor had seduced her, would he have troubled to deny it? It was much more his nature to boast of it and be surprised anyone should object. His mother knew what men were like, he would have reasoned, hadn't her own husband seduced their maid? If Lucio had protested, Victor would have tried to pay him off, and if Julio had protested, he would have been pleased. Oh, yes, Victor would have liked to get back at Julio.

So the doubts had begun to take hold in Jack's mind, for Victor had done none of the things he'd expected. And his mother had talked in that strange way of Paola and if she were right, well, there was the explanation for Isabella's behaviour. She was so young, though, could she really have worked such spite on his family? Even to suspect her caused him as much pain as her rejection of his own love. He had thought her so sweet, so innocent, he had put her on a pedestal and he could not bear to take her down. For the first time, he felt he truly understood his mother's feelings for his father. But then they had shared love, as he and Isabella had never shared love. He knew that if she came to him and said she loved him, he would marry her tomorrow; he still did not know how he was to live without her.

Maria came gliding on to the patio to tell him there was a visitor.

He looked up without interest. 'Say the family is not at home,' he instructed.

Maria made a little face. 'Is Julio,' she announced, with a smile. Lucio and his son were favourites in the household.

'Julio?' Jack went cold. 'Here?'

'You wish to see him?'

'Yes.' Jack stood up, putting out his cigarette. 'Please show him in, Maria.'

Julio seemed to have grown, even since Jack had last seen him, and though he was wearing some sort of school uniform, he appeared no schoolboy. Here was a young man, with Jack's father's face, and the likeness, now so plain, brought the blood to Jack's cheeks.

'Julio,' he got out, 'it's good to see you.'

'I come to see Don Victor.'

'I'm afraid he isn't here. Won't you sit down and talk to me? I'll ring for some tea.'

'No tea,' Julio said contemptuously, 'but I wait. You permit?'

Jack, gripped with apprehension, nodded and Julio, after some hesitation, sat down.

'You've heard from your father?' Jack asked hopelessly.

'Yes, he send message with Vittoria.'

Of course. Vittoria must have got in touch with Julio's school as soon as she had returned to BA.

'So you know what happened?'

'*Cómo no*! Vittoria tell me all my sister say.'

'It is not necessarily true, Julio, what your sister said.'

'Is true. Please, I wish to speak only with Don Victor.'

'Listen, Julio –' Jack leaned forwards – 'I think you should go. There is no point waiting to see my brother, there is no point in trying to – take revenge.'

'I decide that, Don Juan.'

'For God's sake, call me Jack! We were friends once. I

never did you any harm, all I wanted to do was help.' Jack swallowed, as the sweat broke on his brow. 'Did Vittoria tell you I wanted to marry Isabella?'

Julio's dark-blue eyes flashed in surprise. 'You? Ask for my sister?'

'Yes, I love her, but she doesn't love me. She has refused me.'

'Of course, you are a Wintour. She would not marry a Wintour.'

'Yet she said she was betrothed to my brother?'

'Don Victor take her honour, is right she marry him. I come today to make him.'

'It's not possible, Julio, it can't happen. Oh, please, leave here now. Forget all this and start a new life with Lucio. If you see my brother, there will only be more trouble, more violence –'

'I wait for Don Victor,' Julio replied.

Time passed. Julio, refusing all offers of refreshment, sat like a statue, his fine Wintour head held straight, his eyes cast down, while Jack, smoking cigarette after cigarette, sat slumped in despair. When Alice at last appeared, followed by Victor laden with packages, Julio leaped to his feet and stood before them, as taut as an archer's bow, and Jack stood beside him.

'Here is Julio, Mother,' Jack said, trying to sound natural, then added, hoarsely, 'He knows what has happened.'

'The devil he does,' said Victor, throwing down the packages, but Alice managed to smile and put out her hand.

'*Buenas tardes*, Doña Alicia,' Julio murmured, bowing. 'I wish to speak to Don Victor.'

'Well, I don't wish to speak to you,' Victor retorted. 'Your sister made a false accusation, that is all I have to say. Now I think you should leave.'

'Don Victor, will you marry my sister?'

'No, I will not marry your sister. Now, what do you want to do? Knock me down? Or something more? We've had experience of revenge in this family, you know. Are you going to wait for me to turn my back?'

'Victor!' cried Alice, but he laughed.

'Come, you're only a boy, Julio, don't get yourself mixed up in violence, it never does any good. Be a sensible fellow and go and there's an end to it.'

Julio was silent, standing calmly now, almost relaxed, his eyes never leaving Victor's face.

'Will you go?' asked Victor.

'Don Victor, you once say to me, "I will get even with you." Are you remembering this?'

'Did you say that, Victor?' asked Alice swiftly.

'Did you?' cried Jack.

Victor stared from one face to another. 'Oh, look, it was after the race, I was angry –'

'Did you say it?' Alice snapped.

'Yes, I did, but it was absolutely in the heat of the moment. It didn't mean anything.'

'Didn't it?' asked Jack.

'No, of course it didn't. Oh, for God's sake, you're not going to rake up those accusations again, are you? I tell you, it didn't mean anything, and I certainly did not try to get even with Julio through Isabella. Put that right out of your minds.'

'I accused you of it once,' said Jack.

'And I told you I'd never do it. I never did.' As no one spoke, Victor's face flamed. 'You believe me, don't you? Mother? Jack?'

'I believe you,' Alice said after a long, heavy pause. 'It's true, people do say things they don't mean in the heat of the moment.'

Victor's eyes flickered with relief. 'Jack, you see that, don't you? You believe me, too?'

'I don't know, Victor, I don't know what to believe any more.'

'I know,' Julio said quietly. 'I believe my sister, I believe what she say. So I tell you, Don Victor, one day will be my turn to get even with you. Is fair, this, is no revenge, is justice. Doña Alicia, I take my leave. *Adiós*!'

'Julio!' cried Jack, but Julio, flinging back his dark hair from his Wintour brow, strode out without looking back.

The three people he left on the patio exchanged long, troubled looks but found no words to say.

Chapter Fourteen

Belcarron in the spring. Primroses on the cliff and daffodils bending in the drive, high winds and lively sea. Alice and Jack were home.

Tina was stunned by what her mother told her – about her father, about Julio, about Isabella. At first she had found it all too difficult to accept, particularly that Richard, the golden man of legend, should have turned out to be human after all. But then her good sense put the question: If her mother had managed to accept, why shouldn't she? Gradually, her father's memory took on some of its old glory, but it was still hard to think of Julio discovering that he had been given away. No wonder there had been friction, outright conflict. No wonder that Isabella had made trouble. If she had made it. Perhaps Victor was guilty. Tina wouldn't have been surprised, but Mama seemed so sure he was not and it was better to believe her. Whatever the truth, Julio had made himself a threat and Victor must put up with it, the rest of them too.

Poor Mama! Poor Jack, too, who had looked as if he lived with devils ever since his return, but he would get over Isabella, people always did get over unhappy love affairs. After what had happened to Papa, the anxiety for Victor was much more real and so much worse, because he was so far away.

Melissa, of course, knew nothing of the problems of her elders and spent her time happily trying out her new presents, her Spanish shawl and castanets, her fans and trinkets from the famous shops in Buenos Aires. Tina, watching, hoped things would always be so for Melissa, that she would always be free as the breeze, would always travel through life lightly. Her own fear was that Melissa might let slip to her mother how much time George Coxe had spent at Castle Morry, for she had not yet found the right time to tell Alice about his proposal. Nor her other plans!

One morning when they were alone after breakfast, Alice asked about Paul Molloy. Was he still interested in the priesthood?

'He's not at all interested. He says he has no vocation and is to go into the book firm.'

'I should think he'd do well, then. Hester's business is very successful. Did you like him, Tina? Enjoy being with him?'

'Not in the way you mean, Mama.' Tina shook her head at her mother. 'I liked Paul very much, but just as another brother. Caitlin was the one I spent most time with, really.'

'And she is all Molloy, of course. Pretty, as I remember?'

'Very pretty. And strong.'

'As strong as you?'

'Stronger.'

Alice raised her eyebrows. 'Don't tell me you met your match, Tina?'

'In a way I did.' Tina hesitated. 'Caitlin is very keen, you know, on Irish liberation.'

'Oh, of course, they all are, the Molloys.'

'So am I, Mama.'

Alice's gaze sharpened. 'What do you mean? Are you talking about Home Rule? You surely don't want to see it?'

'I do, Mama. I think there's a case for it.'

'Why, I can't believe what I'm hearing, Tina! You think there is a case for denying your birthright?'

'The Anglo-Irish have no birthright to Ireland. If we're talking about rights, it's the Irish who hold them.'

Alice rose from the table and rang the bell for Bridie to clear.

'We'll discuss this another time,' she said frostily.

'Wait, there's something I want to tell you, Mama. George Coxe has asked me to marry him.'

As Bridie came in, cheerfully humming, to stack up the breakfast things, Alice's manner melted into delight and she caught at Tina's hands. 'Why, that's wonderful, Tina! Why didn't you tell me before, you silly girl?'

Tina smiled at Bridie, who removed herself, still humming, with her loaded tray, then turned to Alice.

'Of course, we're not engaged yet. George wishes to speak to you first.'

'Of course, of course,' Alice agreed eagerly.

'And then we may not get married for a while.' Tina took a deep breath. 'You see, Mama, I want to study medicine.'

'You mean to become a nurse?'

'No, a doctor.'

'Have you taken leave of your senses?' Alice threw up her hands as though to ward off this extraordinary news. 'Women are not doctors!'

'They are now, more and more are qualifying and practising. I know just what's involved and, with your permission, I hope to begin studies in the autumn.'

'This is quite beyond me, Tina. Whatever does George think?'

'He's willing to help, he's trying to find me a place now at one of the London medical schools. Oh, please, Mama, don't look like that! I want to do this so much. I have the right to try.'

'George is not young. How long will he wait for you, Tina?'

'I won't make him wait too long. We could marry before I finish the course.'

'You'd be a married woman and a medical student, too?' Alice shook her head. 'Oh, I shall never get used to this modern world! Things are so different from my day.'

'But didn't Cousin Hester marry Daniel Molloy and start her own bookshop? Didn't you always support her, Mama?'

'I suppose I did.' Alice suddenly smiled and kissed Tina on the cheek. 'And I suppose I'll have to support you, too. Go ahead, then, Tina, do as you wish – you will anyway. But don't forget George.'

'I won't, I promise you. You'll see me in satin and orange blossom yet, and Melissa can be a bridesmaid, which is her great dream at the moment.' Tina flung her arms around Alice and hugged her. 'Thank you, Mama, thank you!'

Jack had gone sailing that day and was late coming back. They waited dinner for him, watching from the cliff until the light faded, but Melissa had long gone to bed before they heard his step in the hall. Alice went to chide him for worrying her so.

He only protested, 'Why, you knew I'd be all right. I was with friends, anyway. Where's the danger in a sail?'

'Never mind, now you're back, but dinner's been waiting hours. You'd better just quickly wash, so we can begin.'

In the dining room, where so many Wintours had gathered, eaten meals, drunk their wine, put the world to rights, or Ireland, at least, Bridie lit the candles, not the lamps, and Alice took her place at the head of the table. How many years now had she sat in her father's chair? She scarcely liked to think, time was going by so fast. Here was Jack, suffering from love, when only yesterday he had been a little boy under the table, hiding from the storm. And Tina, who had fought so many battles with Miss Wynne, was now quite grown up and planning to marry and become a doctor! At least, Melissa was still a schoolgirl, although seeing her dancing in her shawl, fixing a flower in her hair, it was certain she would not be a schoolgirl for much longer. Alice sighed, as Bridie served the soup. One should not complain; it was natural for children to grow up and grow away, one could not hold on. If only she had not had the continual worry over Victor pressing on her heart, though ... Alice called on Jack to open the wine.

'What friends?' Tina asked suddenly. 'I thought you'd gone sailing alone, Jack?'

'Oh, they weren't really friends, just some people I met down at the jetty. A brother and sister from Cork, staying with an aunt – she wasn't with them.'

'You'd never met them before and you took them sailing? Rather a strange thing to do, wasn't it?'

'Not really. The brother's up at Oriel, I've seen him once or twice. He's a good sailor. Hoping to make a rowing blue, as well. His sister said she was at school with you, Tina.'

'Oh, what was her name?'

'Paget. Barbara Paget. Her brother's called Terence.'

'Barbara Paget?' Tina's eyes danced. 'I remember her! Plump, with ginger hair and freckles.'

'Not at all. Very slim, dark-red hair, and absolutely no freckles.'

As Bridie brought in the fish, Jack added, 'I thought her

rather pretty, as a matter of fact. Hope you won't mind, Mother, I told them to call. Miss Paget said she'd like to meet Tina again.'

'Why, I hardly know her!' cried Tina, exchanging glances with Alice.

'And would like to be introduced to you, Mother,' Jack finished. 'That's all right, isn't it?'

'I should be delighted, but what's the name of this aunt? Where does she live?'

'She's a Miss Carlow.' Jack, Alice noticed, was eating heartily, as he had not eaten in weeks. 'A great churchgoer, apparently; lives in that old place near the rectory.'

'Why, I do know her!' Alice declared, with some relief. 'Oh, yes, she's one of the old school. Used to visit in Mama's day, I remember. We must ask her to tea.'

The meal wore on, accompanied by pleasant family talk, and just for that time, the troubles of Ireland and Argentina seemed to have no place in their lives.

'Oh, you don't know how glad I am to be back,' Alice murmured, almost involuntarily, 'back here at Belcarron. I don't think I shall travel very far away again.'

'Nor I,' said Jack, with feeling. 'This is where I have to be, I realise that now.'

'I might travel,' Tina remarked, draining her glass. 'I might even live away. In London.'

'London?' Jack raised his eyebrows. 'What's this, then? Have I missed something?'

'Never mind,' Alice said comfortably. 'The great thing is that, wherever you go, Belcarron will be waiting. That's the one sure thing we can always count on, isn't it?'

'Always,' said Jack.

They left the table for the drawing room, where Bridie had already set the coffee tray and drawn the curtains against the night. The lamps were lit, the fire crackled pleasantly, and as she took her chair, it seemed to Tina that the scene was one she should remember. Just in case they were wrong. Just in case one day Belcarron were not waiting as they thought it always would be. What a strange thought! She pushed it from her mind.

'Coffee, Tina?' Alice asked.

'Please, Mama,' said Tina.

Part II
1914

Chapter Fifteen

Carron was changing. In the pearly light of a June evening, 1914, the number of yachts cramming the old harbour made the village seem like another Cowes. So Jack Wintour commented, returning from a sail with his friend Terence Paget. As they moored Jack's dinghy, the *Sea Watch*, and headed for Ryan's, their favourite pub, Terence was cheerful, but Jack's brow remained dark.

'Just look at these people,' he murmured, his eye taking in the yachting crowd sitting with their glasses on the sea wall, smoking their cigarettes and laughing, oblivious of the stares of the children and the few fishermen still mending nets. 'What do they have to do with Carron? The real Carron, I mean?'

Terence, a solidly built, ginger-haired lawyer from Cork, gave an indulgent grin. 'They just want a change, old man. They work hard all the week – so do I – then at the weekend fancy a quiet sail and a drink. Would you stop poor devils like me from enjoying themselves?'

'You know I'm not talking about you. You've been coming here for years without trying to change the character of the place. But these people are building houses here, for God's sake! They're filling the streets with motors, changing the pubs out of all recognition –'

'Oh, come, Jack, the locals aren't suffering, they're delighted to be making a bit of extra cash out of the visitors. Everywhere is changing, anyway. Just because you're lucky enough to live at Belcarron, you can't shut away the rest of the world, you know.'

'Can't I?' asked Jack.

Now in his twenty-seventh year, Jack was thinner than at twenty, but bronzed, fit and very handsome. Looking at him, as they ordered beer in the crowded pub, Terence still found himself amazed that his sister had turned Jack down. 'Barbara,' he had remonstrated, 'just what exactly do you want? The fellow's a Wintour, he's good-looking, he's as nice a character as you could wish to meet –'

'That's the trouble,' Barbara had replied. 'Jack's too nice. I'm sure I could never have a row with him.'

'Why on earth should you wish to have a row?'

'Oh, I don't. I'm putting it badly. All I want is – a little excitement.'

Excitement. Terence shook his head. Women were odd creatures, one could never fathom them, but Barbara had been married for five years now to an officer in an Irish regiment, who presumably provided all the excitement she wanted, while Jack – Jack was still footloose and fancy-free and having to take consolation in his sailing and his Napier motorcar.

'Shall we sit outside?' Terence asked, carrying their tankards.

Jack glanced at his watch. 'Might as well stay where we are; have to go back soon, anyway. Mother will be worrying about dinner.'

'Aunt Eugenia, too. She's a decent old thing, I don't want to upset her when she's been so kind, putting me up.'

'You could always stay at Belcarron, you know, there's plenty of room. At least, until Victor comes.'

'When's he due?'

'Early August.' As they found seats, Jack gave a crooked grin. 'Bringing home the son and heir for Mother to see. Her first grandchild – she's over the moon.'

'There'll be others. I'll stand godfather to your son yet, Jack.'

'Maybe.' Jack lit a cigarette. 'And maybe not. I don't seem to be too popular with the women, do I? Unlike Victor. His wife adores him.'

'And is Victor duly grateful?'

'Who knows? But he made a good match. Evie was Miss Stonefield, only daughter of our banker in Buenos Aires.'

'Very nice. I don't know how it is, I never seem to attract any rich bankers' daughters these days.' Terence grinned. 'I'm afraid I'm like you, Jack. Just not appreciated.'

They sat in companionable silence, ignoring the noise around them, knowing they would have to make a move soon, but unwilling to make it yet. Terence was thinking of Jack's beautiful sister Melissa, now on a visit to her sister in Dublin and no doubt breaking hearts there as easily as she broke them in County Cork. She certainly wouldn't look at an overweight, ginger-haired lawyer, or would she? Well, he could dream, and a dream was all he wanted, really; he was enough of a realist to know he would be happier with someone clever and plain, like Melissa's sister Tina, who was, would you credit it, a doctor. Only she was married too.

'Like a fill-up?' he asked, but Jack shook his head and tapped his watch.

'Got to be going, old man.'

'Right you are.' As Terence nodded and sat back, Jack wished suddenly that he could have confided in him. Terence was one of his most trusted friends, they had known each other for years, were even on first-name terms. But, of course, it wasn't possible. Terence wouldn't understand. There was no point in trying to involve anyone who did not share their views – his, Tina's, George's. All the same, keeping secrets wasn't his style. I shall be damned glad when it's all over, thought Jack.

'I really must congratulate your sister on becoming a doctor,' Terence remarked lazily. 'That is a tremendous achievement. What a successful family yours is, isn't it? Melissa the toast of the county and Victor the great South American rancher –'

'Oh, he's that, all right. To the *estancia* born.' And still in one piece, Jack added to himself, young Julio's threats having come to nothing. In fact, Julio himself seemed to have vanished into obscurity. Although Lucio wrote to Alice every Christmas, he never mentioned Julio or Isabella. But Jack knew that Isabella was married and it didn't hurt, he had got over Isabella a long time ago.

'Sure you won't have one for the road?' pressed Terence.

Jack rose firmly to his feet. 'Terence, I really am going home,' he was beginning, when his eye caught the face of a young man who had just entered the bar. 'Oh, my God,' he whispered, and sat down again.

'Someone you know?' Terence swivelled round so that he might follow the direction of Jack's gaze, but the tall, dark-haired man wearing a tweed suit and carrying his hat meant nothing to him. He turned back to Jack. 'I say, are you all right?'

Jack, very pale, tried to smile. 'Of course. It's only that I've had a bit of a shock. Haven't seen that fellow there in years.'

'And don't want to see him now, from the look of you.'

'No, that's not true, I'm glad to see him. If I'm right – maybe my eyes are playing tricks.'

'Don't think so, he seems to know you, Jack. I'd say he's just as shocked as you are.'

'Wait here.' Jack rose again. 'I'm going over to see him.'

'Julio?' Jack put out his hand. The young man's dark-blue eyes filled with alarm, then flickered and looked away.

'Mr Wintour,' he said, in a low voice.

'Jack, you mean. You remember, don't you? My name is Jack. Come, take my hand.'

'If you wish.' Julio Castillo, after a moment's hesitation, shook Jack's hand. He raised his eyes with great reluctance, extremely ill at ease.

'Why didn't you let us know you were here?' asked Jack. 'You always used to say you'd come one day. I can't tell you how glad I am to see you.'

Julio licked his lips and glanced hurriedly round the crowded pub. 'Jack, I shall not stay. I know I am an embarrassment to you, please forgive –'

He made a move to turn aside but Jack caught him by the arm. 'Of course you're not an embarrassment to me, why do you talk that way? Come, you must meet my friend –'

In spite of Julio's obvious unwillingness, Jack insisted on taking him back to Terence, who, intrigued, stood up to be introduced.

'Terence, this is Julio Castillo from Argentina; Julio, please meet my friend Terence Paget, from Cork.'

'You knew each other in Argentina?' Terence delightedly

shook Julio's hand. 'This calls for a celebration! What will you have, Señor Castillo?'

'Thank you, nothing, Mr Paget. I think I should go up to my room –'

'You're staying here, at Ryan's? Well, then you can surely spare time for a drink – won't you try our good Irish ale?'

'Terence, I think we'd better save our celebrations for later,' Jack put in, trying to speak easily, yet still to Terence seeming not quite in command. 'Julio and I must get back to Belcarron – yes, Julio, my mother will be most anxious to see you. Terence, may we meet again when I return from Dublin?'

'Of course.' Terence politely made his farewells and watched, mystified, as the two young men left the pub together. He felt a little stirring of envy; they were both so handsome, the one so dark, the other so fair, and somehow alike. Alike? He shook his head and drained the beer in his glass. There was no way Jack Wintour of Belcarron could be like Julio Castillo of Argentina. Yet something, he didn't know what, linked the two. Terence's quick lawyer's brain seized on the mystery and worried it as a dog gnaws a bone, but he had not enough facts to go on, he could reach no conclusion, only sense the unrest that gripped both men as they left him alone in the pub.

'I am sorry, Jack, I am not happy, I think I will not come.' Julio stared distractedly down the village street, where the children were still playing in and out of the lines of parked motors. 'After what happened when we last meet, Doña Alicia will not wish to see me.'

'Julio, that was years ago, you were only a boy!'

'Doña Alicia is *madre*, she will think of her son.'

'Well, no harm has come to her son. Victor's done very well. He's married, with a baby boy, and he's coming home in August. You need have no worries about my brother, Julio.'

'Don Victor is married?' Julio raised his fine dark brows. 'And you, Jack, are you married?'

'I'm afraid not.' Jack hesitated. 'I know about Isabella, Julio. I know she's married. I hope she's happy.'

'She is very happy. She also has a boy, she named him Lucio.'

'And Lucio himself?'

'He is retired. He say, why should he not rest, see his grandchildren?' Julio smiled. 'So, he sees his grandchildren, but I think he misses the land. I think he will always miss the land.'

'We have so much to talk about, Julio. Please, let's walk to Belcarron.'

They took the dusty road to the cliff, where the wild fuchsias lined the verge, each walking without speaking, still unsure of the other.

'Look there,' said Jack, as the bay sprang fully into view and on the rising headland, Belcarron stood, white and shining, its windows glittering in the last of the evening sun. 'There's Belcarron, Julio.'

'I know,' Julio answered, 'this I have already seen.' He turned his face to Jack. 'Is beautiful.'

'When did you see it?' asked Jack. 'How long have you been here?'

'Two days. I see it with Bridie.'

'You came to the house? And never called?'

'I never come to the house. Bridie meet me in the village and show me.'

'And she never said a word! That's not like Bridie.'

'I ask her to say nothing. Forgive me. How could I know you would wish to see me?'

'Maybe you didn't wish to see us?' Jack asked bitterly, and Julio flushed.

'I have explained,' he replied with dignity, 'and I do wish to see you, Jack. But I come here to find my mother's home, my mother's people, and is none. No mother or father, no brother or sister, only Bridie.'

'I'm sorry, Julio. I believe Mena's parents died some years ago and the rest of the family emigrated, except for Bridie. She was your mother's youngest sister. At least you have found her.'

'Yes, is wonderful.' Julio smiled and seemed to relax a little, but as they neared the house, he tensed again and kept his eyes on the ground.

'Look, it's all right,' Jack told him, 'my mother will be pleased to see you, I know she will, and you couldn't come here without seeing her, it would hurt her very much.'

'I have no wish to hurt Doña Alicia, Jack, but I think she

will remember that last time in Buenos Aires. Is natural that she should.'

'She understood how she felt, she knew you were only trying to protect your sister.'

'Isabella, yes . . .' Julio bit his lip. 'I have to believe her, Jack, you see that?'

'Of course, I've told you, we all understood.'

At the steps leading to the solid front door, Julio hesitated. 'I think I will not go in, Jack. My mother, she never used these steps. My place is with Bridie.'

'Your place is wherever you want to be, Julio. If I ask you to stay for dinner, why should you not acccpt?'

'I shall not accept, Jack.'

'Lucio often dined with us, why shouldn't you?'

'Not here. Please do not ask me.'

'Very well.' Jack sighed, took out his latch key, then put it away again. 'I'll ring the bell so we can see Bridie. You will come in and meet my mother, Julio?'

'If you wish.'

'You haven't forgotten she has a portrait, the portrait of your mother?'

Julio's face cleared, his eyes shone. 'I do not forget, Jack. Is always in my mind.'

As soon as Bridie saw Julio with Jack at the door, she put her hands to her face and burst into tears.

'It's all right, Bridie, it's all right.' Jack patted her shoulder.

'Mr Jack, wasn't I ever knowing you'd meet him some day, my sister's boy?' Bridie cried. 'And isn't he a lovely, handsome fellow, then, and all Donovan? I can see my da standing before my eyes now, so I can!' She flung her arms around Julio, who laughed and kissed her, as Jack indulgently waited.

'But Bridie, you never told me Julio was here,' he reminded her. 'If we hadn't met accidentally, I'd never have known.'

'Wasn't he after swearing me to secrecy? Isn't that the truth, then, Francis Flynn?'

'Yes, is the truth, is all my fault.' Julio was still smiling, completely at ease with Bridie, seeming to accept that she called him by the name he had before he was adopted.

'Come away with you now,' Bridie urged, 'to see what Maisie has been cooking for your supper!'

'First he must meet my mother,' Jack said gently, and turned at the sound of Alice's voice on the stairs.

'Jack, is someone with you? Have you a visitor?'

The three people in the hall looked up as Alice Wintour came down the staircase. She was nearly fifty, grey-haired and overweight, yet lovely still, her skin smooth, her eyes clear. Her dress that day was pale-blue merino, so narrow-skirted she had to watch her descent carefully; it was only when she reached the last step that she was able to look up and greet the caller. Her welcoming hostess smile all ready, she put out her hand, then her smile froze and she caught her breath.

'Julio?' she whispered.

''Tis Mena's boy, ma'am!' Bridie cried. 'Hasn't he come all the way from the Argentine just to see me? Can you ever believe it?'

'Doña Alicia,' Julio murmured, his gaze intent on her face, 'you forgive – my coming?'

'Forgive? Julio, I'm very glad to see you!' As Julio bent over her hand, Alice began rapidly to recover her poise. 'Bridie, you're right, I can't believe it – Julio here, at Belcarron! But you must come into the drawing room, Julio, take some sherry –'

'He's to have supper with Bridie, Mother,' Jack said quickly, 'but I've persuaded him to talk to us first. He'd also like to see your picture of Mena. May I get it?'

'Of course, fetch it from my room.' Alice put her hand lightly on the visitor's arm. 'But come, let's talk, Julio. You know, we've had no news of you for years.'

As Bridie, a puzzled look clouding her features, disappeared downstairs, Julio allowed himself to be escorted into the long, lovely room where generations of Wintours had entertained and his young mother had once served, as his aunt still served, the Wintours' guests. Sitting stiffly in an armchair, he accepted a glass of sherry and politely answered Alice's questions about himself.

'Yes, I have now finished school and military service,' he told her, 'and in the autumn I go to university, where I shall study languages.'

'Why, that's wonderful, Julio!' Alice exclaimed. 'I must say, your English is very good – isn't it, Jack?'

'Excellent,' agreed Jack, coming in with Mena's portrait. 'You must have worked very hard.'

'Yes, I work hard, is useful to speak English well in Buenos Aires, but I have no wish to go to university.' Julio set his glass carefully on a side table and let his eyes rest on the picture Jack had set down by his chair. 'I prefer, really, to work with the land, but my father say I shall never own land, so is best to try for a profession.' Julio shrugged. 'I do as he wish.'

'Lucio writes to me regularly,' Alice remarked, 'but he has never mentioned you. I've often wondered about you and wished he had told us something of you.'

'He maybe thinks he embarrass you, Doña Alicia,' Julio answered, flushing, 'after what happened.'

'Won't you forget all that?' asked Jack. 'I've told you, we understood. You were a boy at the time.'

'Of course you were,' Alice agreed.

'I threatened your son, Doña Alicia. I was wrong.'

'I say with Jack, you should forget it now. It's all in the past, it's over.'

'I hope Don Victor will forget.'

'He's not Don Victor, he's plain Victor,' Jack said shortly. 'Don't worry about him, Julio, he knows as well as we do, you meant him no harm. Now, let me show you the picture of your mother.'

'Thank you,' Julio said softly.

For a long time, he gazed in silence at Ernestine Wintour's portrait of Mena.

'Is it like?' he asked Alice, at last.

'Very like.' Together they looked at the heart-shaped face, the dark hair and blue eyes, the wicked little smile. 'She was so pretty, Julio, everyone thought so.'

'And like Bridie, I think?'

'That's true, though, of course, Bridie is older now.'

'And my mother will never be old.' Julio set the picture down and bowed. 'Thank you, Doña Alicia, for letting me see this. It makes me very happy.'

She hesitated, then cleared her throat. 'Julio, would you like to have it?'

As Julio stared and Jack caught his breath, she said quickly, 'I should like you to have a likeness of your mother, Julio, it's all you have of her. Please – it would be right.'

'*Muchas gracias.*' Julio shook his head. 'I thank you, Doña Alicia, but I cannot take it. You loved my mother, you must keep her picture. I will always think of it with you.'

Alice, bowing her head, said no more, and Jack, relieved for her, carried the picture away.

'Julio,' Alice said awkwardly, 'I'm so glad to have this opportunity of talking to you. There's something I would like to tell you.'

'Yes, Doña Alicia?'

'It's about your father. I mean your real father, my husband.'

He stiffened and withdrew his gaze from her face. 'You wish to make me feel better, Doña Alicia? It is not possible. He gave me away.'

'To Lucio, who wanted you so much.'

'And Don Ricardo did not want me at all.'

'I've been thinking over the years, Julio, and I don't believe you're right about that. I believe, when he came back that last time to the *estancia*, my husband was looking to you for comfort. I can't explain why I should feel this, but I'm sure it was so. But you see, you were Lucio's son by then.'

'And that was better for Don Ricardo.'

'You remember the codicil to his will? He wanted to take care of you, he left money to Lucio for your education.'

'He did not want to give me love.'

'Please try to think that there might have been love, too. It was always a difficult situation. You see that, don't you?'

'Yes, I see it is difficult for people like me, Doña Alicia, people who should never have been born.'

'It is wrong to think like that, Julio. God has a purpose in all that He does. So we are taught.'

'And I wait to see what it is.' Julio gave a dark smile. 'Do not look so sad, Doña Alicia. I cannot love Don Ricardo to please you, but I thank you for your kindness.' He bent his head over her hand. 'Also for your love for my mother.'

Later, when Jack and Alice were at dinner and Julio was with

Maisie and Bridie in the kitchen, Jack said he felt too disgusted to eat.

'These class distinctions,' he burst out, 'they're absurd! The whole structure should be brought to the ground!'

'Oh, please don't start, Jack,' Alice said wearily. 'Julio would have been welcome to dine with us. He preferred to be with Bridie.'

'And Bridie has to be in the kitchen, when she's not running upstairs to serve us!'

'Do finish your soup, Jack. We can't change the whole world over the dinner table.'

'If everyone were like you, Mother, there would be no changes made at all.'

'Perhaps that would not be such a bad thing, then.'

After a pause during which he did finish his soup, Jack asked, with a wry smile, 'Do you know what Bridie said about Julio? That he was a perfect Donovan. The Wintour nose has quite escaped her.'

'Sometimes people see what they want to see. Julio is all Bridie has left.'

'And he won't be staying. When I walk back with him tonight, I must ask him what his plans are.'

'My plans?' Julio repeated, as they left Belcarron for the road back to the village. 'I have no plans. I came to Ireland to see my mother's country. Is beautiful, but not happy. What can I do? Nothing. I think maybe I just visit Dublin and go home.'

'You'd like to do something? For Ireland?'

'But yes, of course! I tell you many years ago Ireland should fight, as Argentina fight, for freedom!'

'That could mean a civil war, Julio.'

'Is true, and maybe now people think only of the German war.'

'German war?' Jack, striding step for step with Julio, laughed lightly. 'You mean all that stuff in the newspapers? That won't come to anything. The papers have had us at war with Germany since 1901 at least, but we're still at peace. The Irish, though, they may fight their own battle.'

'You would wish to fight with them, Jack?'

'I don't know about that, but I might care to help in other ways. Would you?'

'I am not sure I am understanding, Jack, what would I do?'

'I can't explain now – perhaps tomorrow. Would you come sailing with me tomorrow, Julio?'

'I know nothing of sailing – only horses.'

'You can leave the sailing to me. On the water we can talk freely.'

They were approaching Ryan's now, where people were still sitting, drinking and talking, in the soft summer dusk. Jack halted. 'You said you might go to Dublin. Would you come to Dublin with me? Stay with my sister, Tina?'

'Your sister lives in Dublin now?'

'No, but she's rented a house there. Actually, she lives in London. She's married to a doctor and has just qualified as a doctor herself, we're all very proud of her.'

'A lady and a doctor? Yes, you must be proud.'

'My cousins are coming over from America, there are things we have to do and you could help, if you are willing. What do you think?'

'I say, you have only to ask me.'

Jack hesitated.

Julio waited. 'You know you can trust me, Jack,' he said, at last.

Instantly, Jack put his hand on Julio's shoulder. 'It's not that, Julio, don't think I'm worrying about that. The thing is, there could be danger and what we're planning is not actually legal. I don't know that I have the right to ask you to take risks for us.'

'If it is for my mother's country, you have the right.'

'Well, let me think about it tomorrow, I'll take you sailing and we can talk then.' Jack stood back. 'Go in now, Julio, and look out for me in the morning.'

'Jack, I think I shall not sleep!'

'That's all right, I haven't slept in weeks.' Jack grinned. 'Goodnight, Julio.'

'Goodnight, Jack.'

Chapter Sixteen

While Jack took Julio sailing round the Carron coastline, his American cousins were arriving in Dublin.

Tina's rented house was in a quiet terrace on the south side of the city. It had a Georgian fanlight and six long, lace-curtained windows, and Caitlin and Paul would have been charmed, if they hadn't been thinking of other things. A plump and contented George Coxe had met them in Liverpool and escorted them over on the night mail; now Tina embraced them as they stood among their boxes and blushed as they gave her their congratulations.

'Dr Tina Coxe!' cried Caitlin. 'Oh, it's so wonderful! I can scarcely believe it!'

'Why the surprise?' asked Paul, kissing Tina's cheek. 'I always knew there was a brain behind that pretty face.'

'Oh, Paul!' Tina delightedly took his arm. 'How good it is to see you two again! It seems an age since my wedding, doesn't it, but so much has happened. Would you like to see your rooms?'

'Guess I'd like to wash up,' Paul was beginning, when Caitlin, thin and nervy in a narrow-skirted travelling dress, cut in.

'Never mind about washing, Paul, just let's hear what this is all about.'

'You mean, what I wrote to you about?' asked Tina.

'I mean, what you hinted at.'

'At least take off your hat, Caitlin.' Tina and George exchanged glances. 'Then we'll talk.'

With some reluctance, Caitlin unpinned her hat and followed

Molly, the maid, up the narrow stairs to her room, but she was soon down again, watching Tina pour coffee in the drawing room. It was only natural, she supposed, that her cousin should appear so much like a cat that has swallowed the cream. Not only had she made a happy marriage, she had also pulled off the remarkable feat of qualifying as a doctor and being appointed to 'walk the wards' in a London hospital. So, she looked attractive and satisfied and something else besides. Excited? Yes, that was it. Tina was crackling with as much excitement as an electrical storm. Why?

'Come on,' Caitlin ordered sternly.

'You want to know what this is all about?' Tina's voice was clear. 'I suppose you could say – gunrunning.'

Gunrunning. The word seemed to quiver on the air. Paul's eyes went at once to Caitlin, but she was staring at Tina. 'I guess I see now why you didn't send us details,' she said, after a pause.

'I knew you were coming over –'

'That's right, I plan to work with Countess Markievicz and Paul said he'd come over for the ride.'

'The point is, will you join us?'

'In gunrunning?' asked Paul. 'Tina, I thought you were against violence.'

'I am, but George and I can both see that there's a case for the Irish Volunteers to be armed. The Ulster Volunteers have been arming for some time and are quite prepared to fight over Home Rule.'

'When you say "us", who do you mean?'

'Jack and myself, and people you don't know. Not George, he can't get away from the hospital.'

'Unfortunately,' said George.

Caitlin was frowning. 'You know we'll join you, you don't even have to ask, but what I find strange is that we haven't heard a whisper of this over in the States.'

'That's because it all began in London,' George told her, 'in Westminster, in fact, which is our home.'

Paul drained his coffee and sat back. 'Perhaps you'd better just fill us in,' he suggested.

George had for some time known a group of people in London

of the same type as Countess Markievicz herself – well born, well to do, without personal interest in Irish freedom, but motivated by a great desire to see justice. When Tina mentioned the names of Sir Roger Casement, Erskine Childers, Mrs Stopford Green and others, Caitlin opened her eyes and Paul let out a long, low whistle.

'Never knew the Irish had so many friends in London,' he murmured.

'Sometimes the Irish don't care to admit it,' said George with a grin.

'You can't blame them for that!' fired Caitlin.

'If we're talking about justice, give credit where credit is due.'

'Shall I go on?' asked Tina.

A Home Rule bill was on the stocks again and, as she had said, the Ulster Volunteers were ready to fight if their counties were included. In April 1914, they had taken delivery of a huge consignment of illegally landed arms without interference from the authorities, which had so incensed Childers and the others that they had vowed to provide arms for the Irish Volunteers, who were at present drilling with broom handles.

'Broom handles!' cried Caitlin. 'Doesn't that say it all?'

'There's something to be said for broom handles,' Paul said beneath his breath, but no one heard.

'Who is this Erskine Childers?' asked Caitlin. 'The name's familiar.'

'He's a committee clerk at the House of Commons,' Tina answered, 'but you may have read his spy story *The Riddle of the Sands.*'

'Oh, sure,' said Paul, 'great yarn.'

'That brought in his sailing and he's an excellent sailor. He's worked out a plan that involves two yachts, the *Asgard*, that's his own, and the *Kelpie*, owned by a man named Conor O'Brien. The *Asgard* will land arms at Howth, near Dublin, and the *Kelpie* will land them in County Wicklow.'

'Wait, you go too fast,' said Catlin. 'Have these guns already been bought or not?'

'Childers and a journalist named Figgis bought them in Hamburg with money raised by our committee. There are 1,500 Mauser rifles and 45,000 rounds of ammunition.'

'So where's all that stuff now?'

'Still in Hamburg. Getting them over to Ireland is what we have to do.'

'By sea? But Paul and I don't sail!'

'Sorry, only Jack will be sailing – he's joining the *Asgard*. The rest of us will be landlubbers, helping to unload at Howth.'

'When?' Caitlin's eyes were shining. She was as excited as Tina, yet feeling, Tina guessed, a little piqued that these plans were not hers.

'Timing is critical,' said George, 'all worked out by Childers. He's an odd devil, but highly efficient. The two yachts sail for the continent on different dates but rendezvous in the North Sea on 12 July with Figgis, who'll be bringing the arms from Hamburg by tug. O'Brien will take what he can and land his load on 20 July, Childers will take the rest and land on July 26.'

'July 26?' Caitlin echoed. 'That's weeks away. What do we do until then?'

'Enjoy yourselves? Meet up with the Countess? Weren't you planning to do that, anyway?'

'How much does she know of this?'

'I'm not sure, but the Fianna boys she trains are due at Howth to help unload, that's been arranged. The Irish Volunteers will also be there. They've been marching out every Sunday, so a march to Howth will not seem suspicious.'

'This unloading,' Paul broke in, suddenly, 'it's risky, right?'

'Right,' answered Tina. She fixed him with a direct, blue stare. 'If the coastguards catch us, we run the risk of arrest, that's part of the deal. But you don't have to come in with us unless you want to.'

'He wants to,' said Caitlin.

'It's your decision,' Tina went on, ignoring Caitlin. 'We know your views on violence.'

'I rather thought they were the same as yours,' he replied mildly.

'I've explained why I'm involved. It would be wrong to leave the Irish Volunteers unprotected.'

For some moments, Paul sat without speaking. Then, he pushed back his yellow hair and nodded. 'All right, I'm in.

I've never called myself a pacifist, I guess there's such a thing as a just war.'

'And this is one!' cried Caitlin.

'Except that at the moment, there is no war,' George declared. 'I prefer to think of the whole operation as a form of deterrent. If the Ulstermen know the Irish Volunteers are armed, they may not be so keen to start open war.'

That'll be fine, thought Paul, as long as the Irish Volunteers don't think of starting the war themselves, once they've got their arms.

He was relieved when George, glancing at his watch, suggested it was time for a drink before lunch. 'Caitlin, Paul, what will you have? Sherry? Irish whiskey?'

'If you don't have bourbon, I guess I'll take Irish whiskey,' Caitlin answered coolly. 'Do you have any ice?'

A door banged and there was the sound of a quick footstep in the hall. 'Hello, I'm back!' cried a young voice, and Melissa, in the narrowest of hobble skirts, came teetering into the drawing room. 'Oh, Caitlin – Paul – how lovely to see you again! Haven't met since Tina's wedding, have we?'

'Hello, Melissa,' said Caitlin, accepting Melissa's embrace.

'Hello, Melissa,' echoed Paul, stooping to kiss her cheek. As he straightened up, still holding his cousin's hand, his gaze went from her flushed, lovely face to her hat, which was large, stylish and trimmed with violets. Something clicked in his brain and a memory, sweet as the flowers, came flooding back. Cousin Charlotte had taken him for a drive in her friend's grand carriage, she had bought him a delicious, sticky bun and when they went back, Grandmama had told him he had a new little sister.

'Cousin Paul?' Melissa whispered, and he found he was still holding her hand and everyone was staring. He blushed and cleared his throat. 'I like your hat,' he said hoarsely.

Oh, dear, thought Tina, and refused to meet Caitlin's eye.

It was like the sun going out for Paul when, two days later, he had to bid goodbye to Melissa at the station. She was wearing a different hat but looked, he thought, as enchanting as ever, and the only bright spot in the darkness was that she wanted him to go down to Belcarron as soon as possible.

'You will come and visit me, won't you, Paul?' Melissa murmured, holding him with her green gaze. 'You too, Caitlin?'

At Melissa's polite afterthought, Caitlin gave a sardonic smile.

'It's so terribly dull down there, you know,' Melissa continued, taking her seat in the railway carriage with Paul's helping hand, 'and I'm sure I don't know why Tina is making me go back, especially when I have to travel on my own. It's true, Mama likes one of us around and Jack is coming to Dublin, but that's what I think is so odd. I mean, why should Jack come to Dublin? He hates it.' Melissa took off her hat and patted the waves of yellow hair, the same colour as Paul's own. 'I can't help thinking something is going on that's being kept from me.'

She likes to put on an act, thought Caitlin, but she's the type never to miss a trick.

'I'm not sure we shall have time to come to Belcarron,' she called, sweetly as the train began to move.

Melissa called back, equally sweetly, 'Never mind, I'll be back anyway for the Horse Show! Be sure to make time for that!'

Caitlin's lip curled. 'Horse Show, indeed! As though we hadn't better things to do than go to the Horse Show.'

'I shouldn't mind going,' Paul replied, 'or to Belcarron. Why did you say we wouldn't have time? You know we'll have to visit Cousin Alice.'

'I hate Belcarron,' Caitlin told him fiercely. 'Shame on you for not feeling the same, after all Papa went through there.'

'All he went through? I don't believe he went through very much at Belcarron. From what I've heard, our cousins were pretty easy going with the servants.'

'Belcarron is like all estates in Ireland, filled with Irish suffering. Don't make me go down there just because you want to see Melissa again.'

'All right, then. I'll wait till she comes up for the Horse Show!'

Brother and sister stared with hostile eyes into each other's faces, until Paul suddenly relaxed and took Caitlin's arm.

'Let's not waste time quarrelling, Caitlin. We should be

going back to Tina's place, check on just what we have to do.'

'There'll be plenty of time for that,' Caitlin answered, still unyielding. 'The landing's not for ages yet. I'm going to Surrey House to call on Madame.'

'Madame?'

'That's what Countess Markievicz prefers to be called.'

'Makes sense, I guess, if no one can pronounce her real name.'

'It's her husband's name – he's a Polish count, though I think they're separated.'

'I'll bet.'

'What do you mean by that?' Caitlin cried spiritedly.

'Well, she's a wild one, isn't she? Into everything that's going, from women's rights to Irish nationalism. I think she could be hard to live with.' Paul began to walk with Caitlin out of the station. 'And I'm not sure, Caitlin, I want you to be too involved with her.'

'And what makes you think you have the right to tell me what to do? You're not Papa.' Caitlin pulled her hand from Paul's arm. 'If you were, you'd be glad I'm to work for Madame.'

'As one of her Daughters of Ireland? Or one of her boy scouts? I believe she spends most of her time drilling her Fianna boys.'

'Yes, it's true she has formed a group of Irish boy scouts,' Caitlin replied evenly, 'and she's teaching them to shoot and fight for their country. If you find that amusing, perhaps you and I should part company, Paul. Seems you're more Wintour than Molloy, doesn't it?'

'Caitlin –' he snatched at her hand – 'don't let's be like this. You know I care as much for Ireland as you do. I'm sorry if I tried to make fun.'

Her gaze softened and she again took his arm. 'I'm sorry too, Paul. Guess I was mad at you for wanting to go see Melissa. But I don't know why you shouldn't. She's lovely.'

'Ah, she's got admirers lined up ten deep, I wouldn't have a look-in.' But Paul gave a happy, relieved smile. 'Let's get back and see if Jack's arrived. You know he's motoring up? He's got a Napier, so Tina says.'

'Guess I can always see Madame tomorrow,' said Caitlin.

They saw the car as soon as they turned the corner of the street; with its long green chassis and handsome brass lamps, it could scarcely be missed, especially as it was surrounded by an admiring crowd of small Dublin boys.

'Will you look at that?' asked Paul, in awed tones. 'See the coachwork? Oh, that's a beauty! I thought my Empire was something –'

'Tina's at the door,' Caitlin pointed out, 'seems to be waiting for us.'

'Jack's arrived,' Tina told them. 'Well, of course, you can see his motor –'

'I just hope he'll let me drive it,' said Paul.

'The thing is, he's brought someone with him.' Tina seemed strangely embarrassed. 'It's Julio.'

'Julio?'

'You remember, I told you about him, the adopted son of our *estancia* manager?'

'What's wrong, Tina?' asked Caitlin.

Tina glanced hastily behind her at the half-open front door. 'Look, I'd better explain. He's our half-brother. Papa's son. His mother was Mama's maid Mena.'

'Mena?' Caitlin's face darkened. 'You mean the girl who once worked with my father at Belcarron?'

'Yes. Mama took her out to Argentina and – well, it's not the way you think, Caitlin. Please don't look like that!'

'Poor young devil!' Caitlin whispered, as Paul put his arm around Tina. 'It's the same old story, isn't it? Thank you for telling us, it was right we should know. Now, may we meet him?'

He was as tall as Jack, that was the first thing Caitlin noticed when she was introduced to the young man standing next to her cousin. The second was that he was very handsome, and the third that he had the Wintour nose. Oh, he's all Wintour, isn't he? she thought. No wonder Tina told us who he was; we'd surely have seen, anyway.

As he bent his dark head over her hand, Spanish-style, she went pale.

'I'm green with envy over your Napier,' Paul was telling Jack. 'Now, I've got an Empire, do you know it? Not as grand as yours, but goes well. Little Aristocrat, they call it –'

Caitlin, slowly turning her head, met Julio's gaze fixed on her.

'Like a spin?' Jack asked Paul, delightedly. 'See what you think?'

'Aren't you tired? You've done enough motoring, haven't you?'

'I've never done enough motoring. Come on, we haven't got much time, I have to leave tomorrow to join the yacht.'

'Doesn't anyone want tea?' Tina called, but Jack and Paul had already disappeared, and Julio and Caitlin seemed to want to do nothing but stare into each other's eyes. Only George obligingly held out his cup.

It was thrilling, seeing Jack off next day to join the *Asgard*. Knowing that the yacht was about to begin its journey seemed to bring the adventure nearer, to make it all more real. No one read the newspapers on 29 June. The report of the murder of an Austrian archduke in Sarajevo would not have meant much, anyway.

Chapter Seventeen

It was the morning of 9 July. Julio had gone to the post office, Paul had taken Jack's car to the garage; Tina, missing George who had had to return to London, was alone with Caitlin in the drawing room.

'I don't know –' Tina began, then stopped. Her eyes again went wonderingly over her cousin. So pretty, wasn't she? Much prettier, even, than when she had first arrived, when she had seemed all raw edges willing to cut. Now everything about her had softened, her eyes, her mouth – most of all, her sharp tongue.

'What don't you know?' asked Caitlin languidly.

'Well, whether Paul is in love with Melissa, or just with Jack's motor. I expect he'll be mooning over it at the garage, said he wanted to look at it in the pit. Then there's Julio. He's supposed to be seeing Dublin. All he does is spend time with you.'

'But I'm showing him Dublin.'

'You don't even know it, Caitlin.'

'I guess I know *my* Dublin. Where Papa used to work on Parnell's newspaper, where Mother had her first little bookshop.' Caitlin smiled. 'Heavens, when you think what she has now!'

'And have you met the famous Countess Markievicz yet?'

'Oh, yes!' Caitlin sat up in her chair. 'She was wonderful, Tina, just as I had imagined her. Really striking, with great, fine eyes, you know, and a kind of magnetic way of holding you. We had the most terrific talk and she wants to see me again, so we can decide where I'd be most useful.'

'You didn't mention Howth?'

'No and neither did she.'

They were both silent, thinking of the hazards ahead. The arrangements had been carefully worked out, but on paper. In practice, there was so much that could go wrong. For instance, would the German tug with the rifles turn up at the *Roetigen* lightship which was the rendezvous? If it did, would the *Asgard* and the *Kelpie* be able to manage the cargo? When they sailed back, they would be constantly meeting ships of the fleet – would they be challenged? No one expected the same indulgence from the government that the Ulstermen had apparently received, when they took delivery of 30,000 Mausers the previous April.

Then there were the actual landings. The *Kelpie*'s landing at Kilcoole in County Wicklow might not be too difficult, but it was possible there would be more of a coastguard presence at Howth. The Irish Volunteers would be there, of course, pretending their march was just routine, together with the Fianna boys and a number of young men and women recruited to help who would have travelled out by taxi. Everything would be done to give the impression that all anyone wanted was a pleasant day out by the sea.

'I've been thinking,' said Tina. 'Now that we have Jack's motor, why don't we use that, instead of a taxi? Paul could drive and it would give us greater flexibility.'

'Which we might need. If the police move in, there'll be chaos and we'd do better with our own transport. Especially as we shall be collecting Jack from the yacht.'

'How I wish it were all over!' cried Tina, rising suddenly and beginning to pace up and down. 'At first it seemed so exciting, such a challenge –'

'It still is.'

'Yes, but I try to face facts. Things could go wrong.'

'They could, but they won't.' Caitlin squeezed Tina's hand hard. 'Don't think failure, Tina, think success.'

'It's so easy to say that.'

'No, it's hard. But it must be done.'

'You're right, of course.' Tina sighed heavily. 'It's the only way to face something like this.' She glanced at the small marble clock on the chimneypiece. 'Now, I must do some shopping – want to come?'

'If you don't mind, I think I'll just stay here.'

'To wait for Julio?' Tina's mouth tightened. 'Take care, Caitlin.'

'You mean, of Julio? Or myself?'

'Take care neither of you gets hurt, is all I'm saying.'

'No one is going to get hurt, Tina.'

After a long, steady look, Tina said no more but went to put on her hat. A few minutes later, she left the house.

Caitlin, smoking a cigarette, kept watch at the window for Julio's return. Any moment now he would be back and they would be together. She could hardly bear the pleasure of anticipation, knowing he would be feeling thc same, hurrying home, hoping to find her alone. And she was alone, the house was empty, Tina and the maid both out, and precious time ticking by. Who knew when they would find another opportunity like this?

They could go sightseeing together, go for walks, maybe touch hands, but nothing more, for Julio was far too much of an Argentine gentleman ever to compromise a young lady by attention in public places. Caitlin smiled, as the smoke from her cigarette rose. That was how he regarded her, of course, as a correctly brought-up young lady, which indeed she was. Except that she had ideas of her own on love which did not accord with convention, or with Julio's. It had been difficult to make him forget his upbringing enough to kiss her in the rare moments like these when they were alone in the house. For anything more, when he had put no wedding ring on her finger, there was no hope at all. Yet he thought of it, she knew, and so did she. As she sat and waited for him, she shivered deliciously, thinking of it. Oh, Julio – she stubbed out her cigarette – why don't you come?

Then she saw him and her heart gave a leap. His eyes found her at the window and he waved, smiling, and came into the house, running. 'They're out!' she cried. 'Everyone's out, we're all alone!'

They clung together, kissing and swaying, as time stood still and the world stopped. Then Caitlin, without consciously thinking what she was doing, broke the rule she had made, that she would never, never ask him – and asked him.

'Julio, darling, please, please, let's go to bed, let's go up to my room now. Come, there's no one in, we may never have another chance –'

'Catalina?' He whispered her Spanish name, which he always liked to use. 'What are you saying?'

'You know what I'm saying, Julio. Come, it isn't wrong to make love. What could be wrong about it? It's beautiful, it's something we want to give each other, isn't it?'

'*Amada*, I do not understand. You say is not wrong to make love? Of course, is wrong, outside marriage. Is beautiful, yes, is a wonderful gift, but only between husband and wife. The Church say this, I say this.'

'You refuse me?'

'Refuse? *Dios mío!* Catalina, you know I want you more than anything in the world!'

'But only if we're married?' Caitlin stepped back, her blue eyes stormy. 'What difference does it make? We love each other, don't we? I never thought I could care for anyone the way I care for you, Julio. I thought Ireland was all that mattered, but you want to work for Ireland too, so we are at one, at one in every way. That's why we should make love, make the supreme gift, don't you see that?'

He took her quietly into his arms. 'Catalina, will you marry me?'

She leaned against him, saying nothing.

'Catalina?'

'I don't know, Julio, I can't answer you.'

'So *you* refuse *me*?'

'No, oh no!' She kissed him passionately. 'It's not that, it's my work, what I want to do. I've never thought of marriage.'

'That's because you have not loved as you love now. To love as we love, marriage must follow, *amada*.'

'How could we be together, though? I must be here; you'll want to return to Argentina.'

'Maybe not.' His face darkened. 'What is for me in Argentina?'

'There's your family, your career –'

'What career? I have no career. All I wish is land and I have no money for land.'

'You are an Irishman, after all.' She laughed softly. 'All Irishmen want land.'

'If I stay here, Catalina, will you accept me?'

'Hold me, Julio, hold me!' Her mouth was covering his face with kisses, her arms were around him, straining his body to hers, but he still cried, hoarsely, 'Say we can be married, *amada*, say we are betrothed!'

'Yes, Julio, yes, we are betrothed!'

They were delirious with joy, fast in each other's arms, when the bang of the street door sent them leaping apart.

'The maid!' Caitlin whispered, straightening her dress.

But it was Tina. 'Hello, you two,' she called cheerfully. 'Didn't you want to go out?'

'After lunch, perhaps,' Caitlin answered lightly. 'But how quick you've been! You must have been lucky with your marketing.'

Tina smiled wryly. 'As a matter of fact, I'm rather late. Time must have been passing quickly for you. Will you excuse me, I must take off my hat.'

'Catalina, why did you not say we are betrothed?' cried Julio, when Tina had left them.

Caitlin put her finger to his lips. 'Ssh, let it be our secret, just for a while.'

'I do not wish it to be a secret.'

'No, wait, my darling, until the arms are landed, then we'll really be able to celebrate!'

Chapter Eighteen

The *Asgard* and the *Kelpie* were due to rendezvous with Figgis and the tug from Hamburg on 12 July. As the *Asgard*, with its unusual crew, approached the *Roetigen* lightship in the North Sea, fog came down. There was no sign of the tug, no sign of the *Kelpie*; for a while, they knew despair. Then someone made out the tug coming towards them through the mist and they all heard Figgis shouting that O'Brien had taken as much as he could; there were 900 rifles and over 20,000 rounds of ammunition still on board. 'Can you take them?' came the call, echoing eerily across the water.

'Yes,' they shouted back, 'we'll take the lot!'

On a yacht this size? thought Jack, but he shouted with the rest, 'Yes, we'll take the lot.' Somehow.

Hours went by of hard, manual work, until every rifle and box of ammunition was transferred from the tug to the yacht and stowed away, in cabins, passageways, anywhere a space could be found. Then they looked at one another, the amateurs and the two coopted fishermen, and realised they had done it. Done what they had come so far to do. The arms were aboard. Now, all they had to do was get them back to Howth, but for a little while they gave themselves up to euphoria.

It should have been nerve-racking, the long voyage back, and it was true that every time they passed official vessels, their hearts were in their mouths, but the knowledge that the arms were safely below made them curiously at ease, rather than afraid. It was as though all the fund raising, all the planning, all the physical discomfort, was already worth while, even though the end had not yet been reached. 'Think success,'

Caitlin had told Tina. No one on board the *Asgard* needed that kind of advice.

Jack was of the opinion that he had never been so happy. For the first time in his life, he felt he was achieving something, something that was his alone and had nothing to do with his family. 'What a successful family yours is, isn't it?' Terence Paget had commented, but what had he, Jack, done so far? He had never shone at school or university, he had never trained for a profession, he had not yet found any one who would take him on in marriage. It was true that he was helping his mother in the running of Belcarron, but with the shrinking of the estate, there was less and less for him to do and only the income earned by Victor in Argentina kept Belcarron going. It didn't do to dwell on these things, but sometimes when it was his turn to rest and he couldn't sleep in the cramped conditions of the yacht, this dreary stocktaking occupied his mind and then he took comfort in his new venture. Working for Irish freedom, obtaining for the Irish what they couldn't obtain for themselves, these were tasks that eased his conscience and made him glad he at least had the skill to be able to join in something like this.

Sometimes he felt like thanking the skipper, Erskine Childers, for making it all happen, but he knew Childers would shrink from any such demonstration and it wasn't in Jack's line, either. When the job was done, however, there would surely always be something special between himself and these people he had come to know so well. The British army officer, Gordon Shephard; Molly Childers, the skipper's wife; Mary Spring-Rice, from the London Committee. And Childers himself, lined and weathered, living in a world of his own, yet the driving force behind the whole undertaking. What would become of him, of all of them, when it was all over? Like everyone else aboard the *Asgard*, Jack found he couldn't think beyond the landing at Howth.

The *Kelpie*'s landing, which should have been straightforward, was in fact delayed, owing to damage in the yacht to which the arms were eventually to be transferred at Kilcoole. This was depressing, but only a temporary setback, and the urgent concern for Tina and the others had always been for the

Asgard. As far as they knew, that was still on course for landing on Sunday 26 July.

At dinner on Friday evening, Paul tried to take a philosophical view. 'I really don't think we have any need to worry about Sunday, but if things go wrong and we're arrested, well, we're arrested. I doubt they could pin much on us.'

'I'm not worried about being arrested,' Caitlin said sharply, 'I'm worrying about the loss of the arms. That would be a real tragedy.'

'It won't happen.' Tina poured wine. 'Think success, Caitlin.'

'To success!' Julio raised his glass and let his eyes rest on Caitlin. The others followed his lead and drank the toast, but their nerves were too stretched to enjoy it. They all went early to bed.

During the night, the wind rose. By morning, it was blowing a gale and dark clouds were gathering; by lunchtime, the storm itself had arrived and all that day battered the city and the coast.

'Surely it must wear itself out before tomorrow?' asked Caitlin, her eyes large and shadowed in her white face.

'It will, don't worry,' Paul told her, with a confidence he did not feel. He knew nothing at all about Irish weather in July. Maybe it could go on for days.

'Is like the *pampero*,' Julio murmured. 'At home, we think of horses and cattle in the storm. Here we think of those on the sea.'

'All I can think of is the *Asgard*,' Tina replied. 'Can she ride this out?'

'Childers will get her through,' said Paul, 'everyone says he is an excellent sailor. That's the one thing we can be sure about.'

Sunday's dawn brought no let-up in the storm, but the plan had to be followed and they made their way to Howth with spirits as low as the clouds over Dublin. It had been arranged that the *Asgard* would lie off Lambay Island and wait for Figgis again, who would this time be in a motorboat. In view of the dreadful weather, however, it seemed more than likely that the motorboat would not be able to put out.

'What can Childers do?' asked Tina.

'Wait,' said Paul.

*

For two hours, the *Asgard* cruised up and down outside Howth, while the crew, soaked and buffeted, raked the daytime darkness for a sign of the motorboat. They saw nothing, but suddenly there was a break in the clouds and the rain slackened, then stopped. Now was their chance and they took it. They lowered the sails and as the Irish Volunteers appeared on the quay, the yacht moved quietly into the harbour. Jack looked at his watch. It was a quarter to one. They were on time.

'She's coming in, she's coming in!' cried Tina, who had field glasses. 'I can see her. I can see them all on deck, Oh, thank God, thank God!'

'Can you see Jack?' asked Paul from the Napier, which he had parked among the taxis on the quay.

'Yes, I see him. I can't believe it, he looks so well! They all look so well! And proud – I think I've never seen Jack looking so proud and happy.' Tina lowered the glasses, as sudden tears stung her eyes. 'Oh, dear, I feel such a fool, but I've never been so relieved in my life.'

'Can anyone see the coastguards?' asked Caitlin, her gaze searching the waiting crowds. 'They must surely be here some place, they couldn't fail to see what's going on.'

'They won't interfere at this stage,' said Tina, 'not with all these people. But I shouldn't be surprised if they call the police and that will mean soldiers as well from Dublin Castle.'

'Oh, God, I hope you're wrong,' cried Caitlin, leaping into the crowd. 'Let's help get these arms off as soon as possible. Come on, what are we waiting for?'

Everything went so smoothly it was almost an anticlimax. The whole operation of unloading the arms and distributing them to the Volunteers took no more than half an hour, after which Childers stood chatting to some of the leaders of the nationalist movement who had come to welcome him: Cathal Brugha, who had organised the taxis, Bulmer Hobson, who had marched in the Volunteers, Arthur Griffiths of Sinn Fein. Jack, his hair bleached by the long days in the open air, his face tanned, stood with Tina's arm in his, thinking what a moment of triumph this was for the quiet Englishman. But Childers, as usual, showed no emotion. He had already thanked his crew, shaking them each by the hand, now he and his wife quietly withdrew, to take to the sea again.

'I can't believe it's all over,' Jack muttered, and Tina pressed his arm.

'I say, thank God it is. Oh, Jack, it's so good to see you again! I must get a message to George as soon as possible, to say you're safe.'

'And the arms,' Jack said, with a grin. 'They were the point of the whole thing, remember.'

The welcoming top brass had driven away, followed by the taxis and the Fianna boys, and the Volunteers were beginning their march back to Dublin, proudly displaying their rifles on their shoulders. 'You know,' said Jack, 'I suddenly feel tired.'

'We have your motor right here,' Paul told him. 'I've looked after it like a baby. Guess you'll be wanting to drive back?'

'I think I might just fall asleep at the wheel. How about you taking us back, Paul?'

'If you're sure.'

'Jack, we're so proud of you,' Julio murmured, as they climbed into the Napier. 'You are – what is the word? – a hero!'

'Oh, please, it's Childers who's the hero. He was amazing, cool as a cucumber throughout the whole thing, and at the end coming in like that on time!' Jack shook his head. 'All the rest of us did was to follow him.'

'Don't run yourself down, Jack,' Caitlin told him crisply. 'What you did was truly brave and you did it for Ireland. I want you to know we're grateful.'

'It'll be something to tell your grandchildren, won't it?' asked Paul, from the wheel of the car, but Jack laughed.

'Grandchildren? I'd better get married first. Caitlin, care to take me on?'

'Any time,' she answered, finding Julio's eyes, 'only you're far too nice for me, Jack.'

'You said it,' said Paul, grinning, 'but where are we going? Back to Dublin?'

'Why don't we stop somewhere for a meal?' asked Tina. 'There's a little place on the road back where you can get magnificent beef. I'll guide you, Paul.'

'Will it be open on Sunday?'

'If it isn't, we'll open it up ourselves. Come on, let's go before the coastguards appear.'

It was evening before they drove into Dublin and almost immediately ran into crowds making for one of the quays by the Liffey. Paul stopped the car to ask a man hurrying by what was going on.

'Sure, 'tis the people following the soldiers to Bachelor's Walk,' the Dubliner threw over his shoulder.

'Hey – wait! What soldiers?'

'Them as were at Clontarf. Weren't they called out to the Volunteers, then, to take their rifles?'

'They took their rifles?' cried Caitlin, turning pale, as the others exchanged stricken glances.

'They did not, am I not telling you? The Volunteers got clean away, but the people are following the soldiers. You be driving on, maybe you'll be seeing.'

'It's just what we were afraid of,' Tina said as Paul drove on, following the crowds. 'The police must have been alerted and called out the troops, so now there's trouble.'

'But they didn't get the rifles, that's all that matters,' Caitlin declared. 'Oh, thank God, the Volunteers got away!'

'Bachelor's Walk,' Julio repeated, 'please, what is this?'

'It's one of the quays by the river, where things were landed,' Tina explained. 'The army barracks are not far away and that's where the soldiers must be heading. I'm not sure we should go, I don't think we should be involved.'

'I don't agree,' Jack responded. 'It's the end of the thing, isn't it? I think we should see what happens.'

They reached the quay to find the soldiers drawn up and the crowd hurling stones and bottles. 'Stay in the car,' Jack whispered to Julio and the girls, as he and Paul got out, the better to see what was happening.

'Jack! Paul! Come back!' Tina protested. 'Those soldiers have bayonets and rifles.'

The soldiers, men of the King's Own Scottish Borderers, remained motionless as their officer walked towards them. He gave an order and the rearguard wheeled to face the crowd. Then he put up his hand.

*

Afterwards, they were to learn that he only wanted silence so that he could speak to the people, but the soldiers, who had been given the order to load at Clontarf, and had never unloaded, thought he meant them to fire. There was a single shot, and then a volley, and a number of people fell to the ground. One of them was Jack.

They were around him in seconds – Tina, Caitlin, Paul, Julio – holding him, tearing at his shirt to see his wound, but there was blood at his mouth and his eyes were closed.

'Tina, Tina!' cried Julio in agony. 'Do something, please, you are a doctor, do something to help Jack! *Madre de Dios*, help him, help him!'

Tina looked up from Paul's face to Julio's and Caitlin's, all so ashen, all so afraid.

'I can't help him, Julio,' she answered stonily. 'Jack is dead.'

Chapter Nineteen

A tragic accident was how the authorities viewed the incident at Bachelor's Walk. Several people had been killed and nearly forty injured, but that toll could have been much worse, and though a commission later censured the soldiers, it was clear they had simply misunderstood their officer's intention. The Irish, however, saw things very differently. To them, the shootings were yet another example of British repression when the question of Home Rule was still not resolved, and they were shocked and angry. There might well have been serious repercussions, except that events elsewhere were soon to override even Irish emotion. All that mattered to the Wintours was that they had lost Jack.

On the morning of 3 August, Julio sat alone at Belcarron, on the bench overlooking the sea. He was wearing a new black suit and looked pale and ill, but he was not ill, he was grieving, which felt much the same. Jack was gone. Jack, who had been his friend, who had been his brother. He still could not believe it, even though he had seen Jack die, though he had attended the funeral. How long would it be before he could accept it? He shook his head, staring dazedly at the bay. A long, long time.

It had been difficult, meeting Victor. He had always known it would be. Jack and Doña Alicia might have been ready to forgive his old threats, but Victor would show no forgiveness and Julio wanted none. So the cold stare Victor had given him from grief-filled eyes was only what he had expected and didn't matter at all. Nothing mattered now, except his Catalina, and he had scarcely spoken with her since their descent into sorrow.

'Julio?' He had not heard her approach, but she was beside him and he leaped to his feet.

'Catalina!' In her black dress, with her hair strained back from her face, she seemed a stranger and his heart ached to see her so.

'Cousin Alice would like to see you, please,' she told him quietly, 'if you don't mind.'

'How are you?' he asked gently.

'Like everyone else, I suppose. Trying to come to terms with nightmare.' She held out her hand. 'But it's worse for you. Jack was special to you, wasn't he?'

'Very special.' He put his arm round her shoulders and they stood for some moment in a quiet embrace.

'You should go to Cousin Alice,' she said at last.

'Yes, I'll go,' he agreed.

Victor, at the window of his grandfather's study, where he had gone to smoke a cigarette, watched them both with rising resentment. The two people he most disliked, communing together on the lawns of Belcarron, it was intolerable! Caitlin Molloy he would have to accept, even though her father had once burned down the stables at Belcarron, but Julio Castillo – why in God's name should he be entertained here at a time like this?

Victor drew angrily on his cigarette, his eyes narrowing in the smoke, as Julio and Caitlin turned and began to move towards the house. Come to that, why had Julio been asked to stay with Tina in Dublin? Why had he and the rest of them been down at the quay the day Jack was killed? It was bad enough to arrive from Argentina to find his brother dead, his home plunged in sorrow, his mother stricken, without the suspicion that his family were in a conspiracy he knew nothing about. I'll get it out of George, he thought. Tina could be as obstinate as a mule, but George was reasonable, he would see it wasn't right for the head of the family to be kept in the dark.

'Victor dear?' Evie, his wife, seeming taller and thinner than ever in her mourning, appeared at the door to the study. 'Wouldn't you like to join us for coffee?'

'If you like.' Victor ground out his cigarette. He looked at her with reddened eyes and her heart turned over with compassion. Poor Victor, he wasn't used to suffering and she knew he was grieving for Jack more than he would ever admit.

'Do you think I should bring Rickie down again?' she asked, taking his arm. 'Everyone thinks he should be a comfort to your mother, but when I ask her if she would like to hold him, she scarcely seems to hear.'

'It's far too soon for Mother to take comfort in anything,' Victor replied. 'Leave Rickie upstairs with the nurse. He's better out of all the gloom.'

In the long drawing room, where the air seemed warm and cloying, even though the windows were wide open, Bridie was handing round coffee. Alice was not present, Victor noticed; nor was Julio. Tina was pacing the floor.

'It's Mama I feel so sorry for,' she burst out. 'It took her years to get over Papa, she was like someone with a long illness, wasn't she? She'd just got better and now -' Tina's voice trembled – 'she's back in the sickroom again.'

'Will you not be taking your coffee, Miss Tina?' Bridie pleaded. 'Here, be having a bit of sugar, 'twill be doing you good.'

Tina obediently stirred in sugar. 'I don't see how Mama can get better this time,' she finished despondently.

'I'm afraid there may soon be many more mothers grieving like her,' George said in a low voice. 'The news looks bad.'

'What news?' asked Caitlin.

'Well, what's in the papers. The prospect of war.'

'Guess we've had other things to do than read papers. You mean between England and Germany? They've been talking of that for years.'

'It's different now,' Paul remarked. 'There's been an order for mobilisation all over Europe.'

'Oh, how absurd!' cried Tina. 'An Austrian archduke gets killed in Sarajevo and everyone has to go to war?'

'You know it's more complicated than that,' George told her. 'None of us took any notice of that assassination, but it was the match to the tinder. Germany sided with Austria, Russia sided with Serbia, now France has become involved and if Germany tries to go through Belgium to attack France, we shall be drawn in. Our commitments to Belgium go back a long way.'

'The States will not be drawn in,' Caitlin declared, 'and I see no reason why Ireland should help England. What Irishman would want to fight for England?'

Victor looked at her with cold dislike. 'I think you will find plenty of Irishmen who will want to fight for England. There are already a number of fine Irish regiments in the British army and if war comes, I for one will be ready to go.'

'No!' cried Evie, turning white. 'No, Victor, you can't mean it!'

'Victor, think of Mama,' said Tina, staring at him. 'After what's happened to Jack, you couldn't do that to her.'

'I don't understand you. This is a matter of duty. All the British in Buenos Aires are planning to volunteer if there's a war. Do you think I could stand aside?'

Caitlin took a step towards him. 'How can you say you'd fight for the British?' she cried, breathing hard. 'The British army murdered your brother!'

'Caitlin!' Paul leaped to his feet.

'Caitlin,' whispered Tina, taking her arm, 'don't say such things, please. Those soldiers made a mistake, they never intended to kill anyone. Mama has letters from Dublin Castle –'

'So that makes it all right, does it?' Caitlin's cheeks were burning, her lips trembling. 'Oh, you Wintours make me ill, do you know that? Even when one of your own loses his life because of British repression, you still close ranks, don't you? You still won't admit what's being done to the Irish every day! Oh, I have to go out, get some air –'

Shaking off Tina's hand, Caitlin pushed past Victor and ran from the room, leaving silence behind her.

'I'm sorry,' Paul said at last, sinking back into his chair. 'She's overwrought, so distressed over Jack –'

'That's true of all of us,' Victor replied curtly. He looked round at the watching faces. 'But while we're here together, would someone explain to me why Jack was down on that quay in the first place? And why was he in Dublin for nearly a month when he hated the place? What was he doing there for so long?'

George, Tina and Paul stared at the carpet. Evie kept an unhappy gaze on Victor. Melissa waited.

'George, you're a sensible fellow,' Victor said, making an effort to appear patient, 'you know I have a right to know what's going on. Why was Jack in Dublin? If that's where he was.'

'I'm afraid I can't tell you,' George replied evenly. 'What Jack was doing in the last weeks of his life was his own affair.'

'That's true.' Tina raised her eyes to Victor. 'You actually have no right at all to ask about Jack's private life, Victor.'

'You were all involved, though, weren't you? There was something afoot and as usual, I am the last to know!'

'Victor, just leave it,' said George. 'It's water under the bridge.'

'Why should I leave it?' Victor was beginning, when Bridie, who had taken away the coffee tray, reappeared. 'Mr Victor, sir, will you be going to the morning room, if you please? And Miss Tina and Miss Melissa.'

'Mama wishes to see us?' asked Melissa.

'Isn't it the lawyer, then, come over from Cork?'

'Lionel Pearce!' cried Victor. 'What's he doing here? No one told me he was coming.'

'He arrived some time ago, when you were in the study,' Tina told him.

'But why? It can't be to do with Jack's will, he'd nothing to leave.'

'Except his share of the *estancia*.'

'That has to go to the family.'

'I don't want to know what Jack has left, anyway,' Melissa sighed. 'What does it matter, now that he is gone?'

In just a few days, age had come to Alice. Before the news of Jack's death, she had still retained her beauty, seeming to have defied the years. Now she appeared vanquished. Almost before her family's eyes, she had grown old.

She managed a smile as they filed into the small, shabby morning room, and told them to sit down, adding, 'Mr Pearce here wishes to give us the terms of Jack's will.'

No one was listening. Their eyes were on Julio, sitting, white-faced, by Alice's side. Victor turned a stormy gaze on his mother.

'What is the meaning of this, Mother? Why is Julio Castillo

here? This is a family matter, is it not?'

'Would you be so good as to acknowledge Mr Pearce, Victor,' Alice asked, her smile dying, 'and sit down.'

'I'm sorry.' As his sisters took chairs, Victor remained standing but inclined his head towards the lawyer and murmured a greeting.

'If you would sit down, Mr Wintour, we could begin,' Lionel Pearce said quietly.

'There is no question of beginning until Julio Castillo has left this room. I demand he leave now.'

'I assure you, there is good reason for Señor Castillo's presence. Please, Mr Wintour, sit down.'

'Sit down, Victor,' Alice ordered.

After a long, uncertain moment, Victor did.

Lionel Pearce shuffled his papers and cleared his throat. He too was looking older, with long lines deeply etched on his brow and at his mouth. He had, of course, the Wintours remembered, known Jack since he was a boy.

'This is a very sad occasion,' he began slowly. 'I hope you will permit me to say, for me personally. I never thought it would be my duty to have to read Mr Jack's will. But it's simple enough. He has left some small legacies to the servants here, his dinghy to Dr Tina Coxe, his motor to you, Mr Wintour, his signet ring to Miss Melissa, and his watch to his friend Mr Terence Paget. Otherwise, all his assets go to Mrs Wintour to dispose of as she thinks best, with the exception of his share of the Estancia Sentos in Argentina, which goes to Señor Julio Castillo.'

There was a short, terrible silence. No one looked at Julio, who kept his own eyes down. Everyone looked at Victor, who had risen to his feet.

'I don't believe it,' he said thickly, his face mottling. 'It's not possible. My brother wouldn't have done that to me.'

'What do you mean, to you?' asked Tina at once. 'What has Jack done to you?'

'There must be some mistake, Mr Pearce,' Victor went on, ignoring Tina, 'you must have misunderstood my brother's intentions. He knew he could not leave his share of the *estancia* away from the family.'

'There has been no mistake,' Lionel Pearce replied. 'Mr

Jack came to me shortly before he left for Dublin and told me what he wanted me to do. I followed his instructions to the letter.'

Only then did Victor turn to Julio. 'How did you make him do it?' he asked softly. 'How did you persuade Jack to leave you his land?'

'I know nothing of this, I swear it!' cried Julio. 'Jack never said a word to me. How could I know what he wish?'

'What he wish,' Victor repeated, contemptuously, 'you mean, what you wish. But it's all a waste of time. You are the legally adopted son of someone outside the family, you cannot inherit Jack's share of the *estancia*.'

'I'm afraid I'm not an expert on Argentine law,' the lawyer remarked. 'Are you certain of your facts, Mr Wintour?'

Victor ran his hand over his mouth. He shook his head. 'I am not absolutely certain, but I believe it is so.'

'Jack was a British citizen,' Tina put in quickly. 'Mama made sure we all were. Maybe he would not be bound by Argentine law?'

'As far as the *estancia* is concerned, I am afraid he would,' Pearce returned. 'The land is Argentine land, you see. But I can look into this, I can establish the position –'

'No, that will not be necessary,' Alice said quietly, and Victor swung round.

'What do you mean, Mother? Of course we must establish the position!'

'I already know the position, Victor. It would be extremely difficult for Julio to share legally the ownership of the Estancia Sentos. He is not a member of the family, he is, as you say, the adopted son of Lucio Castillo.'

'There you are, then!' cried Victor triumphantly. 'He cannot inherit!'

'Yet Jack has made it known what his wishes were and we must follow them,' Alice went on. 'I suggest a compromise.' She looked around at the intently watching faces. 'That Julio should receive Jack's share of the profits, in return for which he acts as overall manager of the *estancia*, with full responsibility for decision-making with the rest of the family. This I believe would be legally acceptable and would come as close as possible to what Jack wanted.'

'Manager?' Victor repeated. 'Mother, I already have a manager!'

'Overall manager is what I suggested, Victor.' Alice turned to Julio. 'You would be agreeable to this, Julio?'

'Agreeable?' Julio's voice was trembling. 'Doña Alicia, I do not know what to say to you – but yes, yes, I am agreeable, if this is what you wish.'

'It was what Jack wished, Julio.' Alice turned to her family. 'Does everyone else agree?'

'Of course, it's only right,' Tina answered. 'I'm absolutely in favour.'

'So am I,' said Melissa, 'if I count, that is. I'm not of age.'

'I can vote for you,' said Alice. 'Victor, what about you?'

'You can guess my answer, Mother. I do not agree.'

'You would go against your brother's wishes?'

'Certainly, if I considered them wrong, and I do.'

Alice hesitated. 'You don't think Julio has a moral right to Jack's share?' she asked quietly. 'It is what Jack believed himself, that's plain.'

'Perhaps we should not discuss that now.'

'You may speak freely before Mr Pearce. He knows the facts.'

'Julio has no right to any profits from the Estancia Sentos.'

'We're talking of moral rights, not legal rights,' Tina said sharply. 'Didn't you hear what Mama said?'

'I heard.' Victor moved to the door. 'My answer is that Julio Castillo has by his past behaviour forfeited any right to share with this family in anything. Good day, Mr Pearce.'

When Victor had left, Alice turned to the lawyer. 'Do we need him?' she asked simply.

'That is a question you may have to put to your Argentine lawyers, Mrs Wintour. As you own the major part of the *estancia* and outnumber your son by three to one in this matter, I'd say you need have no worries.'

'I do not know how to thank you, Doña Alicia,' Julio murmured. 'I shall never forget what Jack wished to do for me, or what you do for me. Also, Tina – Melissa –' He bowed and turned aside.

'I've told you, we're only carrying out Jack's wishes,' Alice told him. 'Perhaps we should have thought of something like this before.'

'We should,' Tina murmured. 'It took Jack to show us what to do.'

'Mr Pearce, I will discuss formal arrangements with you later,' Alice said, rising a little unsteadily, 'but now, won't you stay to luncheon?'

She went out on his arm and Tina, watching, tried to hold back tears. 'Poor Mama,' she whispered, 'she keeps going so well, but it's as though it's someone else who is with us and she is elsewhere.'

Melissa pressed her hand. 'I said I didn't want to know what Jack left,' she murmured, 'but I'm glad, now, I have his ring. And you have the *Sea Watch*, Tina. You must come often and sail.'

'All I hope is that Victor sells the Napier,' Tina said fiercely. 'I couldn't bear to see that car again.' She glanced at Julio. 'Why don't you go and find Caitlin, Julio? Tell her the news?'

'You wish?' Bowing courteously over their hands, he left them, still looking grave, but less pale. Tina and Melissa exchanged glances.

'Any hope that Julio might take Caitlin to Argentina?' asked Melissa.

'They're so in love, they won't want to part, that's for sure.'

'She'll probably make him stay in Ireland.'

'We must just wait and see.' Tina blew her nose. 'Now I must go and tell George about Mama's idea.'

'And I'll tell Paul, shall I?' asked Melissa.

Chapter Twenty

Caitlin was walking through the trees that bounded the stables and formed what the Wintours liked to call their wood, though it was hardly that. Still, it provided shade and a screen from the house and she felt the better for being alone in its cool green light, away from the Wintours. When Julio came running, calling her name, she turned and stood still until he reached her, when she took his hands and drew him further into the trees.

'*Amada*, what is wrong?' he asked gently. 'You seem upset, yes, I can tell. What has happened?'

'Kiss me, Julio, just kiss me.'

He looked around. 'Here? I do not like –'

'Oh, please, no one can see. What does it matter, anyway?' Caitlin kissed him on the mouth. 'Oh, I do so hate being at Belcarron! The Wintours are not my kind, they don't understand anything I care about. Let's go back to Dublin!'

'Catalina, I do not understand you. You speak of Doña Alicia? Of Tina? They are my friends, they are your family. Why do you speak of them this way?'

She shrugged, leaning against a tree with her arms folded. 'Tina is all right until she comes here, then she forgets everything that matters, but Cousin Alice, Victor and Melissa – they are all alien to me, Julio, alien to everything I stand for. When I'm here, I feel stifled. I know I must get away. When can we go?'

He gave a small, shy smile. 'First, you must hear my news. I think you will be surprised.'

'Is it good news?'

'Very good. Jack has left me his share of the *estancia*.'

'Really?' Caitlin raised her eyebrows. 'Well, I suppose it will give you an income.'

'Income?' Julio threw his arms wide. 'Catalina, it means much more than money to me, it means all the world! To share in land, to work with land, is all I want.'

'Are they going to let you have it? Is Victor?'

Julio let his arms fall. 'Victor is not important. Doña Alicia say I may be manager, I may take what Jack have from the profits. That is legally permitted.'

'So you can't legally own Jack's share? I thought they'd never let you.'

'Is not their fault, is the law, Catalina. If I am manager, if I am with the land, is all I want.'

'Would have wanted,' she corrected. 'Things are different now, remember? We're engaged.'

'I do not forget, but now I may give you a home, now I look after you.'

'Where? In Argentina? Did we not say we would work together for Ireland? How can we work for Ireland in Argentina?'

'But when we talk before, I have nothing, *amada*, now is all changed. Is changed because of Jack, what he gives to me.'

Caitlin stared at him, her blue eyes seeming dark in the shadow of the trees. 'What are you saying, Julio? You've been offered the post of glorified manager by the Wintours, so you won't stay in Ireland? Is that what you are saying?'

'I say we go back to Argentina as man and wife.'

'And Ireland can go sink in the sea for all you care, is that it?'

'No!' He tried to take her in his arms, his handsome face suddenly filled with the naked fear that all he had was falling through his fingers, but she eluded him and stood apart.

'You are just the same as all men, after all,' she said slowly. 'When it comes to decisions, you make them. You want to stay in Ireland, we stay in Ireland. You want to go to Argentina, we go to Argentina. Well, things are not going to happen your way, Julio. I have work to do in Ireland and I intend to do it. I could never live in Argentina, I should die, thinking of the people here and all that must be done. I guess, if you can't see that, you don't know me at all, and I don't know you, either.'

They stood in silence, looking at each other, and the sunlight striking through the trees showed their faces hard and set, strangely different in their pain, like masks they had put on to deceive. Julio felt sick. Where was the truth? With this hostility? Or their love? Or had there never been real love? He refused to believe it. His love for his Catalina was absolute, it was a rock in all the sea of grief and uncertainty. '*Amada*, you do know me,' he murmured brokenly, drawing her to him, 'you do know my love. All I wish is happiness for you, I do anything for you, anything –'

'Then stay in Ireland with me,' she said quietly, looking up from the circle of his arms into his yielding face. She could see the sweat on his brow, could feel his heart bounding beneath her hand. 'Julio?' she pressed. 'Julio?'

'Is as you wish.' The words seemed forced from his lips. 'I stay in Ireland.'

She lowered her head and pressed her face against him.

'I agree,' he whispered, 'do not worry, I stay with you.'

'No.' She pulled herself from him. 'No, it wouldn't do, I see it wouldn't. I was wrong to ask it.'

'Is not wrong, Catalina. All I wish is to be with you. If it cannot be in Argentina, then must be Ireland. Is all right, I understand.'

'It's not all right, Julio. It wouldn't do, it wouldn't work. You'd be as lost here as I would be in Argentina. All you'd have would be me and I wouldn't be enough.' As he tried to speak, she put her finger against his lips. 'Please, my darling, hear me out. The trouble is, you have no real work here. You'd be helping me because I asked you to, but you'd spend all your time regretting the *estancia* and then . . . I guess we'd end up hating each other.'

'Why do you talk this way?' he cried frantically. 'We love each other, this is all that matter. I agree to stay, now you wish me to go. Is not possible, I cannot live without you. Come, let me hold you –'

'No, it wouldn't help – the more I'm with you, the less I see straight.' Caitlin's eyes filled with rare tears. 'Julio, I'm going to leave you now. Please don't follow me, there's nothing more to say.'

'Say you love me! Catalina, let me hear you say it. Julio, I love you!'

'Julio, I love you. There, I've said it, and it's true. But to give up what really matters, even for love, is wrong.'

'What really matters?' he repeated slowly. 'All that matters to me, Catalina, is you.'

'Oh, Julio ...' She went to him and kissed him, long and passionately, as though she could never leave him. But she did leave him, running through the trees with tears on her face, and he stood where she had left him, letting the bitterness flow over him, thinking never again would he come to trees in sunlight. Once before, he had stood like this, when he had learned that Don Ricardo was his father. Jack had come to him then and tried to comfort him, as he had tried to comfort him again all these years later in his will, but now there was no Jack, no comfort. He had been happy for a little while, thinking of the land, but now the truth rolled over him. He had lost Jack and he had lost Catalina. Why had he ever called her Catalina? Her name was Caitlin, an Irish name, and she was Irish. She belonged to Ireland, she would never, ever, be his.

That night, as he lay sleepless in his room at Ryan's, listening to the old clock in the bar chime midnight, Great Britain and Germany moved officially into a state of war.

Chapter Twenty-One

'It's happened, then,' said Tina, 'just as you said, George.'

'As I feared.' He threw down the newspaper, his face heavy and grey. 'God, the stupidity of it!'

'Men have always been stupid,' Caitlin snapped, 'particularly politicians.' She was very pale, her eyes shadowed, but showing her usual fire.

Victor poured more breakfast coffee. 'But going to war for Ireland would not be stupid, would it? In your eyes?'

'Of course not, that war would be just.'

'If you were a Belgian, wouldn't you consider this war just?'

'It's true, small countries must be protected from aggression,' said Tina. 'Germany has invaded Belgium, so we must attack Germany, but couldn't the matter have been managed some other way?'

'I absolutely agree!' cried Caitlin. 'Some other way should have been found. Think of the men who will be killed, the women wearing black –' She stopped, as Alice put back her chair and stood up.

'If you will excuse me,' she whispered, and left them.

'Victor, you'd better tell Mama,' Tina said quickly. 'I mean, if you're really planning to join up.'

'Oh, Victor, don't!' Evie wailed. 'It's not necessary, really it isn't. We'll be going home to Argentina, no one will expect you to go –'

'I expect it of myself,' he said shortly. 'Yes, you're right, Tina, I'll tell Mother now.' He strode out.

'How can he be so cruel?' Evie burst into tears. 'If he doesn't think of me, of Rickie, shouldn't he think of her?'

'Victor has his faults, but he's no coward and doesn't want to be thought one,' Tina said, with a sigh. 'I'm afraid he's made up his mind on this; you won't change him.'

'You don't need to tell me,' Evie sobbed. 'When have I ever changed Victor's mind on anything?'

At first, Victor could not find his mother. Then he saw her small, black-dressed figure descending the path to the sea and quickly scrambled down after her.

'Mother, wait! I want to talk to you!'

She had reached the little strip of sand at the foot of the cliff when he caught up with her and gave her his hand, as she stepped across to sit on a smooth rock, baked dry by the sun. The air was sultry again, the breeze over the sea scarcely moving the waves. Alice put up an old sunshade and looked up at her son. 'It will soon be your birthday,' she murmured. 'Do you remember your twenty-first? We were all here then, weren't we? Marianne and Everard, Frederick and Cecily. And Jack.'

'Mother, please –'

'Marianne was so sorry not to come to the funeral, but she's been nursing Everard's mother, who is very ill. Did I tell you that?'

'Yes, you did, I was sorry to hear it. Listen, I have something to tell you, Mother, and I know it will upset you, but if you could just try to understand –'

'Is it something to do with the war?'

'Why, yes, yes, it is. How did you know?'

'When I saw your face at breakfast, it was plain you had decided to go. You have, haven't you?'

He found himself a rock and sat down, wiping his brow. 'I thought I'd try for a commission in one of the Irish regiments, maybe the Royal Rifles.'

'They'll be sure to take you.'

'I hope so. Oh, look, I know it seems hard, after what's happened, but you do understand, don't you? I couldn't just go back to Argentina and leave my country in the lurch?'

'I'm glad you think of England as your country, Victor.'

'Thousands of Irishmen will be volunteering, Mother. When it comes down to it, England is the mother country, they'll want to fight for her.'

'The fact is, Victor, you do have commitments in Argentina. You needn't go to war.'

'I have a manager for the *estancia* –' his face darkened – 'as you very well know.'

'Yes, and I have appointed another. I'm surprised you want to leave Julio in charge.'

'He will not be in charge!' Victor shouted. 'I have not agreed to your appointment, Mother. Things will stay as they are until I return.'

'Until you return?' she repeated, her voice trembling. 'You know what the chances of that will be.'

'Oh, Mother –' As he looked into her ravaged face, his heart was touched with sudden compassion. 'I'm sorry, I just wish there was something I could do.'

'There is, Victor. You can accept Julio.'

He leaped to his feet and stood staring out to sea, his face working.

Alice rose and quietly took his arm. 'It's what I want more than anything, Victor. Because Jack wanted it. Because I want Jack to lie in peace. Do you understand?'

He said nothing.

'It is right we should do something for Julio, Victor. Jack saw that, I want you to see it too. You said you wished there was something you could do. Please do this for me.'

'Very well.' He turned and looked down at her, his face in the sunlight hard and forbidding. 'If that's what you want, I will do it.'

'Thank you,' she said simply.

As they made their way back up the cliff path, Alice paused to take breath. 'It would be nice, you know, if you were to tell him yourself,' she murmured, gasping a little. 'I mean, Julio.'

'You surely don't mean me to go down to Ryan's to see him?'

'Well, he's there. I asked him to stay at the house, but he insisted he wished to give no trouble. Do go down there and speak to him, Victor, give him your hand.'

'I'll think about it,' said Victor.

After dinner that evening, he walked down to Ryan's, where the talk in the bar was of nothing but war, and asked for Señor Castillo.

'Sure, he's up in his room, packing, Mr Wintour, sir,' Pat Ryan told him. 'He's not after drinking these days, but he'll be glad to be having a word. 'Tis up the stairs and second on the left.'

When Julio answered Victor's knock, his face showed his surprise and distaste.

'May I talk to you?' asked Victor stiffly.

'Please, come in.'

The room was small and low-ceilinged; both men had to stoop until Julio, pushing aside his boxes, placed a basket chair for Victor and took a sagging armchair for himself.

'I'll come to the point,' Victor said at once. 'First, I'd better tell you that I intend to join one of the regiments.'

'You go to war? Argentina will not be involved.'

'I think you know that I am not an Argentine. It's hard on my mother, I feel guilty, but as I see it I have no choice.'

'So, where is this point?' asked Julio.

'The point is, to make my mother happy, I have agreed you should manage the *estancia* and take Jack's share of any profits.'

'To make Doña Alicia happy? I see.'

'Of course, it doesn't make *me* happy. I've made my views plain.'

'Very plain.'

Victor leaned forwards as the basket chair creaked beneath his weight. 'But it's occurred to me that there is an alternative to this. Maybe my brother was right, you should have been given something, compensation of some sort, but you're a practical fellow, you'll be able to see as well as I that it would never work, you and I in harness. What I've come to ask is, will you agree to take cash instead? Enough to buy something of your own elsewhere?'

'A long way from you?' Julio laughed, his eyes shining. 'The answer, Don Victor,' he said distinctly, 'is no.'

Victor drew back. 'You refuse? Without even considering?'

'I do not need to consider, Don Victor. You remember, many years ago, I say I will get even with you? Everyone think I mean you harm, but that was not true. I just wished to wait for some time like this. And now it has come. *Gracias a Dios!*' He laughed again, as Victor sat like stone.

'You know why I wait? Not because of my sister. I think, now, you spoke the truth and never touch her. No, is because of what you say to me that day we race.'

'For God's sake, what did I say?'

'"You bastard" is what you say.' Julio's face was white. 'Jack, he called me his brother, but you say "bastard". So I say to you, no, I take no money from you, I take Jack's share, because he was my brother and I was his, I do what he wish and not what you wish.' Julio stood up and opened the door. '*Buenas noches*, Victor. I think now I may call you that? Please to go. Tomorrow I come to Belcarron to say goodbye.'

Victor, his face thunderous, strode to the door and slammed it behind him.

'Goodnight, sir!' Pat Ryan called from behind the door, but pushing through the yachtspeople crowding the bar, Victor made no reply.

The following morning, as he said he would, Julio went to Belcarron to say goodbye. He did not look for Caitlin – even to think of seeing her again filled him with anguish – but made his way to the kitchens to find Bridie. She was having her mid-morning cup of tea with Maisie and the new kitchen maid, Agnes, but leaped to her feet when she saw him and flung her arms around his neck.

'Ah, now, you're not leaving?' she cried. 'Oh, but I can see it in your face, you are coming to say goodbye, isn't it the truth, Francis Flynn? I'll not be forgiving you for leaving me, so I won't.'

'I am leaving, but I am not saying goodbye,' he whispered against her face. 'Dear Bridie, I cannot say goodbye to you. I will see you again, I promise.'

'When? When? Ah you devil, you know we'll never be meeting again!'

'Sure, Bridie, you could be going to Argentina yourself,' Maisie put in eagerly. ''Tis money you have now, why not be spending it?'

'My money from Mr Jack?' Bridie's eyes filled with tears. 'I'll not be spending it, I could never be leaving Belcarron. 'Twould fall down, so it would, if I were to go.'

'She's thinking of the mistress,' murmured Maisie, ''tis the mistress would miss Bridie.'

'I know.' Julio kissed Bridie on the cheek. 'But we will meet again somehow, Bridie. You are my own mother's sister, I will not forget you.'

'Be going, then, 'tis too hard to be seeing you when 'tis not staying you are.' She turned him round and pushed him towards the door. 'And be writing, Francis Flynn!'

'I promise, I promise!' Bowing hurriedly to Maisie and the astonished Agnes, Julio left the kitchen, his hand to his eyes, and Bridie, finding her chair, sat down. 'Ah, Francis,' she said forlornly, ''tis a beautiful young man you are and the finest nephew but 'tis never again I'll be seeing you. Not in this life, I'm thinking.'

Agnes, without being told, moved the kettle over on the stove, to make more tea.

Julio, recovering his composure, joined Paul and Melissa, who were standing together on the lawn, not looking out to sea but at each other. At Julio's approach, Paul reluctantly turned his head.

'Hello, Julio. Are you looking for Caitlin?'

'I have come to say goodbye,' Julio answered obliquely.

'That's too bad. As a matter of fact, Caitlin's gone down to the post office to send a telegram. Seems almost everyone is sending telegrams this morning.'

'Is the war, I suppose.'

'Yes. Then Victor's off for a board with one of the regiments, Evie's arranging her passage home –'

'And Paul is going back to New York,' Melissa said, with a sob.

Paul held her hand. 'How about you, Julio? Are you going straight back to Argentina?'

'Yes, I am leaving today for Liverpool, I wish to get a sailing as soon as possible.'

'You might have waited and travelled with Evie,' said Melissa. 'She'd be glad of your help.'

'I think not.' Julio bowed and held out his hand. 'May I please say goodbye?'

Melissa, to his astonishment, held him close and kissed him

on the cheek. 'They don't like me to speak of it, but I know you're my brother and I do wish you well, Julio. Don't break your heart over Caitlin, you're sure to find someone easier to live with back home.'

'Melissa!' cried Paul, glancing apologetically at Julio, but she only shrugged her elegant shoulders.

'Anyone can see they've parted, Paul, and I'm only trying to make Julio feel better. Not that any of us can really feel better,' she added despondently.

'It's been good knowing you, Julio,' Paul assured him, shaking his hand. 'We've been through a bad time together, something we'll never forget.'

'That is true.'

'Which means that there'll always be something between us, those of us who are left. If you ever find yourself in the States, you'll come and see me, right?'

'Thank you, I shall.' Julio again bowed and kissed Melissa's hand. 'Now I must find Doña Alicia.' He took a last look at the bay, and the view his mother must have known; at the sea – so calm today – where Jack had taken him sailing. '*Adiós*,' he murmured, and left them.

'Poor devil,' Paul said to Melissa. 'I guess you're right, Caitlin has turned him down.'

'I know she's your sister, Paul, but really it's just as well.'

'I don't like to think of any fellow being turned down, though.'

Melissa linked her fingers in his. 'Let's walk in the wood,' she murmured, 'people can see us here.'

Alice was in her father's study, writing letters. At one time it had been a place of unhappy memories for her – it was there she had found Richard and Charlotte together long ago – but now it reminded her of Jack, for it was where he had worked on the Belcarron accounts. One kind of painful memory had faded and another had taken its place, but the thought of Jack soothed as well as hurt and she liked to be where he had been.

When Julio entered at her murmured 'Come in', she looked up and smiled with a hint of her past beauty and his heart warmed towards her, Jack's mother, his own patron. Why were Caitlin's feelings so bitter? There was a gallantry about Alice in her grief that he could not fail to admire, and now she had a new anxiety. Victor was to go to war.

'Oh, Julio, my poor boy.' As she motioned him to a chair, it did not surprise him that she had read the signs of a new sorrow in himself. 'Is it Caitlin? I thought she was looking very unhappy.'

'Caitlin goes to Dublin,' he answered, looking at his feet, 'I go to Argentina.'

'I know it's no consolation, but perhaps it is for the best. She could never have settled away from Ireland.'

'But I offer to stay in Ireland, Doña Alicia.'

Alice looked horrified. 'Stay in Ireland? But what of your family, and your new life on the *estancia*?'

'I know, I know.' He put his hand wearily to his brow. 'Is not my wish to stay here, but I offer, and –'

'She still refused you? Oh, I'm so sorry, Julio, but things will seem different when you're back home, they will, you'll see. Now, shall we go to the drawing room and take a glass of sherry? You're staying for luncheon, of course?'

'Thank you, Doña Alicia, but I must go, I must say goodbye. I leave tomorrow.'

'You will not have dinner this evening? A farewell?'

'If you will excuse me –'

'I understand.'

Alice walked with him to the door, where they looked down at the drive together.

'Will you say goodbye for me to Tina and George?' he asked. 'I regret I miss them.'

'Of course, Julio.'

He hesitated. 'You know I shall never forget you, Doña Alicia, and what you do for me. You know I shall never forget Jack.'

'Mr Pearce and I will be in touch with the lawyers in Buenos Aires as soon as possible. Everything will be made formal and legal, you need have no worries about your future.' Alice, stretching up, kissed Julio on the cheek. 'You'll come back one day, to see Bridie and me? This was your mother's home, you know, and also –' her voice shook – 'Jack's.'

'I think of that, Doña Alicia. Maybe, one day.'

'Belcarron will be waiting. Goodbye, my dear, and good luck.'

'Goodbye, Doña Alicia.' He kissed her hand and went down the steps.

At the end of the drive, he turned and looked back at the small, dark figure in front of the white house. He raised his hand, Alice waved her handkerchief, then he strode away down the road to the village. If he had feared to see Caitlin returning from the post office, he did not and he told himself he was glad, he could not have borne seeing her again. Yet knowing he would not, he felt no better; she was as dead to him as Jack, and with Jack was in his heart for ever.

Chapter Twenty-Two

'Has Julio gone?' asked Melissa, entering the drawing room.

'Yes, I've just said goodbye to him, poor boy,' Alice replied.

'Why do you call him that? I think he's been very lucky that Caitlin turned him down, she'd have made a dreadfully prickly wife.' Melissa moved listlessly to the drinks tray. 'Mama, may I have a sherry?'

'If you wish. But where's Paul?'

'Packing.' Melissa, after glancing at her mother, who shook her head, poured herself a glass of sweet sherry. 'Everyone is packing.'

Alice stared into space.

'I know I shouldn't talk of missing Paul, with Jack gone and all the sorrow, but I am so very miserable, Mama.' Melissa set down her glass and broke into sobs.

'Why, my dear, I never knew you cared so much for Paul,' Alice murmured, leaving her chair and putting her arms around Melissa.

'It's not just Paul, it's Jack, it's everything.' Melissa looked into her mother's face with beautiful, tear-drenched eyes. 'But I do love Paul, Mama, I know I shouldn't tell you, shouldn't bother you –'

'Ssh, you're not bothering me. Jack has gone, but you're here and I must look after you too. Do you think I don't care about your happiness?'

'I shouldn't have said anything, except that Paul is going away and I don't know how I shall bear it!'

'You've had so many admirers, my dear, I must confess, I never thought . . .'

'Thought what? That I could care for someone like Paul?' Melissa sat up and dabbed at her eyes with her handkerchief. 'Oh, I know people have always thought I was looking for a title or money, but it's not true, I only wanted the right person and that's Paul. The wonderful thing is, Mama, we both feel the same way.'

'Do you, dear?' Alice smoothed back Melissa's yellow hair. 'Why don't you ask Paul to speak to me, then?'

'Speak to you, Mama? The way things are? How could he? There's no way we could marry.'

'Not now, of course, you're in mourning. But there is nothing to stop you thinking of the future.'

'You haven't forgotten that Paul is a Catholic, Mama?'

'No, I haven't forgotten. It might have been important once. Now all I care about is your happiness.'

'I dare say Paul's father will object.'

'Hester will try to make him understand.'

Melissa looked closely into her mother's face. 'He's not my real worry, anyway, he doesn't affect me.'

'You're looking at me as though I affect you.' Alice gave a faint smile.

'You do, Mama. How could I ever leave you?'

Alice rose and returned to her own chair. 'Finish your sherry, Melissa. Time is getting on.'

'I haven't upset you, have I, Mama?'

'Do finish your sherry.'

'Mama, don't look so lost! You know I'd never, ever leave you. Not now.'

'Melissa, the last thing I want is to come between you and your happiness. Do you think I could allow you to sacrifice yourself for me? If it's what you want, you must go to New York and go with my blessing.'

'How could I, Mama, how could I?' cried Melissa, then was silent as George, followed by Evie and Caitlin, came into the drawing room.

'All arrangements made?' asked Alice, when she had invited George to pour sherry.

'Yes, we return to London tomorrow,' Tina replied.

'There, you see, Mama, there'll be just you and me left at Belcarron,' Melissa said quickly. 'Caitlin is to go to Dublin and Evie has booked her passage to Argentina.'

'As a matter of fact, I haven't.' Evie's tone was strangely defiant. As she drank her sherry, her colour rose and her pale-blue eyes glittered. 'I mean, why should I go back to Argentina?'

'Surely, my dear, your family will want you home?' asked Alice. 'No one knows how difficult things will become, you may not be able to travel later on.'

'Yes, but if I went home, I should never see Victor! When he got leave, I'd be thousands of miles away, it would be absurd.' Evie leaned forwards, her thin face more animated than anyonc had ever seen it. 'I've been thinking, why shouldn't Rickie and I stay on here, at Belcarron? We'd be safe here and I shouldn't have to make that long voyage back all alone. Oh, please, Mrs Wintour – I mean, Mama – do say you agree! If you were to put it to Victor, I know he'd accept it.'

'I'm thinking of your parents, Evie. You might be away for years.'

'No, no, everyone says the war will be over in no time and they know my place is with my husband. While Victor is here, I should be here too.'

'Well, then, I think it is a sensible idea. It's true that if you were here, Victor could perhaps see you from time to time, and Rickie, too. I'm sure that's very important.'

'Oh, you agree – that's wonderful!' Evie sat back, breathing quickly as though she had been running. 'You'll be sure to speak to Victor? He thinks I've already made arrangements.'

'I'm sure he won't need persuasion, Evie, to let you stay with me.' Alice looked across at her younger daughter. 'And when Melissa goes to New York, we shall be company for each other.'

Caitlin, who had been taking no interest in the conversation, jerked up in her chair and swung round to look at Melissa, whose green eyes were wide.

'You're going to New York?' Caitlin cried. 'When? I thought you were to stay at Belcarron?'

'I – nothing has been decided –'

'Yes, it has, Melissa, you're to stay with my cousin Hester,' Alice said firmly. 'I want you right away from this war and it would be convenient for you to travel with Paul.'

'With Paul?' Caitlin repeated, drawing her dark brows together, her eyes still fixed on Melissa. How like she is to her father, thought Alice, watching; how difficult she will always be!

'Yes, why not?' Melissa flashed. 'What's it to you, Caitlin?'

'Tell me why you're going,' Caitlin retorted. 'I don't believe it's just to get away from the war. Tell me the real reason.'

'All right, then, you may as well know. Paul and I are in love. We want to be married.'

'Oh, Melissa, I thought as much!' cried Tina with delight. 'Oh, that's the best news I can imagine!' As she ran to her sister and embraced her, no one looked at Caitlin, standing quite still beside her chair.

'Of course, we have no plans for marriage for ages,' Melissa was saying happily, 'or even a formal engagement. We're in mourning for dear Jack and would not even consider it. But now Mama has suggested it, I can go back with Paul, meet Cousin Hester and Paul's father, see New York –'

'For God's sake, stop babbling!' cried Caitlin. 'I don't believe a word you're saying. You've made a mistake, misunderstood Paul's intentions. I shall go and speak to him now!' Knocking over her chair in her haste, she flew from the room, leaving Melissa to turn angrily to her mother, while the others exchanged glances.

'How dare she speak to me like that?' stormed Melissa. 'She hates me, she always has, she doesn't think me good enough –'

'Hush,' Alice whispered uneasily. 'Of course Caitlin doesn't hate you, Melissa. This has just come as a surprise, that's all. After Paul has talked to her, she'll understand.'

'Paul!' Caitlin burst into his room without knocking, to find him drying his hands at the washstand. He turned round, smiling.

'Hello, Caitlin, I was just about to come down.'

'Is it true, Paul? Is it true what Melissa is saying? You are to be married?'

'Married?' He looked at her with almost comical astonishment. 'She said that? When?'

'It's not true, then? You don't know anything about it? I

thought as much, the silly ninny has made a mistake!'

'There's no mistake,' Paul said seriously. 'I do want to marry Melissa, I've asked her and she's accepted me.'

The colour rose and burned angrily in Caitlin's cheeks. She took a step backwards. 'I don't believe what you're saying, you're not making any sense. You couldn't possibly want to marry Melissa.'

He was not listening. 'I must go down and see Cousin Alice. Melissa must have spoken to her, after all, though we never thought there was a chance, not after poor Jack died, it's been tearing us to pieces – Caitlin, will you excuse me?'

'Wait!' She held his arm as he attempted to pass her. 'Look, maybe you are in love with Melissa – she's pretty enough – but you'd be crazy to marry her. I mean it, you'd regret it in a week.'

'No, that's not true.' Paul pulled himself free of Caitlin's grasp. 'I could never regret marrying Melissa, she's the only one I've ever wanted to spend my life with, the only one I've felt like this about. There may be difficulties –'

'You're right there. What about Papa? What's he going to say if you want to marry a Wintour?'

'He married one himself, didn't he?'

'You're comparing Melissa with Mother!' Caitlin's eyes flashed. 'That's absurd and you know it. Mother has a brain, she thinks things out for herself. She wanted to work for Ireland before she ever met Papa, she changed her religion because she thought it was right, she's always had her own ideas. But Melissa's only interested in clothes and materials and hats. How is she going to fit into your life?'

'She is interested in materials,' Paul said thoughtfully, 'as a matter of fact, she's thinking of going to art school to study textiles and design. She's actually very talented, Caitlin, and intelligent, even if you can't see it.'

'Oh, I see her intelligence, all right, just rather differently from you.' Caitlin gave Paul a last bitter look, before turning away. 'Goodbye, Paul, and good luck. You're going to have to find out for yourself what sort of mistake you've made. Thank God I shan't be around to see it.'

'Caitlin –' Paul tried to catch her as she left him, but she evaded his hand and ran to her own room, where she slammed the door behind her with a crash that echoed through the house.

Downstairs, people winced and looked at Alice. She rose.

'Melissa, would you find Paul? I think Bridie is ready for us.'

Melissa gladly sped away and Caitlin, locked in her room, heard her light footsteps on the stairs.

Before she left for Dublin that afternoon, Caitlin had a last word with Tina. 'You haven't forgotten what you used to say in New York, that you'd help if you were needed? Help Ireland's cause?'

'Haven't I already helped?' asked Tina levelly.

'In the Howth landing, yes, but I'm talking about the future. You said you'd train as a nurse; in fact, you've become a doctor. You know how useful that could be.'

'Surely this war has changed things, Caitlin? Ireland will not try to force independence at a time like this?'

'This war has changed nothing. It may even make things easier.'

Tina hesitated. 'I still want to see Ireland free, I feel as strongly about that as ever, but . . .'

'But what?'

'But I can't see a rising happening and I'm not sure I could be involved.'

'Tina, you promised! Remember Jack, and all that he did for the Irish Volunteers. You wouldn't go back on your promise after his sacrifice, would you?'

Tina, looking troubled, shook her head.

'All right, then, it's arranged. If the call should ever come, you'll answer it?'

'Very well, I shall do what I can. Short of violence.'

'You won't be expected to fight, Tina, just look after those who do. What about George? Will you speak to him for me?'

'George is planning to offer his services to the army.'

'Oh, of course.' Caitlin smiled faintly. 'He's an Englishman, isn't he?'

'Caitlin . . .' Tina touched her cousin's arm. 'I just want to say I'm so sorry about Julio and that you're upset about Paul and Melissa. It may seem a strange match, but I think they'll be very happy –'

'Thank you, Tina, I don't wish to discuss it.' Caitlin put out her hand. 'I have to go now, the taxi's due. Goodbye, I'll write to you in London. Keep in touch.'

'Where will you stay in Dublin? What will you do?'

'A room is being found for me, and I'm sure you can guess what I'm going to do. The Irish have an army too and I'm joining it.'

'The Irish Citizen Army?' Tina whispered.

'That's right. Wish me luck, Tina.'

Chapter Twenty-Three

Nothing could have better soothed Caitlin's heart than her activities in Dublin. While she went marching and drilling, wearing her green uniform and slouch hat, she was able to forget her parting from Julio and her chagrin over Paul's love for Melissa. She knew, of course, that men were always falling for girls such as her cousin, she had just never imagined that her intellectual brother would want to marry one. There was no doubt that he would be lost, not only to his family, but also to the cause she had always thought mattered as much to him as it did to her. Accepting that loss had been painful in the extreme, and as if to make up for Paul's defection, Caitlin threw herself into Irish politics with an abandon that would have delighted Daniel and worried Hester. But Hester was in New York and Caitlin was in Dublin, and in those heady days, Dublin was all that mattered.

She revelled in the company that now welcomed her: such people as Sean O'Casey, who was to become a playwright, Jim Larkin, the labour leader, James Connolly, the Socialist politician, and, of course, Countess Markievicz herself. Madame, of extravagant personality and striking looks, was a natural leader, adored for her selfless energy in working for Irish freedom and the Irish poor, and though there were those that disliked her, no one could deny her achievements. She might have been born a lady and married a count, but during the great lockout of 1913, when 25,000 men were put out of work, it was she who worked day and night to feed the families. 'Madame's not just an idealist,' Frances Tarry, a new friend of Caitlin's, told her. 'She's practical, too, she wants to put food in bellies, as well as setting Ireland free.'

Frances was thin and freckled, with fine ginger hair that was always escaping from its knot. Her parents were dead but had been staunch Republicans and Frances, alone in the family house, carried on the torch of their beliefs and let rooms to people who shared them, Caitlin among them. She was also a member of the Citizen Army and had done much to ease Caitlin's way in her first days in Dublin. They had watched together with cynical amusement as the British prime minister, Asquith, pushed a Home Rule bill through Parliament. It seemed too good to be true – and was, for as soon as it received the royal assent, it was suspended for twelve months or until the war was over. Bonfires were lit, bands played, the newspapers declared this was Ireland's Day of Triumph, but all it meant, as far as the nationalists could see, was postponement of trouble and a carrot to make Irishmen join up for England's war. Ireland was as much in thrall as it had ever been.

Yet life was pleasant enough for Caitlin at that time. She and Frances, in common with half Dublin, it seemed, liked to go to Madame's house in Leinster Road, where there were fine pictures but no carpets, set meals or servants, and where everyone talked half the night and Madame was everywhere, lighting the house with her presence. There was open talk of rebellion, though when it came down to facts, secrecy sprang up like a hedge of thorns, the sort of secrecy that had prevented Madame from taking part in the Howth landing, even though her own Fianna boys had been involved.

'She holds no grudges,' Frances told Caitlin, 'though really it makes my blood boil. It's because she's a woman, you know, she's excluded from so much and so are we.'

'It's true,' Caitlin agreed, 'only the Citizen Army accepts us on equal footing. Why shouldn't Sinn Fein recognise we're as good as men?'

'Madame admits she's only a member of the Irish Volunteers on sufferance. She sometimes says what the men would really like her to do is to cut sandwiches and make the tea!'

'When Madame can shoot as well as any of them!' cried Caitlin. 'Doesn't that kind of attitude drive you crazy?'

They were in Madame's kitchen and Frances laughed.

'Better do what we were born to do, Caitlin. The kettle's boiling, let's make the tea.'

Later, back at home, Frances said she had picked up a new rumour.

'Seems the Irish Volunteers may be splitting, some are planning to form a new group with Sinn Fein. They may even join forces with the Citizen Army.'

'With us?' cried Caitlin. 'Frances, how would you feel about that?'

Frances shrugged. 'Might have to happen. If the rising is to be successful.'

'The rising? That's as far away as ever, isn't it?'

Frances looked mysterious. 'Don't despair, my dear. It could be on the cards sooner than you think. With German help.'

'German help?' Caitlin was incredulous. 'I don't understand.'

'Nor do I, fully. But it's not so hard to believe, is it? With German help, we might really become separated from England. I thought you might have heard something of this yourself; the hint is that it's an American idea. Have you heard of John Devoy?'

'Of course, my father knows him well. He edits the *Irish American*.'

'And Roger Casement?'

'He helped organise the gunrunning. Is he in this too?'

Frances put her finger to her lips. 'Let's say no more, let's wait and watch. But those guns your poor cousin helped to bring over may well come into use, after all.'

'Caitlin seems happy in Dublin,' Tina told George, as they read their letters at breakfast in their London house. 'Seeing a great deal of Countess Markievicz.'

'I'm not so sure that that's such a good thing,' George observed. 'The Countess is a very fine person, but the sort to attract trouble. Caitlin needs calming down, not encouragment.'

'They are the sort to win wars, George.'

'And make mistakes. The last thing Ireland needs is some

crazy plan that will destroy all that's been achieved.'

'The point is, nothing has been achieved. The Home Rule Act is a piece of paper, nothing more. That will be made clear when the twelve months run out. Or before, if the war is over.'

'Not much chance of that. Have you seen the casualty lists?'

Tina rose and walked agitatedly to the window, where she stood looking out at the quiet Westminster street.

George followed and put his arm around her. 'Victor will be all right, darling, I feel it in my bones. He's a survivor.'

'I'm not just thinking of Victor, but if anything did happen to him, I don't think Mama could recover. Not after Jack.'

George kept his hand on her shoulder. 'On the credit side, we did win the Battle of the Marne, that could be a hopeful sign.'

'Maybe.' Tina blew her nose. 'I must go, George. No news for you, I suppose?'

'The consensus of opinion seems to be that I should stay put. Though I could work in a field hospital as well as the next fellow, I suppose. Don't worry, they may take me yet.'

'Don't worry?' She tried to laugh. 'Darling, my worries will begin when they do take you. Unless I join you.'

'Oh, no! That's out of the question, Tina, put that right out of your mind.'

She gathered up her letters from the breakfast table and moved to the door. 'If only there weren't Ireland to worry about as well,' she said, in a low voice.

'You wouldn't get involved in anything there?' he asked in alarm.

'You'd have been all in favour once.'

'Not now. We must get this war over before we can think of political change in Ireland.'

'But isn't this war about political change, George? People moving flags on maps?'

'True, and that's what Ireland wants. A national flag on the map of Ireland.'

Tina shook her head. 'Ulster will never let it happen. Oh, sometimes I feel so depressed ... Let's go back to Belcarron soon, sail Jack's *Sea Watch* and see Mama. She's on her own, you know, now that Melissa has gone to New York.'

'I thought she had Evie with her?'

'Oh, yes.' Tina looked shamefaced. 'I'd quite forgotten Evie.'

Tina did not go back to Belcarron, she could not be spared, and Terence Paget laid up Jack's dinghy for her before going away to the front. The autumn gales came and as the sea pounded the land and the yachts quailed, Belcarron, so exposed, took the brunt and sent Evie running to Alice. Would they be safe? Would Rickie survive in his nursery? Would the roof come falling about their ears?

Of course they would be safe, Alice soothed her, these gales came every year and Belcarron had always withstood them, there was no need to be afraid. What were a few flying tiles and shaking windows, anyway? Alice did not add that they had other things to worry about and neither of them spoke of Victor, but Evie, wrapped in shawls, walked the house like a wraith.

They lived for their letters, which came regularly from Victor and Tina, and it was a particular relief to Alice when she at last heard from Melissa in New York. Victor's notes were so short, they scarcely needed censoring, but Tina sent long missives, full of hospital chat she thought might be of interest, and promises to visit very soon. Hester wrote that she had been so happy to welcome Melissa, the dear child, but was still worrying about Alice and how she was managing after Jack's death. She longed to come over, but Daniel had not been well and would take no care of himself, so she must postpone her trip, perhaps until this terrible war was over; she could only hope Caitlin was safe in Dublin and prayed every night for the safe return of Victor from the front.

No mention was made of Daniel's views on Melissa, but when Melissa's first letter arrived, she said he had not been unfriendly and though he had not yet been told of the engagement, she and Paul were hoping for the best. In view of their mourning, they were, of course, living very quietly, but she could tell already that New York was wonderful, and Cousin Hester had been so sweet and helpful, finding her a college place to study textile design, assuring her she could make a splendid career in the future. 'I can't wait for you to come over, Mama,' Melissa finished.

Oh, please, do consider it. It's terrible to think of you all alone at Belcarron – well, with Evie, of course, but if the war ends soon, and everyone thinks it will be over by Christmas, she will go back to Argentina and then what will you do? Please say you will come. Perhaps next year, for my wedding?

'Terrible to think of you alone at Belcarron.' Alice read Melissa's letter again, then carefully folded it away. But to be alone was all she wanted. No one ever seemed to realise that. It was for Evie's own sake she had encouraged her to stay on, and of course, if she left, Alice would miss her, little Rickie too, but she herself would never leave Belcarron, for Melissa's wedding or anything else. This was her home and the home of her ghosts. They must never be left.

The gales abated and there came a day of warm autumn sunshine and strange calm. Alice and Evie walked together on the lawn, watching Rickie staggering ahead, the sunshine glinting on his fine blond hair. His features were still soft and unformed, neither Wintour nor Stonefield, yet he reminded Alice of her own sons, playing in the garden at the Estancia Sentos, walking and falling and smelling the flowers. She felt a stab of compunction that she had so far paid so little attention to her grandson, which was not because she didn't love him or wasn't proud, only that her heart was so frozen by sorrow, even Rickie had been unable to touch it.

Now Evie threw his coloured ball and he ran after it, arms outstretched, laughing with delight, then, while they watched, stumbled and fell and began to wail. Evie was quick, but Alice was quicker. Swiftly, she was with him, gathering him into her arms, pressing her cheek against his damp little face. 'Poor little boy, did you hurt yourself, then? No need to cry, you're safe now, safe with Grandmama.' Safe, safe ... As she felt his plump arms winding themselves around her neck, sudden tears blinded her own eyes, tears she had never been able to shed for Jack. The hardness of her grief began to melt and she knew she was coming back, slowly, painfully, to the world.

'What is it, Mama, what is it?' cried Evie. 'Are you ill? Tell me what's wrong!'

'Nothing, my dear,' Alice murmured, quietly relinquishing Rickie to his mother's arms. 'I'm sorry, I didn't mean to worry you. I've just begun to mourn Jack, that's all, I've been able to weep.'

Evie, holding her son, put out her hand and grasped Alice's. 'I'm glad, Mama, I'm so glad, now you can get better.'

'One day.' Alice touched her grandson's soft hair. 'Evie, whatever happens, here is something worth living for – we must remember that, mustn't we?'

'Whatever happens, yes.' Evie shivered in the warmth of the late sun.

'I think it's going to be all right, you know,' Alice went on. 'Sometimes one has feelings about these things. Maybe I shouldn't say so, but I think Victor will come back to Belcarron.'

'No, don't say so, Mama, don't say so.'

'Very well, my dear.' As Evie set down Rickie, who had quite forgotten his woes, Alice threw his ball again and watched as he ran after it, but this time he did not fall down.

Part III

1915–1918

Chapter Twenty-Four

In spite of her cheerful letters home, Melissa was not finding life in New York easy. She missed her mother, she grieved for Jack, she did not see Paul as often as she wished, for he had his own apartment and when he came to his parents' home, well, of course, there was always someone else around. Hester was sweet, could not have been kinder, and Daniel, thank heavens, was often away, but it was all rather constraining and not what she had expected. New York itself was wonderful, exactly as she had imagined, but because they were in mourning the family did not go out much and if it had not been for her days at college, Melissa did not know how she would have got through. College was her saviour, the admiration of her fellow students balm to her disappointment, the work itself a window opening on to a whole new world.

'It's so exciting,' she told Paul, 'to know I can really do something! All my life, people have thought me pretty but rather silly – yes, it's true, and it's what Caitlin thinks, isn't it? Don't tell me she hasn't said so. But now I've found what I'm good at, working with materials, designing, making ... I just seem to know what's right, and I'm so grateful, Paul, you have no idea!'

'Darling, I'm so happy for you,' he answered fondly. 'Everyone needs to have belief in themselves and now you've found yours. I used to worry what you'd find to do, I knew you'd never want to help run the bookshops –'

'Heaven forbid!' she cried, laughing.

'And I didn't somehow see you as a homebody.'

'Not now Tina's a doctor and women are doing so many things.'

'But you still want marriage?' he asked quickly. 'You're not going to whizz away from me up to some dizzy heights in a career?'

'Oh, don't be absurd! I love you, don't I? Or why would I have come here?'

He hesitated. 'May I ask you something, then? You needn't answer now. Think it over. It's . . . quite a step.'

'Whatever can it be?' Melissa was intrigued. 'Don't look so serious, Paul, tell me what it is.'

'Well, I wondered if you would consider becoming a Catholic?'

She knew she should have been expecting it but, all the same, was taken aback. He saw her look and grasped her hand.

'You knew this was something we'd have to face one day. I mean, where do you think we'd be married?'

'Well, it's usual to be married in the bride's church, isn't it?'

'Not with a mixed marriage. It would be very difficult for me to marry outside the Catholic Church.'

'Why? You've always said you weren't religious.'

'Not devoutly religious, but I am a believer. I could never be anything other than a Catholic.' Again, Paul hesitated, still holding Melissa's hand. 'There's also the question of my father.'

'I thought it would come round to him.'

'As you know, he doesn't even realise that we love each other, he thinks you're just visiting, the way Tina did. If I were to tell him we wanted to marry, I'm not sure . . . I'm not sure how he'd take it.'

Melissa withdrew her hand. 'You're saying he doesn't like me?'

'It isn't that, it isn't that at all. He has nothing against you as a person.' Paul ran his hands through his hair. 'Oh, you know what the trouble is, Melissa, we've discussed it – you're a Wintour.'

'I just thought, after he'd got to know me, he'd accept me. I mean, your mother's a Wintour.'

'Yes, but she wanted to work for Ireland before she met him, he knew that. And she changed her religion.'

Melissa sat very still, so grave and lovely in her plain black dress, Paul's heart was in his mouth in case she should say no to him. When she finally met his eyes, however, she said, 'All right, if it's what you want, if it's something we have to do, I'll change my religion.'

He would have swept her into his arms, except that Hester came in at that moment and he contented himself with taking Melissa's hand again, as he told his mother the good news. A smile of undisguised relief lit Hester's features. She had aged, Paul noted, since his father's illness and Jack's death, and he was full of contrition that he had added to her worries by bringing home Melissa, but what could he do? He and Melissa were in love, it was natural that they should want to marry. A way must be found. Thank God, she had agreed to join the Church. That, at least, was something.

'Oh, my dear!' Hester folded Melissa in a warm embrace. 'You won't regret becoming a Catholic, I promise you, I never have. My faith has brought me so much love and consolation, it has helped me in so many ways. But that's only part of it. The real beauty of belonging is that you are part of truth, you see, you are at one with God.'

'What do I have to do?' Melissa asked, politely returning Hester's embrace, then releasing herself.

Hester glanced at Paul. 'I think we should see Father Kelly, don't you? He's young and enthusiastic, he'll make it interesting and easy –'

'I don't necessarily require things to be made easy,' Melissa said coldly, and Hester, quickly agreeing, said she had only meant that Father Kelly would make some of the drier parts understandable, which, heaven knew, was what most people required. 'When you've finished your instruction, you'll be formally received into the Church, with sponsors and so on. It would be nice to make it a special day, wouldn't it? Perhaps your twenty-first birthday?'

'I think that's a wonderful idea,' Paul put in. 'Don't you, Melissa?'

'Yes, of course. It will give me time, anyway, to inform Mama.'

'Oh, yes, Melissa, you must tell your mother as soon as possible,' Hester said seriously. 'For a long time, you know, my mother did not approve and it was so sad, but she accepted in the end, and I think Alice will see it straight away from your point of view.'

'I hope so,' Melissa replied.

Later, when Paul had left them, Hester told Melissa she was worried about Daniel. For some time now, he had had health problems, but she had kept from Paul how serious they were. Caitlin, in Dublin, knew nothing, was indeed something of a worry herself, but there was nothing Hester could do about Caitlin.

'What are these health problems?' Melissa asked uneasily.

'They're to do with the heart and circulation. The doctor says there is a risk of a seizure if he does not take care, but my husband has never taken care –' Hester tried to smile – 'he's unlikely to begin now.'

'You think he should not be told about Paul and me, then?'

'No, he must be told. You have a right to your marriage, of course you have, but I must try to keep the tensions down, if I can. I'll have to admit, your decision to become a Catholic will be a tremendous help. After all, I changed too!'

'I can't pretend I'm like you, Cousin Hester. I'm not really interested in Irish freedom, or religion either, if I'm honest.'

'I know, I know, but the main thing is you're doing all you can and I want you to know that I am particularly grateful.'

They kissed affectionately, but when Melissa was alone in the room once used by her sister, angry tears stung her eyes. It did not seem fair to her that she should have to change her religion, and she was sure Paul would not have asked it of her for himself. It was all being done for the sake of Cousin Daniel, and why should any member of the Wintour family do anything for him? But Daniel was Paul's father and she loved Paul. If this was the only way she could marry Paul, then she must submit.

She dashed away her tears and stared at the framed prints of Ireland lining the walls of her room. They reminded her of home, of Belcarron, with its upstairs candles and roof that leaked, no matter how much money was spent. So different from this pleasant American apartment, where electric light had replaced the gas mantles and everything was so charming and comfortable and just what Melissa normally enjoyed. Tonight she felt herself an alien, as Tina had once felt before her, sitting in that same room, thinking of home. To cheer herself up, she began to brush her long, fair hair, taking comfort in her beauty, and wondering vaguely how she would get on with Father Kelly.

She did not get on with Father Kelly. He was second-generation American Irish, with large, heavy features and staring blue eyes that reminded her of Daniel's. Though quite polite, he managed to make it plain he was only instructing her on sufferance, and that anyone of her background and looks could not possibly be sincere about changing her religion. And the truth of it was, he was right. How could she convince him, when she was not convinced herself?

Meanwhile, the war beyond America's horizon continued to spread to the different fronts around the world like some terrible disease. No one talked now of an early end to the conflict and it seemed only a matter of time before America would be drawn in. Originally, there had been resentment felt towards Britain over the blockade of German ports which was seen to affect American shipping, but when the *Lusitania* was torpedoed in May 1915 with the loss of 1,100 people, many of them Americans, opinion swung the other way. 'We shall have to go in now,' said Paul, which made Hester and Melissa turn pale, both thinking of him. But another thought came without warning into Melissa's mind. Now she would never get home. But why should she want to?

Her own problems were, she knew, tiny, antlike compared with the sufferings of those involved in the war, yet they were real enough. As the months dragged on and her twenty-first birthday drew nearer, her heart grew heavier and heavier. The worst of it was, she could not let anyone see.

It had been arranged that she would be received into the Roman Catholic Church at early-morning Mass in the Molloys' local church. After she had taken her first Holy Communion, there was to be a special breakfast, to which Father Kelly and other clergy had been invited, together with a few close friends. In spite of all the anxieties over Victor and the war, and the fact that they were only just out of mourning, Hester said she wanted to make this a very joyful occasion for Melissa and Paul, and Paul himself suggested it would be the best possible time to announce their engagement. There would be legal documents in connection with the *estancia* for Melissa to sign, there would be presents to open, and in the evening a dinner party to be preceded by cake and champagne. It would be one of the most wonderful days of her life. One she would remember always.

On the morning of her birthday, a perfect June day, Melissa got up very early. She sat for some time looking out at the clear sky and the street slowly coming to life beneath her window, before bathing and braiding her hair. From the corner of her eye, she could see the white dress she had designed and made herself hanging on the back of her closet door, but she did not take it down. Instead, she put on her half-mourning dark-grey blouse and skirt and went slowly to the living room.

'Happy birthday, happy birthday!' cried Hester, hurrying to kiss her. 'See, here are all your presents and your mail – did you ever see such a pile? Daniel, come and greet Melissa!'

Daniel, who had returned from a speaking tour only the day before, rose slowly from his chair. He had become heavy-jowled over the years, his colour was high and he did not look well, but he advanced on Melissa with something of a smile and shook her hand. 'This is a great day for you, a great, sacred day,' he told her, in his rich Irish brogue. 'May you gain spiritual comfort for many years to come.'

'It's her birthday too,' Hester reminded him, 'wish her a happy birthday,' but he returned to his seat, breathing hard, evidently feeling he had done quite enough.

'He's tired, it's all the travelling,' Hester excused him. 'Oh, but my dear, how pale you are, as white as a lily! I wish you could have had some tea, but of course it's not allowed before Communion. And were you not going to wear your lovely new dress today?'

'Where's Paul?' Melissa asked huskily. 'Why is he not here? He said he would be here early, I want to talk to him.'

'He will be here in a moment.' Hester was studying Melissa's pallor with fast-growing apprehension. 'What is it,

Melissa? Don't you feel well? There's no need to feel nervous, you know exactly what to do, and we'll soon all be back here for breakfast –'

'Cousin Hester, will you ask Paul to come and see me in my room?'

'In your room?'

'Yes, it's very important.' Whether it was proper or not, Melissa did not care; if she were to stay a moment longer in the drawing room with Daniel in his chair and the presents piled high, she felt she would suffocate. And she must speak to Paul alone.

The Irish maid had already made Melissa's bed and opened the windows to let the morning sun come streaming through, but Melissa drew the venetian blinds and, when Paul found her, was sitting in shadow.

'Melissa, my darling, happy birthday!' he cried, flinging himself on his knees beside her chair. 'Oh, I've waited so long for this day, let me kiss you!'

'No, don't, don't kiss me.' She turned her head away. 'Don't kiss me, Paul.'

'What's the matter? Are you worried about Communion? It's all right, darling, we'll all be there to support you.'

'I'm sorry.' She turned her beautiful eyes on his face. 'I don't know how to tell you, but I can't go through with it. I lay awake all night, thinking what I could say, but there's no way of not hurting you, is there? Of not hurting Cousin Hester, and everyone?'

Paul had risen to his feet. He had taken a small box from his pocket and was turning it in his fingers. His face was grey.

'How long have you known?' he said at last.

'I suppose, a long time, but I wouldn't let myself believe it.'

'What are we talking about here, Melissa? Not being a Catholic? Or something else?'

'I don't understand you. What are you saying?'

'I'm trying to find out what you're saying.'

Melissa gave a little nervous laugh. 'I thought I'd told you.'

'You told me you couldn't change your religion, but before that you wouldn't let me kiss you. I'm getting the feeling that means something more.' His voice was very quiet. 'Have you stopped loving me, Melissa?'

'No! No, of course I haven't!'

He drew her to her feet, pulled up the blind and let the light shine fully on the face she tried to avert. 'It wouldn't be the end of the world for me if you didn't become a Catholic,' he whispered. 'I love my Church, I love my parents, but I'd never give you up and you know that, don't you? So why wouldn't you let me kiss you?'

She closed her eyes against the light and said nothing.

'Do you want to see the ring I chose? I have it here, in this box. Do you want it, Melissa? Will you put it on?'

It seemed she could not look at him, could not speak, and as he looked down at her face, at the heavy, closed lids and the fringe of dark lashes lying against the pale skin, a shudder went through him. He closed the blind and let her go.

'It's over, isn't it? And how long have you known that?'

Her eyelids flew open, her green eyes blazed at him. 'I haven't known it, I don't know it now, why do you talk to me so? As though I'd been keeping something from you!'

'What happened, then? Tell me what happened.'

'I can't explain. It was just that those lessons with Father Kelly went on and on and I began to feel I couldn't do what everyone was wanting me to do. I didn't know why, because I knew that all that mattered was you.'

'And suddenly you found I didn't matter, after all?'

'No, no, that's not true, it's not true!' Melissa put her hands to her eyes, as Paul's face cracked into a stricken grin.

'Come on, my darling, face it. Better now than later.'

'All I've told you is that I can't become a Catholic –'

He took her hands from her eyes and made her look at him. 'I know what you've told me, and I congratulate you, you have courage. Plenty of girls wouldn't have been able to speak out, they'd have gone through with it and then there'd have been hell to pay. We've been spared that, haven't we?'

'The trouble is, I don't know how I feel, I really don't. You're talking as though I've given you up –'

'And haven't you?'

She burst into tears and for some moments he held her, soothing her, until she grew calmer. 'Oh, Paul, how am I to face Cousin Hester?' she whispered. 'And your father? He'll never forgive me.'

'I'm afraid we had better go and tell him now, there's no point in putting it off. Everything must be cancelled.'

'No, no, I can't, don't ask me! You said I had courage, but I can't do that!' Melissa leaped away from Paul, staring at him with her hands to her lips. 'I can't face your father, Paul.'

'I haven't asked you to, I'll tell him myself.'

'And I must pack, I must find somewhere to stay. You do see, don't you, that I can't stay on here? It would be unthinkable, wouldn't it?'

'Melissa, what are you talking about? You can't leave here, my mother would never allow it. She's responsible for you.'

'Not now, I'm twenty-one, remember?' Melissa ran to her closet and began pulling out clothes, throwing them on the bed. 'There are plenty of places I can stay while I think out what to do. Suzie Leifson, for one, would like me to go back to Westchester, and other people have invited me too. Don't worry, Paul, I'll be all right.' Suddenly, Melissa halted her feverish packing. 'I'm glad, you know, your parents will never forgive me. I can never forgive myself for what I've done to you.'

As Paul quietly left her, the white dress Melissa had made for her reception into the Catholic Church swung unnoticed from its hook.

An atmosphere of funereal calm settled over the apartment. Melissa had left by taxi, sobbing. Daniel had gone to church, supposedly to pray, actually, Paul believed, to offer up thanks for the departure of a Wintour who need never darken his door again. While Hester, white-faced and drawn, went about doing all the things that had to be done, Paul himself felt strangely light-headed, as though he had been anaesthetised yet still remained conscious, the result perhaps of having eaten nothing all day. Or, more likely, because the blow he had received had been so severe, he was still reeling.

'You must stay and have dinner here,' his mother urged. 'Please, Paul, you must take something.'

'A brandy, perhaps.' Paul poured himself another drink. 'How about you, Mother?'

'You know it will do no good to drink.' Hester regarded him with anxious eyes. 'Oh, I'm so sorry, so sorry . . . For Melissa too, I suppose; she must be going through a bad time.'

'Only you could think of Melissa, Mother.'

'The truth is, I'm not thinking of her, I'm trying to be fair and reasonable, but all I want is for her to understand what she has done to you. How could she? How *could* she? To wait until the last moment before Communion to tell you!'

'She knew she had to do it then, if she was going to do it at all.'

'But to give you up, Paul!' Hester's eyes flashed. 'I could understand her deciding against changing her religion, she's young and we may have pressed her too hard, but to –'

'Give up your son? Unthinkable!' As Paul drank more brandy, Hester rose and crossed to the bell.

'Would you like a sandwich? Cheese or ham or something?'

'No sandwich.' Paul set down his glass. 'I don't know why, but I can't feel anything. Do you suppose it will hit me tomorrow?'

'Oh, Paul!'

'I guess I always thought it was too good to be true, that she should choose me. She had the pick of Ireland, you know, whole counties at her feet, and all the fellows at the art college here are in love with her.'

Hester's lip curled. 'Really? I'm afraid I'm not in the least interested. The problem now is to get her home, she will have no reason to stay in New York.'

'It's not safe to cross the Atlantic these days, Mother. I think she'd best stay on and finish her course, go home at the end of the war.'

'And when will that be?' Hester gave a long, troubled sigh. 'Poor Alice has enough troubles without this. What a worry children are, from the time they are born onwards! I sometimes lie awake, thinking of Caitlin.'

'Caitlin can take care of herself, I shouldn't waste time worrying about her.'

'But if there's a rising, Paul?'

He stared. 'Who says there might be a rising? Ireland's just been given Home Rule.'

'Suspended Home Rule, no one is deceived by it.' Hester shook her head. 'There are things going on we know nothing about, Paul.'

'Does Papa?'

'He knows my views on force. All I can do is pray. Oh, if only Caitlin had married that young Julio! Then she would have been safe!'

'She'd never have settled in Argentina, he's better off without her.' Paul rose and put his hand on Hester's shoulder. 'Will you excuse me? I think I'll go out for a bit. Walking, or something.'

'You won't stay to dinner?'

'Not tonight.'

As he moved towards the door, she followed him. 'You won't . . . try to see Melissa?'

A hard flush rose to his cheekbones. 'You know me better than that, Mother.'

'I'm sorry.' Hester also flushed a little. 'But I shall have to call on Mrs Leifson. I must be able to tell Alice that Melissa is all right. And then we must plan what she is to do.'

'Just don't tell me,' said Paul, going out and closing the door.

Chapter Twenty-Five

Hester decided to wait until the following Saturday, when Melissa would not be at college, before visiting the Leifsons' home in Westchester. She did not want to see Melissa, but felt that she should, and of course it was necessary to speak to Suzie Leifson's mother and discover just what arrangements were being made. Suzie herself, a friendly girl with the cool blond looks of her Scandinavian forebears, had several times visited the Molloys' apartment and Melissa had spent a weekend at Acrepoint, the Leifsons' house, which meant that Hester at least knew something of the family. Knew that Henry Leifson owned textile factories in a dozen major cities, that his wife came from Boston, that Suzie had two younger sisters and an older brother already in the family firm. No doubt he will fall in love with Melissa, too, Hester thought bitterly, but that was not her concern. All she wanted, for Alice's sake and her own, was to check that Alice's daughter was safe and had practical plans for her future. If only she could have been given a passage home! But Hester did not want even Melissa to risk travelling the Atlantic at that time.

Mrs Leifson had been welcoming on the telephone and Hester arranged to call at three. Having booked a car and a driver, she spent some time deciding what to wear, for she felt she should look her best when she met Melissa, for Paul's sake – as though he would care at all! The day was hot and she finally settled on a cool grey silk two-piece, with dark-grey hat and matching gloves – subdued colours, but she was after all just out of mourning for Jack.

Westchester, the home of the prosperous, was looking

delightful that June afternoon, with the trees surrounding the estates in full leaf and the lawns smelling sweet and fresh, but Hester's spirits did not rise. She felt no better when she reached Acrepoint, a fine large house, built in modern style with thin-framed windows and tiled roof. Its drive and surrounding grounds were immaculate, its atmosphere monied and comfortable. The sort of place to suit Melissa, thought Hester, then was a little contrite, for she knew Melissa loved shabby Belcarron as much as anyone in the family. Whatever else I do I must be fair, Hester told herself, but the memory of Paul's blank, suffering eyes made her heart swell with indignation. It took all her self-control to present her usual serene image to Melissa's hostess.

Gwendoline Leifson was an attractive, self-assured woman; her dark hair was carefully dressed, her brown eyes bright and enquiring. She greeted Hester in her private sitting room, which, like the rest of the house, was furnished with the kind of simplicity that cost a great deal, and apologised for her husband's absence, he was away on business. 'He would so much have liked to meet you, Mrs Molloy,' she added.

'Really?'

'Of course. Because of Molloy's Books. He always admires enterprise.'

Hester, pleased, lowered her eyes. 'I'm so grateful to you for your help with my young cousin. The situation is very difficult.'

'It is, and I sympathise, but you really need have no worries. We are only too happy to have Miss Wintour here, she is very welcome to stay as long as she likes.'

'That's so kind, I appreciate it very much. Only, I feel my cousin, Melissa's mother, would prefer her accommodated – how shall I put it? – in a formal arrangement, if you understand me.'

'Of course, I should probably feel the same myself. But what do you have in mind?'

'I don't really know, that's the problem. With the war, it's not safe for Melissa to return home at present, and she feels it would be too difficult to stay with me.' Hester sighed. 'I'm afraid we're being something of a nuisance to you, Mrs Leifson.'

'Not at all. As I say, we are happy to have Melissa. Why not leave her with us until something else is found?'

'I should be most grateful,' Hester said sincerely.

'That's settled, then.' Mrs Leifson rose. 'Now, would you like me to send Melissa to you, to have a quiet word here? My daughters have arranged a tennis match today with some of the other girls from Oakdene. Perhaps you would care to join us later for tea?'

'That would be delightful. Thank you again for all your kindness.'

'I'm only too glad to be able to help. These things happen, don't they? Young people fall in and out of love – both Tim and Suzie have broken a few hearts from time to time, and had theirs broken, too. It's all a part of growing up.'

'As you say.'

'Well, I'll find Melissa.' Mrs Leifson smiled uncertainly. 'Will you excuse me, Mrs Molloy?'

It was pleasant in the elegant sitting room, with the windows open to the garden and the sound of young people's voices echoing from the distant tennis courts. Hester stood up and in some agitation, as she waited for Melissa, studied the family photographs about the room. Suzie with her father, a heavy-faced, middle-aged man with hair that might have been blond or grey. Two young girls, who looked liked Suzie. A dark-haired, bright-eyed young man, who looked like Mrs Leifson. Heartbreakers, Mrs Leifson had called her son and eldest daughter. How easily the word had slipped off her tongue. But their own hearts had been broken, too, and they had recovered. Would Paul?

'Cousin Hester?' Melissa had quietly entered and was standing inside the door. She was wearing a white, ankle-length tennis dress and had tied a coloured band around her hair.

'Melissa.' Hester took a deep breath. 'Perhaps we should sit down.'

Melissa took a chair some distance from Hester and pulled the band from her hair, bringing down pins she had to replace with shaking fingers. Her eyes were red and she did not look well, but Hester felt no sympathy. After what she had done, it was right Melissa should show signs of being upset.

'I know there's nothing I can say,' said Melissa, at last.
'No, there isn't.'
'So why have you come?'
'You didn't expect me to come? You know I'm responsible for you while you are in America. I'm responsible to your mother.'
'I am twenty-one now, you don't need to feel responsible for me.'
'Is that all you have to say?'
'No, no, it's not.' Melissa raised her eyes to Hester's. 'Oh, Cousin Hester, I just wish I could make you see I feel as wretched as Paul over this, I really do.'
'I don't think so. The pain of rejection is quite different from what you are feeling.'
'But what you don't understand – what no one seems to understand – is that I've lost Paul! I've lost him and there's nothing I can do to bring him back!'
Hester was silent, sitting with bowed head.
'I didn't want to stop loving him,' Melissa went on in a low voice. 'I was happy, I was truly happy. Then it all went. It died. I don't know why.'
They both sat, hearing but not listening to the cries of the tennis players. There was an argument, voices were raised, then peace again. Insects droned in at the open window. Someone was rattling china.
Hester tried to focus her eyes on Melissa. It's true, she thought, she has suffered. I should try to be kind to her. But the words she might have said would not come.
'If you did understand, Cousin Hester, it would help,' Melissa murmured. 'I know I shouldn't expect it, but it would make me feel better.'
'Well, it's true, love can die,' Hester said jerkily, 'and it's nobody's fault.'
'Nobody's fault,' Melissa agreed eagerly.
'But you see, I am Paul's mother, I think of him.'
'And so do I. Don't you know I'm thinking of him all the time?' Melissa took a step towards Hester. 'Does he hate me?' she whispered.
'It's not his way to hate.'
'No, but he won't ever want to see me again, will he?'

'Melissa, what do you expect? Paul doesn't hate you, I don't hate you, but there must be time to heal, for all of us.' Hester picked up her bag and gloves. 'Now, we had better decide what you are to do. I suppose it's quite out of the question for you to come back to me?'

Melissa shook her head. 'I couldn't do that, you know I couldn't.'

'Well, we must sort out something. It's not safe for you to return home by sea.'

'That's what I'd like to do. Not every ship is torpedoed, I'd take the risk.'

'For your mother, too? You know how she'd feel if anything happened to you.'

Melissa looked down. 'No – I couldn't risk that.'

'Mrs Leifson has said you're welcome to stay here until something else is settled, so perhaps we should leave things like that.' Hester managed to put her arm round Melissa's shoulders. 'Shall we go to tea?'

Tables had been set under trees near the tennis courts and maids were already serving sandwiches and lemonade to the players, when Suzie presented her brother Tim and her young sisters to Hester. Pamela and Josie bobbed politely and melted away with Melissa in tow, but the tall young man of the photograph put Hester into a chair, saw that she had tea and was in every way so charming and courteous, Hester's heart sank. Has he fallen for Melissa already? she wondered. Then she was distracted by Mrs Leifson's bringing up a strong-jawed fair-haired woman who took Hester's hand in a firm grip. 'Remember me, Mrs Molloy? Meg Wynne? I came to dinner once, when Tina was with you.'

'Of course you did, and then I'm afraid we rather lost touch.'

Hester's spirits rose as she welcomed Tina's one-time governess, someone who would remember Alice and Belcarron, who was a link with her family when, in spite of Mrs Leifson's kindness and Tim's charming manners, she was feeling very much alone. 'What a pleasant surprise to find you here, Miss Wynne!'

'Well, as you may recall, I teach at Oakdene, which is just

down the road from here. Suzie was one of my pupils and her sisters are with me now. I often bring girls over for tennis; Mrs Leifson is extremely hospitable.' Miss Wynne took a chair near Hester's and bit heartily into a cucumber sandwich. 'I hear you've had a little trouble with Melissa.'

'I had no idea you knew Melissa was here.'

'I didn't, I only met her this afternoon at the tennis, but I've heard about Paul. Oh, what a shame, Mrs Molloy – such a nice, steady young man! I remember him when he was a little boy at Belcarron, so sweet and old-fashioned.'

'Yes, it's very distressing, but there's nothing anyone can do.'

'Even when she was a very small girl, it was clear Melissa would be a beauty,' Miss Wynne remarked, 'and beauties can cause problems.'

'There's no harm in her, Miss Wynne, I know she never intended to hurt Paul.'

'Yet you can't forgive her? I'm sure I don't blame you. But what happens now? Is she to go home?'

'The way things are, it can't be risked.' Hester gave a deep, troubled sigh. 'You will have heard that my cousin lost Jack, just before the war?'

'Yes, Tina wrote to me. I was so very sorry. He was a very dear child.'

'So, with Victor away at the front, there are enough anxieties without Melissa crossing the Atlantic. She's doing an art course at the moment and should finish it.'

'And live where?'

Hester sipped the tea Tim had given her. 'That's just what I don't know, Miss Wynne. Mrs Leifson has kindly offered to let her stay on here, but I don't think that would be practical.'

'No, it's never a good idea to stay too long with friends.'

'And of course she doesn't want to come back to me.' Hester stared hopelessly at the young people chattering around her. They seem so carefree, yet who could tell? They probably all had troubles of their own.

'An apartment would not be suitable, of course, for a girl on her own,' Miss Wynne was murmuring, 'but I do know of another possibility, I don't know if you would consider it –'

'I should consider anything, Miss Wynne!'

'Well, there's a place in downtown New York that might just suit. It's not a boarding house, more a kind of club, for young women who are students or have to go out to business. There's a secretary and a warden and quite strict rules.' Miss Wynne smiled grimly. 'Maybe it wouldn't be Melissa's cup of tea.'

'I don't know. I think we should look into it. Do you have the address, Miss Wynne?'

'Yes, it's called the Regency. Several of my ex-pupils are residents, though on the whole it's more for girls of less wealthy backgrounds, those who have to make their own way in the world.'

'It wouldn't do Melissa any harm to know people not as fortunate as she. Miss Wynne, I'm very grateful to you. We must meet again soon and talk about the old days.'

'I shall look forward to it, Mrs Molloy.'

To Hester's surprise, Melissa seemed not to mind the idea of living in a club for young ladies. 'I suppose I have to live somewhere,' she sighed, 'and I'd have my own room in that sort of place and be independent.'

'I don't know about independence,' Hester replied. 'There are rules and regulations, you know.'

'I shouldn't mind. But will you go with me to see it, Cousin Hester?

Now she's unhappy, she's really missing Alice, thought Hester; she talks of independence, but she's always been the baby of the family, she can't get used to facing things alone.

Aloud, she said, 'Of course I'll come with you, Melissa. We're still family, in spite of all that's happened. I'll always come if you need me.'

'Cousin Hester, I don't deserve you,' Melissa said gravely.

'It doesn't do to talk of what any of us deserve,' Hester couldn't resist saying.

The Regency Club, if not luxurious, was comfortable enough, with a good menu and a decor Melissa said she could live with. The residents, all about Melissa's age, seemed polite, well-brought-up girls who satisfied Hester's private criteria.

'You think you'll be happy here?' she asked Melissa.

'Yes, I'm sure I shall. After all, it's only until the end of the war, anyway, then I'll be going home.'

'You haven't thought about staying on? Would there be the same opportunities for your career in Ireland?'

'Not in Ireland, but I could go to London. Tina has said she would love to have me, after the war.'

After the war. Even in America, people felt they were in a kind of limbo until the conflict ended. Hester lived in dread of America's joining in and prayed every night that Paul would not volunteer. A selfish prayer, she felt, but she made it, anyway.

Melissa's room at the Regency was large and high-ceilinged with windows facing an enclosed square, where there were a few trees and benches among dark city grass. Suzie Leifson helped her move in, hanging up clothes in the roomy closets, hammering in nails for the two pictures Melissa was allowed, one a view of Belcarron, the other a watercolour of the Cork countryside.

'Of course, I can put my photographs on the chest here,' said Melissa. 'I think I can make the place look mine, don't you?'

'Yes, it's not too bad.' Suzie looked around at the flowered wallpaper and chintz curtains. 'Maybe they'd let you change the drapes.'

'Oh, I don't think so. I'm sure they have a rule about it.'

'Seem to have a rule about most things. It's a bit like school, isn't it, Melissa? No smoking, no drinking?'

'I don't smoke or drink.'

'And no gentleman callers except in the public lounge?'

'I shan't be having gentleman callers, Suzie.'

'You will, you know. Tim for a start.'

Melissa paused in her arranging of photographs. 'He said that?'

'Sure he did. He's a friend, isn't he?'

'I really don't think I want him to come, Suzie. It's nothing to do with him personally, I just don't want to be seeing young men at the moment.'

'That's absurd. You'd die if you didn't go out some time, anyone would,' Suzie said earnestly.

'I just want to get on with my work.'

Suzie put back her fair hair and frowned. 'Melissa, any girl who looks like you won't be allowed just to get on with a career. I know you're very talented – makes us all so green – but the fellows will be wanting to see you and you won't be able to stop them.'

'I've seen quite enough of fellows,' Melissa said in a low voice, 'and I don't want any more trouble, it's as simple as that. If I'm talented, I should be allowed to make something of it.'

'Well, if you stayed here you probably could. I showed some of your stuff to Father and he was pretty interested. I guess he'd give you a job, if you wanted one.'

'A job?' Melissa's green eyes glowed. 'You really think he would?'

'If you were here, but you want to go home, don't you?'

The light faded from Melissa's eyes. 'Yes, I do. I love New York, I love my friends – everyone's been so kind – but I have to think of Mama. If I were in London, I could go home any time. Here there's the Atlantic between us.'

Suzie nodded sympathetically. 'Guess I'd feel the same. But to get back to Tim – you really don't want him to call?'

'I really don't.'

'I'll tell him that, then, shall I?'

'Please.'

The following day, Tim called.

'A Mr Leifson to see you, Miss Wintour!' Alison Hammond, one of the residents, came banging on her door. 'He's downstairs, in the lounge. Gee, what a stunner!' At the vexed expression on Melissa's face, she added cheerfully, 'If you don't want him, I'll have him!'

'I'll go down,' Melissa said, trying to smile.

Tim was reading a magazine in the corner of the lounge, where several other young men were also turning over pages, self-consciously waiting for their dates.

'Miss Wintour!' Tim bounded up and put a large bunch of dark-red roses into Melissa's hand. 'A few flowers for your room.'

'They're very beautiful. Thank you, Mr Leifson.'

'Oh, come, you did once say you'd call me Tim, and I should be allowed to call you Melissa, shouldn't I? You were our house guest, remember?'

'We still don't know each other very well,' Melissa replied uneasily. 'But thank you for these, it's very kind of you to call.'

He looked down at her, his brown eyes glinting. 'Is that it? I don't get to take you for a cup of coffee?'

'I have my unpacking to do, thank you all the same.'

'Oh, come on.' He drew up a chair. 'Suzie helped you with that yesterday, how much stuff do you have?'

'Didn't Suzie tell you? I'm not interested in going out with young men at the moment.'

'You don't mean that includes me?' Tim lay back in his chair and took out his cigarettes.

'I'm sorry, they don't allow smoking,' Melissa said apologetically, and he put his case away.

'Go in for rules here, don't they?'

'I suppose they have to.'

'Which simply means we go out. Come on, it's a lovely evening. Get your hat, Melissa, and walk with me.'

'Please, you haven't been listening, I don't want to get involved.'

'Who's talking about getting involved? I'm offering a little stroll along the sidewalk and tomorrow, maybe, dinner with Suzie and her beau and me.' Tim put his head on one side and grinned. 'Not love and marriage, Melissa.'

She blushed angrily. 'I wasn't talking about love and marriage.'

'Well, what are you talking about? You can't call it getting involved, to have dinner with a guy and his sister.'

'I'm really in mourning for my brother, Mr Leifson.'

'I'm very sorry about your brother, but I think you're more in mourning for Paul Molloy. What happened was tough, but it's over. Life goes on, Melissa. You're young, you're beautiful, you need to go out, you need friends. Suzie's one, I'm another. What do you say?'

She hesitated. 'I suppose it wouldn't do any harm to go out occasionally. But I do need time, you know – I feel that I do.'

'Sure you do, and we have all the time in the world.' Tim pulled her to her feet. 'Now you go put those flowers in water and I'll wait here. All right?'

'All right,' said Melissa.

Chapter Twenty-Six

Time, Melissa had said she needed, and time Julio had taken to settle back home in Argentina. Although his new life offered everything he wanted, learning the skills of running an *estancia* was proving harder than he had imagined. Victor's manager had not taken kindly to the arrival of Julio, who was neither a member of the Wintour family nor an employee. He removed himself from the Estancia Sentos, saying he wished Don Julio the joy of it, to which Julio replied that joy was just what he intended to achieve. He had called back Lucio from retirement and, though Lucio had already expressed doubts about the wisdom of Julio's working for the Wintours, he had been only too delighted to return to the *estancia* itself. After all, Don Victor was away at the war, Isabella was happily married, there was no reason why Lucio should not instruct his son and at the same time work again where he had been so happy.

'How I've missed this place!' he told Julio. 'This is where I was young, where Don Ricardo and I planned and worked. While Don Victor was here, I never thought to see it again, but here I am and I pray things will work out for us.'

'Forget Don Victor,' Julio replied. 'He's Victor to me now. Doña Alicia wished me to work on equal terms with the family and, though you may find that hard to accept, *Papá*, that's how it's going to be.'

'I do find it hard, but it's not my place to argue with Doña Alicia's wishes.'

'Because they are Jack's wishes, my brother's wishes. You understand, *Papá*?'

'I understand, Julio.'

Thoughts of Jack were always with Julio, but as the months went by, the memory of Caitlin, which he had believed would live in his heart for ever, began to fade. He hardly liked to admit it, it seemed so strange to be without the sweet ache that had possessed him for so long, but the time came when he could think of her without pain, when even to recall her lovely face was difficult. Lucio told him he should get out more, try to meet people, take trips to Buenos Aires, he would never find anyone to marry otherwise.

'*Papá*, I'm not looking for anyone to marry,' Julio told him, 'and I make trips to Buenos Aires anyway.'

'To the bank? What kind of excitement is that for a young man?'

'Some men find banks very exciting indeed.' Julio laughed.

By 1916, the war fever that had gripped Buenos Aires had somewhat died down as it became clear that the conflict was not going to end in one quick burst of glory, but some expatriates still went off to enlist and women still knitted socks for the trenches. In spite of the sinking of Argentine ships by German submarines, the government stayed officially neutral, its aim being to make as much profit as possible, and certainly there were profits to be made. All those soldiers needing meat – who better to provide it than Argentina?

This was a good time for *estancieros*, as Arthur Stonefield told Julio, his manner a little distant, for he could not for the life of him see why the Wintours had gone along with Jack's absurd will and given young Castillo more than was necessary. He might make a good manager, but he was legally Lucio Castillo's son, and to allow him to take what Jack would have taken was simply not right and just showed the way the world was going.

'Yes, times are prosperous,' Julio agreed, well aware of what was going through the banker's mind. 'I hope to take full advantage of prices and bring production levels as high as possible. I do not forget the trust that has been put in me, Mr Stonefield; I shall not let the family down.'

'I hope not,' Arthur said, regarding him with a pale-blue stare, 'especially as my son-in-law is still in the trenches. Did you hear he had been awarded the Military Cross?'

'Yes, Doña Alicia wrote to me. You must be very proud.'

'Of course, although I'd far rather he were back here in the Argentine with my daughter and grandson.' The banker stood up and extended a cold, dry hand. 'Thank you for coming in, Señor Castillo, these routine reports are helpful. Please give my regards to your father.'

Julio, smarting under Stonefield's thinly disguised condescension, walked out into the splendid streets of downtown Buenos Aires and tried to soothe his feelings by window-shopping for a while. Luxury goods did not interest him, however, and it always annoyed him, as it had annoyed Jack, to see only the rich in this part of the city, as though no other *porteños* existed. It was not, of course, a logical attitude, for the poor could not be expected to come where they could afford nothing, and now that he had money himself, wasn't he being just a shade hypocritical? He shrugged, knowing that however much money he made, he could never be at one with the rich, could never be *gente decente*. Jack had done all he could to ease his path, but it had been Jack's father who had put him half in one world, half in another, and content in neither. He took a taxi back to the house on the Avenida Lila, where he always stayed when in BA, deciding he would let Vittoria cheer him up with one of her excellent lunches. She still liked to spoil him, as though he were a little boy.

They were drinking *mate* tea on the back patio when the outside bell clanged. Vittoria, heavy now and inclined to be asthmatic, struggled to her feet, but Jorge raised his hand, he would answer it.

'Can't be for me,' Julio murmured. 'No one knows I am in BA except Señor Stonefield.'

'A letter, maybe,' said Vittoria, fanning herself. She gave him a sidelong glance. 'You should go out more, Julio, meet people –'

'Some nice girl?' He smiled wryly. 'Just at present, Vittoria, I have no wish to marry.'

Jorge reappeared. 'A lady has called. She asked for the señora or a member of the family, so I said you would see her, Julio. I hope I did right?'

'Did she say who she was?'

Jorge shook his head and grinned. 'She is young and attractive, so I showed her into the *sala*.'

'Now why is she alone?' Vittoria wondered. 'Correct young ladies do not visit alone.'

'Times are changing,' Julio answered, getting to his feet. 'I suppose I'd better see her.'

He found the mysterious visitor looking up at the portrait of Don Enriques, which hung over the chimneypiece. She was tall and slender, wearing a grey belted dress and a straw hat pressed over rich black hair. Though the face she turned at his entrance was too thin for beauty, it was true that she was attractive, even striking; her dark eyes, shining in a magnolia pale face, were like eyes Julio had seen before but could not place.

He bowed and introduced himself. 'I am Julio Castillo, manager of the Estancia Sentos. May I be of assistance, señorita?'

'Thank you, I wish to speak only to a member of the family.' Her voice was very pleasant, her Spanish very pure.

'I am afraid the family is in Ireland at present,' Julio told her.

'I see.' She stood with her hands folded, keeping her intense gaze on his face, although he had the feeling she had already noted everything in the room. 'Then I must not take up any more of your time. Thank you for seeing me.'

'Please, won't you sit down for a moment?' He placed a chair, feeling a strange reluctance to let her go. 'May I offer you some refreshment? Tea? Fruit juice?'

'Thank you, nothing, but I should like to rest for a little.'

As she gracefully seated herself, she smiled. 'You must be wondering who I am, Señor Castillo.'

'I presumed – a friend of the family?'

'No, we have never met. My name is Sofia Almedo, I come from Mendoza. This is my first visit to Buenos Aires for some years.'

'You are alone, Señorita Almedo?'

'Yes, alone in BA, alone in the world. Both my parents are now dead. I did have an uncle –' she paused, watching his face – 'but he died in Paraguay.'

'In Paraguay,' Julio repeated, feeling he should be understanding something and failing.

'Are you close to the family?' the young woman asked abruptly. 'Do you know their history?'

'I know their history.'

'Then you will understand if I tell you that my mother's maiden name was Sentos.'

Sentos. Julio's gaze moved to the portrait of Don Enriques. There were the eyes, the same dark eyes, painted there, bright, alive and watchful here. He felt a long, cold finger move down his spine.

'Your mother was a Sentos, then it was –'

'Her brother Antonio Sentos, my uncle, who killed Richard Wintour.'

Julio went white. He bent his head, aware that Sofia Almedo was watching, but unable to conceal his reaction. To come so close to one whose blood relation had killed his father was affecting him more than he would have thought possible. Thank God, he thought, passing his hand over his brow, Doña Alicia is not here to meet this girl.

'You seem very concerned,' she said softly. 'Did you know Don Ricardo? Surely not, you are too young.'

'Why did you come?' he asked hoarsely. 'What good did you think it would do, after all these years?'

'I came because so many years have passed.'

'But why? Why?'

'That I cannot tell you, Señor Castillo.'

'If any member of the family had been here, your visit could only have caused them pain. You know that, don't you?'

She flinched, drawing back in her chair. 'I never wish to cause them pain! I know – no one better – what my uncle did to them. But don't you think my family suffered too? What he did ruined our happiness. My grandmother never recovered from the disgrace, nor did my mother, but no one thought of us. The Wintours were the victims, it is true, but we did not escape.'

'I never thought of that before,' Julio murmured.

'My mother adored her brother and he was lost to the family just as much as Don Ricardo was lost to the Wintours. He fled to Paraguay, where he died in an accident with his horse. All this my mother told me; of course, I wasn't even born at the time.'

'Your uncle was like your grandfather, I believe. He also thought he had a right to Sentos land.'

'It is true he thought it wrong our forebears sold their share and went to Tucumán.' Sofia Almedo shrugged. 'It was said to be legal at the time, but it was a terrible thing to do, all the same.'

'To part with land?'

'Don't you agree?'

'I do. I'd never give up land.'

There was a silence, as Julio sat with his head resting on his hand and looked at the floor, while the young woman looked at him. Then she stood up and he stood up with her. She put out her hand.

'Thank you so much, Señor Castillo, for listening to me. It has made me feel better.'

He held her cool hand until she gently removed it. 'Would you like me to give you Doña Alicia's address in Ireland, so that you could write to her?' he asked.

'No, thank you. I should prefer to speak to her personally.'

'Señorita Almedo, I have no idea when any member of the family will return to BA. There is war in Europe, you see –'

'Of course, but I can wait.' She gave a last look at the portrait of Don Enriques and moved to the door. 'Now I must bid you good day, Señor Castillo.'

'May I escort you to your hotel?'

'That is kind, but there is no need. I shall take a taxi.'

'Please, allow me to accompany you. Unfortunately, there is no car or carriage here at the moment, but I shall myself find you a taxi – yes, I insist.'

Ignoring Vittoria's knowing smile at Jorge, Julio called a taxi and, with an excitement he had not felt for a long, long time, took his seat beside Señorita Almedo.

'How beautiful BA has become!' she remarked, as they were driven through the city.

'Some of it,' Julio replied. 'What's Mendoza like?'

'Warm and pleasant. Very green during summer, dry in winter. Lots of fruits and vines. As a matter of fact, my father was a wine grower.'

'I'm afraid I've never been up to the northwest.'

'I don't suppose many *porteños* have.'

'I don't think of myself as a *porteño*. I spend my life on the pampas.'

'Yet, you know –' she hesitated – 'you don't look at all like an Argentine.'

'Don't I?'

'No, you look quite English.'

'Lots of Argentines have blue eyes,' he countered lightly, trying to cover his embarrassment.

'It's not the blue eyes, it's something else, something I can't quite place – but, please forgive me, I should not be talking to you like this . . .'

'That's all right.' The taxi was slowing down; they must be nearing her hotel, Julio thought, and asked quickly, 'Please tell me, how long are you in BA, Señorita Almedo?'

'A few days, I think, but I have made no plans.'

The hotel was in a quiet street off one of the fashionable thoroughfares and when Julio had paid off the taxi, they stood at its entrance, looking uncertainly into each other's eyes.

'Thank you for all your help,' Sofia Almedo said at last.

He glanced up at the façade of the hotel. 'You say you are alone here? Alone in Buenos Aires?'

'I have my maid.'

'Would you permit – would you allow me the honour of calling on you? I know it would not be considered proper, but you are alone here, without family or friends, and that is not good. I should very much like to call on you and show you something of the city, before you leave for Mendoza.'

He thought he saw a flash of pleasure in her eyes before she lowered them.

'May I call?' he pressed.

'I . . . yes. Yes, please do.'

'What time would be convenient?'

'Any time. I shall be here.'

'I shall come tomorrow, then, tomorrow morning.'

'I shall look forward to it, Señor Castillo.'

He watched her slender figure disappear into the hotel and knew he was strongly attracted, was almost on the edge of falling in love, which would be crazy. Not only crazy, but wrong. She was the niece of the man who had killed Richard Wintour; to become involved with her could only lead to complications he could not face. What would Doña Alicia's reaction be, for instance, if she were to learn he was in love with a Sentos? What would Sofia Almedo herself say, if he were to tell her Don Ricardo was his father? He shuddered, fanning himself with his hat. His imagination was running away with him, he must put on the rein now, take a hold of himself. What after all had happened, so far? He had escorted Señorita Almedo back to her hotel and asked if he might call. If there was a great pit opening up before him, if he saw himself sliding, hurtling, to disaster, it was not too late to step back. He need not call on Sofia Almedo tomorrow, he need never see her again. But as he replaced his hat on his head and turned away from her hotel, he knew he would see her again, he knew he would spend a sleepless night waiting for morning, waiting to call.

They met the next day and the next and the next, and what they saw in the city, Julio could not afterwards remember. Parks and gardens, famous old buildings, shining new ones, shops, cafés – had they actually danced the tango? That would certainly not have been considered proper at one time, but since the tango had swept the west, no one any longer disapproved of the dance from BA's underworld. All the same, he could not believe he had actually asked Sofia to partner him in it, the very thought made him dizzy. Holding her close, running his hand down her back, feeling her slim body moving in a thin silk evening dress . . . Yet, he might have done. Everything had taken on the nature of a dream, and it was not until their fourth day together that he even tried to wake up and talk about his work.

'You know I must be returning soon to the *estancia*?' he murmured, as they sat together at an open-air café table. It was evening, the March air still warm and silky, the scent of Sofia's flowers heavy between them. 'I've been wondering – couldn't you come back with me?'

'To the *estancia*, Julio?'

'Why not?' He drank some wine, still thrilled at her use of his first name, though it seemed quite natural; they had crammed so much into their short acquaintance, they felt they had known each other for ever.

'How could I? It isn't possible.'

'Look, we get on a train, we get off a train, we ride horses – you ride, don't you?'

'Oh, be serious!' She was laughing at him, her eyes tender. 'I am saying it wouldn't be possible for me to go with you alone.'

'My father would be there.'

'But we must travel alone.'

'You'd have your maid. Come, who is to know?' Julio leaned forwards eagerly. 'Please, Sofia, come with me to see your family's old home. You know it's what you want.'

'Yes, it is, I want it more than anything, to see Sentos land, the Sentos house.' Sofia clasped Julio's hand. 'Julio, I will do it, I'll come with you!'

'That's wonderful, wonderful!' He couldn't believe his luck, when from the blue, the thought of Don Ricardo came to him and he sat back, his brow clouding.

'What is it?' she asked quickly. 'Julio, what's wrong?'

'Nothing. It's just that I've remembered something I must tell you.'

'About some woman?'

'Why do you say that?'

'Well, you're so handsome, Julio, I can't believe there have not been women in love with you.'

'I could say the same about you, Sofia. You're so attractive, there must have been men in your life before me.'

She smiled and took up her glass, her eyes dancing. 'Yes, there were some who were interested, but I was not, so that's the end of that story. What about you?'

'There was one girl,' he answered, after a pause, 'an American girl. She was my cousin, actually, but I met her in Ireland.'

Sofia's smile faded. 'An American girl? Was she pretty?'

'Very.'

'And she loved you very much, but you didn't love her?'

'We loved each other, but she didn't want to come back with me to Argentina.'

'She turned you down?' Sofia drew her brows together. 'She was mad, that girl.'

'No, she was sensible. Everything she said was right and I'm glad now that things worked out the way they did. Otherwise, I should not have met you.'

Sofia's smile returned. 'Oh, Julio,' she said softly.

'I still haven't told you what I want to tell you,' Julio said, looking away from her. 'I'm afraid it isn't going to be easy.'

'Tell me quickly, then. I don't want to be afraid.'

Afraid. He wondered why she had used that word. A premonition that what he had to tell her might destroy the magic of the spell they had cast over each other? He kept his eyes down.

'The fact is, Sofia, I am illegitimate. Lucio Castillo was manager of the Estancia Sentos and he and his wife adopted me, but my real parents were Doña Alicia's maid and –' his tongue seemed suddenly heavy, unwilling to move – 'and Don Ricardo.'

She had been right to be afraid. When he finally raised his eyes, he saw that he had dealt her a terrible blow. She was flinching before him, as though he had hit her with his hand.

'Don Ricardo! Oh, my God, how can you tell me that? How can we be here together, at this table? How can you even look at me?'

'Sofia, my darling –'

'You call me darling!' She was horrified, still wincing in her chair.

'I call you that because I love you. Does that mean anything to you?'

'Everything.' She leaped to her feet. 'But let's leave here, Julio, let's go where we can be alone.'

They walked through the lighted streets towards Sofia's hotel. There was a small garden nearby, scenting the air with jasmine, and they sat there together on a bench, arms entwined, not speaking. No one was close, though there were people in the distance, and Julio, with a sigh of desperation, turned Sofia's face to his and kissed her. He had thought about this first kiss so often, wondering how it would be, how she would respond; and now it had happened. It was wrong, of course, that he should kiss her when they were not even betrothed; as he had tried to explain to Caitlin, such behaviour could damage a girl's reputation for ever. But he was in too deep to think of Sofia's reputation now and could only hope she understood that the kiss was a symbol of what he offered, which was marriage.

At least, she did not seem offended, did not move from his

arms, though her body felt stiff and unrelaxed against his.

'I had to kiss you, Sofia, as a sign of my love,' he whispered. 'Won't you kiss me now?'

'No, I can't.'

'You don't love me?'

'How can we talk of love, after what you've told me?'

'Sofia, what happened in our families need have nothing to do with us.' He withdrew his arm from her shoulders. 'Unless you mind that I am illegitimate?'

'No, no, I don't care about that at all, I swear I don't! And I do love you, I've loved you from the first moment I saw you in the Avenida Lila. But if I love, I want to marry, and how could we be married, knowing that my uncle killed your father?'

'Lucio Castillo is my father. Richard Wintour gave me away.'

'But you must care that he died the way he did!'

'Yes, I do, especially for the effect it had on the family, but in a way I feel it's worse for you than me.'

'Yes.' She gave a sob. 'That's because I carry the guilt. It's the guilt that would always come between us. Don't you feel that, Julio?'

'No, because it isn't true. You carry no guilt, you are not responsible for what your uncle did, any more than I am responsible for what Richard Wintour did. We have to live our own lives and I want you to say you'll still come to the *estancia* with me, because that is your family's home and it's going to be yours.'

'Mine?'

'Ours,' he said firmly. 'Come, I'll take you back to the hotel and tomorrow we'll make arrangements to travel.'

She said no more, but when they reached the hotel, she put her hand softly against his face.

'Till tomorrow,' he whispered, and she nodded and left him.

Chapter Twenty-Seven

As Julio had known she would be, Sofia was an excellent horsewoman. Elegant and straight-backed, she rode beside him on the track from San Vincente as though born to the saddle of her criollo mount, thanking God, she told him, she did not have to travel with her maid by ox cart.

'One of these days, they will make good roads across the pampas,' Julio said with a smile, but Sofia shook her head.

'I believe the pampas has been changed enough. Let us enjoy it as it is.'

Julio knew that Sofia's mother, who had been dead only a year, had once taken her daughter on a train trip across the plain, but they had never touched on Sentos land. Perhaps Sofia was remembering that trip and her mother, for a shadow crossed her face and she fell silent. Julio, too, rode in silence. As the meeting came closer, he was beginning to realise just what it would mean to present Sofia to Lucio. In Buenos Aires, he had put the thought of it from his mind, but now he could not do that. Lucio had admired, even revered, Don Ricardo. How would he regard Sofia, the niece of the man who had killed him? How would Julio tell him that this was his betrothed? Sweating in the warmth of the March sun, Julio could not even imagine.

'Is that the house?' Sofia asked suddenly, and, as the Wintours had so often done before her at this point on the track, she shaded her eyes and stared at the distant poplars marking the site of her family's one-time home.

'That's it,' Julio answered. 'Of course, it's much changed from when it was first built.'

'Yes, yes, but at heart it will be the same, I know it, I feel it. Julio –' she turned wild eyes on him –'I have the strangest feeling that I'm coming home, that all my life this has been waiting for me. It is absurd, isn't it? But, you know, my mother always said my grandfather felt he did not belong in Tucumán, it was not in his blood, the way this land was in his blood. And all the time in Mendoza, I used to think, One day I shall return to the pampas. Do you think I was foolish to think that way?'

'No, I can understand it. I feel the same about land myself, but then I'm half Irish. Someone once told me all Irishmen are crazy about land.'

'Then we'll be crazy together!' Sofia cried and galloped ahead.

He caught her easily, and together they rode up to the house and dismounted. Sofia's eyes were everywhere, taking in the long, low building, the new roof the Wintours had built, the poplars and willows and climbing plants, the little garden at the side, made years ago by Doña Alicia.

'How beautiful!' Sofia whispered. 'It's just as I imagined it.' Her eyes were gleaming, her pale cheeks unusually flushed, as she swept off her hat and put her hand to her dark hair. She seemed oblivious of Julio, but he took her arm, as the peons came up for the horses.

'Come and meet my father,' he said huskily. 'His house, you know, is behind this one. It's where I used to live when I was a boy.'

When Lucio appeared at the door to his cottage, his handsome face lit up at the sight of Julio. 'You're back!' he cried. 'Oh, what a relief! So many days away in BA, I thought surely some harm had come to you!' His eyes turned wonderingly to Sofia. 'But, Julio, you have brought a visitor – a lady! Please introduce me.'

'*Papá*, may I present Señorita Sofia Almedo, from Mendoza? Sofia, this is my father, Señor Lucio Castillo.'

Sofia gave Lucio her hand with a charming smile. 'Señor Castillo, I am so happy to meet you. Your son and I met in BA. He asked me if I should like to visit the *estancia*, but I hope I do not inconvenience you?'

'Inconvenience – no!' Lucio, immediately yielding to her

manner, bowed over Sofia's hand. 'But you must excuse us, señorita, we are not prepared for your visit and the house is small, it may not be suitable –'

'*Papá*, I thought Señorita Almeda would be more comfortable in the main house,' Julio put in quickly. 'There's more room and I'm sure Maria could soon prepare something.'

'Of course. Señorita, permit me to escort you,' said Lucio, and Sofia, smiling over her shoulder at Julio, followed him into the Sentos house.

'So, Julio, you are late back from BA,' Lucio murmured, as he and Julio returned to the cottage, 'and of course now I see why. The señorita is charming. Where in BA did you meet her?'

'*Papá*, may we talk?'

At the expression on Julio's face, Lucio's eyes were suddenly watchful. 'Is there something wrong?'

They moved into Lucio's small study, where Lucio lit a cigar and Julio drank some fruit juice thirstily.

'First, *Papá*, I wish to tell you that I have asked the señorita to marry me and she has accepted.'

Lucio stared at the end of his cigar. 'And how long have you known each other? Four days, or is it five?'

'I know it sounds crazy, but we both knew, as soon as we met, that there could be no one else.'

'Love at first sight is not necessarily the best basis for marriage, Julio.'

'I know, but our love is not a matter for discussion. It is settled that we are to be married. The señorita has no parents, no one she need ask for consent –'

'And you are not asking for mine,' Lucio observed dryly.

'No – I mean, yes, I do want your consent, *Papá*, but I am of age and I know my own mind.' Julio wiped his brow with a shaking hand. 'The trouble is – the thing that may upset you is – oh, God, I don't know how to put this.'

Lucio waited, patiently smoking.

'*Papá*, the fact is, Señorita Almedo is a Sentos. It was her mother's brother who killed Don Ricardo.'

Lucio's face went yellowish white, his sombre eyes burned.

'And she is here? You brought her here?'

'*Papá*, she is only nineteen, she wasn't even born when

Antonio Sentos did what he did. She cannot be held responsible.'

'Family is family, Julio, and she has Sentos blood.'

'I have Wintour blood,' Julio said steadily, 'yet have I ever been considered a Wintour? I am your son, *Papá*, I am Castillo.'

Lucio looked down at his cigar and put it out. 'Oh, Julio, what can I say to you?' He rose and moved to the window. 'You see there? You see the house? Your señorita is there now, where her uncle came and put his knife into Don Ricardo. For the sake of Sentos land. What does *she* think of Sentos land?'

Julio bit his lip. 'Her father was a wine grower in Mendoza.'

'So?'

'So, I don't know what she thinks of Sentos land!'

'You bend your head, you don't look at me, why are you lying to me, Julio?' As Julio made no reply, Lucio came close. 'Tell me, when did you meet the señorita in BA?'

'She . . . she came to the house.'

'The house on the Avenida Lila? Why? Why should she do that?'

'She hasn't told me. I think she wanted to make her peace with the family.'

'Make her peace? Apologise?' Lucio laughed contemptuously. 'And how would she, a Sentos, apologise to the Wintours?'

'You don't understand what it has been like for her family, *Papá*. They have borne the burden of guilt, they have suffered.'

'As Doña Alicia has suffered?' Lucio sat down as though he were suddenly too weary to stand, and put his hand to his brow. 'Julio, I can never refuse you. All I have ever wanted is your happiness, you know that, don't you?'

'I know it, *Papá*.'

'Things seemed to be going so well. Your sisters married and settled; you here, I with you – I thought for once I could relax –'

'I'm sorry,' Julio cried. 'I wouldn't for the world have brought this pain to you!'

'Yet you have.'

'I can't help it, I can't help it – I'm in love.'

'And people in love can never think straight.' Lucio sighed and put out his hand, which Julio grasped as though it were a lifeline. 'Whatever I say, I can't prevent you doing what you want to do. You are of age, you have your own income. If I leave you –'

'For God's sake don't leave me, *Papá*!'

'Then I lose you.' Lucio shrugged. 'You hold all the cards, and I admit it. Marry your señorita, but please tell Doña Alicia yourself. I cannot.'

'I'll tell her as soon as possible.'

There was a light tap at the door. 'May I come in?' Sofia called.

Lucio, dropping Julio's hand, drew back, then slowly rose to his feet as Sofia, changed into the grey silk dress she had brought with her, came into the room. Her colour had faded, she looked pale and apprehensive, her eyes very large and luminous; her beautiful black hair, brushed and oiled, was twisted into a knot. As soon as she saw the expression on Lucio's face, she turned to Julio. 'You have told him?'

'I had to tell him.'

'Of course, he is your father.' Sofia looked at Lucio. 'Señor Castillo, please forgive me, I know I should not have come here. I am deeply sorry I have caused you distress.'

He inclined his head. 'There is distress for all of us in this, señorita, but it is true what Julio says, you're not to blame for what happened.'

'My presence is to blame for hurting you. I shall leave tomorrow.'

'There's no need. I have accepted your betrothal to my son.' With a supreme effort, Lucio took Sofia's hand. 'I hope you will both find happiness together.'

Julio could not speak. He went to Sofia and put his arms around her shoulders, as tears welled into her eyes and she tried to smile.

'Please, will you excuse me?' Lucio murmured. 'I shall be pleased to see you at dinner.'

Sofia turned her tragic gaze on Julio. 'My dear, you should have told me – I never realised how much your father cares.'

'He thought the sun shone for Don Ricardo. Doña Alicia too.'

'He is devastated, Julio, devastated! Oh, is this how it is always going to be? I said, didn't I, we should not marry? I said it would be impossible and it is!'

'No, it's not!' Julio shook her lightly by the arms. 'What I said stands. We're not to blame for other people's actions, we have a right to our own happiness. Trust me, Sofia. Everything will be all right, you'll see.'

'If only I didn't have to see your father again!' she moaned. 'He looks so very, very unhappy, and I am the cause.'

'Antonio Sentos was the cause, Sofia, and he is dead,' said Julio.

In the days that followed, Lucio kept out of the way of his son's guest, seeing her only at dinner, when he was always his courteous self, and afterwards quickly retiring.

'He'll come round,' Julio kept saying, 'give him time, he only needs time.'

'I think he's come round as far as he can,' Sofia replied, 'and I'm grateful for that.'

Anna, her maid, a grave-faced, incurious woman who had previously been maid to Sofia's mother, arrived with Sofia's luggage, making her feel, she told Julio, more at ease.

'More at ease?' he cried, stung. 'When you have me?'

'Oh, I know, and you're all that matters, but when a lady has her maid, she feels right, somehow, as though she can face the world.'

'With me you can face the world, maid or no maid,' Julio replied.

He felt ill at ease himself until he had written to Doña Alicia, and spent much time writing and rewriting drafts until he was satisfied he had done all he could to make her understand. Sometimes, as he took his thoughts back to Belcarron, Caitlin came into his mind and he hoped she was not too obsessed by her work for Ireland to find someone else to love. How different his life would have been if she had accepted him! He thanked God she had not, for in spite of his guilt over causing pain to Lucio and Doña Alicia, his heart and mind were wholly Sofia's. He could not imagine a future without her.

He took pleasure in showing her around, in introducing her to their few gauchos and other workers, in riding the land, not only where the herds grazed, but also where the crops were grown and the tenant farmers had made their homes. She revelled in it all, but principally in those aspects her forebears would have known, the old bakery and the dairies, the wood they had planted, the *pulperío* in San Vicente, where they would have bought their candles, flour and saddles. She even at one point suggested riding out to *rodeo* with the gauchos, saying she wanted to see the way the cattle had been rounded up in the old days, but Julio firmly declined to take her. Women had their place, gauchos would tell her, but it was not at the *rodeo*, or twirling the *lazo* and the *bolas*.

'So what would I have been doing in the old days?' she demanded. 'Having babies, I suppose? Making clothes and salting beef? You know, I should have been happy in that life.'

'Life's a little easier now, though.'

'There'll still be babies. We must have lots of sons, Julio.'

'I want a daughter, just like you.'

They rode out together one warm morning, when Julio was once again playing truant from his work, but unable to resist the lure of a few hours alone with Sofia. This was what they both liked best, to be alone together under the high sky, on the open sea of the pampas, feeling close to nature, close to each other. When they stopped to rest, Sofia spread a rug under the *ombú* trees, as Alice has always done, to avoid sharing the dry grass with snakes and lay back with her hands behind her head. 'I do belong here,' she murmured, sighing with satisfaction. 'It's true what I say, this land is in my blood.'

Julio stirred uneasily beside her, thinking of Lucio's words. 'There's something you still haven't told me,' he murmured, with an attempt at lightness. 'Why did you call that day on the house at the Avenida Lila?'

'Now why bring that up?' She plucked a blade of grass and tickled his face. 'It was just a foolish impulse, it didn't mean anything.'

'It didn't seem like an impulse to me.'

'You're suggesting I'm keeping secrets from you?'

'No, of course not, I'm just curious.'

'Well, it's not of any importance, I can assure you.' She threw away her blade of grass and sat up. 'But is there not something else you'd like to ask me, Julio?'

'Something else? I don't think so. What should there be?'

'If you can't think of it, it's not my place to remind you.' She laughed. 'Ah, I'm so happy here, but one day you must come to Mendoza, to see where I used to live. I still have my mother's house there, you know.'

'I should like very much to see your home.'

'Then let's go north for our wedding tour. I suggest we marry very quietly in BA, then I take you to Mendoza and Tucumán. How does that sound to you?'

'It sounds wonderful. But then we return here, Sofia, we settle here?'

'Of course.' She looked at him thoughtfully. 'It's a shame, though, you could not have had a share of the land. Don Ricardo's son wished you to have it, didn't he?'

'I have explained the position. I have the income.'

'But it is unfair, Julio. You should have been alllowed to share on equal terms.'

'We can't change it, so let's not talk about it.' Julio drew her gently towards him. 'Sofia, we're wasting time.'

He began to kiss her, lightly at first, then with passion, as the sun beat through the glossy leaves of the trees and the horses moved patiently where they had been tied. Suddenly Sofia broke free and began to undo the jacket of her riding habit.

'No, Sofia, don't,' Julio murmured.

'Why not? It's too warm, that's all. How can I kiss you properly, dressed like this?'

He knew he should stop her, she was inexperienced, she didn't know what she was doing, but it was too much for him and, like a man in a dream, he slowly took off his clothes as Sofia rapidly slipped from hers. They made love on the rug which Sofia had laid against snakes and for a while entered such ecstasy they seemed to lose themselves and the world. Yet, the world was still there, waiting, and when she came back to it, though she and Julio still clung together, Sofia suddenly burst into tears.

Julio instantly released her, staring with horror at her tears. 'Sofia, I'm sorry! I'm so sorry! I didn't mean that to happen, I swear I didn't!'

'I know, I know.'

'Then, please, don't cry, I can't bear to see you cry. Let's get dressed, let me help you –'

'No, I can dress myself. Don't! I said I could dress myself.'

She did accept his help to mount her horse and was calmer then, her tears drying on her cheeks, but Julio suddently buried his head against the horse's side. 'All these years, I've blamed Richard Wintour for thinking of his own pleasure, for doing what I've now done myself. Oh, God, Sofia, I wish I were dead!'

'I don't.' She bent down and kissed his dark head. 'It's all right, my darling. We love each other, we're going to be married, we shouldn't think we've done wrong.'

'Suppose you have a child?'

'We'll be married soon. No one will know we didn't wait.'

They were married on Easter Saturday 1916 at the Church of Santa Teresa in Buenos Aires, with Vittoria and Jorge as witnesses, and Lucio and the maids as guests. Afterwards, there was a small reception at the old Sentos town house; then they left for their honeymoon in Mendoza.

Chapter Twenty-Eight

On that same Easter Saturday when Julio and Sofia were married, Caitlin met Tina at Dublin railway station. 'Oh, Tina, you came!' she cried, snatching up Tina's case.

'I said I would.' Tina, who was wearing a raincoat over her tweed two-piece and carrying her medical bag, did not smile as she returned her cousin's embrace, a fact that Caitlin did not fail to notice.

'What's wrong?' she asked urgently.

'We can't talk here.' Tina unbuttoned her raincoat and threw it over her arm. 'It's so warm, isn't it? Much warmer than I expected.'

'You got my message, you know what's going to happen. Just tell me what's the matter.'

'Let's find a cab,' said Tina.

In the cab, Caitlin kept her strong gaze on Tina's face, while Tina put on a show of enjoying seeing Dublin again, in a cheerful mood at the end of Holy Week. Neither spoke until the taxi stopped outside 28 Clock Street, the house Caitlin had rented for Tina.

Caitlin said, 'This is it. I hope it'll be all right.'

'Looks fine,' Tina replied, paying off the driver and turning to run her gaze over the small, stone-built terrace house. 'Have you the keys?'

'Sure.' Caitlin let them in and set down Tina's case in the narrow entrance passage. 'Now, explain.'

'Explain? You need me to explain? You know I'm not happy about this and neither is George. He tried to persuade me not to come, but I promised, so I'm here, but I want to make it plain, I shall assist on the medical side and that is all.'

Caitlin flushed darkly. 'After all the years of waiting, I tell you the rising is tomorrow and you say you're not happy? I don't understand – isn't this what we've been waiting for?'

'Yes, but it's the wrong time, Caitlin. To rise against England at a time like this is only going to cause more suffering, more deaths, and will get nowhere. Look, I don't want to upset you, I can see you're over the moon –'

'Yes, and where are you? Over in the English camp, it seems.' Caitlin strode down to the little parlour at the end of the passage and flung herself into a chair. 'I never thought you'd turn traitor on us, Tina.'

'I beg your pardon,' Tina said icily, 'what did you call me?'

Caitlin shook her head moodily. 'Oh, you know I don't mean you're really a traitor, it's just that you're so half-hearted and half-hearted support is no support at all. This is the rebirth of Ireland, Tina, the start of a new republic. You either believe and stay, or you go. There's no halfway house.'

'I believe in an Irish Republic, Caitlin, nothing would make me happier than to see Ireland free. But why start a rising now? Why not wait until the war is over?'

'I should have thought that was obvious. With England otherwise engaged, we'll have a better chance of success.'

Tina's eyes narrowed as she studied her cousin's face. 'You know the force the government can put against us, war or no war. There's some other reason, isn't there, for starting now?'

'What other reason should there be?' Caitlin leaped up. 'Look, let's go see what Maggie has left for you to eat. I told her to prepare something cold. And I guess you'd like some tea, wouldn't you?'

'Oh, please.' Tina relaxed a little. 'I'll take my things upstairs and wash first, if you don't mind. It's very good of you, you know, to find me a house and a maid, considering –'

'Considering I'd one or two other things on my mind?' Caitlin laughed. 'I'm only sorry you couldn't have stayed at my place, but as you know, I only have a room. I thought you'd be better off here.'

'It's perfect,' said Tina.

Over a meal of thick, delicious Irish ham and salad, Caitlin talked of the events of the previous few days. It was only on

Tuesday that the leaders of the Citizen Army had been told that Easter Sunday was to be the day of the rising. Caitlin knew because Countess Markievicz, a staff lieutenant, had told her. 'I guess I'm no star, I'm still one of the rank and file,' Caitlin added, 'but Madame knows Frances and I can keep a secret.'

'Frances is the one with the boarding house?'

'Yes, my landlady.' Caitlin grinned. 'And friend. Well, the crazy thing is that Eoin MacNeill, who is commander of the Irish Volunteers, wasn't told, though his Volunteers would have to be involved anyway. He went rushing round, saying he would countermand all orders to mobilise, until Sean MacDermott told him there was to be –' Caitlin stopped short and busied herself adding hot water to the teapot.

'Was to be what?' asked Tina.

'Oh, God.' Caitlin for a moment rested her brow on her hand. 'I guess you're going to have to know some time, Tina. There's German aid promised, men and arms. They've been organised by Roger Casement – you remember, he helped in the Howth affair –'

Tina had turned white. 'German aid? *German* aid, Caitlin? When we're at war with Germany? You can't mean what you're saying – tell me it's not true!'

'It is true.' Caitlin sat with her face averted. 'Oh, I knew you'd be upset, with Victor at the front –'

'This is about much more than Victor!' Tina jumped to her feet and began to pace the small, stone-flagged kitchen. 'This is about a just war against an aggressor, a country that means to dominate, has already dominated –'

'Exactly!' cried Caitlin. 'If you're talking about England! England is no better than Germany, where Ireland is concerned, and the English war is not Ireland's war. If Germany is willing to help us, why should we say no?'

'Because thousands of Irishmen have already gone to war against Germany and died. They care as much as the rest of us about aggression and tyranny, and if your people invite the Germans to Ireland, that would mean they'd died for nothing. It's wrong, it's despicable, and I won't be a party to it!'

'You withdraw your help?'

'I withdraw my help.'

The two women stared at each other, both white, both trembling.

'Very well, then, there's no more to be said.' Caitlin shrugged. 'You might as well turn round and go home to George. It's what you want, anyway, isn't it? Why in God's name did I ever think I could trust a Wintour? I should have listened to my father.'

'How dare you?' Tina whispered, scarlet flooding her face. 'How dare you accuse me again of treachery? You should have listened to your father, yes, who would once have burned down my home. But what about your mother? How do you think she'd feel to hear you speak of her family that way? You're a Wintour yourself, as well as a Molloy; you should be ashamed!'

Caitlin lowered her eyes. 'I'm sorry, I shouldn't have said that. You're a fine, true person and I know it. Guess I was only trying to hurt, because you don't want to join us any more.'

'How could I, Caitlin, how could I?'

'Oh!' Caitlin gave a long, bitter sigh. 'I suppose you couldn't. You were right, of course. One reason why we're rising now is because of the offer of German help. But there are other reasons, too. All those loyal Irishmen you talked about, giving up their lives for a just cause, they've not been rewarded, have they? There's still no real hope of Home Rule. Ulster still holds all the cards, always will. Unless we do something. Oh, Tina –' Caitlin stretched out her hands. 'Don't you see, we had to have those men and arms, to get anywhere at all? Please won't you reconsider?'

Tina was silent, her colour still high, her eyes stern, when a violent knocking sounded on the front door. 'Who can that be?' she asked quickly. 'No one knows I'm here.'

'They know I'm here, I left this address.' Caitlin was already on her way to the door, Tina following.

A thin-faced, red-haired young woman dressed in a military-style jacket and long black skirt, stood on the doorstep. 'Oh, Caitlin, thank God you're here!' she gasped. 'The news is bad, really bad. May I come in?'

'This is Frances Tarry,' Caitlin said over her shoulder to Tina, as she drew the young woman inside and closed the door. 'Frances, my cousin, Dr Tina Coxe. Now, calm down,

Frances, and tell us what's happened.'

'The ship's gone down – two Volunteers have given the news. The *Aud* was scuttled in Tralee Bay yesterday.'

'What ship?' asked Tina, 'what is she talking about?'

Caitlin was holding her hand to her lips, she had turned a strange greenish white. 'It's the arms, the ship with the German arms. Oh, my God! Twenty thousand rifles at the bottom of the sea. I can't believe it . . . What can we do?'

'There's worse,' Frances went on. 'There'll be no men either. Sir Roger Casement's been taken, taken where he landed on Banna Strand from the submarine. They're saying that's his message; no men, no arms. So we're on our own.'

'No men, no arms.' Caitlin rounded on Tina. 'Looks like you needn't worry, Tina, there'll be no Germans to help us. I'd better get back to Madame, see what's going to happen. Frances, do you know what James Connolly is going to do?'

'No, but I know what MacNeill is going to do, he's rescinding all orders to move. There's to be a notice in the *Sunday Independent* tomorrow.'

'My God, do we take our orders from the newspapers now?' cried Caitlin, fastening her jacket. 'Frances, I'm coming back with you. Tina, wait for me here. I'll get a message to you as soon as I can.'

When Caitlin and Frances had hurried away, their faces dark with despair, Tina left the house and hurried rapidly through the streets until she found a garage where she could hire a motorcar.

'And is it your husband who'll be driving it, ma'am?' the garage owner asked politely.

'I shall be driving it myself.'

'Sure now, there's not many ladies can drive, but I've the very thing for you, if you'll just come over here, taking a look.'

'What's the make?' asked Tina, studying the solidly built four-seater, which boasted a hard top for the back seats and an adjustable cover for the front.

''Tis a Lancia, ma'am, a 1913 model, and the wonderful thing I'm telling you is you'll be needing no starting handle! 'Tis all electric, the latest thing, and grand for a lady like yourself!'

'I don't suppose it's cheap, but whatever it is, I'll take it,' said Tina, taking out her wallet. 'Can you let me have some petrol?'

'I can, but 'tis a thing to be worrying about these days. Will you be going far, are you thinking?'

'I'm not sure yet where I'm going,' Tina answered. She added to herself, 'I only wish I were.'

On Easter Sunday, Tina bought the *Sunday Independent* and read MacNeill's announcement:

'Owing to the very critical position, all orders given to the Irish Volunteers for tomorrow, Easter Sunday, are hereby rescinded and no parades, marches, or other movements of Irish Volunteers will take place.'

She folded the newspaper and put on the kettle, glad that the maid did not come on Sundays, glad that she was alone in the house, for she found she was trembling with relief. She made tea and opened the damper on the range, so that she might get a good glow to make toast, still feeling shaken, as though she had brushed with danger that had touched her and moved on. 'Thank God,' she murmured, 'someone's had some sense at last, it's all off.'

The toast was finished and she was buttering it when the front door knocker sounded again throughout the house and she dropped her knife with a clatter. Caitlin, she thought, in some vexation. Well, if she is disappointed, I am not. She closed up the range and went to the door.

'Tina!' Caitlin swept in, wearing her uniform of green jacket and a dark divided skirt. 'Tina, it's all right! Connolly's announced we're going in tomorrow instead!'

'Going in where?' asked Tina, her heart plummeting.

'To our stations as planned.' Caitlin was radiant. 'The Citizen Army and the Volunteers are to be joining together, we're to be the Army of the Irish Republic, taking up our battle stations!'

Tina sagged against the wall of the narrow entrance passage-way. 'Oh, no – no, Caitlin!'

'Don't look like that! It's all arranged. Connolly will be taking the General Post Office and Pearse will proclaim the Republic from the steps, then we'll march to our stations. I'll be with Madame at St Stephen's Green, near the College of Surgeons. You could be with our other doctor, Kathleen Lynn, or just wait and see where you're most needed when the fighting begins.' Caitlin looked at Tina's long tweed skirt. 'I don't suppose you'd want to wear trousers, would you? Or a divided skirt? Better than an ordinary one because we'll be using bicycles –'

'Come into the kitchen,' said Tina.

'Madame is saying she may be needed as a sniper,' Caitlin went on, as she followed Tina, 'but I'm not sure exactly what I'll be doing. With my nursing experience, I might even do best to stay with you, Tina – what do you think?'

'I shall not be working with you,' Tina said distinctly.

Caitlin stood very still, all the warmth and animation dying out of her face.

'You're not joining us?' she asked quietly.

'No.'

'May I ask why not?'

'You know why not.'

'But, Tina, there's to be no German aid, you heard that yourself yesterday! The ship was taken into custody and the captain scuttled it himself. Devoy tried to send a message to the States to tell the Germans they mustn't land before Sunday, but the damned ship had no radio. Can you imagine? No radio? As for the men, it seems there never were any troops coming. Casement knew and was trying to stop the rising, but, of course, he was arrested.' Caitlin looked imploringly into Tina's eyes. 'But, don't you see, there's no reason why you shouldn't help us now! We have Dr Lynn, but we need you, too, we're going to need all the medical help we can get.'

'If there had been a radio on that ship, wouldn't you be planning to use those German rifles now?'

'Didn't you once unload German rifles yourself at Howth?'

'Those were for the protection of the Volunteers, and we were not at war then with Germany. You were hoping for German soldiers too, weren't you? You were prepared to let Germany use Ireland for its own purposes.' Tina set her chin in the way Caitlin knew so well. 'I'm sorry, Caitlin, it's just not possible for me to work for the rising now.'

'You realise this is the end of everything between us?'

'It needn't be.' Tina stretched out her hand. 'You said you understood my views. Can't you just accept them? Let us still be friends? You mean a great deal to me.'

Caitlin began to walk from the kitchen, her heavy boots ringing on the stone flags. 'Goodbye, Tina,' she said over her shoulder.

'I'm not going home!' Tina shouted, as Caitlin flung open the front door. 'Caitlin, remember, I'll be here if you need me!'

Caitlin made no reply and Tina, watching, saw her running down the street; she did not look back.

Chapter Twenty-Nine

Every day during the long week of the Easter Rising, Tina braved the streets, hoping to see Caitlin, knowing she would not, yet feeling it was something she must do. George said on the telephone she owed Caitlin nothing. She could not really accept that, for in her mind Caitlin had become one with Ireland, an Ireland making a terrible mistake, yet still deserving somehow of her compassion. It was not a logical view - most of the Irish people themselves were out of sympathy with the rebellion - yet Tina battled on, fleeing with the crowds before gunfire, flinching from the looting, still determined not to go home until she had seen the end of it.

'Don't you care at all about me?' George asked.

'I do, I do, please believe me. It's just that I must see this thing through, I must see what happens to Caitlin.'

'I don't know about Caitlin, but the leaders will certainly be shot.'

'Shot?'

'What else can they expect? They're shooting people themselves every day. And there's no hope they can win, they know that already. They're on a suicide mission and the quicker you leave them to it, the better.'

Tina knew George was right. They had no hope of success, they were looking for death or glory. Connolly, Pearse, Plunkett, Countess Markievicz and the rest - but not Caitlin, Tina prayed, please God, not Caitlin.

Every day, there were fires, as looted shops were set alight, and by Thursday the artillery fire of British troops had set half the centre of Dublin ablaze. When an incendiary shell sent the

General Post Office up in flames, it was clear the end must come soon. This was the rebels' headquarters, it was from here they had proclaimed the Republic, now it was collapsing around them, they would have to give in. For a time, they tried to carry on. James Connolly, although shot in the ankle, formed a new HQ in Moore Street, but the flagpole they left bearing the new Irish tricolour had already fallen. It seemed an omen that there would be surrender, and on the afternoon of Saturday 29 April surrender came. Patrick Pearse in his Volunteer uniform handed his sword to General Lowe on the steps of the ruined post office. The Easter Rising was at an end.

Tina was out in the crowds, seeking for any scrap of information she could pick up. What would happen now? An elderly Dubliner with bloodshot blue eyes said, sure, all the different Volunteer posts would have to be told. Weren't they sending a nurse off now, with a soldier to guard her and a white flag and all?

'A nurse?' Tina repeated. 'To give orders of surrender?'

'From James Connolly, am I not telling you? Did I not see her with my own eyes marching down the street?'

'Has she been to the College of Surgeons yet?'

'Now that I can't be saying. Sure, she'll never get round all them Volunteers today!'

So Caitlin might not even know yet that the surrender had been made? Tina moved on through the shattered streets, her nostrils filled with the acrid smell of smoke, her blue coat and skirt grey with dust. She was filled with a great longing now to get away, to get out of Dublin, to be back with George and free of this terrible responsibility. But the responsibility towards Caitlin hung around her like a chain. She could not go. For a time she stood still on the pavement, debating what to do, while people hurried past her. She could go back to the house and wait, wait until tomorrow, then try again. By tomorrow, the nurse with the white flag would have reached the College of Surgeons, everyone would have to come out, obey the order to surrender.

Raising her eyes, Tina saw Caitlin coming towards her down the street.

Her face was very pale and she was hatless. A man's

overcoat had been slung round her shoulders and beneath it, Tina could see her left arm hung limp. Though she appeared to be staring straight at Tina, her eyes had the dazed, unfocused look of someone in a dream. A nightmare, thought Tina, and flew to her side.

'I saw the nurse,' Caitlin said, 'she was carrying a white flag, I couldn't believe it . . .'

'That's all right, Caitlin, let's go home. Lean on me.'

'No, I can't go with you. I have to see Madame, I have to tell her –'

'Tell her tomorrow. Come, take my arm.'

Caitlin could walk, except that she seemed not to want to walk in a straight line, but Tina, finding a strange strength, supported her, moving with her through the people as though everything were completely normal, they were only Dubliners, out like everyone else to see the end of a crazy rebellion, going home now for a cup of tea. In the circumstances, of course, anyone could look as white as Caitlin, anyone could lose a hat. An empty taxi drove by, and Tina would have given any money to have taken it, but dared not. On they went in their wandering way until, as though it were sanctuary, they fell against the door of the house in Clock Street. As Tina fumbled with the key, Caitlin seemed to recognise her for the first time.

'Tina, what are you doing?' she asked in a loud voice, which Tina tried to muffle with her hand. 'Stop it! Take your hand away. I'm not coming with you, don't try to make me. I have a message for Madame –'

Tina, with one last giant effort, picked her up, carried her into the house and locked the door.

Tina was relieved to find that though Caitlin had been shot, the wound was superficial. A bullet, probably from a sniper's rifle, had skimmed the upper part of her left arm but had not lodged in the wound, and she had been saved from losing too much blood by someone's having tied a large, white handkerchief around her arm. No doubt the same person who had torn away the sleeve of her jacket and lent her the overcoat, thought Tina, as she boiled up water to dress the wound, while Caitlin lay on the sofa in the parlour. She had been lucky, but she might still need hospital treatment.

'I feel so sick,' Caitlin whispered later, to the face that floated before her. 'Where am I?'

'In my house. Don't worry, you're quite safe.'

'So who are you?'

'A friend. Try to rest now. I'm going to give you something for the pain.'

'I don't feel any pain.' Caitlin drifted into sleep.

When she came round again, her arm felt on fire, but her head was clear. She looked again at the face near hers. 'You shouldn't have brought me here, Tina, I don't want to be with you – you wouldn't help us.'

'Don't want, don't want!' cried Tina, losing patience. 'Why should I care what you want?'

Caitlin closed her eyes.

She was aware of someone waking her, trying to make her drink. Except for one gas lamp, the room was dark, so it must be night, but the voice in her ear was telling her she must get up, must hurry, they must leave as soon as possible.

'Where are we to go?' asked Caitlin.

'To Belcarron.'

Then Caitlin knew the voice belonged to Tina. 'Not Belcarron,' she said wildly, 'no, I won't go to Belcarron!'

'You must. You'll be safe there for a while.'

'I can't. Cousin Alice won't accept me.'

'Of course she'll accept you.' Tina helped Caitlin to sit up. 'It's not ideal, but I think we must risk it. There's no difficulty, I have a car at the door, but I want to leave before dawn, so we must hurry.'

'Where did you get a car?' asked Caitlin, as Tina prepared to give her another injection.

'I hired one.'

'But why?'

'I don't really know. Premonition, maybe. Come on, let's get you up.'

'Tina, wait! I want to say I'm sorry, I shouldn't have spoken to you that way – you've been very kind –'

'That's all right. I shouldn't have lost my temper, either.'

'But you do understand, don't you, that I can't come with

you? I can't leave Dublin, I have to go to Madame.' Caitlin's shadowed eyes were enormous in the pallor of her face. 'I have to tell her about the nurse, about the surrender. It's my job.'

'My dear, she'll be told today, you don't have to worry.'

'No, but I was sent out to see what was happening. We saw the smoke from the GPO. We knew there'd be talk of surrender, but Madame wouldn't have it, she wouldn't admit it. I went out, I think it was in the afternoon –'

'Please, don't tell me this now. We must hurry –'

'No, wait, I have to explain. I was hurrying, trying to get to the post office, and someone said Connolly was in Moore Street. I didn't know what to do. Then I felt the pain in my arm. One of our people came to me, he put something on my arm. He said he'd take me to Vincent's – that's the hospital – but we saw the nurse, we saw the nurse with the white flag –'

'Oh, Caitlin,' Tina whispered, 'this will do no good, no good at all. We must leave before someone finds you –'

'I don't know what happened then,' Caitlin murmured shakily. 'I guess I must have passed out for a while. When I came to, the guy had gone, but he'd put his coat around me. I set off to find Madame –'

'Instead, I found you. Look, Caitlin, it's hard, but you must realise that there's nothing you can do for Madame now. The nurse will go to the College of Surgeons today and then it will all be over. But if you come with me, you'll have a chance to work again. That's what you want, isn't it?'

Caitlin seemed too exhausted to answer. She allowed herself to be dressed in a skirt of Tina's and a blouse from which Tina had cut the left sleeve; then she sat quietly while Tina draped a jacket around her, brushed her hair and pinned it up.

'All over?' she repeated. 'You think it's all over?'

'I'm afraid it is. Can you lean on me as far as the car?'

'But what will happen now? What will happen to – the others?'

'I don't know. There'll be trials, I suppose.'

'Tina, I can't go with you! I can't leave them, don't you see that?'

'This way,' Tina said calmly, 'the motor's just here. You can lie in the back and I'll cover you with a rug. You'll sleep soon.'

'I'll never sleep!' But Caitlin had not the strength to fight any more and she lay still, where Tina placed her, listening to the noises of the city, watching the lights in the sky from buildings still burning. When Tina came out with her case and a basket in which she had packed some food, Caitlin's eyes were closed.

There were army patrols everywhere in the city and sweat rose on Tina's brow every time they passed one, but she was stopped only once when a soldier flagged her down and passed his torch over her face. He asked her who she was and where she was going.

'Miss Daisy Morry,' she replied, 'travelling to Castle Morry in County Cork.'

Reassured by her confident English accent, the soldier nodded, but still looked in the back at the sleeping Caitlin. 'And that lady, miss?'

'My sister. We were spending Easter in Dublin. Now we're trying to get home.'

He waved her on and she smiled and gave a regal nod, but at the next corner, out of his sight, had to stop and rest her head on the wheel for a moment until her trembling stopped. Then she drove on, following the route she had worked out, which, because of the state of the Irish roads and the fear of breakdowns, unfortunately had to follow main roads as far as possible. There would also be the problem of finding somewhere to stay for the night; with Caitlin as weak as she was, they could not travel too far. Finding a safe place would not be easy.

The sun came up and the countryside was revealed in all its spring beauty, but Tina had no eyes for anything but the road ahead, with its hazards of potholes and wandering animals, and, what she most dreaded, approaching army vehicles.

They made good time through the flat plains of County Kildare, though Tina was made uneasy by the openness of the terrain and relieved to see nothing more threatening than race horses being exercised. County Kilkenny was prettier, with trees and small, lush fields, and they stopped for a while in a lane off the main road, where Tina ate her sandwiches and Caitlin managed a few sips of water.

'You'll be feeling more like eating by tonight,' Tina told her, 'but the problem will be finding somewhere to stay. I don't think we should risk a guesthouse or hotel.'

'There are places,' Caitlin murmured, 'places with friends.'

'Where? Can you tell me where? Please, Caitlin, try to remember!'

Caitlin moved her head restlessly. 'Where are we now?'

'Some miles from Callan, County Kilkenny.'

'There's a house near Clonmel. In a village – a tiny village a few miles past Clonmel.'

'Clonmel.' Tina bent her head over the map. 'That's on the border of Waterford and Tipperary. It would do, anywhere near there would do. Can you remember the name of the village?'

Caitlin wiped her brow with her good hand. 'You can see the mountains,' she offered, 'the Comeragh Mountains.'

'Yes, but the name of the village?' Tina pressed.

'I guess I could take you there.'

'Right!' Tina packed up the picnic and started the car. 'Keep awake!' she called over her shoulder. 'Just till we get there.'

They reached Clonmel, an attractive little town with a pretty river setting and the views Caitlin had mentioned of the Comeraghs. The village could not be far, then, and Tina drove slowly, expecting to see it round every bend, but it was when they came to a solid stone house standing alone that Caitlin called, weakly, 'That's it.'

'I thought you said it was in a village?'

'Guess that must be further on. But that's the house.'

Tina pulled up. The house was well decorated, with a prosperous look; there was a garden full of spring flowers at the front and a wide drive leading to the rear. It was not at all the sort of place she had expected. She turned to look at the mountains in the distance – yes, the windows of the house would have excellent views. Also, of any vehicles coming up or down the road.

'What's the name of these people,' she asked, 'these friends?'

'No names,' said Caitlin.

'So, what do we do? Just go up and ask to stay?'

'They expect it, from time to time.'

'It seems so odd, though, just to do that. Unless you know them very well?'

'I don't know them at all.'

Tina, puzzled, got out of the car and pushed open the garden gate. It bore a name, Knock House, she noticed, but there was no name plate on the front door. She rang the bell.

A tall, middle-aged man with thinning grey hair and horn-rimmed glasses answered. He looked like a professional man, a lawyer or a schoolmaster. His gaze went past her to Caitlin looking out from the car. 'Are you from Dublin?' he asked. His voice was educated and authoritative, with just a hint of Irish lilt.

'Yes, I'm Dr Tina –'

'Please.' He raised his hand. 'No names. Bring your friend into the house, then put your motor at the back of the house out of sight.'

Of all her experiences, this seemed to Tina to be one of the strangest. Perhaps because her host and his wife, a stout, comfortable woman with curling white hair, seemed so very normal, the circumstances of their hospitality appeared even more odd. She and Caitlin might have been old friends being greeted for a usual visit, instead of dust-stained strangers arriving out of the blue. Oddest of all was that no names or details of any sort were exchanged. From the time they met until they said goodbye, Tina never knew what their benefactors were called or what they did, and they never knew her name or Caitlin's. No mention was made of the rising, except by Caitlin, who eagerly asked if there was any news of Dublin. The grey-haired man said no.

Hot water was provided for washing, followed by a meal: boiled chicken and vegetables for Tina, who ate with their hosts in an oak-furnished dining room; something light for Caitlin, who was early given a bed.

'I don't know what to say to you,' Tina murmured, when she rose to say goodnight. She looked around. Everything was so comfortable, so ordinary, she blinked her eyes, thinking it might vanish and she would find herself back on the road, searching every oncoming car for soldiers or police. 'I wish I could thank you.'

The couple smiled her thanks away.

'Now, have you everything you need?' asked the woman. 'Be sure to say.'

'If I could just have some boiled water?'

'Of course. Do you require bandages?'

'I have plenty, thank you.' Eyes went to her doctor's bag, but nothing was said.

The boiled water was brought and the grey-haired man carried it upstairs for her – there appeared to be no servants in this strange house. 'What about petrol?' he asked, at the door to the room Tina was to share with Caitlin.

'It's a problem. We have to get to –'

Again he held up his hand. 'Don't tell me. I know where I can get a gallon or two. Will you let me drive the motor?'

'Surely.' As Tina gave him the keys, she asked, 'Are you real?'

'Real enough,' he answered. 'Goodnight now.'

The bedroom was large, with flowered curtains and wallpaper, two brass-ended beds and highly polished mahogany furniture. No gas or electric light, only candles, which made Tina think of Belcarron and catch her breath for a moment with apprehension, wondering if they would ever get there. Caitlin was lying with her eyes closed and Tina, setting down the hot water, touched her gently.

'I'm sorry, I'm going to have to dress your arm again. I'll try not to hurt.'

'Don't worry.' Caitlin was stoical as Tina stripped off the old bandages and studied her wound. 'How is it?'

'Not too bad. You've been lucky, it's only a flesh wound, but you should still have hospital treatment.'

'Why, if it's not serious?'

'Well, I'm doing what I can and I don't think there's any danger of infection, but you need a surgeon to do a proper repair.'

'Tina, I'd be arrested if I tried to go to hospital here.'

'Which is why I want you to come to England with me. George and I know private hospitals where you'd be safe.'

Caitlin shook her head. 'It's out of the question,' she said, with a gasp, as Tina continued to work on her arm. 'I can't leave Ireland, I can't leave my friends.'

'You can't help them by staying here, and you'll be more use out of prison than in.'

Caitlin was silent until Tina had rebandaged her arm, when

she asked quietly, 'Why are you doing this for me?'

'I don't know. Because you're family, I suppose.'

'I've said some pretty terrible things about the family.'

'You're my cousin, I couldn't just leave you, could I?'

'Even though you hated what I was doing?'

'I know you thought it was right, I know it was for Ireland.'

'You haven't asked me,' Caitlin said slowly, 'but I want you to know, I didn't shoot anyone.'

'Didn't you?'

'No. It's funny, I learned to shoot, I wanted to be the same as the men, but in the end I only nursed people. That's what most of the women did, that and cooking, if there was anything to cook. Frances and I did hold up a bread van –' Caitlin dissolved into tears. 'Oh God, what's going to happen to Frances?'

Tina gave Caitlin two sleeping tablets and a little water. 'I'd like you to take these to get you through the night. Try to rest.'

Caitlin swallowed the tablets. 'I'd rather have a cigarette – don't have one, do you?'

'I'll get some tomorrow.' Tina undressed and put out the candle. 'Now I'm going to try to get some sleep myself. We have a long day ahead of us before we get to Belcarron. Goodnight, Caitlin.'

'Goodnight, Tina.'

They both lay staring into the darkness of the unfamiliar room. Then Caitlin added stiffly, 'And thanks.'

They left their anonymous hosts next morning. Tina had thanked them again and was walking to the car, when Caitlin turned back.

'You have a telephone,' she said, looking directly at the man with grey hair. 'Are you sure there's no news from Dublin?'

'Only that thousands of suspects are being rounded up. Some are being sent to England.'

'But what of the leaders? What's happening to the leaders?'

'I'm afraid I have no information.'

The woman who had taken such good care of Tina and Caitlin shook her head. 'They're saying there will be executions.'

'Executions!' cried Caitlin. 'When they're prisoners of war?'

'The authorities don't regard them as such.' The man offered

Caitlin his arm. 'Let me help you to the motor.' When she was installed once more on the back seat of the Lancia, he waved his hand and returned to the house, swiftly closing the door.

'Drive on,' said Caitlin, 'drive on, quickly.'

'Strange couple,' Tina observed when they had driven some miles. 'Not the sort you'd expect, somehow, to be offering – what they offer.'

'Not everyone who supports our views lives in a cabin with the pig,' Caitlin retorted.

'That sounds like the old Caitlin. Are you feeling better?'

'I'm sorry, it just annoys me when people expect all the Irish to be the same.'

'All right, I apologise.' Tina drew into the side of the road and took out her maps. 'What we have to decide now is our best route home. I'm very much afraid that we'll have to go through Cork. We can't afford the petrol to do anything else, even with the extra our friend managed to find.'

'You do as you think best,' said Caitlin.

'I don't really see why they should stop us, do you? I suggest we go from here to Mitchelstown, not Fermoy, because that's a garrison town, then to Mallow and down into Cork from there.'

'If there was a rising, we could run into trouble.'

'A rising?' Tina dropped her map and stared in consternation at Caitlin. 'You didn't tell me there was to be a rising in Cork!'

'Oh, Dublin wasn't the only one planned. But it may not have come off. Anyway –' Caitlin looked into space – 'it'll be all over now. Just as in Dublin.'

Tina bit her lip. 'We'll just have to hope for the best, that's all. If we're stopped, I'll give my own name, in case anyone knows me. I'll say you're Evie. No one knows Evie.'

'How do you know they won't be expecting me to make for Belcarron?'

'Because they know my mother's views. She's no nationalist, you know that.'

'And you still say she'll accept me?'

'You're Hester Wintour's daughter, aren't you?'

'Hester Molloy's daughter,' said Caitlin.

*

At any other time, their route to Cork would have charmed, for the countryside was soft and beautiful and the little towns full of character, but their minds that day were not on scenery. They stopped in Mallow, a quiet watering place, where Tina found a dairy and bought milk, cheese and rolls. Caitlin was looking white again, with dark bruises under her eyes. After they had eaten, she fell asleep on the back seat of the car. Perhaps it was just as well, thought Tina as she headed for Cork, her heart hammering.

Yet all seemed normal in the old city and port, built between the two channels of the river Lee. There were soldiers and Royal Irish Constabulary men about, but no more than usual. Knots of people, mainly men, were standing around chatting, but then in Ireland there were always knots of men standing around chatting, especially if they'd had a drink or two. People with children were strolling through the eighteenth-century streets, enjoying the spring afternoon, and there was the usual traffic to and from the quays, but as far as Tina could tell this was just the same old Cork she knew, and if there had been a rising in the 'rebel' city, as people called it, she could see no signs of it. Her spirits rose a little, except that she still had to worry about petrol and was nowhere near the only garage she knew, which was by the station. Obviously, to get out of Cork as soon as possible would be best, but to get out of Cork and find no other garage before they got home would be disastrous. Tina took the decision and turned the car towards the station.

'Thank God, you are open,' she told Sean Heenan, as she parked before his garage, 'I thought you might be closed on Sundays.'

Sean, large and sandy haired, looked closely at Tina, then gave a grin of recognition. He remembered her from the past when she and Jack had filled up the Napier and George had called with a hired car. 'Ah now, when we've petrol, isn't Sunday our best time, ma'am? Is it petrol you're wanting?'

'It is, Mr Heenan.'

'You're in luck, then. Be driving over to the pumps.' He looked in at Caitlin, who had stirred in the streets of Cork, but was now asleep again. 'Now, is it your sister you have in there, ma'am?'

'No, my cousin from America, just over for a holiday. A little tired with the crossing.'

'Ah, now 'tis a terrible time to be picking a holiday, with them mad Shinners up in Dublin and all!'

'There's been trouble here?' Tina asked, cautiously.

'Sure, there was talk of a rising, but weren't they saying they had nine different letters telling them what to do and in the end, didn't they do nothing? I've no patience, I'm telling you, 'tis them boys gives Ireland a bad name and are getting us nowhere. Now would you be wanting me to do a few little checks on this grand motor you're driving, ma'am, seeing as you're still a long way from home? Don't you be disturbing the young lady, she can stay where she is.'

Tina was walking to and fro, glad to stretch her legs after the constriction of driving the car, when a tall, thin woman, dressed in a wrinkled grey coat and skirt and a black velvet hat, came out from Sean Heenan's office. She seemed to hesitate for a moment, then approached Tina.

'Excuse me, I hope you'll forgive me for speaking to you, but are you by any chance travelling to Skibbereen?'

Her voice had the Anglo-Irish accent Tina knew so well, yet she spoke slowly, as though finding the words were an effort. Beneath her hat, Tina could see that her hair was yellow and as she looked directly into Tina's face, her eyes were the same green as Melissa's.

'Where in Skibbereen do you want to go?' Tina asked, her voice trembling a little with excitement.

'Oh, just to another garage where I can hire a car. I've just come off the City of Cork packet, missed my train, and thought I could get a car here, but there's nothing available for hours. I should be for ever in your debt if you could give me a lift.'

'I should be delighted to give you a lift. Perhaps I could take you further than Skibbereen?'

'Oh, I don't think so. It's very kind of you, but it's rather out of the way. I'm going to Belcarron.'

'Hello, Aunt Charlotte,' said Tina.

Chapter Thirty

They were on their way, threading through the streets of Cork again, Charlotte beside Tina, her green eyes alight, her Gladstone bag, her only luggage, stowed away.

'I can't believe it,' Charlotte kept saying, 'I simply can't believe it! Little Tina! You were only a child when I last saw you, you know.'

'And now I'm married and a doctor.'

'A doctor? Good heavens!' Charlotte took off the velvet hat and put her hands to her yellow hair, which was only slightly tinged with grey. 'How strange everything seems! I can't believe I'm here with you, driving like this . . . But who's the girl sleeping in the back? Your sister?'

'No, my cousin, Caitlin Molloy.'

'Oh, God, Caitlin Molloy! I remember the day she was born.' Charlotte tried to laugh, then stopped as though she might cry. 'It's all a little too much for me. I never thought I'd be meeting anyone from the family this way. I had it all worked out, what I was going to say to Alice, and it's all so difficult because even speaking English is something I have to think about. I've come from Germany, you know. I'm what you might call a refugee.'

'From Germany? How? I mean, how did you get away?'

'It's a long story, I'll tell it to you later.' Charlotte looked back at Caitlin. 'Your cousin seems to be sleeping very well. Is she all right?'

'Actually, she's a little bit sedated.'

'She's ill?'

Tina hesitated. 'This is our road,' she murmured. 'I mustn't miss it.'

'Bandon. How these old names come back to me!' Charlotte stared curiously as Tina's eyes went from side to side, checking for army patrols. 'What's wrong, Tina?'

'Nothing.' Tina let out a long sigh. 'I think we're going to be all right, Aunt Charlotte. At least for the time being.'

'It's a funny thing, you know –' Charlotte's gaze slid again to Caitlin – 'but you almost give the impression of being refugees yourselves. I've been reading the Sunday papers, they're full of the Dublin Rising.'

'Oh, yes? I haven't seen them.'

'You wouldn't have been involved in that, by any chance?'

'Oh, Lord, Aunt Charlotte, you're quick. No, I wasn't, but Caitlin was. She was wounded in the arm.'

'Fighting for Ireland. Like father, like daughter. What about her brother? Was he in it, too?'

'He's in the States, he wasn't involved.'

'And you weren't involved, but you managed to rescue Caitlin. How did you do that?'

'I don't think the details matter, Aunt Charlotte, but maybe I should tell you that Mama doesn't know anything about it. She doesn't even know I'm on my way, she thinks I'm in London with George.'

'George?'

'George Coxe. He's a cousin of Mavis Morry's. I married him.'

'George Coxe ... I remember him, too. Oh, dear, so Alice doesn't know you're coming. She doesn't know I'm coming, either.'

Tina snatched a quick glance at Charlotte, then turned her attention back to the road. 'Poor Mama, seems she's in for some surprises.'

'You're not at all like her, are you, Tina? You know, you remind me of my aunt Constance, has anyone told you that before?'

'Frequently,' said Tina.

It was dark by the time they reached Belcarron. Not too dark for Charlotte to miss the changes to the village as they drove through, which she found exciting. But when she saw the house, she fell silent. Stepping out of the car, her eyes went up to the face of her old home, the white walls, the square, sashed windows, the roof that always cost a mint, as she told Tina, again trying to laugh and failing.

'Tina, this hasn't changed.'

'No, it hasn't changed.'

'Do you know, I'm really not sure what to do. I haven't seen your mother since 1893. Can you believe that, Tina? Not since Christmas 1893.'

'Aunt Charlotte, could you give me a hand with Caitlin? She's awake, but she may not be able to walk very well.'

'Who's there?' cried an Irish voice from the suddenly opened door. 'Now don't be coming any further, we've guns here, so I'm telling you!'

'It's all right, Bridie,' Tina cried. 'It's only me!'

She could see her mother standing on the steps of the house and rushed to her and threw her arms around her, as though she were a child again, being welcomed back after absence. 'Oh, Mama!' She dragged out a handkerchief to wipe her eyes.

'Tina, whatever is it?' Alice cried, holding her fast. 'I thought you were in London. Oh, it's so lovely to see you –'

'I'm all right, Mama, I'll explain everything later, but Caitlin's outside, she's been hurt, and there's someone else –'

'Someone else?'

'Aunt Charlotte, Mama.'

Alice stood very still, her back rigid, as Charlotte, carrying her velvet hat, came into the hall. The lamplight shone on her straw-coloured hair and caught the flash of her green eyes, and to Alice time stood still. Twenty years and more dissolved, and she was looking at her sister again, ordering her to go, to leave Belcarron, and Richard was there and she wouldn't speak to him, wouldn't listen to him, and then all the pain and emptiness of the long years seemed to rush past her and she was back in the hall with this new, older Charlotte, swaying on her feet.

'Charlotte – you're here? You've come back?'

'Alice –' Charlotte was swaying, too. 'Will you take me in?'

Caitlin came into the house on Bridie's arm, and Alice went to her and kissed her pale cheek. 'Caitlin, I'm so sorry you've had an accident. Tina, take Caitlin upstairs, she looks as if she should be in bed. Bridie will help you.' Alice turned back to

Charlotte, standing with her eyes on Alice's face and her Gladstone bag at her feet.

'You'd better come into the drawing room,' Alice said stiffly.

'Thank you,' Charlotte replied.

Here in the long drawing room were the same shabby chesterfield and chintz-covered chairs, the good rugs on the polished floors, the portraits and photographs, even the same mellow oil lamps set on the tables. Alice had kept everything the same.

Although the evening was not cold and a small fire was burning in the grate, she drew a white shawl around her shoulders as she politely invited her sister to sit down, as though she were a stranger. Again, Charlotte said, 'Thank you.'

They sat down, each warily eyeing the other, knowing the ice between them must be broken, wondering if it was possible.

'You haven't changed,' Alice said, clearing her throat. 'I'm afraid I have.'

'Not really. You're a little plumper.'

'And you're a lot thinner. Do you want to tell me what's been happening to you, in all these years?'

'How much do you want to know? It's been a long time.'

'I suppose I want to know why you've come back.'

'That's easy. I wanted to come home.'

Alice's eyes flashed. 'You think of Belcarron as your home?'

'Oh, I know it's yours, but when there's trouble, one thinks of where one's been safe.' Charlotte gave a long, shuddering sigh. 'There's no point in not being straight with you. I haven't got anything except what I'm wearing and what's in my leather bag. In Germany I have money I can't touch. Here, I'd just about enough left to hire a car from Cork. In fact, Tina found me at the garage and gave me a lift, so I'm a few pounds in credit.'

'Oh, Charlotte!' Alice sat back in her chair. 'Would you like some tea? Or something stronger?'

'Better make it tea. I'm quite light-headed enough as it is.'

While Caitlin lay quietly in one of the guest bedrooms, and Tina luxuriated in a long, hot bath, Charlotte drank tea and talked and Alice listened. Slowly, the ice between them began to crack.

'I won't tell you how I felt when I left Belcarron,' Charlotte began. 'You won't want to know, but it was pretty bad. I had the money you'd given me for my share of the estate, so I was feeling very flush, which of course was always fatal for me. I never could resist spending money when I had it. I took a flat in London, met up with a few old friends from the time Dudley and I were there, and, well –' she laughed – 'had a good time, I suppose. What I was really doing was trying to forget, put as much distance as I could between myself and what I'd done, which was rather impossible. One or two fellows proposed, but I wasn't interested, and then the money began to run out and I didn't know what to do next. I don't know if you'll remember Priscilla Letton? My friend from Dublin?'

Alice nodded, keeping her eyes on her sister's face. 'Of course I remember her, the one who said she could never bring herself to marry.'

'That's right.' Charlotte's eyes danced in the old way. 'She did say that. And she swore she'd never have any children either, and now she's married and has four. But I'm getting ahead of myself. Priscilla asked me to go to Germany with her, to take the waters at one of the spas – at least, her mother wanted to take the waters and Priscilla wanted to enjoy herself. So, we all went to Bad Homburg and I met Rolf von Eberbach.'

'He wasn't a baron?'

'A baron? Is that what people said? No, but he did have the von and he was wealthy. Actually, you may not believe this, but that's not the reason I married him. I wasn't in love with him, but I liked him, I really liked him, and I knew he would be a good person to be with. He was more than twenty years older than me and a widower.' Charlotte poured herself some more tea. 'Unfortunately, with two grown-up daughters, Trudi and Herta. As you might guess, they didn't take to me at all.'

'The wicked stepmother?'

'Exactly. But they married, we didn't see too much of them, we had a very pleasant country home and a flat in Berlin, we really had a good life. Until the war. You can imagine what it was like for me then, being considered English. Rolf was wonderful, supported me in every way; I really didn't worry. Then, one afternoon, he – he had a heart attack and died.' Charlotte lowered her eyes. 'Alice, I know you hate smoking in here, but would you let me have a cigarette?'

'Of course. As a matter of fact, I've quite given up worrying about it.' Alice watched as Charlotte gratefully lit a cigarette. 'Charlotte, I'm very sorry about your husband.'

'Things were pretty difficult after that. Rolf had left me half his estate, including the Berlin apartment, but his daughters wouldn't accept the will. Both their husbands were officers in the German army and they began to make accusations against me, saying I was a spy, trying to obtain military information, and I don't know what.' Charlotte laughed grimly. 'Fortunately, I had some good friends. They came to me one night and said if I didn't want to be arrested, I should leave, just with what I could take. They helped me to get to Holland and from there I bought myself a passage in a Dutch trawler. Don't ask about that, Alice, it doesn't bear thinking about, but I got to Suffolk and that was all I wanted. As I told you, I had a little English money. I got to Cork, met Tina.' Charlotte blew smoke. 'Now I'm here. Do I thank God, or not?'

'You might have gone to Marianne's from Suffolk,' Alice commented obliquely. 'She would have helped you.'

'Marianne? She hates me. I'd never have gone to Marianne's.' Charlotte leaned forwards. 'Do you hate me, Alice?' she asked softly.

Alice was silent. 'Did you know that I'd lost Jack?' she asked at last.

Charlotte's face changed. 'Jack? Oh, no, Alice, I didn't! Oh, that dear little boy! Was it in the war?'

'No, just before. A freak accident.' Alice shook her head, staring into the fire. 'It hit us all pretty hard, as you can imagine.'

'Alice, I can't bear thinking about it.'

'Plenty of people are facing what we faced.' Alice looked up. 'And I'm lucky, I still have three children. Melissa is in America at present, and Tina lives in London. Did she tell you that she'd married George Coxe, Mavis Morry's cousin?'

'Yes, she did. I remember George quite well. Big, nice,

fair-haired doctor. And Tina is a doctor too? That's wonderful, Alice, you must be so proud. What about Victor?'

'Victor is in the army. He married Evie Stonefield, a very sweet girl, daughter of our banker in Buenos Aires.' Alice gave a tender smile. 'And I'm a grandmother. Victor and Evie have a son, Rickie – I wish you could have seen him, but Evie is visiting her aunt in England.'

'A grandmother?' Charlotte threw her cigarette end into the fire. 'I envy you. I didn't tell you, but Rolf and I had a child. A daughter. We called her Lotte, a little bit after me, you see. If she'd lived, she would have been seventeen now, but she died at five weeks.'

'Oh, Charlotte!' Alice, stricken, stretched out her hand and clasped her sister's. 'Oh, I'm so sorry. I used to have such nightmares about losing a child!'

'It is a nightmare,' Charlotte said quietly, 'whenever it comes. You've suffered a great deal, Alice.'

'I'm not the only one.' Alice let go of her sister's hands. 'But maybe I've been remembering things too long, Charlotte. Maybe I shouldn't let the past come between us any more.'

Charlotte sat very still, keeping her eyes on Alice's face.

'If you want to stay on at Belcarron, you're welcome.'

Charlotte immediately let her gaze fall. 'I don't know what to say. Alice, you're all I have in the world now, you know that, don't you?'

'It's good we'll be together, then.'

Charlotte leaned forwards and kissed Alice on the cheek. 'Thank you,' she said simply.

Alice's smile was warm and glowing, as she made to rise. 'Now, we mustn't say another word,' she began, but Charlotte put out her hand.

'Just one,' she whispered, 'well, one or two. It was all envy, you know, it was all caused by envy.'

Alice stared in surprise. 'Envy, Charlotte? Why should you have been envious of me?'

'Because you had the Wintour nose. No, don't laugh. I'm sure I'd have been quite a different character if I hadn't had this bump.' Charlotte ran her finger down the bridge of her nose. 'You were always so beautiful and Papa's favourite, I knew I could never compete. I was sure it was all the fault of my nose.'

'Why, you always had far more admirers than I!' Alice exclaimed. 'Young men used to hang around you like flies round honey.'

'All I wanted was to look like you.'

'You also had Richard,' Alice said, in a low voice, 'at one time.'

'No, that's not true. He was attracted to me, like other men, but he never loved me as he came to love you. That was what I saw when he came back to Belcarron. I saw what you both had and I seemed to have nothing. So, I tried to take him from you.' Charlotte turned her head away. 'You'll never know how much of my life I've spent regretting it.'

'Charlotte, it's all over, it's past. You're home now and we can make a fresh start – that's what we both want, isn't it?'

'It's what we want,' Charlotte agreed.

'So, come up and see your old room now, before I see what can be done about dinner.'

'My old room? It hasn't changed, has it?'

'I'm sure you've already noticed, nothing at Belcarron has changed,' Alice answered with a smile.

Tina came down and they had an informal meal which they ate in the drawing room, seemingly relaxed, except that Alice kept looking at Tina, waiting for her to speak of Caitlin, and Tina kept looking away.

'Where's Evie?' Tina asked suddenly. 'I've only just realised that I haven't seen her. And where's Rickie?'

When it was explained that Evie was visiting her aunt Lucinda in England, Tina nodded.

'Perhaps she should stay there for a while, until things settle down.'

'You think there'll be more trouble?' asked Alice.

'Well, it's possible. People here never approved of the rebellion, but they won't want executions.'

'I thought we had enough troubles with the war.' Charlotte turned to Alice. 'But tell me, Alice, why is your younger girl in America? I was so looking forward to meeting her.'

Alice and Tina exchanged glances.

'It was a love affair that didn't come off, Aunt Charlotte,' Tina said, 'and all because of the violets in your hat.'

'What are you talking about?' asked Charlotte, laughing.

'Paul saw Melissa with violets on her hat and fell for her like a ton of bricks. To be honest, he'd have fallen for her anyway. She's really lovely.'

'He actually remembered my hat?'

'So Cousin Hester told us.' Tina grew serious. 'Actually, it's all very sad. Melissa went to New York to marry Paul, then fell out of love, and now it's all over. But Melissa can't get back.'

'She never meant to hurt Paul,' Alice said quickly. 'These things happen. But now, Tina, we've talked round the subject long enough – what is the matter with Caitlin?'

'If you'll excuse me,' Charlotte said tactfully, 'I think I'll go to bed, I'm absolutely exhausted.'

'Of course, Charlotte.' Alice found her a lamp and escorted her to the foot of the stairs, where they exchanged kisses.

'Welcome home, Charlotte, and sleep well.'

'Goodnight, Aunt Charlotte,' Tina called from the drawing-room door.

'Goodnight, Tina; goodnight, Alice!'

When they had watched the slender figure climb the stairs, pause for a moment at the landing window, then disappear, mother and daughter faced each other alone.

'How is Caitlin?' asked Alice.

'She's sleeping. Bridie took her a little supper and she managed to eat it.'

'Just what has happened to her, then?'

'She's been shot.'

Alice returned to her chair by the fire and sank into it. Tina went to kneel beside her.

'It's not too bad, Mama. I mean, she's not going to die or anything, but her left arm needs more treatment. I must take her back to hospital in England.'

'Was she involved in the Dublin Rising, Tina?'

'Yes, she was.'

'Were you?'

'No, but I shall have to tell you that I had intended to give medical aid.'

'Aid to those people? Tina, how could you? While your brother fights for his country, you would help to bring it down?'

'I believe in Irish freedom, Mama, but not in violence. In any case, when I heard they had tried for help from Germany, I withdrew.'

'Oh, Tina!' Alice rocked to and fro. 'That you might have been involved at all breaks my heart – breaks my heart, do you know that?'

Tina scrambled to her feet. 'All right, the rebels were wrong, they took lives, but maybe people like us have already broken Ireland's heart, Mama. The thing is, I haven't got time to go into the rights and wrongs of it all now. I must get Caitlin away from here as quickly as possible and I must have help.'

'Are you saying the authorities might come looking for her?' cried Alice. She put her hand to her lips. 'Are we committing an offence, harbouring her?'

'What do you want to do? Throw her out?'

'Of course not. I abhor what she has done, but she is Hester's daughter and I shall protect her if I can.'

'All right, if the police remember Caitlin's connection with us, they might come here. I don't think it's likely, but it's possible. That's why I want to get her away tomorrow.'

'But how? You won't be able to risk the ordinary steamers?'

'No, they'd be a last resort. I was thinking we could sail privately to the English coast.'

Alice's eyes widened in horror. 'You're surely not planning to use Jack's dinghy, Tina? You could never sail that alone!'

'I can handle it all right, but it's not big enough and there's no cover. Caitlin must be under cover.' Tina's gaze was wary. 'Cavan Morry's *Speedwell* would be much more suitable.'

'You would ask Cavan to help Caitlin?' Alice cried.

'Why not, Mama? It's why I brought her here, so that I could ask him. He's the only person I could trust and there's no real risk for someone like him, so well known and respected. If anyone could get us through, he could.'

'I'm sorry, Tina, it's not possible.'

'You think he'd refuse me? He'd do it for you, Mama, and you'd ask him, wouldn't you, for Cousin Hester's sake? I don't say for Caitlin's.'

'Tina, Cavan isn't here. He and Mavis are in London.'

'In London!' Tina's face was blank.

'Yes, they've gone to see the girls who are doing volunteer nursing, they won't be back for a week or more. And the *Speedwell* has been laid up. For the duration of the war.'

'I see. Well . . .' Tina laughed shortly. 'That's the end of that then, isn't it?'

'What will you do?' Alice asked apprehensively.

'I don't know, Mama. I'm afraid I haven't the faintest idea.'

Chapter Thirty-One

After a sleepless night, Tina rose early and went down to the village to put through a long-distance call to George, but could not reach him. She had to content herself with leaving a message and returned home, feeling strangely alone. It was wonderful, of course, to be back at Belcarron, to have a comfortable bed, good food and fresh clothes, but in the matter of getting Caitlin away to England, she was on her own and had never been more conscious of it.

Charlotte, on the other hand, was relaxing in the atmosphere of her old home like a cat who has been given a place in the sun, wearing a pretty dress of Alice's which she had drawn in at the waist, making plans to have new clothes made, to go round the old haunts, to visit old friends. 'To think I used to find Belcarron boring!' she cried after breakfast. 'Alice, being back here is heaven!'

Alice smiled, but her eyes on Tina were watchful. 'I thought we might go down to the village this morning,' she told Charlotte, 'there are so many changes you should see. What will you do, Tina?'

'I must dress Caitlin's arm, Mama.' Tina stood up. 'Will you excuse me?'

She ran up the stairs, her face burning. How could they sit there, the two of them, making plans to do this, to do that, when no plan at all had been made for getting Caitlin away? She knew she was being unfair to her mother, who was as eaten up by anxiety as she was herself, but her frustration was so intense, she could have screamed. The trip to Belcarron had been a complete and utter waste of time. Caitlin might as well have stayed in Dublin and been arrested there, if Tina could do nothing for her here.

Caitlin seemed better. After the long sleep of yesterday, she said she felt refreshed and ready to go, wherever it was they were going.

'I don't know where we're going,' Tina snapped, as she finished dressing Caitlin's arm. 'All my plans have fallen apart.' She found a fresh blouse and cut out the left sleeve. 'Here, let me help you to get ready.'

'I don't look too bad,' Caitlin observed, studying herself in the mirror, when Tina had helped her into the blouse and one of Melissa's old jackets, and brushed and pinned up her hair. 'Quite respectable enough for the steamer, if that's what we're taking.'

'I had hoped to borrow a yacht, but it's not possible, we'll just have to forget it.' Tina laid a blue cloak that had once been Alice's over the back of a chair. 'That might be useful for concealing your arm.'

'Are we going to risk the steamer?'

'Would you be prepared to do that?'

Caitlin shrugged. 'Seems we don't have much choice.'

'We could still call ourselves the Morry sisters, I've heard they're in London.' Tina had begun packing her case and a small bag for Caitlin. 'I think we may as well leave as soon as possible. Will you stay here while I go down and write a note for Mama? She's gone to the village with Aunt Charlotte and I haven't said goodbye.'

'I'll stay here if you'll let me see the newspaper.'

'There's nothing in the newspaper.' Tina quickly put her hand on Caitlin's. 'Only that all the rebels are now in custody.'

Caitlin's eyes grew dark. 'Except me,' she said, with a sob.

Tina wrote her note and propped it on her mother's desk, then ran down the back stairs to the kitchens. Maisie had taken Agnes to the village for vegetables, but Bridie was at the table, reading the paper and drinking her mid-morning tea.

'Bridie, I'm away,' Tina said, flinging her arms around her. 'Oh, it's been so lovely to see you! Take good care of Mama for me, won't you, while I'm gone?'

'Sure, you're never away already, Miss Tina? Why, 'tis only yesterday you came!'

'I know, but I have to take my cousin to England. Could you possibly cut us some sandwiches? For the journey, you know?'

''Tis a fine picnic I'll be putting up for you, Miss Tina, and that poor stem of a girl up the stairs.' Bridie's eyes were bright on Tina's face. 'You be taking care,' she said slowly. 'I'll be saying no more.'

'I know you understand everything, Bridie, you always do.' Tina kissed her cheek. 'We'll take care all right, don't worry.'

Feeling better now that she had something to do, Tina ran back to the hall, where she picked up the luggage and took it out to the car at the front of the house. Her thoughts were on the eternal worry of petrol, when the sound of approaching footsteps made her turn her head. Then all the blood in her body seemed to freeze. A British army officer was coming up the drive.

It was too late to do anything. Tina could only stand helplessly until he reached her, but her thoughts were racing, racing up to Caitlin, willing her to look out of the window and see him and go. But Caitlin's room faced the sea, not the drive, she would not be able to see him.

'Dr Coxe – Tina – don't you remember me?' The solidly built, broad-faced young man was beaming at her. 'Terence Paget from Cork.'

Jack's friend. Tina felt her blood begin to flow again and she held out her hand. 'Terence! How lovely to see you! Won't you come in?'

'Thanks.' He took off his hat, revealing close-cut ginger hair. 'But whose is that splendid Lancia? Not yours, is it?'

'Only hired, I'm afraid. Do come in, Terence, and let me give you some coffee. I'm afraid Mama is not at home at present. Did you want to see her?'

'Well, I usually call when I get some leave.' He followed her into the hall, where they met Bridie, carrying a picnic basket. 'Morning, Bridie, what's that you've got there? Looks good.'

Bridie, sending a quick glance to Tina, said, 'Sure, 'tis just a few buns. Will I be getting you some coffee, Miss Tina?'

'Please.' Her heart still thumping so loudly she was sure Terence would hear it, Tina took him into the drawing room.

He told her he had driven over that day with his uncle, who

was buying a couple of things in the village and would be along shortly. 'Then we'll be going for a sail,' he finished cheerfully. 'Still prefer Carron to Cork for sailing.'

'Oh, yes, I know you're a great sailor,' Tina said, her eyes thoughtful.

'How about you? You and George still sailing Jack's *Sea Watch*?'

'Yes, except that George isn't with me this time, he couldn't get away.' She leaned forwards, studying Terence's uniform. 'I say, Terence, I see you're a major now - congratulations!'

'So's Victor, isn't he?' He grinned. 'But don't think I'm going sailing togged like this, I'll change before I sail. Trouble is, if a fellow goes around in mufti these days, he's liable to end up with a handful of white feathers.'

'That's shameful. How can women do that sort of thing, when they don't know the facts?' Tina poured the coffee Bridie had brought. 'You'll wait for Mama, won't you, Terence? She won't be long, she's only taken Aunt Charlotte to the village.'

'Aunt Charlotte? I didn't know you had an Aunt Charlotte.'

'She's been away for some time ...' Tina's voice died, the colour drained from her face. Caitlin, wearing Alice's cape, had come into the drawing room.

'I didn't know anyone was here,' she said.

Terence leaped to his feet with another beaming smile. 'Hello, isn't this your cousin, Tina? Miss Molloy?' He advanced towards Caitlin, holding out his hand. 'How are you, Miss Molloy? Terence Paget - we met at Tina's wedding, remember?'

'I remember.' After a moment's hesitation, Caitlin brought out her right hand and shook Terence's. 'You were a friend of Jack's, weren't you?'

'I was, yes, and you're from New York? I seem to remember you gave me quite a lecture on Ireland over the champagne.'

'Caitlin, perhaps you should go back and rest?' Tina asked lightly. 'My cousin hasn't been at all well since she arrived from America, Terence.'

'Oh, but couldn't you at least stay for coffee, Miss Molloy? I'd so much like to talk again.'

'About Ireland?' Caitlin fixed him with a cold stare. 'Some people have done more than talk lately, haven't they?'

'You mean in Dublin? You're right, and I'm afraid those fellows will shortly be paying the price for it.'

'They weren't all fellows.'

'No?' Terence stopped smiling. 'Won't you sit down, Miss Molloy?'

Tina didn't see how it happened, but as Terence placed a chair for Caitlin and tried to help her towards it, he touched her left arm. She gave a thin, piercing scream and backed away, her cape slipping from her shoulder to reveal the sleeve of Melissa's jacket hanging loose. There was a short, appalled silence, then Terence put aside the sleeve and looked at Caitlin's useless, bandaged arm.

'You were right, weren't you?' he asked quietly. 'They weren't all fellows in the Rising.'

'Terence, please let me take my cousin upstairs.' Tina hurriedly replaced Alice's cape around Caitlin, who was still shuddering with pain. 'Please, Terence.'

'I'm sorry, Tina, I don't think I can do that. Would you and your cousin sit down? We must talk.'

'There's nothing to say, you've guessed the situation.'

'Please do as I say.'

At the edge in his voice, Tina helped Caitlin to the chesterfield, where they sat exchanging hard, blue stares with him.

'Miss Molloy was in the Rising. Were you, Tina?'

'No, but I was in Dublin.'

'And you rescued your cousin and brought her back here? What did you think you were playing at?'

'I thought I was doing my duty.'

'Don't you know the authorities will have her name? They'll know of her connections with your family. How could you bring her to Belcarron? To your mother's home?'

'The authorities know my mother is not a nationalist. They won't expect to find Caitlin here. And would you please stop talking over her head, as though she were not here?'

'I've no desire to have him speak to me,' Caitlin said shortly, 'and anything you say to a British army officer will be a complete waste of time, Tina.'

'Tell me what you're planning to do,' Terence said to Tina, ignoring Caitlin.

'I was planning to borrow a yacht, but it wasn't possible.' Tina laughed. 'In fact, when I first saw you and remembered how much you were Jack's friend, I thought you might help us. I thought you might want to help Jack's cousin.'

Terence's freckled face went red. 'Jack's cousin?' he cried. 'I wouldn't help her if she were George the Fifth's cousin! She's been shooting British soldiers.'

'As a matter of fact I haven't,' Caitlin snapped, 'but perhaps I should remind you, it was British soldiers who shot Jack.'

'That was an accident!'

'He shouldn't have been in an Irish crowd, you mean?'

Terence strode to the door. 'Tina, you spoke just now of duty. Well, I'm going to do my duty. I'm going down to the village to inform the RIC that your cousin is here. Don't try to stop me.'

Neither Tina nor Caitlin said a word, but watched from the drawing room as Terence marched down the hall. They could not see the front door from where they were, only knew he must be opening it.

'I'm sorry, Caitlin,' Tina murmured.

'What do you have to be sorry about?' asked Caitlin.

'Why, Terence, there you are!' came Alice's voice, echoing through to them. 'We found your uncle and have brought him back to lunch. Tina, where are you?'

In a moment, they were in the drawing room, Alice, Charlotte and Bill Paget, a serious-faced, middle-aged lawyer from Cork, while Terence stood in the doorway, his face set like stone.

'Caitlin, how nice to see you up!' Alice exclaimed. 'May I introduce Terence's uncle, Mr Paget? Bill, this is my young cousin from New York. My daughter, from London, I believe you know?'

As Bill Paget shook hands and presented Terence to Charlotte, Tina's heart was in her mouth. What would Terence do? Surely his ramrod back and unsmiling expression must be alerting everyone that something was wrong? Caitlin rose from the chesterfield and excused herself. 'I'm so tired, Cousin Alice, would you mind if I went upstairs?'

'Of course not, my dear. Would you like Tina to help you?'

'That would be fine.' With surprising grace, Caitlin bowed

to the company and withdrew, leaning on Tina's arm, while Terence, now very pale, stood in silence.

'Don't forget to come back for a sherry, Tina!' Charlotte called. 'I'm just ringing the bell.'

Tina smiled and carefully closed the drawing room door behind her.

'Mrs Wintour, I'm afraid I can't stay,' Terence said urgently, 'I am required – I have something to report.'

'Oh, come, Terence, I've hardly seen you! I know you want a sail, but there's lots of time for that and we haven't talked at all. Sit down and tell me about your sister. How is her baby?'

Terence, after hesitating a moment, sat down staring at the closed drawing room door, but in a moment was up again, hurrying to the window, which in fact showed no view of Tina's car.

'What's the matter with you?' asked Bill. 'You're jumping round like a cat on hot bricks!'

Terence glanced back at Alice, who was taking a glass from the tray of drinks brought in by Bridie. She raised it to him with a smile, as Charlotte came up and took his arm.

'You're surely not thinking of leaving before lunch, my dear boy? You're on leave, aren't you? What can be so urgent that you must miss our good Irish beef?'

'Always so restless, these young people,' Bill murmured, looking from Terence to Charlotte. 'Can't seem to settle for five minutes!'

'I sympathise, I've always been so restless myself,' Charlotte was beginning, when Terence suddenly jerked his arm from her hand and went leaping for the door.

'Will you excuse me?' he cried, over his shoulder.

'Terence!' Bill roared after him, but Terence ignored him, taking the stairs two at a time and racing along the upstairs landing. Agnes, carrying towels, shrank back as he went past her.

'Which is Miss Molloy's room?' he called to her. 'Show me now where it is!'

'Sure, it's here, sir.'

She flung open a door, watching apprehensively as he stormed in and immediately out again, crying, 'Oh God, I'm too late!' and ran back down the stairs. Bridie was crossing the hall and he caught her roughly by the arm.

'Where are they, Bridie? Where are Miss Tina and her cousin?'

'Didn't they go down the back stairs five minutes ago?' she answered coolly. 'And it's my arm you are hurting, Major Paget.'

'Terence, will you explain yourself?' his uncle shouted. 'What's this all about?'

'I'll show you!' Terence answered, flinging open the front door. Alice, Charlotte and Bill watched with him as Tina's handsome Lancia disappeared down the drive.

'It's no good,' said Terence, breathing hard, 'they won't get away, you know, they were foolish to try.'

'Get away? Get away from what?' asked Bill.

No one answered him. Terence found his hat and put it on. Beneath its brim, his stern, righteous face was the face of a stranger.

'Mrs Wintour, I'm sorry, but there's nothing I can do. I must find a telephone. There isn't one here, I believe?'

She shook her head, and with a brief nod, he left them, marching smartly, as though he were on parade.

'Wait! Wait for me!' Charlotte was running after him, the May Day sunshine catching her yellow hair, as Bill, even in that time of stress, couldn't help noticing. Terence turned, in exasperation.

'What is it, ma'am? I can't stop, every minute counts.'

She caught his arm. 'Major Paget – Terence – do you really want my niece and her cousin to go to prison?'

'Tina knows what she's doing. If she wants to risk prison to assist a rebel, that's her decision. It's my duty to see that the law is not flouted. Now if you will excuse me –'

Charlotte still kept her hand on his arm, her narrow eyes holding his. 'Don't you think Jack's mother has suffered enough?' she asked softly.

He was silent.

'What good will it do, if they do go to prison? Tina will be prevented from doing her work. Caitlin will come out no better than when she went in. The people who will really suffer will be my sister and my cousin, Caitlin's mother.'

'It's not the point who suffers, Frau von Eberbach –'

'Oh, no, it's the principle of the thing, isn't it? I've always hated principles.' She released his arm. 'Well, do what you think best, Major Paget.'

'I will,' he said, hesitating, as she began to walk back towards the house, 'it's my decision.'

Chapter Thirty-Two

By evening, Tina and Caitlin were back in Cork, still free. They left the Lancia with Sean Heenan, with money to drive it back to Dublin, and took a taxi to Penrose Quay, one of the many quays on the river that circled the centre of the city. Tina had found from a timetable that the City of Cork Steam Packet Company had a boat that night leaving for Fishguard on the Welsh coast, and they bought two tickets. Neither spoke of the chances of being stopped by the RIC, now so high they could scarcely hope they wouldn't be, but took some satisfaction in knowing they were at least battling to the end. The authorities would be looking for two women travelling together; therefore they had decided, if Caitlin could manage it, to separate until after their arrival in Fishguard, always supposing they got as far as that. Tina, with her wedding ring in her purse, would be Miss Daisy Morry, and as they could not both be Morry girls if they were not to travel together, Caitlin would be Miss Cecily Lister. Her Dorset cousin's name, Tina remarked, sounded very English, very respectable, at which Caitlin gave an exasperated sigh.

They looked at each other in the lights of the quay, as they waited to embark on the *Herald of Cork*.

'You think you can do it, Caitlin?' asked Tina.

'Sure I can.'

'You're not in too much pain?'

'The stuff you gave me worked like a charm.'

'This is the last hurdle. If we get on board, I think we'll be all right.'

'They could be waiting for us at the other end.'

'I know, but it's less likely.' Tina handed over Caitlin's bag, which contained some of the huge picnic Bridie had put up, so that Caitlin need not struggle with a meal in public. 'I wish we could have got you a cabin.'

'I'll be fine, don't worry.'

'I'll wave to you in the saloon, then.' Tina swallowed and turned to look at the waiting steamer. 'There are police there, I can see them. I'll go first and if they stop me, you leave at once, you understand?'

'Agreed, but if they stop me and you're on board, you don't come back, there'd be no point.'

'Caitlin, I couldn't sail without you!'

'You're needed in London.' Caitlin's gaze was fierce. 'Don't come back, Tina, I mean it.'

Outwardly calm, inwardly in turmoil, Tina moved to the gangway and presented her ticket to the official of the company. Next to him, two RIC men - large, burly, fresh-faced men - were standing together. Their eyes went over her without interest. The official nodded, gave her back her ticket, and she walked on to the boat, her legs and hands trembling as though she had a fever.There was a crush of people around her, she longed to get away, to breathe, but she could not go below, she must wait to see Caitlin aboard.

So many bad moments in the past few days, but this must surely be one of the worst. The light was poor, making all the faces below look greenish, like faces in a nightmare. Caitlin's, hidden beneath the large, black hat Tina had lent her, could scarcely be seen at all. As her cousin's caped figure approached the gangway, Tina leaned forwards, straining her eyes, then drew back in terror as Caitlin seemed to stumble and one of the RIC men put out his hand. Oh, God, if he touched her arm! But Caitlin steadied herself and the man's hand dropped. She set down her bag and with her right hand held out her ticket. The official said something to her. She replied. The RIC men appeared to be staring at her, perhaps wondering why on this mild night she was enveloped in a long, thick cape. Sweat was breaking out on Tina's brow, and for a second or two, she closed her eyes. When she opened them again, Caitlin was coming towards her. She had got through.

Half-remembered prayers of thanksgiving went through Tina's mind as Caitlin passed her, her face expressionless, and went on down to the saloon. Terence hadn't turned them in, then? That was the only explanation; he had remembered Jack, or Mama, and he had not turned them in – oh, thank God, thank God! They were, of course, not safe yet. As Caitlin had said, they could be stopped on arrival at Fishguard, but Tina was now wonderfully confident that they wouldn't be. Giving herself up to elation, she took long breaths of the salty, oily air. As the steamer began to glide from the quay, to the accompaniment of its hooter and all the various knockings, clankings and mysterious noises a boat can make, she went below.

Sitting up in the dimly lit saloon, a leather cushion at her back, her medical bag on her knee, Tina passed a long night. The sea was calm, its motion only enough to lull people to sleep, but she could not sleep. Her thoughts were a merry-go-round, lurching her through the past few days, taking her in and out of Dublin, Cork and Belcarron, sending her driving again on all the potholed country roads, on and on, on and on. Her eyelids drooped, closed, and opened again, and she sat up with a start, looking down at the saloon to Caitlin, sitting wrapped in her cloak, her hat in her hand, her head sunk on her chest. How pale she was! Her wound should have been dressed, but Tina could do that tomorrow, if all went well, before they caught the train to Paddington. She must also telephone George, but at the thought of George her conscience stabbed and she moved uneasily in her seat. She had put him through the mill, it couldn't be denied, and all in the name of this strange duty to Caitlin and Ireland. Maybe her first duty should have been to him. He had wanted her to go back home as soon as the Rising started and she had not done that, she had taken her own way, confident as usual that she was in the right. Oh, George! Had she failed him? No, she truly believed she had not, she had done what she had to do, and he would understand. As soon as they were together again, he would understand. But would they be together again? In the watches of the night, the elation she had felt at first, coming aboard, faded.

Morning brought cold light, people stirring, stewards

moving. 'Had a good night, sir? Not too bad, was it? Taking breakfast, madam? Soon be in, now.'

Tina sat up, rubbing her eyes. So she had slept, after all; she didn't feel as though she had. There was a large, heavy feeling pressing on her spirit. For a moment she couldn't think what it was, then it came back to her. Fishguard. They would be coming in soon. Would there be anyone waiting? Her eyes went down the the saloon again for Caitlin, but she was not in her place. Probably in the washroom, or maybe up on deck. Tina picked up her bags. She'd better find her, not to speak to her, of course, just to check that she was all right.

There were so many people about, it seemed impossible to find her. Several times, Tina thought she saw her in the distance, a young woman in blue, a white face under a black hat, but when she came close, it was never Caitlin. She snatched a cup of coffee and a roll and went up on deck, where the air was still cold and a mist was wreathing the Welsh coast and rolling round the passengers. Figures covered in moisture loomed in and out of view, but none was Caitlin. Tina, shivering in her ulster raincoat, walked the deck. This would be the place to wait, this was where Caitlin must come. Suddenly Tina saw her, standing quietly at the rail. As though she sensed Tina's presence, she turned and their eyes met. Then the mist swallowed her and Tina stepped back.

By the time the steamer came in, the mist had gone and a pale sunlight showed British police mingling with the people waiting below. Tina's heart began to thud but she straightened her back and put up her chin, keeping her eyes fixed on the passengers moving down the gangway. A black hat, a blue cape, there was Caitlin, walking well, not stumbling this time. She reached the quay and hesitated. A policeman was close, he was looking at her, he was calling a colleague. Tina leaned against the rail. But Caitlin was moving again, the policeman talking to his colleague could not be talking about her, she was keeping going, not looking back, she was lost in the crowd. For long moments, Tina stood watching the quay where she had been. It seemed too good to be true. No one had stopped her.

Nor did anyone stop Tina. No hand was laid on her shoulder, no voice said, 'Dr Ernestine Coxe? May we have a word?'

They had done it. After the nightmare of anxiety and fear, they had walked off the boat and no one had stopped them. All they had to do now was to catch the train.

They had arranged to meet in the ladies' waiting room on the station platform, and Tina, her spirits soaring, made her way there on wings. Caitlin wasn't there, but that was no surprise. With so many people pouring off the steamer, she would be going carefully, not wanting to risk any more damage to her arm. From the window of the waiting room, Tina looked out, watching a train for Paddington pulling away. It didn't matter about missing it, there would be plenty more and anyway she had first to telephone George.

The minutes ticked by; women came and went, banging the door, and every time Tina thought one of them would be Caitlin. She really was late, wasn't she? A little cold hand began to clutch at Tina's heart. Had they caught her, after all?

A porter's head came round the door and a Welsh voice called, 'Any lady here, name of Morry?'

'I'm Miss Morry,' said Tina, turning pale.

'Lady asked me to give you this, miss.' He put an envelope into her hand and she gave him a coin. He touched his cap and left her and she opened the letter.

It was written on ship's notepaper. Caitlin must have obtained it from the steward while Tina slept.

> My dear Tina,
> I have decided, if we get as far as Fishguard, not to go with you to London. You have risked enough for me, I don't want you to risk any more. I know people in England who will look after me and see that my arm is fixed if it needs it, though it seems fine to me. I have a little money – I borrowed some from Bridie. Tell her I'll be sure to pay it back. Tina, you know there's nothing I can say to thank you, but I am saying thank you, anyway. I'm sorry I won't be in touch for a while, guess it's better you don't know where I am. No names, remember? Give my best wishes to George.
> All my love,
> Caitlin.

Tina folded the letter and put it in her bag. She felt very tired, as though all the tiredness she had been putting aside for so long had suddenly taken shape and knocked the breath out of her. A train came steaming in to the platform outside and she remembered the one she had seen pulling out.

'Goodbye, Caitlin,' she said flatly, and went out to find a telephone, to ring up George.

Chapter Thirty-Three

'For Caitlin,' Paul whispered, as he placed a lighted candle at the statue of the Virgin in St Stephen's Church. He crossed himself and returned to his pew, to kneel in a prayer of thanksgiving for his sister's safety. It was a weekday, the congregation waiting for the Mass to begin was sparse, but somewhere in it would be his parents, come like him to offer up prayers for Caitlin and for the souls of the men executed after the Easter Rising. All the leaders had been shot, even James Connolly, who could not stand and had been shot seated in a chair; only Countess Markievicz had been spared and she had been sentenced to penal servitude for life. Paul groaned inwardly at the foolishness of it all, at the disregard for life displayed by the rebels and authority alike. The rebels had gained nothing, the government had gained nothing, Ireland was once again plunged into sorrow and there seemed no way out, no light yet at the end of the tunnel.

At least, Caitlin was safe. Clan-na-Gael had its channels and had been able to confirm that she was not among those taken prisoner. Then had come her cable, sent, for the sake of security, to an old school friend, saying she was well and they need not worry. Thank God for that, for the weight lifted from all their hearts, though the fury which had consumed Daniel since the news of the executions had not abated. As soon as Mass was over, he would be off somewhere with his friends, discussing ways of making the English prime minister see reason before the whole of Ireland went up like a tinderbox. But I shall speak to Papa first, thought Paul, rising as the priest came out to celebrate Mass. Across the aisle, he suddenly caught sight of his mother's face, smiling at him, then she looked down at her prayer book and he too looked away.

The Mass progressed and ended. As the priest left the altar and the congregation filed out, Hester and Daniel waited to speak to Paul.

He had moved up to the altar rail where a little while before he had taken Communion. He could still taste the wafer on his tongue as he raised his eyes to the figure of Christ and made his special prayer. Not because he needed guidance or reassurance. He was certain now what he wanted to do.

'Paul, will you come back to breakfast?' Hester asked, taking his arm. When he said he would, her face lit up with delighted surprise, but Daniel growled, 'Come on, then, 'tis not all day we've got. I've things to do.'

'Taking your pills, for a start,' Hester told him. 'You know your blood pressure is up.'

He refused to answer, but strode ahead of them, his shoulders bowed, his head, more grey than black, thrust pugnaciously forwards.

'He's so relieved about Caitlin,' Hester whispered to Paul, 'but of course at a time like this, we mustn't think only of ourselves.'

'All the same, it's wonderful that she hasn't ended up in an English prison,' said Paul. 'How she escaped is a mystery.'

'I know. Consider the poor Countess – penal servitude for life! And she a Gore Booth.'

'That won't do her much good in Holloway, or wherever they send her.'

'She wouldn't want it to.' Hester shook her head. 'But why get involved in violence, a lady such as she? They say she marched like a soldier, draped in guns and ammunition. Do you suppose Caitlin went around like that?'

'Mother, Caitlin's safe, that's all we need think about at the moment. Let's eat breakfast and give thanks.'

But no one ate much breakfast. They drank coffee and crumbled rolls, but Daniel's thoughts were too dark for him to care about food and Hester was still too much on edge, still too wrought up over the whole situation, even though Caitlin was safe. As for Paul, he had a secret on his mind which he knew he must disclose.

'That's it, then,' said Daniel, rising and pushing back his chair. 'I'm away, Hester, and when I'll be back, I cannot be saying. Goodbye, Paul.'

'Wait a bit, Papa.' Paul, too, had pushed back his chair. 'If you could just spare me a moment –'

Daniel glanced at the clock, shrugged and sat down. 'Now, if it's to do with the bookshops –'

'It's not to do with the bookshops – when have you ever been involved with the bookshops?' Paul could sense his mother's gaze on him as he looked at Daniel. 'The fact is, I want you to know – want both of you to know – I am thinking of going into the Church.'

Hester set down her cup with a crash. Her face was white, but Daniel's was scarlet. His blue eyes wide, he was looking at Paul as though he had never seen him before, and to Paul's embarrassment, large tears suddenly formed and jerked their way down his father's face.

'Paul –' He came round the table, taking Paul's hands in his own. 'Is it the truth you are telling me? I never in this world thought to hear you speak such words. Oh, I'm not believing it, I can't be believing it. Paul, are you telling me you have the call?'

'I am. I wish to become a priest.'

'Oh, Hester, are you hearing this?' Daniel turned to her, still holding Paul's hands, his face wreathed in smiles so rare, they made him seem a different man. ''Tis just like my poor sister used to say, he'll be a cardinal, so he will!' Daniel released Paul's hands in order to cross himself. 'Paul, I am thanking God I have lived to see this day.'

'What do you say, Mother?' Paul asked, turning to her. 'You're very quiet.'

'I don't know what to say,' she answered simply. 'I had no idea anything like this was on your mind.'

'It's been in my thoughts for some time.'

'And you never said anything?'

'I wanted to be sure.'

Daniel, still smiling to himself, was prowling the room as though he would never settle again, and Hester, watching, longed for him to go. She wanted to talk to Paul, alone.

'Ah, we've been in the Vale of Tears,' Daniel cried, his face darkening, 'and still are, don't be thinking I'm forgetting it, but to be hearing something like this –' he shot a new smile at Paul – ''tis a ray of sunshine, so it is, and I can't be waiting to tell the world! Now will you shake my hand, Paul, before I'm away?'

Paul, still embarrassed, shook his father's hand. 'I'm not going to be a cardinal, Papa, or even a monsignor, just an ordinary priest, there's no need to shout it from the housetops.'

'An ordinary priest, is it?' cried Daniel. 'No need to shout it from the housetops? 'Tis not what I'm thinking, Paul, no, indeed, 'tis a miracle, and I'm giving thanks to God for it. Now, I'll be leaving you – Hester, maybe I'll be telephoning. Paul, you've made me a happy man, so you have.' He grasped Paul's hand again and, with his eyes still full of tears, tore himself away.

'Phew!' Paul gasped. 'I think I'll take some more coffee, Mother, if there's any in the pot.'

'Paul, we must talk.' Hester poured the coffee and watched him as he drank it. 'I can see you're serious about this, but I'm not sure you're doing the right thing. You've been badly hurt over Melissa –'

'This has nothing to do with Melissa. I got over my feelings for her long ago. I realise now that they were never real, anyway, not in the way my vocation is real.' Paul looked closely into Hester's face. 'Aren't you happy about it? Even if it's what I want?'

'It's a shock, Paul. You talk of your vocation, but you always used to say you had none.'

'Maybe I hadn't then, but even before I met Melissa, I sometimes felt the Church might be for me. Then, when she seemed to want me, I guess I went a bit crazy. Couldn't believe my luck.'

'You took it hard enough when she gave you up.'

He shrugged. 'That sort of feeling doesn't last. When I heard she was dating Tim Leifson, I assure you I didn't feel a qualm. When she announces her engagement, I'll probably send her flowers.'

'I'm glad to hear it.' Hester stood up. 'But this new decision of yours will have consequences for me, you know.'

'You mean the bookshops? I'm sorry, Mother, I really am. You've worked so hard to build up the chain, I know you always thought I'd take it on.'

'It's not just the bookshops.' She gave a wry smile. 'There'll be no grandchildren.'

He laughed, colouring a little. 'Why, there's Caitlin, isn't there? She's sure to get married one day.'

'Is she?' Hester moved to the window and stood looking out. 'I shall have to hope so. Paul, I'm sorry, but I just can't understand why Catholic priests have to be celibate. My father was a man of God, yet he married and had a family and I don't think he served God any the worse for it.'

'I'm sure you've every right to think that, only the Catholic Church thinks differently and I have to do what they want of me.'

Hester turned round to look at him. 'You've quite made up your mind, haven't you? So, what do you do now? Apply to some seminary?'

'Unless America enters the war. Then I'd enlist.'

'Paul, please don't talk of it. Isn't there enough suffering –'

'It's a question of what we ought to do. Oh, look –' He went to her and put his arm around her shoulders. 'It may never happen, let's think of the good things. Caitlin's safe, Papa is happy –'

She ran her fingers down his cheek and smiled. 'You're so like my father,' she murmured, 'he was always trying to see the bright side.'

'Isn't it the case, though, that Ireland defeated him? He had to go and live in England.'

'That's true, but he was a good man, Paul. There is always a certain goodness in the Wintours.'

'In some of the Wintours.'

'My father, you and Jack.'

'And you, Mother,' Paul said quietly.

'Oh, no, no, not specially in me, Paul.'

'Specially in you.' He nodded. 'Yes, we all know it. Papa too.'

'Oh –' Hester turned away, embarrassed. 'Come, we should be at the office.'

'I'm on my way now.'

'I'll join you later.' As Paul moved to the door, Hester called his name and he stopped. 'Paul, thank you for making your father so happy. It's not the right thing to say, I'm sure, when a son announces his vocation, but it does mean so much to me to see your father smile.'

Paul smiled himself and waved his hand in salute.

He took the elevator down and was leaving the apartment block, feeling relieved he had at last broken his news to his mother, when he saw a young woman getting out of a taxi and stood transfixed. It was Melissa.

'Paul!' She was looking very lovely, in a softly tailored green suit with a matching beret pulled over her bright hair. On the hand that held her gloves, he saw the flash of an enormous diamond.

'Hello, Melissa,' he said casually. 'Were you on your way to see Mother?'

'I – yes, I was hoping to see Cousin Hester.'

'And didn't expect to see me? Sorry about that, but I'm just leaving.'

'I'm very happy to see you, Paul, I guess it's you who's not happy to see me.' Melissa was having difficulty looking him in the eyes. 'The thing is, I have some news of Caitlin. From Tina.'

'From Tina? That's wonderful.' Paul lowered his voice. 'We know she's safe, but that's all we know. Look, why don't I buy you a cup of coffee and you tell me what you have?'

'I'd like that,' she said with some relief, preferring to feel guilty with him, he guessed, rather than with his mother. Not that she needed to feel guilty at all.

Over the coffee, in the nearest soda fountain, Melissa showed him Tina's letter. 'I guess she wrote to me rather than your parents because she thought it might be safer. Letters are censored these days, aren't they?'

'Yes, but this would defeat any censor. There isn't a name on it.'

'Well, but you can figure it out, can't you? You see she says a friend has been hurt –'

'Hurt?' Paul repeated. 'We didn't know that.'

'But is now safe.'

'And it's not possible to say where, but there's no need to worry.' Paul raised his eyes from the letter. 'Do you suppose it was Tina who got her away?'

'I'll bet she did. She could always pull anyone out of anything.'

'Yes, she's strong. I saw that when she first stayed with us and we tried to bully her into working for Ireland. She said she'd make up her own mind and I guess she did.'

'I'm sure she wasn't involved in the Rising, she doesn't believe in that kind of violence.'

'No, she'd just be around to pick up the pieces.'

'Like you, Paul.'

'I'm not sure about that. I'm against the use of force wherever possible, but some wars have to be fought. Wilson seems to have kept us out of the German war so far, but if it comes to it, I shall go.'

Melissa shivered. 'Don't let's talk of the war. You didn't read the last page of Tina's letter. There's a name mentioned there.'

'Is there? Whose?'

'Aunt Charlotte's. She's come back to Belcarron.'

'Cousin Charlotte?' Paul gave a reminiscent smile. 'The lady with the violets ... Ah, what trouble she caused me, didn't she?'

'You mean, if I'd never worn that hat –' Melissa stopped, her colour rising. 'I'm sure I don't know why you say that.'

'You mean, I'd have fallen for you anyway? Of course I would, but that's all water under the bridge now, isn't it?' Paul stared down at the diamond on Melissa's finger which was sending out great flashes of fire. 'I see you're engaged, we must have missed the announcement. Who's the lucky man?'

'Tim Leifson, and you don't really think he's lucky, do you?'

'Of course I do. I can still say that, Melissa, even if I'm not still in love with you myself.'

'I see,' said Melissa, stirring her coffee. 'If you've found someone else, I'm very pleased for you.'

'Someone else? Not exactly.' Paul leaned forwards. 'The truth is, I've made up my mind to become a priest.'

She looked at him in horror. 'Oh, Paul, no! Oh, how can you? Become a Catholic priest? You won't be able to marry, have a family –'

'I'll have something better.'

'No, no, you mustn't do this!' She grasped his hand across the table. 'Oh, please, Paul, change your mind. It would be such a terrible mistake!'

He looked at her lovely face, her pleading green eyes, her trembling lips, and he knew that for him the mistake would have been to marry her. She was beautiful, she was talented, she would make Tim Leifson very happy, but he himself had grown away.

'Don't be sad for me,' he told her gently. 'I'm very happy. I've found what I wanted, and so have you. We're both happy, aren't we?'

When he put her into a taxi, he kissed her lightly on the cheek and smiled at her, but her eyes were still sorrowful.

'I didn't see Cousin Hester, after all – will you give her Tina's message?'

'Of course I will, and thank you for coming. We appreciate it.'

'You'll keep in touch, Paul? Promise?'

'I'll keep in touch.'

A white lie, he confessed to himself, as she was driven away at speed; he had no real desire to keep in touch with Melissa. He took a streetcar to the downtown office, his thoughts moving to Caitlin. Should he tell his parents she had been hurt? Tina had said there was no need to worry; Caitlin herself had said there was no need to worry. He wished to God she could come home. How long would this war go on? There was an uneasy quietness between the United States and Germany, but he couldn't see it lasting. He decided he would try to get accepted by a seminary as soon as possible, so that he could get some training in before he had to enlist.

Chapter Thirty-Four

The war years rolled on.

In September 1916, during the capture of Ginchy on the Somme, Victor was badly injured in the leg and told he would spend the rest of his service at the War Office. 'Which means I can't look my ghosts in the eye,' he told Alice, on his first leave from hospital in England.

'Ghosts?' she repeated, troubled. The remark seemed so out of character for Victor. Yet, she knew what it was like to face ghosts. 'Perhaps it's worse to face the living,' she murmured, thinking of Bill Paget. Terence had been killed in July.

'He never gave you away,' she whispered to Tina, after the memorial service for Terence in Cork. 'Charlotte said he thought of me, but I don't think he'd have done it, anyway.'

'Nor do I,' Tina replied.

'Do you ever hear from Caitlin?' Alice asked.

'No.' Caitlin was lying low, but Tina no longer worried about Caitlin. Her thoughts were with George, who had finally got what he wanted and was serving in a field hospital in France. The Morry girls were somewhere in France, too, working with an ambulance unit, while Hugh, in the navy, was still miraculously safe.

As he had said he would, Paul enlisted when the United States entered the war in April 1917. Hester was devastated, she had prayed so hard. Yet why should she expect God to answer her prayers? News came of Marianne's Freddie, lost at Vimy Ridge; there seemed no point in praying at all. Perhaps there is a pattern and we can't see it, thought Hester. She did not give up praying.

Melissa, as Mrs Timothy Leifson, prayed, too. She and Tim had married at Westchester on his first leave and, though she would have preferred a wedding at Belcarron, what did it matter, after all, where one was married? Alice, who had always pictured Melissa coming down the aisle of St John's on the arm of someone right, didn't spend any time regretting the old daydreams. She wrote at once to Melissa, telling her, 'all that matters is your happiness, everyone sends their love and congratulations, and prayers for Tim's safe return. Come back to us when the war is over.'

People who did come back, but not from the war, were those prisoners taken after the Easter rising. A general amnesty in June allowed Countess Markievicz and Frances Tarry, among others, to return to a triumphant welcome, after which Frances opened up her lodging house again and Caitlin, surfacing at last, came back and took possession of her old room. 'Can you believe it?' she exclaimed, 'my passport and all my things are still here? I feel I've never been away.'

'You've been away,' Frances replied solemnly. 'So have we all, but now we're back and what we're going to do is pick up where we left off. Connolly and the rest won't be allowed to have died in vain.'

Caitlin, opening accumulated mail, fervently agreed, but her face darkened as she read in a letter from Paul that he had enlisted. 'Oh, the fool!' she groaned. 'Why did he have to go and risk himself for the British?'

'Perhaps it'll all be over by the time he gets there,' Frances suggested.

It was not over. When the American troops arrived in Europe in January 1918, nothing had changed. Offensives and counter offensives were continuing their seesaw, there seemed no reason why they should ever end. Yet gradually as the year wore on, it became apparent that Germany and its allies were failing. A British blockade was weakening central Europe, the countries of the eastern sector were on the brink of defeat, Austria-Hungary, Germany's great partner, wanted peace. In October, President Wilson of the United States was invited to work out a peace plan, and on the morning of November 11, the unbelievable happened – the Armistice was signed. The worst war in the history of the world was over.

For the first Christmas of the peace, Alice decided she would like as many as possible of the family to come to Belcarron. Charlotte, Victor, Evie and Rickie were already there, of course, and Paul, who was not yet demobilised, promised to come over from his American army base. Tina and George would come from London, but though the Atlantic was safe again, Hester said she would not leave Daniel, whose health was still an anxiety. Melissa also wrote that she would not be able to make the trip; the Leifsons were planning a grand welcome-home party for Tim; she did hope Mama would understand. They would definitely be over in the spring, that was a promise, unless, of course, Mama would come to them, which would be just perfect!

'I have absolutely no intention of going to America,' Alice declared. 'Melissa knows Belcarron is waiting, she can come here.'

'Quite right,' Charlotte agreed, 'and she should come soon, before she starts a family.'

'I'm not sure Melissa will have a family,' Alice said gloomily. 'She's a career woman, you know, like Tina.'

'I'm sure the Leifsons will expect an heir to all that lovely money, Alice! Anyway, you have dear Rickie, remember.'

'My greatest comfort,' Alice sighed. 'But Charlotte, give me your advice. Should I invite Caitlin? Paul is coming and she is Hester's daughter, after all.'

Charlotte made a face. 'She's as prickly as a porcupine, I can't see her enjoying Christmas with us.'

'I could ask her, and she might refuse?'

'And then your conscience would be clear. Ask her, then, and we'll hope for the best.'

Caitlin did refuse, with a polite note saying she appreciated the invitation, but she would probably be spending Christmas in England. They were puzzled at first, until Tina reminded them that Countess Markievicz was back in Holloway prison again, having been arrested during fights over conscription for the Irish earlier in the year. Rather astonishingly, she had been returned as Member of Parliament for St Patrick's in Dublin, in the December election; no doubt, Caitlin was going over to visit her to celebrate her triumph.

'The first woman MP, but still in prison,' drawled Charlotte, 'that does seem a shame. At least, Caitlin wasn't arrested too. Why you ever got yourself involved with her, Tina, I can't imagine.'

'It's all in the past, Aunt Charlotte, let's not discuss it.'

'As you wish,' said Charlotte, mildly. 'Did I tell you that Bill's agreed to join us for Christmas?'

'That's no surprise,' said Tina. Now that Bill had lost Terence, whose parents and aunt had been dead for some years, Bill's only relative was his niece Barbara. She would certainly have invited him for Christmas, but if Charlotte was to spend Christmas in Belcarron, everyone knew Bill too would spend Christmas at Belcarron.

'Why don't you marry him, Aunt Charlotte?' Tina asked bluntly, but Charlotte only laughed and said she'd had enough of marrying.

Alice had been hoping that Marianne and Everard would come over from Dorset with Cecily, but was not really surprised when Marianne wrote that they would be having a quiet Christmas at home. Everard was not up to taking many services now, but he wanted specially to preach the sermon on Christmas Day, Marianne hoped Alice would understand.

'Of course I understand,' Alice murmured, folding Marianne's letter at the breakfast table. 'Poor Marianne.'

'Poor Freddie, you mean,' Victor said shortly. 'Why the hell we didn't turn the guns on the top brass is beyond me.'

'Victor!' Evie murmured, glancing quickly at Alice.

'You object to my saying hell? I do apologise. Some of us went there, you know, and some of us didn't come back.' He stood up, threw down his table napkin and limped from the room, slamming the dining-room door behind him.

'Evie, it's best not to upset him,' Alice murmured. 'Victor hasn't really recovered yet.'

'I was only thinking of you!' Evie cried, leaping up. 'I don't care what he says, I'm just so glad to have him home!' She too left the room, slamming the door behind her.

'Oh, dear,' said Charlotte. 'I think I'll ring for Bridie to clear.'

Alice's eyes went from Tina to George. 'I know Victor's leg

will never be better than it is, it's not that that worries me –'

'What does worry you?' George asked gently.

'Well, Victor's been so tetchy and irritable since he came back, and sometimes he talks so strangely – I mean, he'd never have said that about the top brass in the old days, would he?'

'Wanting to blow up the top brass doesn't seem so irrational to me, after what Victor's been through. If you're thinking about shell shock, I can assure you there's nothing of that sort wrong with him. He's just taking time to adjust, that's all, as we all are.'

'Yes, of course.' Alice smiled. 'Oh, I'm like Evie, you know, I'm just so glad to have him home.'

'Let's go and get the holly this morning,' Tina cried, after a pause. 'Let's have the whole place looking really Christmassy before Paul arrives!'

'Paul,' Charlotte murmured. 'I'm so looking forward to seeing him again. He was such a dear little boy.'

'You know he still intends to become a priest?'

'What a waste!' said Charlotte.

It was Christmas Eve before Paul arrived. Charlotte, descending the stairs as Bridie let him in, stood very still when she saw the tall, yellow-haired man shaking moisture from his coat, handing Bridie his hat. As when she had met Victor, a stabbing recognition of likeness to Richard rushed over her, the same sickening memory of the past rose up to confront her all over again. Then she saw that this man was more like her uncle Matthew or the photographs of Jack. He had the Wintour features, the Wintour hair, but a certain sweetness of expression that was not Victor's and had not been Richard's. He had not changed, Paul Molloy, he had the same old-fashioned charm he had had at three, after all these years of growing up.

'Paul, do you remember me?' she called.

He turned and, in the dim light of the hall, saw a slim woman in a green silk dress moving towards him, her hair still yellow, still plentiful, her eyes a sparkling green that matched her dress.

'Cousin Charlotte,' he whispered, 'ah, now where are the violets?'

'You don't really remember me, do you? It's quite impossible, you were only a tiny boy when we last met.'

'I remember you, I always have. Do you know, you haven't changed at all?'

'Didn't I always say you were a charmer?' She laughed delightedly. 'Come, let's join the others in the drawing room.'

It was an amazing scene – the long elegant room decked with evergreens and streamers, the glittering tree with its candles, the log fire burning in the hearth – the sort of scene men at the front had dreamed about, which no one believed could exist any more, except in memory. Yet here it was, waiting for him, and if Paul knew that behind the charm lay death and suffering, he was ready enough not to think beyond the fact that he was alive and so were they, all these members of his family who came up to greet him now. Alice, charming in lavender and white; Tina, beautiful because she was happy; George, stout and at ease, smoking a cigar; Evie, holding Rickie's hand; Victor, handsome as ever, no sign of the pain he felt every day of his life, leaning on his stick. And Charlotte, beside him, more lined than she had seemed in the shadowy hall, but still as attractive as he remembered her, he had been telling only the truth about that.

A middle-aged man who seemed vaguely familiar came up to shake Paul's hand.

'You know Bill Paget?' asked Charlotte. 'His nephew was a friend of Jack's.'

'I remember,' said Paul, and at the thought of Jack found his eyes filling with tears.

But no one minded tears that first peace-time Christmas. When Victor made the toast at the Christmas dinner the next day, 'to absent friends, to those we have lost', it seemed natural to everyone that their ghosts should be with them and they should weep for them.

It was two days after Christmas. People were sitting about, lazily making plans to go walking, though a fine rain was falling and the afternoon was dark. Victor, nursing the handle of his stick, said he and Evie must be thinking about packing. They had a passage booked for Buenos Aires, they would be sailing in a few days' time.

Alice, who had been adjusting holly on the chimneypiece, swung round.

'What did you say, Victor?'

'I said we should be doing our packing, Mother.'

'Because you're returning to Buenos Aires?' Her voice trembled. 'Why didn't you tell me this before?'

'You knew we'd be going back some time, it was no secret.'

'Why should you go back? I thought you would be staying here, at Belcarron.'

'You know that's impossible, Mother.' Victor's expression was settling into obstinate lines. 'My work is on the *estancia*. That's where I'm needed.'

'You think you're not needed here? With Jack gone?'

Victor stood up, letting his stick fall to the floor. He retrieved it and limped towards his mother. 'I'm sorry, I truly am, but I can't be in two places at once and there's nothing much left here now, is there? What there is, you can run yourself, you don't need me.'

'Victor, how can you be so cruel?' cried Tina, leaping to her feet. 'Would you leave Mother here on her own?'

'I don't notice you volunteering to give up your work in London.'

'I'm not the heir to Belcarron!'

Victor lowered his eyes. 'All right, I stand to inherit Belcarron, what's left of it, but that won't be for many years yet and in the meantime, Julio Castillo has married a Sentos – a Sentos, if you please – and is doing God knows what on the *estancia*. I have to go back, I have to see what is happening, surely you can see that?'

'Calm down, Victor,' George said quietly. 'As far as we know, nothing is going wrong on the *estancia*. Profits are being made as usual, no one appears to be suffering financially. As for Julio's marriage, the girl can't help what her uncle did, can she?'

'No, but Julio needn't have married her. Mother, you were upset at the time, weren't you? You must be thinking he's not to be trusted?'

Alice took her chair by the fire. 'I was upset, of course, but it's true what George says, Sofia can't be blamed for her uncle's actions. Julio wrote to me and explained that her family had suffered a great deal over . . . over what happened.' She turned her gaze on Victor. 'I am quite certain the *estancia* is running perfectly well, Victor, and the only reason you're going back is because you want to.'

'Have you forgotten me?' Evie suddenly asked. Astonished eyes turned on her and she put up her chin. 'I've been very happy here, you've all been very kind, but I haven't seen my parents in years, I haven't seen my own home. Shouldn't I have the right to go back now?'

There was a long silence. 'I'm sorry, Evie,' Alice said at last, going to her and kissing her cheek, 'I'm afraid I haven't been considering your feelings. Of course you must go back.' She smiled and gave a little shrug. 'It's only history repeating itself, isn't it? Richard and I always wanted to be able to cut ourselves in two. But decisions have to be made and they can't suit everyone.'

'Thank you, Mother,' Victor said awkwardly, and Evie put her arm round Alice's shoulders.

'Who's for a walk, then?' asked George, making no move.

'Oh, let's have tea and Christmas cake and cheer ourselves up,' said Tina.

'Excellent idea,' Charlotte agreed, and rang the bell.

Once again, the steamer trunks and boxes came down the back stairs and were loaded on to O'Dowd's taxi. The farewells were made, the tears shed, first for Tina, George and Paul, then for Victor, Evie and Rickie. Finally, Bill took himself away to Cork and Alice and Charlotte were left to go back into the quiet house together.

'Let's have a drink,' Charlotte suggested, leading the way to the drawing room. She poured a sherry for Alice and a whiskey for herself.

'Whiskey, at this time of the day?' asked Alice. 'Maybe I should have had one.'

'For medicinal purposes, I have a cold coming,' Charlotte explained.

They sat in silence, each wrapped in her own thoughts. Charlotte's were of Paul and her last talk with him after dinner, the night before he left. Alice had gone early to bed; the others were upstairs, finishing their packing. Charlotte and Paul had sat together over a nightcap.

'Are you really going to be a priest?' she had asked him.

'It's my intention.'

'Yet you once planned to marry Melissa.'

'That was a mistake. Only happened because –'

'Of my hat?' She had smiled.

He had looked startled, then returned her smile. 'That was the joke, but I guess there was some truth in it. She did have a hat with violets, it made her special to me.' He shrugged. 'Then she became special for herself.'

'But now, like me, she's part of your past.' Charlotte had finished her drink. 'When you are a priest, will you be allowed to remember us?'

'I don't know about being allowed.' He stood up. 'I'll remember you anyway, Cousin Charlotte.'

She had kissed him on the cheek and said goodnight.

'Why are you smiling?' Alice asked suddenly.

'Was I? Maybe I was thinking how nice it was to be a reformed character.'

'You used to say things like that in the old days.'

'And I didn't mean them? I mean them now.' Charlotte caught at Alice's hand. 'Look, I'm sorry, don't think I don't know how you are feeling.'

'It's the future that's worrying me, Charlotte.'

'We can't do anything about that.'

'But who is to take on Belcarron? Victor won't come back, Tina will always want to work in London, Melissa is in America, Paul is to become a priest. Who is there left? Poor Marianne's Freddie is gone and I don't see Cecily running Belcarron.'

'Or Caitlin.'

'God forbid!' Alice shuddered. 'So I must leave it to Victor. He is the eldest son, it should go to him, but it's clear he doesn't want it. I was talking to Cavan the other day, telling him how lucky he was to have Hugh back and willing to take over the estate. When we go, Charlotte, Belcarron may die.'

'Houses don't die, Alice. They may take on new roles, but they don't die.'

'If Belcarron were to change, it wouldn't be Belcarron. Look at the village, it's not the place we know any more. All those yachts, all those strangers –'

'You may be wrong about Victor, he may want to come back. This is his home, after all.'

'No, it never meant as much to him as it meant to Jack and me, and he has chosen the Argentine, he won't come back.' Alice looked seriously into Charlotte's face. 'If anything happened to me, you'd look after the house, wouldn't you? You and Bill?'

'Alice, I'm only two years younger than you, and I'm not married to Bill.'

'He'd marry you tomorrow, if you wanted it. Listen, you're not thinking of me, are you? You're not staying on here because of me?'

'Certainly not. I'm perfectly happy as I am. I might go back to Germany, though, when things have settled down, just to see if I can salvage any of my property. I'd rather not sponge on you if I can pay my way.'

'Don't talk like that. This is your home.'

'I know it.' Charlotte's eyes softened. 'Please, Alice, don't worry yourself over what's going to happen to Belcarron. Things have a way of working out. There's always Rickie, remember.'

'Rickie? He'll be brought up in the Argentine, he won't think of coming here.'

'You don't know what he'll think. If there's one thing I've learned, it's that you can never tell what people want to do.'

'You're right,' Alice agreed thoughtfully, 'one can never tell.'

Part IV
1919–1923

Chapter Thirty-Five

On a soft, humid day in March 1919, Julio was waiting at San Vicente for the train from Buenos Aires. His arms folded, his hat pressed down on his brow, he stood with the peons and the horses under one of the few shade trees at the halt, his heart thudding with apprehension. Victor Wintour was returning.

'You've been worrying about this for far too long,' Sofia had told him as he prepared to leave.

'I'm not worrying,' he answered coldly.

'No?' Sofia swept up their son Francisco, a handsome, dark-haired child of two. 'I say you've been worrying for years. From the time you took over the *estancia*, you've been worrying about this day.'

'Naturally, I've had to think about the Wintours' return. On our own, we've been free to do as we please; we always knew that couldn't last.'

Sofia's eyes flashed. 'I don't see why we have to concern ourselves with the Wintours at all. Why should I give up my house to them? My old family home?'

'It's easier, that's all. Now that *Papá* has returned to Rosario, his house is available, and you know you wouldn't have wanted to share with Victor and Evie.'

'Why should *they* not take the cottage on? Oh, it's all so unnecessary!'

Julio stopped to kiss his son's round cheek, then Sofia's lips. 'We must just try to get on with them,' he muttered. 'I know it's not going to be easy –'

'Easy!' Sofia set Francisco down and held his hand as they

walked out to watch Julio mount his horse. 'The problem is, you won't let me make things easy.' She raised her eyes to Julio's face. 'You understand me, Julio?'

'I understand you, Sofia, but I don't wish to discuss the matter. There must be no quarrel.'

'I never wish to quarrel, Julio. And you may rely on me to be as charming as possible to the Wintours.'

'You'll have no trouble with Evie, she's quiet and sweet. Victor is the problem.'

'Only if you allow him to be!' cried Sofia, as Julio rode away.

The early-autumn sun was hot, the air motionless. Under the dry-leaved trees, the horses' tails switched and Julio took off his hat and wiped his brow. One of the men from the *estancia* drew on a cigarette, his deep-set eyes narrowing in the smoke. He touched Julio's arm and pointed. The train from BA had appeared on the horizon.

Julio replaced his hat, feeling the palms of his hands slippery with sweat. He knew Sofia had been right, he was worrying about this meeting. He couldn't help it, couldn't stop going over and over the last time he and Victor had met in that room over Ryan's bar, the naked antagonism that had flared between them, the hard things that were said that would surely rise up between them now. There had always been a contest of sorts between himself and Victor, but when Victor had made his offer of money and he, Julio, had taken such pleasure in turning it down, there was no doubt, whichever way you looked at it, that he had won that round. But then the fight had been postponed. Victor had gone away to another war and had suffered, as Julio had not. Would he still want to fight? As the British-made locomotive steamed up to the halt and brought its carriages to a juddering stop, Julio told his men to stay with the horses and walked forward. He would soon know the answer to that question.

Several people alighted, but none was Victor. Then a railway steward appeared at one of the doors and jumped down, giving his hand to a tall man in dark jacket and riding breeches who very slowly followed him. The steward passed him a small valise and a stick, accepted his tip and swung himself back on the train, as the tall man began to look about him. A wide-brimmed hat concealed his hair, but Julio was sure it was yellow, he was sure the man was Victor. Yet he seemed so much older. In spite of all Doña Alicia's letters, Julio was unprepared for Victor's stick and Victor's limp. The arrogant young man of five years before would still be there – oh, yes, people did not change – but in the older wearier man, searching faces at San Vicente, he was not so easy to recognise.

Julio took off his hat, ran his hand through his damp hair, and bravely called, 'Victor?'

The cold, blue eyes found him. 'Julio,' Victor said, after a moment's hesitation, and put out his hand. 'It's good of you to meet me.'

'Not at all. I'm – glad to see you.'

They stood in the sunlight, exchanging long, cool glances of recognition.

Is he remembering Ryan's? Julio asked himself. Of course he was. Their last meeting hung between them like a thick curtain. 'How is Evie?' Julio asked aloud. 'And young Rickie?'

'Both well, thank you. As I said in my note, my parents-in-law wanted more time with them in BA; they'll follow later.'

'I look forward to seeing them again.' Julio bowed and replaced his hat. 'I have the horses here, but perhaps you wish to rest before we ride?'

'Thanks, I'd rather press on to the *estancia*, I don't need a rest.'

One of the peons came forward and took Victor's bag, and Victor, leaning on his stick, followed Julio to the horses. *Madre de Dios*, thought Julio, how is this fellow going to ride with that leg? He turned away his head as the peon assisted Victor to mount. 'Are you all right?' he asked, when Victor was up.

'Perfectly,' Victor replied, settling himself into the broad saddle of his criollo horse.

'We go then,' said Julio, and, mounting his own horse, led the way out of San Vicente.

It soon became obvious that riding was a form of agony for Victor, particularly with his British style, which was never easy on a criollo horse and on Argentine roads. He could not bend his knee and as he bounced in his saddle over every rut, his damaged leg bounced with him and his face grew whiter and whiter. Neither he nor Julio attempted to make conversation, Victor clearly needing all his concentration for managing his horse, and as the peons silently observed his ordeal, Julio suffered with him, every measure of the way.

It was a relief to them all when the *estancia* house came in sight and they rode up to find Sofia waiting for them, holding Francisco by the hand. She had taken pains to look her best, Julio thought, and was looking very attractive in a dark-red, low-waisted dress with matching combs in her black hair. Her face, however, was pale and he knew her nerves were stretched as taut as his own, whatever she might say about not needing to concern herself with the Wintours. As Victor was helped to dismount and she saw his difficulty, her eyes showed her dismay, but only for a second; then she was ready, with her charming smile, to be presented.

'Sofia, this is Victor Wintour,' Julio said in a low, hurried voice. 'Victor, may I present my wife, Sofia?'

For a long moment, Victor's eyes rested on Sofia's face and she knew, as Julio knew, what must be going through his mind. This woman was a Sentos. Her uncle had killed Richard Wintour. Now she must be greeted as a member of the family. It's too much, Julio groaned inwardly. Of course we're asking too much.

'I am so happy to meet you,' Sofia said in faltering English. 'Please, I understand, is difficult.'

She put out her hand and Victor, taking off his hat, bowed over it.

'Thank you for your welcome,' he replied in Spanish. 'Is this your little son?'

Sofia picked up Francisco, whose beautiful, dark eyes were fixed wonderingly on the strange, golden hair of the gentleman who smiled at him.

'Yes, this is Francisco,' Sofia murmured, 'our greatest joy.'

'I see he has your eyes,' Victor said, a little stiffly.

'But Julio's nose,' she cried delightedly.

'Ah. Yes,' said Victor, 'that is the Wintour nose.'

The awkward moment had passed. Julio, scarcely believing it possible, again mopped the sweat from his brow, as, at

Victor's pace, they moved into the house. 'This all seems much the same,' Victor observed, leaning on his stick and looking around, remembering. 'I thought you would have made changes.'

'No, we have not made changes. You do not mind, we live here while you are away? Doña Alicia gave her permission.'

Victor shrugged. 'Where else would you live on the *estancia*?'

'My father – Lucio – built himself a house, if you remember.'

'Lucio . . . where is he, Julio? I thought I would be meeting him today.'

'He visits my sisters in Rosario, he sends his apologies.'

Victor smiled. 'Very tactful.'

'No, not tactful, he wish to see my sisters. But soon he will return to welcome you, Victor.'

'I'll look forward to it.'

Sofia said they must go into the *sala*, Victor must rest, she would bring *mate* tea. 'You are very kind,' said Victor sitting down gratefully and stretching out his injured leg as best he could. 'But, Julio, you're not telling me you've moved into Lucio's house, are you?'

'Why not? We leave this house for you.'

Victor's eyes were glassy with surprise. 'I never expected it, you know.'

'But is better, we think, than two families under one roof.'

'Then it's very generous of you, I appreciate it.' Victor turned to Sofia, who had returned with a maid carrying a tray with tea things. 'Does this arrangement suit you?' he asked in careful Spanish. 'I mean, the move to Lucio's house?'

'I have accepted my husband's wishes.'

'If you're not happy about it, I'd rather we discussed it.'

'Let us say, I am happy.' Sofia inclined her head. 'Please, Señor Wintour, take *mate*.'

Victor hesitated. He cleared his throat, then raised his direct blue eyes to Sofia's watching face. 'Sofia,' he said quietly, 'you must call me Victor.'

Dinner, which had been served in the dining room of the *estancia* house, was over. Sofia, smiling radiantly, had excused herself and retired with a light step to Lucio's house. Julio poured a last brandy for himself and Victor.

'You must be exhausted, Victor, we should say goodnight.'

Victor lit a cigar. 'Julio, my leg is a mess, but you don't need to worry about me, I'm all right.'

'Is good, I'm glad.'

Victor looked down at his brandy. 'Your wife is charming,' he said hesitantly. 'I'm sorry if there was some constraint when I met her. You understand how it was?'

'Believe me, I do,' Julio answered earnestly. 'When I first meet Sofia, I feel like you. I think, this woman is a Sentos, how can I speak to her? But Sofia wasn't even born when her uncle did what he did, and she and her family, they have suffered too, you see, they suffered a great deal.'

'I suppose they did.'

'Of course, they are all dead now. Sofia is the last.'

'Except for your son.'

'Except for my son.'

'He's a fine child, Julio.'

Julio's eyes shone. 'Thank you, Victor. He means all the world to me.'

'I feel that way about Rickie.'

'Julio, there's something I should have said earlier,' Victor announced, finishing his brandy. 'You've done a good job for the *estancia*. You don't mind if I say I was worried about that? To be away so long –'

'No, is natural. But you have not even looked at the books. I plan to show you everything tomorrow.'

'I've gone into the financial position very thoroughly with my father-in-law at the bank. He gives you and Lucio a very good report and I want to say I'm grateful to you.'

'Is the least we can do, when you –'

'Were otherwise engaged.' Victor laughed grimly. 'From what I've heard, not everyone is coming back from the war to find things exactly as they would like them.'

'Victor, was easy for me. I am not proud of it, but we stay neutral, you see, we make the profits.'

'No one expected Argentina to come into the war, Julio.'

'Even when the Germans sank our ships?' Julio shrugged. 'But we sell beef to the Allies, we sell grain elsewhere, we do very well. Now, though, I must tell you, things are not so good.'

'No more sales of bully beef? We'll weather that, don't worry.'

'Yes, but commodity prices are falling everywhere, there may be a slump. Then, here, we have also the labour unrest, is very bad, Victor.'

'There's always been unrest in Argentina,' Victor said easily, 'never comes to anything.'

'This time is different. The Radicals are in power. Hipolito Yrigoyen is elected by one vote.' Julio held up his finger. 'One vote! But it means the Radicals are in power and the *estancieros* are not. Some say the military may become involved.'

'The army?' Victor drew his fair brows together. 'Can't have the army running the country, it's not their job.'

'I hope you're right.' Julio drew back his chair. 'Victor, you look weary. I think I will say goodnight.'

Victor sat on, studying his cigar. 'You've changed, you know,' he said bluntly.

'Changed? You mean grown up?'

'I expect that's it. Yes, you've grown up.' Victor gave a bitter smile. 'So have I.' Suddenly he ground out the cigar and dragged himself to his feet. 'I said once we couldn't work together. Do you think I was wrong?'

'Perhaps,' Julio said cautiously.

'At any rate we have to try. Might mean forgetting the past.'

'You want to?'

'Oh, God, yes.' Victor's eyes had lost all expression. 'These days, I always want to forget the past.'

'Let me get you a lamp,' said Julio, as they left the dining room. 'You really ought to get some rest.'

'Yes, I must admit, I feel like sleep now.' Victor tapped away down the passage to the room Sofia had prepared for him. 'Goodnight, Julio.'

'Goodnight, Victor.' It was on Julio's tongue to say, 'and welcome back', but somehow the words did not come. He meant them, he wished he could have said them. Already, it was too late. Victor had closed his door.

*

'Well?' asked Sofia, brushing her hair in their bedroom. 'Did I charm him?'

'Victor?' Julio looked over her shoulder into the mirror and let his eyes meet hers. 'Oh, yes, I think so. He has accepted you.'

'I don't think he's as bad as you made out, you know.'

'That's because he appears to have changed.'

'You think people can change?'

Julio moved away and flung himself on the bed, sinking into the little lace pillows Sofia had arranged on the bolster, knowing he would soon be in trouble because he had not taken off his boots.

'Julio!' came Sofia's voice, and he obediently sat up. 'All right, all right, I'm taking them off now. Can people change? Maybe after something like the war, though I'll admit I'm surprised. I thought Victor would be the type to go through it without turning a hair.'

'That shows you don't really know him, Julio.'

'Maybe not.'

'And now you're feeling happier? About the future?'

'I am, yes. I think we'll be able to work together, Victor and I.'

Sofia laid down her brush and ran to Julio, flinging her arms around him. 'Oh, I'm so glad, so relieved! I've been so worried, you've no idea –'

'Sofia, the last thing I want is for you to be worrying about me. I said I would give you a home and provide for you, and that's what I've tried to do, there should be no need for you ever to worry.'

'What affects you, affects me,' she said quietly. 'It's foolish to try to pretend otherwise, whatever the circumstances.'

They exchanged long, significant glances. 'Things have worked out better than we expected,' Julio murmured. 'Let's be grateful for that.'

While Julio and Sofia made love – 'After all, we have something to celebrate!' cried Sofia – Victor lay in his Spanish bed and stared into the darkness. His leg hurt and to try to gain relief, he moved it to and fro, but the pain seemed worse and he debated with himself whether it would be worth getting out of bed to take a dose from his brandy flask, deciding in the end that it would not. After what he had put it through today, his leg was going to give him hell anyway; no amount of brandy or exercise was going to help, he would just have to endure it. But this homecoming, in spite of Julio's unexpected friendliness and Sofia's charm, had been much worse than he had anticipated. Looking into the shadows of the room that had once been his parents', listening to creaks and shudders of the old house and the cries of the wild things outside the windows, Victor knew he had that day learned a bitter lesson. The life of the *estanciero*, the life he loved, which his father had loved before him, was no longer for him. He might as well go back to Buenos Aires tomorrow.

He would not, of course. He would give it a respectable try, listen to the arguments that would undoubtedly be put up concerning the ability of lame men to ride, would nod his head and agree that everyone would understand his situation, no one would pity it; after all, he was a hero, wasn't he? Victor's face in the darkness contorted with disgust. He had already seen that day the looks on the peons' faces, and he knew he would see the same on the faces of the gauchos, looks not of pity or contempt, but just a recognition of inferiority. When it came to riding, second best did not exist for the gauchos. Nor did it exist for Victor. What he did he must do well or not at all, and though he should perhaps be thanking his lucky stars he was able even to attempt his old life and was not lying under a white cross in a military cemetery, he knew he was not strong enough to accept his shortcomings. Better by far to give up, return to Buenos Aires, which would suit Evie anyway, who had never much cared for *estancia* life and now would be able to see more of her parents and see Rickie settled in a good day school.

As for the *estancia*, Victor had no worries there. Julio had turned out to be a tower of strength, everything would be safe in his hands and the astonishing thing was, Victor was sure he wouldn't even crow over it. Yes, the boy had grown up, had turned into a man one might even admire; not once, for instance, had he offered facile sympathy on Victor's injuries and for a civilian, that was good going. Sofia Castillo had been a pleasant surprise too; attractive, a perfect lady, Sentos or no

Sentos. A little too intense for Victor's own taste, he could imagine she might be difficult to live with, but both she and Julio had certainly made the best of a situation that could have been very awkward and Victor was grateful.

A longing for sleep suddenly overcame him and he concentrated his thoughts on Evie and Rickie so that when his eyes closed he would not see the Somme, always his great fear at night-time. Fortunately, he was tired enough now not to enter into that nightmare, and with the pain of his leg at last slipping from his consciousness, Victor slept.

Chapter Thirty-Six

When Evie arrived some days later, she expressed horror at Victor's decison to return to BA.

'Why, I thought you'd be pleased,' he cried, nettled. 'Seems you're just as contrary as all other women.'

'Oh, please don't talk like that, Victor. Of course I'd prefer to live in BA, for all sorts of reasons, but I'm thinking of you, not myself. Without the *estancia*, you'll be lost.'

'I've always liked BA, you know that.'

'Yes, for the social life, but what about your work? Your work's always been on the *estancia*; if you give it up, you'll be making a terrible mistake.' Evie leaned forwards, looking persuasively into Victor's face. 'After all, you don't have to ride all the time, do you?'

'Oh, no, I can sit in the office and do the accounts any time I like!' Victor scowled and lit a cigarette. 'Paperwork is not for me, Evie, never has been. What I like is hunting, riding to *rodeo*, riding the pampas. I'd rather die than work in a bank, like your father.'

Evie lowered her eyes. 'You'd never want to take over Stonefield's, then?'

'Take over Stonefield's? Why ever should I?'

'Well, Mama and I were just talking, you know. Papa has no son to inherit, only me. He's going to need someone to hand things on to.'

'He has never once hinted it should be me, probably because he knows it's the last thing I'd want. Anyway, he's nowhere near ready to hand over anything at the moment.'

'I'm not so sure. He sometimes doesn't look well.'

'All the more reason we should return to BA, then.' Victor drew on his cigarette. 'The good thing in all this is that I needn't worry about the *estancia*, Julio can take care of it.'

'Oh, I'm so glad you two get on now! I was so terribly worried at one time about how things would work out. And Sofia is so charming, isn't she? So much nicer than we ever thought she would be.'

'Yes, she's an attractive woman and has certainly tried to please. We've been lucky.'

'And Julio obviously dotes on her.' Evie gave a little sigh. 'He must spend all his money on her, she's always so beautifully dressed.'

'You're well dressed too, Evie.'

'Yes, but I have no style. Not as Sofia has, that's something inborn.'

'Can't say I even know what it is,' Victor grunted, putting out his cigarette and getting slowly to his feet. 'Now, you must excuse me, my dear, I still have some work to do around this place.'

Julio, too, was disturbed by Victor's desire to leave the *estancia*.

'No one here cares about the riding,' he assured Victor. 'You're a brave man, everyone knows that and understands.'

'Save your breath, Julio, I know what people see when they look at me.'

'I tell you, they see a brave man, one who fights for his country!'

'They see a cripple,' Victor said distinctly, 'a cripple trying to do things he has no right to do.'

'That's not fair, Victor. You're only trying to do your job.'

'And not doing it well, not doing it with any pleasure. What's the good of being here, if I can't do any of the things I used to enjoy doing? I might as well be back in BA.'

'Yet you wish to be here, don't you? This is your place, where you belong.'

'I don't belong anywhere, Julio, that's the trouble.' Victor's long-sighted eyes stared into the distance, at the vast grasslands beyond the boundaries of the garden his mother had made when he was a small boy.

'When I was at the front, I wanted to be in Belcarron. When I was at Belcarron, I wanted to be here. Now I'm here, I want to go to BA. I'm a misfit, you see, I have no place where I really want to be.'

'Victor, I think these feelings will pass.'

'A lot of men share them; maybe most of us who came back.'

'You have your wife and little son, and they're all that matter.'

Victor ran his hand through his hair. 'And Evie wants another child, you know. I say, is it right to bring more people into this world?'

'Of course, of course it is! A new life brings hope.' Julio's face lit up. 'And think of having another son!'

'Evie wants a daughter,' said Victor. 'Maybe I do, too. At least she wouldn't have to go to war.'

When he and Evie returned to Buenos Aires, Victor wanted to go directly to the Avenida Lila. After Blanche's persuasions, he first agreed to spend time at West Gate, the new house Arthur had built in the Belgrano district. It was his great joy, a copy of his family's country seat in Shropshire, lost to them since 1820, when Henry Stonefield, Arthur's great-grandfather, had sold it to pay his gambling debts. Henry had later gone out to the Argentine and founded the family bank, so was not a complete black sheep, but Arthur said his family had always regretted the loss of the English house and he was delighted that it had fallen to him to recreate it. Throughout the long years of war, filled for others with death and suffering, he had therefore busied himself with architects and builders, landscape gardeners and decorators, to produce a beautiful white elephant only he wanted. The cost, Victor decided, must have been colossal, and though in his younger days he might have thought it rather a lark to spend so much, now he found it not at all to his taste. He would never, of course, say so, but as he looked around at the honey-coloured Georgian façade of the new house, at the lines of the twelve-paned windows so harmoniously placed, at the fine roof with its pediment and flagpole, he thanked God that he had never had the slightest desire to create another Belcarron in Buenos Aires.

'It's so sweet of you to agree to come here, Victor,' Blanche murmured, as she poured tea in the handsome conservatory, 'but Evie does need a little extra spoiling, doesn't she? I mean, at this time?'

'Mama, it's only June and the baby's not due until December,' Evie protested. 'I don't need spoiling yet.'

'But you are feeling a little sick, my dear, and that old Sentos house is all uneven floors and awkward steps. Suppose you were to trip and fall?'

'Evie's not going to trip and fall,' Victor said firmly. 'We'll stay here for a week or two, but then I must insist we go to our own home.'

'And what of Evie's confinement?' asked Blanche.

'That's up to Evie.'

'Of course I'll come here for that,' Evie said, pressing her mother's hand, and Blanche's smile returned.

'Oh, what a relief! I know you were born there, Victor, but really the Sentos house is no place to have a baby.'

Victor, biting back the retort that what had been good enough for his own mother should be good enough for Evie, rose, and bowed and limped away to smoke a cigarette in the grounds. Here Arthur joined him, saying it was too cold to walk outside now, he must come into the study where there was a log fire and they could have a drink before dinner. Not that dinner would be served for hours yet, but one could always start drinking any time, especially good whisky.

'Taste that, my boy.' Arthur set down a Scottish malt before Victor. 'I have that specially imported. You won't find anything to touch it, I'll wager my last penny.'

'Very good,' Victor agreed, letting the spirit move in his mouth. He set down his glass. 'But talking of last pennies, seems to me what you've been having here is something of a boom time. Last pennies must be very far away for most Argentines.'

'For those who did well out of the war,' Arthur agreed.

'Young Julio at the *estancia* thinks there might be leaner times ahead, though.'

Arthur looked down into his whisky. 'Actually, they're already here. Germany lost, of course.'

Victor's eyes flickered. 'You're saying that was a bad thing?'

'No, no, of course not, but we were neutral, you see.'

'And made money out of both sides? How convenient!'

'Don't put it that way, Victor. You know how much this country contributed to the British war effort.'

'I'm sorry, I do, indeed.'

Arthur sat back, his face paling a little, and it seemed to Victor that it was true what Evie had said, he was not looking well. But then he was older. Weren't they all?

'What do you think of the house?' Arthur asked, suddenly rousing himself. 'I know I've asked you that before, but you've had a chance to get to know it now, haven't you? You understand what I've been trying to do?'

'Yes, and as I said when we arrived, it's splendid. You must be very proud.'

'I am, Victor, I am.' Arthur offered Victor a cigar and took one himself. 'I just wish my father could have seen what I've achieved. It's very sad, you know, when people go, they never know what you've done.'

Victor lit his cigar without speaking.

'We always had the same goals, my father and I,' Arthur went on, 'always the same goals. Did you know your parents were great admirers of Papa, Victor?'

'I did know that, yes. I remember my mother talking of him often.'

'What a beauty she was, when she was young!' Arthur shook his head. 'I often used to think they were the handsomest couple I knew, your parents, Victor. But now, I want to tell you how glad I am you've come back to BA. Living on the *estancia* is all very well until you get yourself a wife and family, then it becomes just too damned difficult.'

'It had certainly become too damned difficult for me.'

'I'm glad you agree with me.' Arthur leaned forwards. 'I've been meaning to ask you, how's that leg of yours for polo?'

'It isn't,' Victor answered steadily, 'for polo.'

'What, you mean you can't ride?'

'I can't ride.'

Arthur's pale eyes went to Victor's stick. 'Oh, look, my boy, that's just defeatist talk. I can put you in touch with the best surgeons in the country, I'll make an appointment for you tomorrow –'

'It's very kind of you, sir, but there'd be no point. Some of the best surgeons in the world have already seen my leg. They said I was lucky to have kept it, but the way it is now is the way it will stay. It won't improve.'

'Well, this is a blow and no mistake.' Arthur drew furiously on his cigar. 'And here I'd been looking forward to showing you my ponies – they're all down at the club, you know –'

'I can still look at ponies,' Victor said acidly. 'It's only my leg that doesn't function.'

'Of course, of course, we'll drive down tomorrow. But all your friends are going to be so upset, Victor –'

'I've come back,' Victor said simply, 'what more do they want?'

The months went by and with the returning heat of summer Evie wilted like a flower out of water. Victor was relieved in the end to see her back in the airy comfort of her parents' home. On the day the baby was due, he went up to sit with her for a while as she rested on a chaise longue in her room. She told him she was feeling in very low spirits.

'It's only natural, darling. I'm sure most women feel the same at times like these.'

'I keep thinking I might not pull through.'

'Oh, come! You're very well, the doctor says so, there's no need to talk like that.'

'Anything can happen in childbirth, Victor.' Evie rested her hands on her bump and sighed dolefully. 'Remember Julio's poor mother.'

'That was years ago and she was out on the *estancia*! You're in BA, you have one of the best doctors available, everything to hand in case of an emergency –'

'If anything does happen,' she went on, not listening, 'my will is all in order, you won't have any trouble with the trustees.'

Victor looked distractedly about him. 'Why are you talking like this?' he cried. 'It's only distressing, it doesn't do any good. Look, I think you should get some proper rest. I'll leave you for a while, come back later –'

She caught at his hand as he bent over her. 'Do you love me, Victor? Really love me? I mean, you didn't marry me just because of the bank?'

'How can you ask me that, when you know what you've meant to me?' He sat awkwardly beside her on the chaise longue, not looking at her, and she knew he was thinking of those times at night when he returned to the front, saw things she couldn't imagine, heard the guns again and the shells, and came back at last, drenched in sweat, to let her hold and comfort him until true sleep claimed him. She had never told anyone of these night returns, nor ever would, and she had his gratitude for that. His gratitude and his love? Yes, his love too. It was foolish to press him on his feelings in the early days, maybe he wouldn't have married her without Papa's money, but there was love between them now and only these dark days before her confinement made her want to make him admit it. Much better not to put things into words, much better just to know and accept what one had. She kissed him gently and said perhaps he should leave her now, she really did feel tired, she thought she might sleep.

'I'll just be downstairs if you want me. You have your bell?'

'Of course.' Evie smiled wearily. 'And Mama is ready all the time to run in and see me on my way. She'll tell you if anything happens, though I'm sure this one is going to be late.'

'Aren't second babies often on time?'

'Fingers crossed, darling.'

Poor Evie, Victor hoped to God the baby would come soon. This waiting around, it was like waiting to go over the top ... It made him uneasy that she wanted to talk about love, but women always did. What could he say? He didn't think he could do without her. Did that add up to love? In his book, yes, and Arthur's money didn't come into it. At least, not now. He made his way painfully through the house and out by the side french windows into the garden, where the December sunshine made him screw up his eyes and find a bench under the trees. A letter from his mother had arrived that afternoon, and this was his first opportunity to read it.

Her first news was of a death. Daniel Molloy had died in September, not of the seizure that had been expected, but very quietly of heart failure, just sitting in his chair at breakfast. Poor Hester was being very brave and had taken comfort in the grand Irish funeral Daniel's colleagues had arranged, even though he had always said he wanted no fuss. Caitlin and Paul had been of great support, of course, and though Caitlin had returned almost immediately to Dublin, the good news was that Hester herself would be coming over in the spring, to pay long visits to Alice and Marianne.

Alice could not tell Victor how much she was looking forward to having her cousin at Belcarron again – dear, gallant Hester, who had seen qualities in Daniel her family could not see, but which must have been there, or how could Hester have seen them? Victor, turning the page, frowned at that and shook his head. As far as he was concerned, Daniel Molloy had had no good qualities of any sort, but of course his mother would never bring herself to speak ill of the dead and she had to consider Cousin Hester's feelings.

At the time of writing, Alice went on, Charlotte was in Germany, trying to salvage something of her inheritance, but between the opposition of her in-laws and Germany's present economic situation, it wasn't likely she would end up with very much. Bill Paget, Terence's uncle, was still hopeful of marrying her, and Alice wished she would accept him, but so far nothing had been arranged. 'She worries about leaving me here alone,' Alice added, as though Alice had ever minded that! I mind, thought Victor.

Probably Victor would have heard from the newspapers, Alice went on, of the new troubles in Ireland. There was this man named Michael Collins, who was mounting a terrible campaign of violence against all officers of the Crown, or indeed anyone who held different views, and the talk was that it would only be a matter of time before there was total civil war in Ireland. Sinn Fein had been banned in Cork, which had only made matters worse, and Charlotte had said, before she left for Germany, that Alice should leave too, if only for a time. As though she ever would! Her ancestors had never been intimidated by violence and she was not going to be the first Wintour to run away from Belcarron. 'I do not write these things, Victor, to make you think you should come home,' Alice finished.

> I realise now that your place is with Evie in the Argentine, looking after our interests there, so please do not worry, these troubles in Ireland will blow over, they always do.

Give my love to the Stonefields and to Evie and dear Rickie, there's not a moment when you're not in my thoughts and I long to hear soon of the baby's safe arrival and that Evie is well.
Your ever loving
Mother.

Victor folded the letter and put it in his wallet. He felt pretty bad. Maybe, once the baby was born, he should go back to Belcarron, not to stay, just to see the situation and make his mother feel better. He put his head on his hand and gave a groan. She would not feel better. Whatever she said, what she needed was a replacement for Jack and he was not that replacement, never could be. As he stared at the beautiful new turf of Arthur's lawn, so well watered it was not even yellowing in the summer heat, he could see no solution.

'Victor!' cried Blanche, hurrying from the house, her face pale with excitement and anxiety. 'It's started, the baby's started, and I think it's going to be quick. The doctor and midwife are on their way, but would you telephone Arthur?'

'I want to be with Evie,' Victor answered, leaping to his feet. 'I said I'd go back when she needed me.'

'Oh, Victor, you know that's not your place now.' Blanche patted his hand. 'Don't worry, we'll take care of her and you'll be much more help looking after Arthur. He always works himself into a terrible state at times like these.'

Only two hours later, the baby was born, a beautiful daughter with a fringe of red hair. 'Which might become fair, or might be coppery like mine,' said Blanche, proudly holding the wrapped bundle for Victor to see. 'Oh, what a relief it's all over! I feel like thanking God on my knees. Such a darling baby and she gave Evie no trouble at all. Rickie, dear, what do you think of your little sister?'

Rickie looked down his handsome nose. 'I was hoping for a brother, Grandmama, but I suppose she'll be all right. What's her name?'

'Claire,' Evie whispered, as Victor kissed her. 'We did decide that, didn't we?'

'Yes, it's a lovely name. Not a family name, of course.'

'Well, why should it be? I want Claire to be a person in her own right.'

'A person in her own right.' Victor smiled as the nurse removed the tiny new Wintour and placed her in her crib. 'I suppose she will be, one day. But now you must rest, Evie, you've done very well. You see, there was nothing to worry about after all.'

'Nothing to worry about,' she repeated, and lay back gratefully against her pillows.

'Now, Blanche, my dear, and Victor – downstairs for champagne,' Arthur whispered. 'Doctor, you'll join us?'

'Why, thank you, I should be delighted.' Dr Hall, the English doctor, gave Arthur a quick professional glance. 'May I say it's good to see you looking so well today, Mr Stonefield?'

'You know what they say, doctor,' Arthur replied with a beaming smile, 'happiness is the best tonic, and this is a very, very, happy day.'

He led the way downstairs to the drawing room, where the champagne was already cooling in its bucket, waiting for them.

Chapter Thirty-Seven

Evie had made such good progress that she was allowed to come downstairs for Christmas dinner. By New Year she was up and about, seeming taller than ever without her bump and talking of having her hair bobbed.

'Evie, don't you dare!' cried Blanche. 'No one is taking that new style seriously!'

But Evie was not to be deterred. 'I don't often get my own way, but this is something I really want. It must be wonderful not to be always worrying about pins and chignons, having a maid pulling and twisting every time one wants to go out.'

'You do as you please,' Victor told her. 'All I want is to get back home; we've been here long enough.'

'I suppose we should go back, especially as Sofia and Julio want to come to see us, but it's so lovely for me, you know, being cosseted.'

'You'll be cosseted all over again by Vittoria,' Victor said with a grin. 'Wait till she sees Claire!'

When Sofia and Julio were eventually greeted at the Avenida Lila by an Evie so transformed by her new hairstyle she seemed a different person, they were almost too astonished to admire the baby.

'Oh, Julio, is for me!' cried Sofia, putting her hand to her heavy knot of black hair. In spite of Julio's look of gloom, she declared she would go next day to Evie's hairdresser and have all her locks scissored away so that she too could be *elegante*!

'Don't try to argue,' Victor advised, as Sofia and the boys accompanied Evie and the baby to the nursery. 'It won't do any good and Sofia can always grow her hair back again, you know.'

'But why do women always want to change themselves?' asked Julio. 'They look perfect, so they want to be different. This I never understand!' He looked up at Victor from his chair, as Victor offered him a cigar. 'And how are you, Victor? Am I right, you are feeling better?'

'A little. Though I'm too damned idle. I'd give a lot to be back on the *estancia*.'

'Is still there, Victor.'

'But not for me. At least, not yet.' The telephone rang outside in the cool, tiled hall and Vittoria put her head round the door. Someone at Stonefield's Bank wished to speak to Don Victor.

'Is good you have the *teléfono*,' Julio remarked, as Victor went to answer it. 'How I wish is on the *estancia*!'

'It'll come,' Victor said cheerfully, 'one of these days. Will you excuse me, Julio?'

He was away only a few moments. When he returned his face was grey.

'*Madre de Dios*, what is it?' cried Julio, rising to his feet. 'Victor, what's wrong?'

'That was John Fleet, from the board,' Victor said slowly. 'Something's happened, something bad, he wouldn't say what, exactly, but I must go to the bank right away. Julio, you'd better come with me.'

'What about Evie?'

'Evie.' Victor put his hand to his brow. 'My God, I don't know what to tell her. It may involve her father –'

'Tell her we are needed on a business matter, we come back as soon as we can.'

'Yes, yes, we could say that. While I speak to her, will you tell Jorge to get the car out? We mustn't lose any time.'

Seemingly without conscious effort, Jorge drove them through downtown Buenos Aires like a man firing a gun. One minute they were in the Avenida Lila, the next they were hitting the target of the splendid Stonefield building, where already it seemed to them there were more people than usual standing at the entrance and in the vestibule.

'We must take the lift,' cried Julio, but the lift was far away.

'The stairs,' snapped Victor, turning.

'Victor, your leg!'

'To hell with my leg!'

'Will be quicker in the end to wait,' Julio said quietly. 'See, the lift comes now.'

White-faced, breathing hard, they stepped into the lift, oblivious of the stares of the men leaving it, but the air was heavy with tension. Something was wrong and the whole building knew it. 'One can almost smell it,' Victor murmured, as the lift carried them upwards.

'Smell what?' asked Julio.

'Disaster,' said Victor.

They came out on the executive floor into a crowd of blank-faced men in business suits, members of the bank's board of directors, accountants, secretaries, clerks, and felt the wave of anxiety rush and engulf them as they were recognised. John Fleet, the Anglo-Argentine member of the board who had telephone Victor, came hurrying towards them, his face clay-coloured.

'Wintour, thank God you're here! And Señor Castillo – I'm so glad to see you. This is a terrible business, terrible –'

'Just tell us what's happened,' Victor said tersely.

'The worst, the worst ...' Fleet put a large trembling hand to his lips. 'I think you had better come and see.'

He led the way through the crowd, which divided before them, and halted at the door to Arthur Stonefield's office, which was open. 'We had to break this lock,' he said over his shoulder, 'when we heard the shot.'

'Shot?' Victor repeated.

'Come through,' Fleet muttered, 'please – come through ...'

Arthur Stonefield was sitting at his desk. There was no doubt that he was dead. The shot the bankers had heard had taken most of his head away and the gun he had used, which had fallen from his right hand, lay on the floor.

Julio turned away. 'Excuse, excuse –' he stammered, and ran from the room. It was his first sight of violent death, no one blamed him; Victor, who had seen such death for years on end, also had to turn aside and could not speak.

'There are letters,' Fleet whispered, 'for his wife and daughter and for you.'

'Thank you.' Victor's hand closed round the letters and he stared down at them, unseeingly. 'Has – has a doctor been called?'

'Yes, our own doctor was in the building, he came at once. There was of course nothing he could do.'

'And the police? Have you called the police?'

Fleet licked his dry lips. 'They are on their way.' He found a chair and sat down heavily. 'Wintour, I never thought I should live to see this day. I remember my father telling me of the troubles of the nineties, bankruptcy, financial crash, failure everywhere – now it comes again.'

'Only to Stonefield's, I think,' Victor said quietly. 'You're going to have to tell me why.'

Fleet raised his eyes. 'Your letter will tell you why.'

'Is it the end of the bank?'

'Just read the letter. I don't want to say any more at present. When this news gets out, we shall be besieged.'

After a long, terrible silence, Victor braced himself to take one last look at his father-in-law, and limped to the door. 'I must go to my family,' he said in a low voice. 'I shall return later.'

Fleet pulled himself from his chair. 'When the police come, they will take charge, there'll be nothing we can do.'

'What should we need to do?'

Fleet shrugged and wiped his brow. 'There may be papers ... papers we could take –'

Understanding sparked in Victor's eyes. 'It's too late for that now, Fleet. Whatever my father-in-law has done, it can't be concealed. Please take care of things here until I get back.'

'You look so pale – won't you take something? A brandy? Whisky?'

Victor had already gone.

At West Gate, time seemed to have stopped. Blanche had been having a bridge party when Evie arrived with Sofia and the children to tell her what had happened. The cards were still scattered on the tables, the chairs pulled back, as Evie took her mother upstairs to her room and her friends, appalled, hurried away.

'Here is Papa's letter, Mama,' Evie whispered. 'Would you like to read it?'

'Why should he write me a letter?' cried Blanche, her hazel eyes blank. 'I don't understand, he's only at the bank, why should he write to me?'

'Oh, Mama!' Evie burst into tears. 'I have a letter too. I really think we should read them; it will help us, you see.'

'Help us to do what?'

'Well, to know what's happened.' Evie wiped her tears and opened the letters, first her mother's, then her own, and after a long, accusing stare, Blanche agreed to read what Arthur had written.

'It doesn't make any sense!' she exclaimed. 'He asks me to forgive him, but doesn't say what for. He is always so vague, you know, all my married life. I have never been able to pin him down.'

Later, when the doctor had arrived and given Blanche a sedative, Evie tried to drink the tea Sofia brought her. 'I don't know when Mama will be able to accept this,' she murmured. 'It's not just that Papa has gone, her world has gone, too.'

'No, no, there must be something left, Evie, it's not possible that a bank should just go under!'

'Banks have crashed before in Buenos Aires.' Evie set her cup aside. 'But I don't care about the bank, I don't care about the money, I just want Papa!'

'It's all in here,' Victor told Julio, pointing to Arthur's letter. 'He explains it all quite sensibly and logically. You must read it.'

'No, I do not wish to read it.' Julio, still deathly pale, would not look at the letter. 'Nothing will make me believe this has happened. Nothing!'

They were alone in a small room at the bank. Arthur's body had been removed to the mortuary and his office sealed, pending investigation by the authorities. Senior bank officials were still dazedly walking the floors of the building, although the clerical workers had been sent home, leaving by the back entrance to avoid the crowds gathered outside. John Fleet had already suggested that Victor and Julio should go home too, but they still sat on, as though unable to break the spell of horror that bound them to the bank, and he had returned to the boardroom and the other directors. They too would not go home.

'I've pieced together what's been happening,' Victor said quietly, 'partly from Arthur's letter – he was very frank – partly from what Fleet has told me. You must try to understand, Julio, it affects you as well as the rest of us. Are you listening?'

'I'm listening,' Julio replied.

It appeared that things had begun to go wrong for the bank as soon as Edward Stonefield died. He had been one of the old school, the sort who would rather die than use a penny of clients' money, but he was clever and shrewd and knew what he was doing. Arthur wanted to be the same, he imagined he was; in fact, he totally lacked his father's acumen and under his leadership the bank began to slide. It was true that he had a board of directors and financial advisers, but he preferred not to listen to them. It was his bank, he would make the decisions, so the board did what he said and the accountants covered his tracks. For years, he sailed close to the wind and got away with it, but when war came, like a lot of other people, he thought Germany would win. He invested heavily in German industry and armaments, he thought he would make a tremendous killing and left himself no margin. When Germany lost and he could see what was going to happen to the economy, he panicked, tried to save the situation by more borrowing, more speculation, but it was too late, he'd used too much of the bank's money, he could not replace it. He went to other banks for help, but with the recession none could do anything. He even tried the Bank of England, which had bailed out Argentine banks in the past, but they said they could not take on the liabilities. There was one last chance when a Spanish bank seemed willing to make a rescue bid, but in the end they decided against it. When Arthur heard that news, he knew he was facing disaster. As everyone now knew, he faced it in his own way.

Julio lit a cigarette with a trembling hand. 'What does it mean for us?' he asked huskily.

'You know what it means for us.'

'Everything we have is here?'

'Everything.' Victor sat back in his chair. 'We have all lost pretty well all we have.'

'And the *estancia*?'

'Until we know if there's anything at all to be paid out, there will be no working capital to run it. To be frank, I haven't an idea in hell what we are going to do.'

'Borrow, I suppose.'

'If we can. My God, I can see why Arthur did what he did.' Victor raised bloodshot eyes. 'You realise all Blanche's capital has gone as well? And Evie's trust fund? What am I to tell them?'

'They will not be thinking of money, Victor.'

'Well, I am thinking of the money, by God I am! It's all up to me, you know, I am the one who has to work something out, make bricks without straw, find assets that don't exist! Just tell me where I am going to get the money to carry on!'

'I think I know,' said Julio.

Chapter Thirty-Eight

As Victor fixed him with incredulous eyes, Julio's thoughts went back to the first night of his honeymoon nearly four years before. He had not learned the truth then, but he had begun to have his suspicions that Sofia was nursing a secret, was longing to tell him something and was still savouring it, looking forward to the moment when it was revealed. Leaving Sofia's maid to follow later, they had broken their train journey to Mendoza at Rufino, where they had booked into a small hotel, ordered a dinner they did not eat, and made love on a hard bed which seemed to them amazingly soft. 'This is better than that rug on the grass,' Julio had whispered, as Sofia slipped out of her silk nightdress, 'no snakes here.'

'Might be cockroaches, Julio, they are in all these hotels, you know.'

'Sofia, this is no time to be talking about cockroaches!' he cried, laughing as he pulled her towards him.

It was when their eager and confident lovemaking was over that Sofia seemed to him, even for a bride, strangely excited. He felt her tension as she lay beside him, supposedly trying to sleep, and he asked gently, 'What is it? You're as strung up as though on a high wire.'

'It is my wedding night, what do you expect?'

'I think there's something you haven't told me.' He put back her long, black hair and tried to see her face, but it stayed a pale shape in the darkness, he could make nothing of her expression. 'You haven't found out – you know – that you are . . .'

'To have a baby?' she asked, smiling at his embarrassment. 'I can't say yet. I might be.'

'Oh, Sofia!' He gathered her into his arms. 'I'd be so happy if you were, you know, now that we're married. No wonder you are all on edge!'

'I'm on edge, but not for that.'

'What, then?'

'Wait and see. Wait until tomorrow.'

'You have a surprise for me?'

'Yes, a surprise.'

'A nice one?'

'I think so, I think you'll be pleased.'

'Is it something to do with Mendoza?'

'I told you, wait and see.'

Next day, as the train rattled them along towards Mendoza, Julio became more and more intrigued over what was to be his surprise, but Sofia refused to say more. She only looked mysterious and teasing and so very attractive, he longed to take her in his arms and kiss her until she told him what she was up to. Mendoza he knew to be a pleasant city at the foot of the Andes, a place of hot, dry climate which irrigation had turned into a centre for wine and fruit growing. Although the city was full of historical associations – José de San Martín had set off from there to liberate Chile from the Spanish – an earthquake had virtually destroyed its buildings back in 1861 and it was now, Sofia told him, a quite modern-looking city. Most of the houses were one-storey for reasons of safety, but her parents' house was not.

'Papa wished to go upstairs to bed,' she said smiling, 'so we go upstairs to bed, earthquake or no earthquake. Ah, Julio, how lovely it will be to show you everything, everything in my home town!'

'I'm looking forward to it.'

'You know that now is the wine-making season? We may have missed some of the fiestas but there will be plenty more. I think this is going to be the best honeymoon anyone could ever have, don't you?'

'As though you need to ask!'

They held hands for the rest of the journey to Mendoza.

It was evening when they arrived and already dark.

'Too late to do anything but go the house,' said Sofia. 'I shall show you everything tomorrow. Now we had better find a taxi, I did not arrange for the car to meet us.'

'You keep a car?' asked Julio.

'Yes, of course, why not?'

'No reason, I just hadn't realised you owned one.' As they began the drive from the station through well-laid-out, well-lighted streets, Julio looked about with interest. He asked if the house was in the city itself.

'No, some way out, near the vineyards,' Sofia told him, her eyes shining in the shadows of the taxi. As she felt for his hand and pressed it, he could feel her fingers trembling.

'You've been away some time, your friends will have missed you.'

'Yes, but now they will be looking forward to meeting you. I thought we might give a party, a sort of late wedding reception. would you like that?'

'Not much, but if it's what you want, I'll go along with it.'

'Dear Julio.' She kissed him softly, then began to point out various public buildings and things she thought he should see; the marketplace, the park, the monument to San Martín, the Liberator. The autumn air was warm and sweet and when at last they left the city, Julio began to feel pleasantly relaxed, as though he were driving in a dream of paradise with his Sofia. His eyelids were closing, he was drooping against her shoulder, when she shook him awake. 'Darling, we're here!'

He sat up, to see ahead of him in the taxi's lights a long, straight drive lined with trees. At the end was a house, tall and white, with long windows and a portico; a rather elaborately styled house, Julio thought, perhaps of French design, rather than Spanish, and certainly a house that would have cost a great deal of money. He cast a sidelong glance at Sofia and saw that she was watching him, waiting for him to comment.

'It looks –' he hesitated – 'rather a grand place.'

'My father rather fancied building a French-style chateau – you must forgive us if it doesn't seem right.'

'It's not single-storey, you're right about that.'

The taxi halted at the portico and the driver placed their luggage at the double glass entrance doors. As Julio paid him, Sofia flew out and rang the bell and was greeted with cries of joy by a stout, grey-haired woman dressed in black. A middle-aged man in chauffeur's livery also appeared and stood bowing, pulling at his moustache.

'Julio, come and meet Ines, who was my nurse and is now my housekeeper,' Sofia called, 'and this is Domenico, my chauffeur. Ines, Domenico – may I present my husband, Señor Julio Castillo?'

'Don Julio.' They bowed respectfully as their eyes went over him, and he self-consciously returned their greeting. Domenico then turned reproachful eyes on Sofia, demanding to know why she had not asked him to meet the train. What was the use of having a splendid American car, if he was not allowed to use it for her convenience?

'I'm sorry, Domenico, but you know how erratic the trains are. I simply didn't want to keep you waiting around for hours at the station. Next time, I promise, you shall be there!' Sofia patted his uniformed shoulder, then, snatching at her housekeeper's arm, moved into the house.

Julio, without speaking, followed. His heart was thudding, his head spinning; he scarcely needed to see the size of the entrance hall, the length of the curving stairs, the scattered Persian rugs and French furniture, the portraits and ornaments, the flowers and silks and handsome lamps, to know what Sofia had been longing to tell him. His wife was a wealthy woman, and until now she had kept it from him. He felt sick.

'You have followed my instructions?' he heard Sofia saying to Ines, as maids brought in their luggage. 'You've prepared the guest suite for us?'

'Of course, of course. Everything is ready, just as you say, Doña Sofia.'

'My own room is too small,' Sofia told Julio, her eyes still shining in the excited way he had been noticing, 'and, naturally, I did not wish to use my parents' room. You'll like the guest suite, it's most comfortable, so I suggest we have tea sent up there. We can get out of these terrible train clothes and take our baths, then come down for dinner. If I know Ines, she will have prepared something very special.'

As soon as they were alone, Julio turned to face Sofia.

'So this is the secret?' He waved a hand around their luxurious surroundings. 'You are rich?'

'Yes, I'm rich!' Sofia's eyes danced. 'Truly, beautifully rich!'

'Why did you not tell me?'

'You never asked me! Don't you remember, I said to you one day, "Isn't there something you want to ask me?" and you said you couldn't think of anything. Naturally, I expected you to want to know about my dowry, but as you hadn't thought of it, I decided it would be fun not to say anything.'

'I knew you were an orphan,' he said stiffly. 'I assumed you had nothing. It was your place to tell me otherwise.'

'Did it never occur to you to look at my clothes, or my maid? At the kind of hotel I could afford?' Sofia put her head on one side, smiling at him. 'I told you my father had been a wine grower. Did you never think to make a connection with my name?'

'Your name?'

'Almedo, Julio, Almedo.'

He stared at her for a moment, then went white. 'Oh, God!' he murmured, and sat down on a padded silk chair. Almedo Wines. Sofia was Almedo Wines, one of the biggest wineries in the country, one with a large export trade and a financial turnover he couldn't begin to imagine.

'You must think me very stupid,' he said in a low voice, 'very stupid and very naïve.'

'I think you're very sweet.' Sofia went to him and began to kiss his face, but he stood up, putting her aside.

'Why didn't you tell me?' he asked again, very quietly.

'I've explained.'

'No, I don't think so. I think you didn't tell me because you didn't trust me.'

'Julio, I told you my name.'

'You could see it meant nothing to me. You didn't make it plain who you were because you thought I'd try to marry you, didn't you, whether I loved you or not?'

'Yes,' she answered simply, 'that was what I thought.'

He walked dazedly to the vast, satin-covered bed and sank down on the edge. 'You really thought that?'

She knelt before him, taking his hand in hers. 'You must understand how it was, Julio. All my life I was brought up to know I was an heiress, that I must always beware of men who would try to marry me for my money. When my mother knew she was dying, she talked all the time of how I must be careful, of how I must be sure. When I met you, I told you my name, but afterwards I wished I hadn't. I was in Buenos Aires, there was no reason for you to know who I was. I knew I was attracted to you, could easily fall in love, but I thought I'd spoiled everything, giving you my name. Then it dawned on me that you hadn't realised, you hadn't made the connection, you thought I was some poor orphan whose father had happened to grow a few vines. And then I was so happy, Julio, so happy! How could I spoil it?'

'I might have checked up on you. I might have known who you were all the time.'

'No, I knew you hadn't. I made enquiries myself.'

'Oh, yes, of course, you would.' Julio pulled his hands from hers. 'Why did you come to the Avenida Lila that day?' he asked harshly. 'You never would tell me. Tell me now.'

Sofia rose and turned away her face. 'You'll think it foolish.'

'Just tell me.'

'I wanted to ask the Wintours if they would sell me the *estancia*.'

Julio leaped from the bed and pulled Sofia to face him. 'You wanted to do *what*? Were you crazy?'

'Not crazy, no, I thought I was being quite sensible. I had been left a great deal of money. There are sugar concerns in Tucumán, too – I haven't told you about them –'

'No, and I don't want you to. Just tell me how you, a Sentos, could possibly have had the nerve to ask the Wintours to sell their *estancia* to you? If you had actually met Doña Alicia, how do you think she would have felt if you had asked her such a thing?'

'I can see now it was selfish and stupid, but I didn't know whether the Wintours really cared about the Sentos land and I knew that I did. Of course, I'm very grateful to my father for leaving me the winery, but it's just a business, it's a way of making money. The *estancia* is something different, it's something I really want, and down there, where no one knows me, I knew I could be myself, and when you've been brought up the way I've been brought up, that means a lot.

Oh, Julio, do try to see how it was for me!'

He turned away and stood with his arms folded, not looking at her.

'I do so love you!' she cried. 'All I want is to look after you, to give you everything you've ever wanted. Money doesn't mean so much to me because I've always had it, but now I can make up to you for all you've had to do without, I can make you the happiest man in the world!'

He stared at her, his face turning first red, then white, and it was as though she had struck him a mortal blow. For some time he seemed to be searching for words; when he found them he could hardly get them out. 'Maybe it's not your fault,' he stammered, 'it's the way you've been brought up, but you have no idea at all, have you, what you've done to me?'

'Why, what have I done?' she asked, turning white herself, 'what have I done but try to make you happy?'

'I was happy,' he answered slowly, 'when I thought I could offer you a home and an income. All my life, I'd seen my father work for other men, I knew that's what I'd have to do, too. Then I learned I wasn't even Lucio's son, I was the son of a man who'd given me away, I was inferior to his other sons, I was nobody. Jack Wintour put things right for me, and Doña Alicia helped. I became my own man, I held up my head. I met you and I was able to give you what I wanted, a share in the working of Sentos land; I was over the moon. Last night, I think I was what you said you wanted to make me, the happiest man in the world.' He gave a long, dreary laugh. 'Don't ask me what I am now.'

'I don't understand,' she said brokenly. 'I thought you'd be so pleased –'

'Where can I sleep tonight?' he asked, interrupting her roughly. 'Is there some sort of dressing room?'

In the end, he had not humiliated her in the eyes of her servants. They took their baths, they dressed carefully, they went down to dinner and, to please Ines, ate something, then they went to their room and lay in the same bed like two stone figures stretched on a tomb.

'You're not fair,' Sofia sobbed. 'You've ruined everything.'

'Oh, Sofia,' Julio answered, 'can't you see, it is you who have done that?'

*

In the morning, they had breakfast sent to their room and looked at each other with reddened eyes.

'What are we going to do?' Sofia asked. 'We're married, we can't go back on that.'

'No.'

'You won't leave me, will you, Julio? It's true what I said, I do love you.'

'We must try to work something out, something that will not involve using your money.'

'Anything,' she said eagerly, 'I'll agree to anything. Except, we must remember we may have a child. My child must not be deprived.'

'You still wish to live with me on the *estancia*?'

'Of course I do!'

'After this?' Julio glanced about the beautiful guest room.

'I've said so, Julio.'

'Very well, then. What I propose is that we live for the most part on what I earn, in the house I can provide, but that you continue to run your vineyards as you have run them before. I presume you have good managers?'

'The best. You shall meet them.'

'Obviously, you must keep your maid, spend on dress as you have always done, do whatever you like with your fortune, but I will accept no part of it. Do you agree?'

Sofia gave a long, exasperated sigh. 'I really don't see why you should not have my dowry. All husbands expect something, and think how much we could do for the *estancia*!'

'The *estancia* still belongs to the Wintours.'

'And am I not to tell them who I am?'

'No, and you are not to try to buy the *estancia* from them.'

'Of course I shan't do that!' she flared. 'We'll get nowhere if you keep throwing that in my face!'

'I'm sorry.' As Sofia moved to the window and stood looking down at the long tree-lined avenue below, Julio followed her and stood beside her. 'Do you really think we might be having a child?' he asked softly.

'I told you I couldn't be sure yet.'

'But it's possible?'

'Yes.' She moved closer to him. 'It's possible.'

He slowly took her into his arms. 'We'll do everything we

can for him, or her, you needn't worry about that.'

'It will be a boy. I want a boy first and I always get what I want.'

'I think you do.' Their eyes met, then Julio began to kiss her. 'Sometimes I do, too. I couldn't give you up, you know, however much money you have.'

'I promise I'll never offer you any of it.'

With one mind, they moved to the still unmade bed. 'They won't be coming in to make it just yet, will they?' asked Julio.

'Why don't you lock the door?' said Sofia.

Slowly, Julio brought himself back to the present, aware that Victor was still waiting for him to explain what must have seemed an almost crazy statement.

'I'm not crazy,' he said, as though Victor had made the comment, 'it's just that Sofia is Almedo Wines.'

'Sofia is what?' asked Victor, then recognition dawned. 'My God, you're not serious, are you? She has inherited Almedo Wines?'

'I've never been more serious, Victor.'

'But why didn't you tell me before?'

'I didn't want to. I didn't want to have anything to do with it.'

'I'd have shouted it from the housetops.'

'That would have been all right for you, not for me.'

Victor laughed, a little shakily. 'Pride, you know, is one of the Seven Deadly Sins.'

'You think I shouldn't be too proud to live on my wife's money? Well, I'm not too proud to offer it to you.'

'And I'm not too proud to take it, if Sofia is agreeable.'

'I discussed it with her this afternoon. She is agreeable.'

Victor rubbed a hand across his eyes. 'Julio, I don't know what to say. What can I say? We shall have to see the lawyers, of course, to negotiate the loan.'

'It needn't be a loan,' said Julio.

Victor started. 'Look, there's nothing else it can be. We can't talk about giving here.'

'I wasn't talking about giving, I was talking about selling.'

'Selling?'

'The *estancia*.' Julio leaned forwards, his eyes alight, 'Victor, would you consider selling the *estancia* to Sofia and me?'

Chapter Thirty-Nine

'We still have the *estancia*,' said Alice, 'that's what counts.'

She was sitting with Charlotte in their father's study, the Belcarron accounts spread out on the desk before them, Victor's cable and a copy of the *Cork Examiner* underneath Alice's hand. Victor, of course, had given them only the starkest details: 'STONEFIELD BANK CRASHED STOP ARTHUR DEAD STOP HAVE MATTERS IN HAND STOP DETAILS LATER VICTOR'. The newspaper, however, had a full account and it was this that had sent the two sisters, white-faced, to the study to survey the position. Alice, breathing fast, was trying to be optimistic. They still had the *estancia*. The *estancia* could still provide an income, if not immediately, then in the future. They had only to wait for Victor to get things sorted out, raise the necessary loans –

'And in the meantime, you've lost your capital and all your investments,' said Charlotte dryly. 'Alice, we must face facts. It's going to be quite some time before you can expect anything from the *estancia*. What are you going to use to run Belcarron?'

'Belcarron hasn't always been dependent on the *estancia,*' Alice said quickly. 'There are still some rents coming in.'

'You know we haven't been self-sufficient for years. There are wages to pay, there are bills to pay, there's wet rot in the attic –'

'Oh, Charlotte!' Alice rose and irritably poked the fire, as the winter rain slashed at the study windows and sent the bushes bending on the clifftop.

'It's no good saying "Oh, Charlotte", Alice. We must decide what is to be done.' Charlotte groaned and twirled a pen between her fingers. 'Oh, if only I could have brought something back from Germany! I feel such a parasite, living here on you, when you quite definitely can't afford me!'

'You're my sister, I can afford you.' Alice sighed and returned to her chair. 'We're not too badly off, believe me, we can weather this if we just hold on. Consider poor Blanche Stonefield, how she must be feeling. And Evie, with the children ... Thank heavens Victor is capable and experienced, he'll know what to do.'

'I never met Arthur Stonefield, but I must say I don't feel much like forgiving him for what he was brought on so many people.'

'Yet he must have suffered a great deal, before he did what he did.' Alice shook her head. 'Thank God his father did not live to see what happened! He was such a wonderful man, Charlotte, so correct, so dependable –'

'Dependable,' Charlotte repeated thoughtfully. 'Yes, as you get older, don't you begin to feel that trust is the most important thing in the world?' Then she bit her lip and a touch of scarlet stained her cheekbones. 'I'm a fine one to talk about trust, I suppose.'

'Let's have tea,' said Alice, and was rising to ring the bell when Bridie herself appeared, beaming.

'Isn't it Miss Tina who's here, then?' she cried. 'And the doctor, the dear man?'

'Tina?' Alice and Charlotte exchanged glances. 'But we weren't expecting –'

'Hello, Mama – Aunt Charlotte!' Tina came in, cold, fresh-faced, still in her heavy coat, with George following. 'We came as soon as we got Victor's cable – only for the weekend, we couldn't manage longer, but we felt we had to see you, find out how this is going to affect you.'

'Why, Tina, I don't know what to say!' Alice kissed and embraced her daughter as George pecked Charlotte's cheek. Bridie took their coats and ran out, smiling, to see about tea. 'You're a tonic, you're both a wonderful tonic!' Alice cried. 'Just when Charlotte and I were sitting here so depressed!'

'It's bad, then, is it?' asked Tina. 'I thought it might be. I know I've lost everything, but then I haven't got Belcarron to run.'

'You do have your project,' said George. As Alice gave him a questioning look, he explained that Tina had been funding a study on poverty and women's health among her hospital patients, which would now, of course, have to come to an end, unless other funding could be found.

'All thanks to Arthur Stonefield,' Tina murmured. 'I'm sorry for his poor wife and Evie, but really he seems to have been no better than a scoundrel. How do you think Victor is coping, Mama?'

'I've no details, but I'm sure he'll be doing his best for us. The main thing is, as I was saying to Charlotte, we still have the *estancia*; when everything is sorted out, that should still provide an income.'

'But in the meantime, will you be able to manage?' Tina bent over the Belcarron accounts. 'George says he'd be willing to help, and maybe Melissa would, too; her father-in-law has plenty of money.'

'But doesn't like spending it, so Melissa says.' Alice tried to smile. 'George, I appreciate your offer very much but I really don't think –'

'Mama, you know you need it. Don't turn it down for the sake of it, because George really wants to help.'

'What about your hospital study? I'd rather he helped you with that.'

'While the wet rot turns to dry rot in your attic?' Tina took her mother's arm. 'Come on, let's go and have tea and talk about this later. I'm starving, I couldn't eat a thing on the crossing, it was so wild.'

But when they were in the drawing room after dinner, listening to the wind howling round the house like a banshee, Tina said firmly, 'There's something else we wanted to discuss with you, Mama.'

'Oh, dear,' Alice sighed, 'and I know what it is.'

'Don't look like that, Mama. The way things are in Ireland now, we really don't think it's safe for you and Aunt Charlotte to stay here. We'd like you to come back with us to London.'

'For how long?' asked Alice.

'Until things settle down.'

'For ever, then.'

Tina caught her breath. 'Look, you know there must be an end to violence soon. Some political solution will have to be found.'

Alice put some stitches into her embroidery, Charlotte raised her eyebrows, George drained his whiskey.

'You don't agree?' asked Tina.

'I don't see a political solution on the horizon,' George replied. 'All Lloyd George can offer is partition between Ulster and the rest of Ireland. That suits nobody. It's an impasse.'

'So the violence goes on,' Charlotte finished.

'Exactly my point,' said Alice.

'Mine, too, then!' Tina cried, with spirit. 'I didn't say there could be a solution immediately. I know the violence is still going on; in fact, it's worse than ever. Which is why I say you should leave Belcarron.'

It was true that the situation in Ireland had recently deteriorated. So many members of the Royal Irish Constabulary were resigning, rather than become targets for the IRA, that the authorities were having to bring in auxiliary forces from England. These were mainly ex-army men, who, because of a shortage of green RIC uniforms, wore khaki trousers and became known all over the country as the Black and Tans, or, contemptuously, the Tans. They brought a new brutality to their retaliation against Republicans, forcing up the level of violence, making it even more certain that one day there would be all-out civil war. In the meantime, the Republicans were desperate again for arms, taking them wherever they could find them, breaking in and raiding, spreading terror among ordinary householders. That was why Tina had become so particularly anxious to have Alice leave Belcarron.

'No one is going to attack me, my dear,' Alice said calmly. 'They all know who I am, they know I have nothing they want.'

'You have Grandfather's guns, Mama.'

'They're useless, Tina, they haven't been used since before the war, no one would want them.'

'I agree,' Charlotte put in. 'We're not really under any threat. Besides, the village is full of yachtspeople now, they're not the sort to come looking for arms.'

'And your Bill comes over quite a lot, I suppose?' asked Tina, with a grin. 'It's my one consolation, that he's around.'

'So, let's consider this matter closed,' said Alice. 'After all, I couldn't leave Belcarron now if I wanted to. Hester is coming to stay!'

'Cousin Hester?' Tina's face lit up. 'Why, there's the solution, Mama! You could go back to America with her! See Melissa and Tim, see Paul, see New York – it would be perfect!'

'I'm willing!' cried Charlotte. 'Alice, what do you say?'

'I'll see,' said Alice, and at the time-honoured phrase every mother uses to placate a too eager child, Tina gave a sigh of defeat.

Chapter Forty

It was a chill, blustery day in late February when Hester returned to Belcarron. She should have been in Dorset, visiting Marianne, but Everard had bronchitis and her visit had been postponed. 'So here I am, three weeks too early!' she cried, hurrying from the taxi to embrace Alice on the steps of the house. 'You don't mind, do you?'

'Oh, Hester!' Alice held her close, then released her to look into her long, sweet face. 'It's just so wonderful to see you again. How are you, my dear?'

'Well, very well.' Hester blinked away a few tears. 'Oh, it's so good to be with you, Alice. You don't know how often I've pictured myself coming back, seeing you, the house, all the old places.'

'Nothing's changed, nor have you. Still the same dear Hester.'

'Still the same lovely Alice.'

They laughed tremulously, then Alice drew Hester into the house, Bridie appeared and was greeted, the luggage was brought in and Hester took off her hat.

'You're in the same old room,' Alice told her, leading the way slowly up the staircase. 'I'm sorry, I'm not as good on stairs as I used to be – put on too much weight, I suppose. Here we are.' Panting a little, she opened a door and immediately Hester was transported back to that day in June 1885 when she, Richard and Marianne had arrived to visit their cousins. There had been summer flowers in the room that day, there were snowdrops now, but everything else was so much the same that she might have been twenty-one again, outwardly calm, secretly agitated by her first meeting with Uncle John's groom, the handsome, dark-browed Daniel Molloy. The memory pierced so keenly that she gave an involuntary sob, and Alice at once put her arms around her.

'Don't mind grieving,' she whispered. 'It's good to grieve.'

'Daniel used to tell me not to, you know, not even to wear mourning.' Hester glanced down at her grey coat and skirt. 'He said he'd had a good life and was going to a better place, he wanted no tears or black dresses. I suppose he never thought I might cry for myself.'

'You did so much for me when Richard died,' Alice murmured, 'I wish I could help you now.'

'You are helping, Alice, you are, believe me.'

They stood together for another moment or two, then Hester moved to comb her hair at the little dressing mirror and Alice said tea was ready when she wanted it. 'Charlotte sends her apologies for not being here to greet you. She's with friends at the yacht club and will be back for dinner.' Alice smiled. 'Actually, she's just being tactful, she knows we want to talk.'

'Charlotte tactful? Alice, she certainly has changed! Oh, I'm so glad you two have made it up! You'll feel so much better.'

'I do. It's as though something festering has been lanced, all the bitterness has gone. And I really appreciate having her here, though I think perhaps she should get married.'

'Married?' Hester swung round from the mirror. 'There's another admirer?'

'Bill Paget, the uncle of one of Jack's friends. He's a lawyer from Cork, a widower without a family, which would suit Charlotte, after what she's been through with her step-daughters in Germany.'

'No luck with her inheritance, I suppose?'

'No luck at all, and she worries dreadfully about having no money. As though I'd want her to pay to live at Belcarron!'

'Are you managing?' Hester asked cautiously. 'I mean, after the Stonefield crash?'

'Oh, yes, don't worry about that. If you're ready, shall we go down?'

'This beautiful staircase,' Hester murmured, running her hand down the banister. 'I remember coming down with Marianne, that time we all went to the ball. Poor Marianne – I can't think what I shall say to her about Freddie.'

'I feel so sorry for Cecily, too. What is she going to do with her life? There's no one for her to marry, all the young men have gone. It's the same for the Morry girls.'

'You don't mean Edie and Kitty?'

'Hester, you're going back into the past! I mean Cavan's girls, Daisy and Moyra. Both so brave in the war, now back home with nothing to do.'

'Then they must find jobs. Every woman should have a job.'

'There are no jobs for men, never mind women, Hester. And what every woman really wants is a home and a family.'

Hester smiled her sweet smile and said she was looking forward to a cup of tea.

'Poor Bridie,' Alice whispered, when Bridie had lit the flame under the spirit kettle and left them, 'she gets so tired these days, has such a bad back, I feel guilty having her work for me, but it's so difficult these days to get anyone to help. Our last little maid departed to work in a shop in Skibbereen, and all the local girls want to do is to work for the yachtspeople.'

'I suppose the time will come when we have no servants at all. After all, there are better things for girls to do these days than housework.'

'Yes, indeed.' Alice gave a wry smile as she made the tea. 'Do you remember Nora who used to be our parlourmaid? I asked her the other day if one of her daughters would like to come into service at Belcarron. You'll never guess what she said. "Oh, it's kind of you, Miss Alice, so it is, but Deirdre is away to Cork to learn the typewriting and Mollie is up at the university." Can you believe it?'

'Why, I think that's wonderful!' cried Hester. 'I never thought such a thing could happen!'

'Well, it appears the girl is exceptional, has gained all sorts of scholarships, and there she is in Dublin, an undergraduate.' Alice passed Hester her tea. 'I'm pleased for her, of course, but I can't help finding it strange.'

'Only because she's one of the first, Alice. We thought it strange Tina should become a doctor at one time, didn't we? But I wish Daniel could have known about Nora's girl.'

They began to talk of family matters. How was Caitlin, how

was Paul? Caitlin was working as hard as ever for the Republican cause, though she had taken a little time off to entertain Hester while she was in Dublin. Now she was away, Hester hadn't liked to ask where – it was never wise to ask Caitlin her plans. Paul was happy in his training to be a priest and might soon be continuing his studies in Rome. It was a disappointment, of course, that he would not be taking over the book chain, but Hester said one should not expect children to follow their parents' wishes; if the chain had to be sold, it had to be sold.

'Oh, you don't need to tell me what to expect from children,' Alice said, with feeling. 'Victor will never come back now. After what's happened to Stonefield's, he is needed out there more than ever to try to get us back to where we were before. Sometimes, you know, I wonder if Belcarron has any future at all.'

'You mustn't give up,' Hester said earnestly. 'You must never give up! Belcarron will survive, I know it will!'

'Of course it will, I'm just looking on the dark side.' Alice set her chin and stood up. 'Come, let me show you round – it's light enough. I want you to see that nothing has changed.'

Charlotte returned in time for drinks before dinner, looking strikingly attractive in a dark-blue two-piece, her yellow hair still showing only a little grey, her green eyes sparkling at the sight of Hester.

'Hester, it's so good to see you! How many years is it since we met? I have an awful feeling it was Parnell's funeral. Wasn't I with Priscilla Letton? Wasn't it raining?' Charlotte pressed Hester's hand. 'Hester, I'm so sorry about Daniel.'

'Thank you.' A slight flush rose to Hester's cheek; she never forgot that it was in a struggle with Daniel that Charlotte's first husband, Dudley Sarn, had been accidentally shot. 'But you are looking wonderful, Charlotte! Have you really taken up yachting?'

'The yacht club, my dear, is more like it.' Charlotte poured herself a sherry and refilled Hester's glass, as Alice excused herself to see Maisie about dinner. 'Yes, it's a nice way of spending time and I meet my friends there. I suppose Alice has told you about Bill Paget?'

'She has and I'm looking forward to meeting him.'

'You will tomorrow night, he's coming to dinner. Tonight, we thought we'd rather be on our own, just the three of us, so that we can talk about old times.'

Just the three of them. How pleasant it was, thought Hester, as they sat down at the long table in the familiar dining room and the candles flickered on their Wintour faces and the Wintour family portraits looked down. Surely Alice was not right to think that Belcarron might one day go? It mustn't, it couldn't . . . Hester wanted freedom for Ireland as much as Caitlin with all her militancy, but to lose estates such as Belcarron with all that they meant would be too high a price to pay.

They were taking coffee in the drawing room, where Alice and Hester were smiling over old photographs, when Charlotte suddenly experienced a strange sensation of unease. She sat up straight in her chair, feeling instinctively she should say nothing to the others. There seemed to be nothing wrong, nothing to account for the icy dread enfolding her. But a memory was stirring. Her father and Dudley, here in the drawing room, herself on the stairs. She had a book in her hand, she had been going up to bed. Appalled, Charlotte seemed to see as in one of the new moving pictures, her young self running back down the staircase, shouting to her father, 'Papa, I think I hear something outside! Papa, Papa, they're here, the house is surrounded!'

With a crash that made Alice and Hester jump, Charlotte set down her coffee cup and leaped to her feet.

'Why, Charlotte, what is it?' cried Alice in astonishment. 'Are you ill?'

'There are people outside,' Charlotte answered, trembling. 'I know it, I can feel it. What are we to do?'

'People outside?' Hester took her arm. 'What do you mean, Charlotte? I've heard nothing.'

'They're outside, they're waiting, I think they've come for the guns, Papa's guns.' Charlotte turned in agitation to her sister. 'Alice, we must get the guns ourselves! We must get the key to the gun room!'

'I can't see anyone!' Alice was at the window, pulling aside the curtain. 'There's no one there.'

'I tell you they're at the door now. Listen – oh, God! Do you hear?'

The three women stood motionless as the outside bell began to clang and a fusillade of knocks thundered against the front door. Then as Bridie's slow step sounded in the hall, they ran to her together.

'Bridie, don't answer!' Charlotte shrieked. 'Don't answer the door!'

'Holy Mother of God, is it the Shinners, then?' asked Bridie, her face turning white. 'Is it the IRA?'

'It might be,' Alice answered calmly. 'Charlotte, you're probably right, someone must have told them about Papa's guns. I think I shall have to let them in.'

'Alice, don't!' Charlotte cried.

'If I don't, they will only break down the door.'

'Yes, let them in,' said Hester. 'I don't believe they'll harm us, if they get what they want.'

'I say we should get the guns to protect ourselves!' Charlotte cried. 'How do we know they won't harm us? No one is safe!'

'I'm going to open the door,' said Alice.

Four masked men stood on the steps, four dark figures silhouetted against the last of the evening light. Before Alice could speak, they were inside, pushing past her, then one slammed the door with a crash that shook the house.

'Just do as we say and you'll not be getting hurt,' he said in a deep Irish voice. 'We know there are guns here, will you be getting them for us? Quick as you can.'

'All I have are my father's old sporting guns,' Alice replied evenly. 'They haven't been used for years, I doubt if they will even fire.'

''Twill be for us to decide that.' The eyes behind the mask were hard. 'Be getting them, Mrs Wintour.'

'Get them, Alice,' Charlotte said hoarsely. 'Do as he says.'

'Why should I?' Alice asked, trembling. 'Why should I give them guns to use against people?'

'If the guns do not fire, sure we won't be doing any damage,' one of the men said with a laugh and suddenly grabbed at Bridie, jerking back her head so that her cap fell to the floor. 'This one will know where they are, I'm thinking, so come on, don't be giving us any trouble.'

Alice gave a cry of alarm, but Bridie turned in the man's grasp and slapped him hard across his masked face. 'You let me go, you great coward!' she shouted. 'You're no Irishman to treat a woman so!'

Before he could retaliate, she had broken away, and though he lunged to follow, one of his colleagues, a slightly built fellow with a cap completely covering his hair, put up a hand to stop him and shook his head in warning. Hester, who had been staring at the slender figure ever since his entrance, locked her trembling hands together and swayed to and fro. 'Dear God, let it not be true, please, please, let it not be true!'

'Oh, Mother, why are you here? I planned this now because I thought you were in Dorset.' Caitlin pulled aside her mask and stood, white-faced, in the soft light of Belcarron's old lamps. Her mother and her cousins stared at her as though she were a creature of nightmare. So she seemed, in her black sweater and trousers, her hair scraped beneath her cap, her mask swinging in her fingers.

'I can't believe it,' Alice whispered. 'Is it – is it Caitlin?'

'It can't be true,' said Charlotte, horror twisting her features. 'Tina rescued you, didn't she? Tina rescued you – for this?'

'Caitlin,' said Hester, very quietly, 'leave this house and take these men with you. Leave this house now. You know I support your aims, I love Ireland, I want Ireland to be free, but this is not the way to do it. You are on the wrong road, Caitlin, you must go back.'

'Mother, we all have to do what we believe is right.' Caitlin turned to Alice. 'Cousin Alice, will you let us have the keys to the gun room? I know you have quite an armoury in there, so don't waste any more time. You'll be quite unharmed if you just do as we say.'

Alice, standing very straight, calmly held Caitlin's gaze. 'I know you can force me to do what you want, so I will give you the keys, but your mother is right, Caitlin, you are on the road to death and destruction, you must learn to understand that. I shall pray that you do.'

'Just be getting the bloody guns before we lose patience!'

cried the man who had snatched Bridie. 'We've been waiting long enough, so we have. Wasn't I saying it would be like this, bringing a woman along? Talking is all they will ever be doing.'

'Be quiet, Donnie!' Caitlin cried fiercely. 'Wasn't I the one who knew where the guns were? Cousin Alice, please give us the key now. Mother, Charlotte – go over there and sit down with Bridie. For God's sake, don't any of you try anything.'

In ten minutes it was all over. Alice, steadfastly refusing to let her hands tremble, had unlocked the door to John Wintour's gun room and, while Caitlin watched, the men seized the sporting guns and rifles and carried them out. The front door was flung open, there was the sound of a distant car's engine starting, then a shout to Caitlin to hurry. She stood at the door, while the night wind rushed around her, and sought her mother's eyes, but Hester would not look at her.

'Will you be coming?' cried a voice again, and Caitlin whirled about and ran. She left the door swinging open.

After a moment or two, Bridie stepped forward and quietly closed it.

'Poor Maisie, 'tis like the dead she sleeps down by the range. Sure she'll be crazy, hearing what she's been missing! I'll be making some tea.'

'I could have done with missing it,' Charlotte groaned. 'Oh, God, I feel quite sick!'

'Alice, you were wonderful,' Hester said faintly. 'But I feel so ashamed – so ashamed . . .'

'Hester, you mustn't. You are not to be held responsible for what your daughter does.'

'She sees it as right, she sees herself in a war, nothing will change her.'

'I'm so cold, let's go by the fire,' Charlotte murmured, shivering. 'I suppose we are really suffering from shock, we'll be better with the tea. Alice, come and get warm, you're so pale – are you all right?'

'As you say, it's the shock. I think, maybe, I won't wait for tea, I'll go straight up to bed.'

'Very sensible.' Hester found Alice's shawl and put it round her shoulders. 'I'll go and see about a hot-water bottle for you, you must try to keep warm.'

'Would you like me to help you up the stairs?' Charlotte asked, as Hester hurried away. 'You really do look a bit under the weather.'

'No, thank you, I'll do better on my own. I'll take one of my pills.'

'Pills? I didn't know you were taking pills, Alice.'

'Only now and again,' Alice answered vaguely. 'Goodnight, Charlotte. I'm sorry we had such a fright.'

'Don't be worrying about me, I'm feeling better, anyway.' Charlotte, her eyes narrowing, watched Alice begin to climb the stairs. 'I do wish you'd let me help you!' she called.

Alice only shook her head.

How steep these stairs were, how high! They seemed as high as waves threatening to engulf her, and as insubstantial. Finding each step was like treading water. Aware of Charlotte's eyes on her from below, Alice straightened her back and felt for the banister with her right hand, thinking it lucky she didn't need her left, for strange things were happening to her left arm, shooting pains and needle stabs, making her want to cry out, except that she didn't want to alert Charlotte. At last, she reached the landing window and wondered if she should turn back to smile at her sister. Too difficult. Her head was spinning so fast, she could picture herself spinning down the stairs, falling like a ball, bouncing on every step. Better just to go to the window where she had always liked to stand, look at the bay, put her bouncing head against the cool glass and take breath for the remaining stairs. How strange, the night seemed to have gone, the whole stretch of the bay was bathed in light, it must be morning already. She was pondering on this, wondering where the hours had gone, when she heard someone call her name, 'Alice?' and again 'Alice?' Very slowly, she turned her head and gave a cry of joy. Richard was coming towards her. He was dressed in his bridegroom's morning dress, there was a flower in his buttonhole, he looked handsomer even than he had looked on that wedding day. She put out her hands and he took them, and all the light covering the bay moved into the house and surrounded them.

*

'Here's the hot-water bottle,' Hester called, coming into the hall from the back stairs.

'Never mind the hot-water bottle,' said Charlotte.

Hester looked at her, then up at the staircase, and put her hand to her throat. Alice was lying beneath the long window, quite still.

'Charlotte, what are you doing?' Hester cried, in a high, trembling voice. 'Why haven't you gone to her? We must help, we must fetch the doctor –'

'Don't go, Hester, she's with Richard, leave them a little while.'

'You – saw him?'

'No, but she did. Somehow, I know she did. Hester, Alice has gone.'

When Bridie came up with the tea, she found them holding each other. It was some time before she could discover what was wrong.

Chapter Forty-One

The funeral was private, attended only by Alice's family and close friends, but the memorial service, timed for Victor's arrival in May, was a grand affair for the whole county. Charlotte supposed that Alice would have been pleased with the turnout, but to her it seemed something of a parody of her sister's wedding. The same church, the same kind of congregation, the same massed flowers, but now the celebration was for a life that was over. The mourners seemed nervous as well as grief-stricken, glancing over their shoulders as though half expecting armed men to spring out from behind the solid old pews. Who could blame them? This was the way life was in Ireland in 1920. Those who had come today to mourn Alice's passing were mourning the past, too, and all that had been sweet and safe and was no longer.

Afterwards, there were refreshments at Belcarron. Sad as they were, everyone brightened when the wine came in and the sandwiches were handed round. Frail, old people in ancient mourning clothes mingled with the younger set, some of whom had decided not to wear mourning at all. There was plenty of talk and even laughter and if the talk was not of Alice, it was only what she would have expected. To dwell on the deceased after the service was never the done thing.

When the last car had been driven away (by a desolate Cavan Morry), the family sat, exhausted, in the drawing room and looked at Alice's chair. It seemed impossible that they should be together in the room she had loved and she not be with them. Everyone had a picture of her in that chair, working on her tapestry, making tea with the little silver kettle, her blue eyes intent, her white hands busy, always so precise, always so efficient, always there.

There are so few of us left now who remember her when she was young, thought Charlotte. There's Hester, of course, and Marianne. I'm glad Marianne was able to come, I'm glad she was friendly, not too disapproving. Charlotte smiled at Bill Paget hovering near, but her smile was abstracted, for he had scarcely known Alice and, though she knew he would be a lifeline in the months ahead, this was Alice's day.

Marianne, sitting with Everard and downcast Cecily, looked at Charlotte and thought how strange it was to be seeing her again, after so many years, and how cut up she looked over Alice, which, if you remembered the old days, was stranger still. Marianne did not regret being nice to her – it was good to be friendly, not think of Charlotte's old spite – but oh, to be nice to Hester, how difficult that had been! For, to be honest, whose fault was all this, if not Hester's? If she had not married Daniel Molloy, she wouldn't have had such a daughter as Caitlin, and then Alice would have been alive today. What a terrible burden of guilt it must be for Hester to carry, knowing that! No one, however much they wanted to, could ever take it from her.

Hester thought, I wish Paul were here, he would tell me what to do, ease the pain, for people say I am a good person but I can't find it in my heart to forgive Caitlin. My own daughter! How can I endure it? The worst of it is, she does not even understand what she has done, she believes she was only doing her duty. All I can do is pray.

Victor, missing Evie, was wondering if there might be life after death. He had never thought so, but some of the fellows in the war had begun to believe there was a good chance. They were so young, so full of vitality, they couldn't imagine just going into the darkness, just being snuffed out like a light. If Papa were somewhere, Victor hoped he would forgive him. Mother, of course, would have understood, if he had been able to tell her, but she had died too soon. Why did people always die too soon, before one could tell them what they needed to know?

He said, aloud, 'Why ever did Mother leave Papa in Buenos

Aires? He should have been buried here, so that she could be near him. Why did no one think of that at the time?'

No one answered at first, then Tina said, 'I'm sure Mama never thought about dying herself. People don't. As a doctor, I know that.'

'Wasn't it because Mama thought Papa had been happy in Argentina, and would like to rest there?' asked Melissa, taking Tim Leifson's hand. 'Didn't you tell me, Victor, he was buried near Aunt Beatrice?'

'Yes, that's probably what decided Mother to leave him there, but now he's 9,000 miles away from her. It doesn't seem right.'

'He's not 9,000 miles away from you, though. You can visit his grave, can't you?'

'I shall not be there,' said Victor.

Every face in the room turned to his. Tina and George, Melissa and Tim, Charlotte and Bill, Marianne, Everard, even Cecily, all stared at Victor. He bore their scrutiny calmly, drinking a little wine and setting down his glass, moving his damaged leg into a more comfortable position.

'What do you mean?' asked Tina brusquely.

'I mean I'm coming home. That is, if you and Melissa agree to what I want to do.'

Bill half rose. 'Do you wish to discuss family matters, Victor? Would you like me to go?'

'Certainly not. You know our situation. With Mother gone, there are only the three of us left to share the ownership of the *estancia*. After the Stonefield Bank crash, things have been very difficult for me, as you can imagine. When you don't need credit, you can get it; when you're desperate, it's another matter.'

'You always had the land as collateral,' George remarked. 'That should have solved your problem.'

'Since the war, values haven't been quite the same, but yes, I agree, I could have put up the land. After what happened, though, I was pretty anxious not to get into a situation I couldn't control.' Victor hesitated, pulling at his blond moustache. 'In the end, I did borrow, from a source I knew I could trust, and I was able to keep things going, but I also had this offer, you see – this offer for the *estancia*.'

Tina and Melissa exchanged glances. 'Are you saying you want to sell the *estancia*?' Tina asked, her colour rising. 'Victor, I can't believe what I'm hearing! That land's been in our family for years. Papa worked his head off to make it pay. If he could know you were even thinking of such a thing, he'd be broken-hearted!'

'Well, Mother wouldn't be. She'd be glad, really glad, to have me back at Belcarron!'

'Not this way, not by selling Papa's land!' Tina swung round to her sister. 'Melissa, what do you think? You're involved in this too, you have as much right to make decisions as Victor.'

Melissa put her hand through her newly bobbed hair. 'I'm not sure, Tina, that Victor isn't being sensible about this. After all, it's going to take years to build up reserves again, isn't it? Tim was only saying that the other day –'

'Not that I want to interfere, you know,' Tim said quickly, 'guess this is all your affair, not mine, but it does seem to me that Victor is going to have quite a fight on his hands to get back to normal.'

'But to sell Papa's land to a stranger!' cried Tina. 'I can't bear even to think about it.'

'It wouldn't be sold to a stranger,' Victor said quietly. 'The buyer is Julio.'

'Good God!' said George, breaking into the stunned silence. 'And just where is he going to get that kind of money?'

'He hasn't a bean,' said Melissa, 'it's impossible.'

'But his wife has,' Victor replied, 'and his wife, if you remember, is a Sentos.'

'So she is,' Tina whispered. 'Victor, you'd better explain.'

'Almedo Wines!' Bill whistled, when Victor had finished. 'She must be worth a mint.'

'She has sugar refineries, too.' Victor gave an exasperated smile. 'Can you believe that Julio isn't even grateful? Wants to pay his own way?'

'I can believe that, yes,' Tina answered. 'There are plenty of men who like to feel they are the providers. But presumably Julio doesn't mind the idea of using Sofia's money to buy the *estancia*?'

'For the first time, he's actually thanking his lucky stars. All he's ever wanted, really, is land.'

'This all seems extraordinary to me,' Marianne declared. 'I'm not even precisely sure who this Julio is, but what I'm wondering, Victor, is what does your wife think about leaving Argentina? It's her home, isn't it? How will she settle here?'

'And what about her mother?' Hester asked, in a low voice. 'Surely she can't be left without support?'

Victor's expression was sombre. 'In a terrible way, it's worked itself out. Blanche, my mother-in-law, has taken the tragedy very badly. It's not just Arthur's death that has affected her, it's what she feels is the disgrace, it's losing her home, which had to be sold, and her position. When Evie asked her if she would consider coming here, she jumped at it. It would be a new life, you see. Nobody here knows the name of Stonefield.'

There was a long silence, while Tina and Melissa sat thinking, and Victor watched them.

'Take your time,' he said at last. 'No need to decide now.'

'Oh, I've decided,' Melissa announced. 'The *estancia* really doesn't mean anything to me. If that's what you want, Victor, I agree to sell.'

Victor slowly turned his blue stare on Tina. She nodded. 'All right, I say the same. Julio has special rights, I don't mind so much, if it's going to him.'

'I should say his wife has special rights,' George observed. 'I know no one was happy at first about her coming into the family, but it has to be admitted, that land was once Sentos land and now it is returning to a Sentos.'

'I know it was Sentos land,' Victor answered shortly, 'but it was Wintour land, too, I can't forget that.'

'It's strange, though, isn't it, that Mama never changed the name?' Tina asked thoughtfully. 'For years it was ours, but she left it still the Estancia Sentos. It's almost as though she knew that one day the Sentos family would take their property back.'

'You've done the right thing, Victor,' Hester told him later. 'Belcarron means much more to this family than the *estancia*, and you're needed here.'

'I agree.' Victor looked at her uneasily, aware that she was suffering, but what could he say?

'I shall be leaving soon for New York,' she went on. 'Melissa and Tim have asked me to travel back with them, and I've agreed.'

'You're not staying with Cousin Marianne, then?'

A shadow crossed Hester's face. 'Not now. Marianne has been very kind, but I know she blames me for what happened to Alice. Of course, she's not alone in that.'

'Cousin Hester, none of us blames you!'

'Not directly, perhaps, but I understand why people think as they do.'

'You look so tired,' he said awkwardly. 'Try to get some rest.'

'Yes, I'll do that.' She said goodnight and climbed the stairs, not pausing at the landing window, and in her room lay on her bed. 'Try to rest,' Victor had said, and 'rest' was a lovely word. But it was meaningless to her.

Chapter Forty-Two

Work was Hester's anodyne. On her return to New York, she lived, slept and ate Molloy's Books and gradually, though her grief for Daniel and her guilt over Alice did not fade, they became easier to accept. The pace was not one she could keep up, however, and in the summer of 1923, three years after Alice's death, she instructed her accountants to reach a figure for selling the book chain. Facts must be faced, she would be sixty next year, there was no one to take over the reins and she was weary, bone-achingly weary, and longing for the rest which had so far eluded her.

On the day the accountants produced their report, she came home earlier than usual, planning to study the figures after dinner, and was greeted by Jennie, her only maid, who brought her a glass of iced tea.

'Hot, ain't it?' she asked, as Hester changed her strapped shoes for slippers. 'Mebbe you should see 'bout getting a fan.'

'Maybe. Or I might just move. To the ocean, or the country.'

Jennie, a tall, black-haired girl of Irish descent, shook her head. 'No, you'd miss the city, you better stay put.'

'You mean, you wouldn't come with me?'

'Not me, Mrs Molloy, I like the shops.'

As Jennie went out, whistling, Hester smiled and fanned herself with a magazine. She had bought it for an article on Melissa, described as 'young Mrs Timothy Leifson, who combines a busy social life with a highly successful professional career as a textile designer for her husband's firm, and also finds time to look after Timothy Junior, just one year of age!'

Well done, Melissa! Hester thought sleepily. She had to

confess that of all Alice's children, Melissa was the one she found least interesting, but maybe she was prejudiced. No mother could warm to the girl who had refused her son. All that was forgotten now, however, with Paul a contented and successful parish priest, working over in Queens. It pleased Hester to see him so happy, though, of course, if he had not found his vocation, he would have taken over the book chain. No point brooding on that now. No point, either, in trying not to think of Caitlin and what she might be doing, now that there was peace in Ireland.

Peace. Hester came awake. Would it last? Surely it would. The people were weary, they could face no more killings. After the years of violence between the IRA and the Black and Tans, there had been the appalling civil war that followed the Treaty of 1921, when the Irish Free State had been created but Ulster had remained British. Even Ireland had not seen the like of that conflict, when Irish fought Irish, when every day brought murders, burnings and executions. Michael Collins, the Republican military leader, was himself assassinated. Erskine Childers, who had worked so hard for Ireland's freedom, was executed by the new Free State, simply for possessing a firearm. It seemed as though the country had gone crazy. Then, suddenly, as though it could roll no further, the great wheel of violence stopped. It was clear that the anti-Treaty fighters had run out of power and when de Valera, the ex-president, ordered them to lay down their arms, they laid them down. The cause of a united Ireland must wait until strength could be gained. For now, there must be peace.

Pray God it will last, thought Hester, but she knew that even if it did, it came too late for her. Not a word, not a sign, had she received from Caitlin and she did not know how she would have responded, had such a sign been made. Ireland was at peace, a peace Daniel would probably not have accepted. No doubt Caitlin felt the same. Whatever her views, she was lost to her mother.

Hester took her bath and dressed for her solitary dinner in a cool silk two-piece. 'Not too much to eat,' she told Jennie, 'it's too hot.'

'Some soup, a little fish?' asked Jennie, but Hester said just the fish would do.

'And a drink first?'

'Why not?'

Hester relaxed and was sipping a cocktail when the doorbell rang.

'Father Paul,' Jennie announced with a grin, knowing a visit from him would mean more to Hester than any drink.

'Paul!' Hester went to greet her son, handsome in his clerical suit and dogcollar. 'What a pleasant surprise! I had no idea you might come over.'

'Nor had I. Could Jennie possibly stretch dinner, do you think?'

'Of course, there'll be more than enough for two.'

'I meant for three.' Paul turned back in the doorway. 'Caitlin, you'd better come in.'

Mother and daughter looked at each other across the few feet of polished floor – it might have been an ocean.

Mother looks older, thought Caitlin.

Caitlin looks different, thought Hester, perhaps because the cream dress she was wearing was so different from her usual style, perhaps because her dark hair, under the cream cloche hat, was short. Certainly her gaze was the same, fiercely direct, like her father's.

As Hester made no move to welcome her in, Caitlin hesitated, glancing up at Paul. 'I told you this wouldn't work, Paul. I'd better go.'

'No –' Hester put out her hand. 'No, don't go, Caitlin. If you have come here to talk to me, I won't turn you away.'

'May we sit down?' asked Paul.

'Of course.' Hester took her own armchair and Paul and Caitlin sat facing her on the sofa. Hester cleared her throat. 'It's three years since Alice died, Caitlin. If you've come here to say you're sorry, you've left it rather late.'

'I am sorry, all the same.'

'Why didn't you say so before?'

'I knew there'd be no point.' Caitlin leaned forwards. 'But, Mother, I swear to you I never wanted to harm anyone. If I'd known Cousin Alice had a heart condition, I'd never have gone to Belcarron.'

'None of us knew she had a heart condition, she never told

us she'd been seeing the doctor for years. But you knew you'd cause distress anyway, didn't you, by going to Belcarron? You knew, but you were so committed to violence for your own ends, you didn't care who got hurt as long as you got what you wanted.'

'I was never committed to violence, Mother. I saw it as necessary, that's all, as it's necessary in a war. Papa always believed we were fighting a war. So did I.'

'And in wars, innocent people get hurt, is that what you're saying?' asked Paul.

'Yes. If that sounds hard, it's still true. Soldiers are trained to accept it, and I saw myself as a soldier.'

'Saw?' Hester repeated. 'Don't you see yourself as a soldier now?'

'No.' Caitlin took off her hat and ran her right hand through her dark hair, shaped neatly close to her head. 'As a matter of fact, I haven't seen myself as that for quite some time.'

'How long?' asked Paul.

Caitlin shrugged. 'Three years?'

'Since Alice died,' Hester said softly. 'Oh, Caitlin, what have you been doing then, all this time?'

'Nursing.'

'Nursing?'

'I can tell you, I was needed.'

'But what about your work, your friends? What about Countess Markievicz?'

'I still admire Madame!' Caitlin cried. 'I still think she's one of the most wonderful people I've ever known. But when I heard about what had happened at Belcarron I couldn't – I couldn't go her way any more.' Caitlin looked down, her lip trembling. 'I guess Papa would never have forgiven me.'

'Don't say that,' Hester whispered, 'don't. Papa would have understood.'

'Sure he would,' Paul said quickly. 'You don't have to apologise if you've had a change of heart, Caitlin.'

'Why didn't you tell me?' Hester asked. 'Why didn't you come to me and explain? You left me, left us all, to think what we liked for three long years, didn't you? Have you any idea what you put us through?'

'I'm sorry, Mother, I didn't think I could do anything else.'

Caitlin looked up, her blue eyes stormy.

'Why? Why did you think that?'

'Because there are some things you can't say sorry for. How would it have looked, if I'd come to you and Tina and Cousin Charlotte and said, "Oh, I'm so sorry Cousin Alice is dead, but I've taken up nursing, so that's all right, isn't it?" You know I couldn't have done that, Mother.'

'But to let me think you were involved in the violence, doing heaven knows what in the civil war, that was cruel, Caitlin, whatever you say, it was cruel and unnecessary.'

'Guess it was.' Caitlin heaved a long sigh. 'Guess I never was very good at seeing things from other people's point of view.'

'It must have been hard for you,' Paul said, when they had all three been silent for some time. 'I mean, not wanting to be involved any more? There must have been some who didn't take too kindly to that.'

'It wasn't easy,' Caitlin admitted. 'People who drop out are never too popular with the IRA.'

Hester caught her breath; it was plain this was a danger she had never considered. 'Caitlin, you weren't punished?'

'No, I was lucky. Madame supported me, so did Frances and some of the other women. After all, I wasn't trying to run away, I was still around, I was offering nursing and they needed nurses. Then, when the Treaty was signed, they'd other things to think about. Everyone split up on one side or the other, and I just got on with my job.'

'You were anti-Treaty?' asked Paul.

'No, I was for it. I didn't want to see Ireland cut in two, but Michael Collins said we should go for the deal because Ulster couldn't possibly survive and we'd get a united Ireland anyway.' Caitlin shook her head. 'Of course you know what happened to him, but I thought he was right and I still do. One day, we shall have all that we worked for and in the meantime, we have peace.'

'Thank God,' said Hester. Again, mother and daughter looked at each other, but now there was no barrier between them.

'I'm home,' Caitlin said quietly. 'Do you want me to stay?'

'I do.'

'May I get some wine,' asked Paul, 'so that we can drink a toast?'

'Take anything you can find,' Hester told him.

When he had filled their glasses, they raised them.

'To peace in Ireland,' Paul murmured.

'To peace in Ireland,' Hester and Caitlin echoed.

Jennie having successfully stretched the dinner to serve them all, they moved to take their places at table. For the first time Hester noticed the awkward movement of Caitlin's left arm.

'Why, Caitlin, your arm is still not right!' she exclaimed. 'I thought you told me in Dublin it would improve?'

'It never did. All my own fault, I guess. I should have let Tina take me to her man and fix it, but I didn't want to risk any more trouble for her. She'd already done enough for me.'

'You're right there,' Paul commented. 'If it hadn't been for her, you'd have seen the inside of an English gaol.'

Hester winced. 'Caitlin, you owe Tina so much, you should have contacted her, you should have made some sort of apology for what happened.'

'I've explained why I didn't. It would have been insulting.'

'Maybe you could see her?' suggested Paul. 'Maybe when you go back to Ireland you could stop off in London?'

'I have no plans to go back to Ireland. My work there is done.'

'You'll never see Frances again? Or Madame?'

Caitlin looked down at her plate. 'Poor Madame . . . She's been in prison again, you know. And Frances is still running her boarding house. I don't know if we'll ever meet again. Right now, I'm just glad to be home.'

It seemed that Paul had already told Caitlin most of the family news – Melissa's marriage and birth of a son, Victor's return to Belcarron – but he had given no details of Julio's purchase of the *estancia* nor of his marriage. When Hester spoke of Sofia, Caitlin went pale and spent more time than was necessary putting cream in her coffee and stirring it round and round.

'So, he is married, and to an heiress? Good luck to him, I'm glad he's happy.' Caitlin gave a light laugh. 'Seems you've been unlucky, Mother, everyone else in the family is married, except Paul and me.'

'Caitlin, there's still time for you to marry! You have made terrible mistakes, but they're in the past. Your life is in front of you.'

'Yes, and what do I do with it? I don't want to nurse any more and I've no training for anything else.'

'Mother's just about to sell the book chain,' Paul told her. 'Now's your chance to become a tycoon.'

'You're selling Molloy's Books?' Caitlin looked aghast. 'Mother, you can't! You'd be absolutely lost!'

'I'm not getting any younger. It's time for someone else to take over.'

'Why not you, Caitlin?' asked Paul.

'Me? That's ridiculous, I could never –' Caitlin, catching the sudden light in her mother's eyes, halted. 'I wouldn't know the first thing about running a book chain,' she finished quietly.

'It's just like running any other business,' Hester said quickly. 'I remember saying the very same thing to Tina. You could take a course – I mean, if you were interested.'

'Sure you could,' Paul put in, 'like mother, like daughter – you'd be a natural, Caitlin.'

'I don't know . . .' she murmured.

'Think about it,' said Paul.

'Yes, think about it,' said Hester.

'Everything is happening so quickly –' Caitlin looked up uneasily – 'I mean, are you sure, Mother, you can live with what I did? Apart from what you felt for Cousin Alice, didn't I make it hard for you? Didn't everyone blame you for having a daughter like me?'

Hester drank some coffee and dabbed at her lips with a trembling hand. 'Let's not talk about it now, Caitlin.'

'You know we have to talk, you know it will always be there.'

'People change, Caitlin. Sometimes, with God's help. So Paul and I believe.'

'It's the Church's teaching,' said Paul.

'If I were to say I believed I'd changed myself, would you still accept me?' asked Caitlin.

'Yes,' Hester answered simply. 'I want to.'

Later, Paul drove Caitlin back to her hotel in downtown New York. She had promised to think about taking over Molloy's Books and next day would be moving her things into her mother's apartment, though she would eventually be looking for something of her own.

'I can't believe it's all real,' she murmured, standing with her hand on her brother's arm. 'I want to thank you, Paul, for all your support. When you became a priest, you know, I thought you'd be down on me like a sack of hammers.'

'I never condoned what you did, Caitlin.'

'But you understood why I did it?'

'Let's not go into that now. The main thing is, you're back and you're going to stay.'

As the traffic roared by and the lights of her hotel flashed in and out in the night sky, Caitlin said, 'Are you happy, Paul?'

'Perfectly.'

'You don't miss –'

'I don't miss anything.'

'I guess you don't, I guess you're happier than any of us – except Julio, of course. With his lovely rich wife and his lovely big *estancia*.'

'You'll be just as happy yourself one day, I promise you. You'll be running Molloy's Books, you'll be married, you'll have children. Ireland will seem far away.'

'I shall never forget Ireland, Paul.'

'None of us will forget Ireland,' he said gently.

In her bedroom, Hester said a prayer of thanksgiving for Caitlin's return. 'And I don't mean to America, O Lord,' she whispered, 'she's travelled much, much further than across the Atlantic.'

When she rose from her knees, she picked up Alice's photograph. Alice would have understood. Caitlin had made her peace. It was time to forgive. Her gaze moved to Daniel, looking sternly from a framed picture by her bed. 'You would have understood, too, Daniel,' she said fiercely, 'yes, you would!'

A knock sounded on her door and Jennie put her head

round. 'I'm off, Mrs Molloy. Everything's done. See you in the morning.'

'Thanks, Jennie. Yes, I'll see you in the morning.'

Jennie hesitated, swinging the door in her hand. 'Nice to meet your daughter, Mrs Molloy. Real pretty, ain't she?'

Hester smiled her assent.

'She's going to stay now?'

'Yes,' Hester answered firmly, 'she's going to stay.'

Chapter Forty-Three

Julio, with his 'lovely, rich wife' and his 'lovely, big *estancia*', was indeed a happy man. Sometimes he marvelled at his own good luck, for, having known bitterness and sorrow, he felt happiness was a matter of luck and all the sweeter when it came his way. Yet there was a cloud on his horizon. Following the course of the troubles in Ireland in the English-language papers, he was ever more aware of the troubles in his own country. So much had been expected from the Radicals when they took office, and so little had been delivered, that there had been a natural disillusion, which brought strikes and violence and unease to the *estancieros*. Remembering Argentina's dark past, Julio feared his happiness was a bubble that could be pricked at any time.

Sofia, dancing on air because the Estancia Sentos was now returned to her family, could not understand Julio's anxieties. Though her own fortune was not as large as before, it was still considerable; they would never have material worries and, in any case, the markets were picking up, the *estancia* was making a profit. They had their son, Francisco, their baby daughter, Rosa, they had their friends, their houses, everything they wanted – why waste time worrying about politics?

'Politics, Sofia, govern our lives,' Julio told her, one wintry May evening when they were in the house in Buenos Aires. 'Nothing matters as much as politics. Consider Ireland!'

Sofia shrugged. 'Argentina is not Ireland, we are not divided.'

'We could be. I don't mean by a border, I mean if we were to stand against a government.'

'Julio, any government could be voted out.'

Julio stared into the leaping log fire. 'I am thinking of the military,' he said slowly. 'The last war they fought was in 1860. I see them looking around for something else.'

'What sort of thing?'

'Power.'

Sofia smiled. 'That's ridiculous, Julio, soldiers don't govern.'

'Generals do. Or, may want to. The middle class is weak; if the landowners were to side with them –' Julio shook his head – 'anything could happen.'

'I'm sure you're worrying about nothing. You're a landowner, but you wouldn't side with the military.'

'True.' Julio lay back, letting his eyes rest with pleasure on his wife's attractive Sentos face. 'Maybe I'm just not used to being so happy. I'm afraid it might not last.'

Sofia stretched out to take his hand. 'We are happy, aren't we? Oh, I'm just so glad Victor let the *estancia* go!'

'He needn't have done, he could have got a loan to carry on.'

'Why, yes, he got a loan from me!'

'I don't mean from us. With the collateral he had, he could have gone anywhere. Things were never as black as he painted them.'

'Then why did he agree?'

'I think he couldn't face living here, not being able to do the things he used to do. When Doña Alicia died, it was the perfect excuse for him to go home.'

'Thank God!' Sofia's dark eyes rested on Julio. 'It was difficult for him at first, going back to the troubles, but now Ireland is at peace. So will your American friend have gone home?'

Julio sat up and shook a warning finger. 'Sofia, please don't let's get involved talking about her. I never even think of her.'

'I'm sure she thinks of you.' Sofia's brow darkened. 'Would you swear you never think of her, Julio?'

He gave a patient sigh. 'Obviously, with all the violence in Ireland, I've wondered if she was all right. I'd be a callous man not to do that.'

'You still love her!' Sofia cried. 'I know you do! If she had taken you, you would never have come back to Argentina, your own country! Oh, I was so happy a moment ago, now I feel it is the end of the world!'

'Sofia, Sofia . . .' He drew her gently into his arms. 'It's not the end of the world. I don't love Caitlin. I did once, that can't be denied, but she was my first love.' He kissed Sofia on the lips. 'You're my true love, that is the difference.'

'Your true love,' she repeated softly. 'Oh, that's beautiful, Julio. I'm sorry, I'm so sorry, my darling. You are so good, so kind and I have this terrible jealousy – will you forgive me?'

'There's nothing to forgive.' He let her go and stooped to pile more wood on the fire. When he had finished, he looked up again at the portrait of Don Enriques. 'He would have been pleased that you're back here, wouldn't he?'

'Yes, but if he had left a share to my grandfather, there would never have been any trouble.'

'It was his legal right to leave the *estancia* to his wife and he loved her, as I love you.'

Their mouths met in a long, passionate kiss, before Sofia drew away, glancing at the clock in the corner. 'I wish it were not so early, Julio, I wish we could go to bed.'

'We can still go to bed.'

'Foolish boy! Your father will be down any minute for dinner.'

'Ah, yes.' Lucio, who had in theory retired again, was visiting from Rosario and enjoying time with Julio on the *estancia*. 'Let's hope dinner will not take too long, then.'

'You're an Argentine and you hope that?' Sofia teased. 'In this country, dinners are always long.'

Lucio, still handsome, still courtly, though over seventy, came into the *sala* and bowed over Sofia's hand. Julio poured him a glass of fine sherry and he took a chair near the fire. 'How well you both look,' he observed, raising his glass, 'how happy!'

'That's because we are, *Papá*.' Sofia kissed him lightly on the cheek. 'Now you must excuse me, I must check on Rosa before dinner.'

'A lovely woman,' Lucio murmured, when she had gone. 'You've been lucky, my boy, and I do not speak of Sofia's money.'

'You don't need to tell me, *Papá*.'

'Still, the money has been a wonderful bonus. To be able to buy the Estancia Sentos! I still can't take it in.'

'And still don't really approve?'

Lucio raised his eyebrow. 'Now why say that, Julio? You know I'm delighted for you. To own such land – it is what every Argentine dreams of!'

'Yes, but you remember Don Ricardo. There is a part of you thinks the land should be Wintour land still.'

'Maybe.' Lucio set down his glass. 'It is true I can't forget Don Ricardo, or Doña Alicia, God rest their souls.'

'Doña Alicia would have been happy that Victor is back at Belcarron. I know she wanted that more than anything.'

'Yes, that is so true.' Lucio raised melancholy eyes. 'And if anyone should have the *estancia*, it's Sofia and you. Don Ricardo would have seen the justice.'

'You believe that?'

Lucio gave a solemn nod. 'Sofia is a Sentos, but you're a Wintour. I do not often say this, but it is true.'

'I am Castillo, *Papá*,' Julio replied quietly, and was rewarded by the flash of pleasure lighting his adoptive father's face. 'That also is true.'

When Sofia returned from the nursery, she was struck by the flow of contentment that surrounded her husband and her father-in-law as they sat either side of the chimneypiece, the light of the flames showing their so different faces to be touched by a strange likeness. For a moment, she felt a little apart, then Julio looked up and saw her and an expression of a different love shone in his eyes.

'Like a sherry?' he called.

'Oh, please, there'll be just time before dinner.'

Lucio stifled a yawn. 'I shan't keep you late tonight,' he murmured. 'When you get to my age, you value your sleep.'

As Julio passed Sofia her glass, their fingers touched, their eyes met, and they smiled.

Chapter Forty-Four

It had been unfortunate for the Wintours that the time of their return to Belcarron coincided with the horrors of the civil war. When they arrived in 1922, together with Blanche, it was to a country where murder and crime were painting the land red, where bridges were blown up and houses burned down, where all normal living seemed no more possible than in a town under siege.

'What have we done?' cried Evie. 'We've brought ourselves to a madhouse! How can we bring up our children in a country like this?'

'It's bad,' Victor agreed, 'but in a way, that's our one hope. It's so bad, it can only get better.'

'How?' asked Charlotte. 'Who will help us?'

'I don't know, but no situation can continue like this for ever. It will have to burn itself out.'

'What an unfortunate choice of words! Let's hope we're not burned down ourselves first.'

Charlotte had finally become engaged to Bill Paget, but while the city of Cork, where he practised as a lawyer, was the centre of appalling fighting, there was no question of a wedding. On 11 August, the Free State troops defeated the Republican forces and took the city, which might have been encouraging except that only a few days later, Michael Collins was ambushed on the road to Bandon and assassinated. Charlotte was more terrified than ever that Bill would be caught up in violence when he drove out to see her.

'It's all a nightmare,' she told Evie, 'a complete and utter nightmare.'

'I know. Mama has shut herself into her room and will not come out. She was so keen to come to Ireland, now she weeps for Buenos Aires. I am at my wits' end.'

'I suppose you could always go back to Argentina?'

'To what? We've sold the *estancia*, if you remember.' Evie sighed. 'Anyway, Victor doesn't want to go back, he says there's no life for him there now. It's strange, Charlotte, at one time he never cared at all for Belcarron. Now all he wants to do is to stay here and look after it.'

'He's a true Wintour, after all,' said Charlotte.

Victor was right. The situation did get better, it did eventually burn itself out. The anti-Treaty men gave up the fight, the scarlet faded from the green, and Ireland woke up to an unknown, untried peace.

'Can one trust it?' asked Evie.

'Yes, this time we can,' Victor replied. 'It was a war and it's over. We have another armistice.'

'And plenty of casualties.'

'Oh, yes,' Victor said shortly. 'You don't avoid casualties by calling "Pax". But we have to be grateful – Belcarron has survived. Other families haven't been so lucky.'

'I suppose they can rebuild?' she ventured.

'I'm not sure there'd be any point,' he replied. 'Are people like us going to fit into this new Irish Free State?'

She stared at him. 'Victor, you're not thinking of giving up Belcarron?'

'Good God, no! Why ever should I?'

'Well, I just thought – the way you were talking –'

'Look –' Victor stabbed the air with his finger, as his face went red – 'whether the new state thinks we fit in or not, we stay here! Let them fit themselves round us, if they like. We are the Wintours of Belcarron and they'd better not forget it!'

'All right, don't get worked up,' Evie said calmly. 'I understand you.'

'Just as long as they do!'

Like everyone else, the Wintours had to pick themselves up after the civil war and try to adjust to a new way of living. 'When you've been under siege, it's not so easy to think you can just come out and walk down the street,' Charlotte commented.

'Maybe not,' Evie replied, 'but it's heaven all the same.'

'No regrets now for Argentina?'

'Not really. Especially as Mama has come out into the light of day. She has really been enjoying meeting all the county, you know – calls them "*gente decente*" . . .' Evie gave a tremulous smile. 'Oh, but it's so wonderful to see her happy again, or, at least, not quite so sad.'

'And now I expect you'll be wanting to make changes?' Charlotte asked, after a pause. 'Couple of new brooms like you and Victor?'

'More repairs than changes, I think. But talking of changes, Bridie and Maisie have asked to have a word. I think they must be wanting to retire.'

'Retire? Bridie and Maisie?' Charlotte's face showed her concern. 'Oh, no, that's not possible, Belcarron would never be the same! They're the last link with the old days.'

'With Victor's mother,' Evie said quietly. 'I know, but they're tired, they need a rest. I feel I must let them go.'

''Tisn't that we're not wanting to work for you, ma'am,' Bridie sighed in the cavernous Belcarron kitchen. 'As the Lord says, 'tis the spirit that is willing, but the body that is weak. Maisie and me are weak, ma'am, and that's the truth of it.'

'The truth,' Maisie agreed. Her gaze went over the vast cooking range and the scrubbed table, the dresser with its plates and cups on hooks, the rows of knives and ladles and wooden spoons, and a tear coursed down her cheek. 'Though 'tis missing this I'll be, and wondering who'll be using my things when I'm away.' She glanced at Evie. ''Twas me cooked the dinner for Mr Victor's twenty-first, ma'am, you'll not be knowing that.'

''Twas me served it,' said Bridie, 'haven't I served dinners at Belcarron for more than thirty years?'

'Oh, Bridie,' Evie murmured, taking her hand, 'must you go? I don't think we can do without you.'

Bridie's mind was made up, however, and so was Maisie's. With the money Jack and Alice had left them, they could afford to buy one of the cottages facing the harbour, they could live together and still see Belcarron. And wouldn't the family be coming down to see them, then? Miss Charlotte and Miss Tina, Mrs Wintour herself and the children? Bridie raised drenched blue eyes to Evie. 'Sure, 'tis not goodbye we'll be saying, ma'am.'

'So, I must be finding new staff,' Evie told Victor, 'which won't be easy. As your mother used to tell us, girls don't like working in these old houses now.'

'Money will buy any staff you need,' Victor replied. 'Mother probably never understood that. Just offer high wages and see what happens.'

Evie took his advice and found it good. By the time Bridie and Maisie had tearfully moved out, Belcarron had a new cook, a parlourmaid, a housemaid and a kitchen maid, though how she was to manage with everyone new at the same time, Evie said she couldn't imagine. Still, Mrs Fahy, the middle-aged cook from Cork, seemed very competent and said she would soon have Millie Brennan and the Duffy sisters up to scratch, while Joey Moore from Skibbereen would get the grounds into shape and Terry Gilling, an ex-soldier Victor had found, would look after the two motors and Rickie's pony. For the first time in years, it seemed, Belcarron was operating on something more than a skeleton staff, though Victor said it still wasn't as good as the old days, when the place had been full of servants, all costing a fraction of what he had to pay out now.

'Times have changed,' Charlotte told him. 'Everything has changed, haven't you noticed?'

And I wonder if you'll be the next one to make a change? thought Evie, who had caught a restlessness in Charlotte's manner and occasionally a small, secret smile that made her think something might be up. Sure enough, the day came when Charlotte and Bill appeared, beaming, and on Charlotte's left hand, next to her engagement ring, was displayed a thin gold band.

'Married!' cried Victor, dropping the *Cork Examiner*. 'Aunt Charlotte, you dark horse! Why didn't you tell us? We were planning a big do!'

'Exactly what we didn't want, old man,' Bill said, his serious gaze scarcely straying from Charlotte, who was looking supremely elegant in a blue and grey two-piece with a white hat. 'We preferred to slope off to a register office and have a quiet little ceremony with a couple of my clerks as witnesses, then drive away, we're not saying where.'

'But first we had to come back to you to say goodbye,' Charlotte added. 'Evie, I'll move my things out when I come back.'

'You're going to live in Cork?' asked Evie. 'Oh, Charlotte, this is awful, I shall miss you so much.'

'Bill has given me carte blanche to do up his house just the way I want. But you won't be getting rid of me, don't worry, we're planning to buy one of those weekend cottages in the village.'

'The ones Jack disliked so much?' asked Victor dryly.

'Did he?' Charlotte shrugged. 'Well, they're there, aren't they? I think one has to take a practical view. As a matter of fact, Tina and George are thinking of buying one too.'

'But you could all stay here!' Evie cried. 'You know we'd love to have you!'

'You've got enough to do without putting up guests all the time.' Charlotte glanced at her watch. 'But we must fly – where's your mama, Evie? I'd like to say goodbye.'

'She's resting, I'll say goodbye for you. Oh, Charlotte, Bill – all the best to you both, all the very best!'

There were kisses and embraces all round, then Charlotte and Bill were waved away down the drive of Belcarron, with Rickie jigging and asking if people didn't usually throw stuff at weddings. 'I could have thrown some rice,' he suggested, 'or else those bits of paper. I'm sure we should have thrown something.'

'I don't think Aunt Charlotte really wanted anything thrown today, darling, but the next wedding we go to, I promise you'll be given a bag of confetti.' Evie put her arm around her son and went with him slowly up the front steps. 'I shall really miss Charlotte, you know,' she said over her shoulder to Victor, 'but I'm glad she's married Bill, he's so nice and steady.'

'Third time lucky,' said Victor cheerfully, and followed them into the house.

*

Later, after dinner, when Blanche had gone to fetch her embroidery, Evie asked Victor if he would mind if she cleared his mother's room. It had been kept since her death just as she'd left it, but it was such a lovely room, it was a shame in a way not to use it and it would be so nice for Blanche. Of course, there would be Charlotte's room going, but Rickie's was scarcely bigger than a cupboard, he could really do with the extra space of Charlotte's, what did Victor think? 'If you'd rather,' Evie said cautiously, 'we could leave things as they are.'

Victor looked for some moments at his cigar. 'No, you'd better clear it,' he said at last. 'Life goes on. It would be absurd to keep Mother's room as a museum, she'd never have wanted that.'

'Tina and I will do it, then, the next time Tina comes.'

'Just as long as I'm not involved.'

'I thought we might give a dinner party for Charlotte and Bill when they return,' Evie went on. 'Tina and George could come over for it and we could invite the Morrys. Hugh's just got engaged, so it could be a combined celebration.'

'Fine, go ahead. I suppose it's time we did some proper entertaining.'

'Yes.' Evie poured herself another cup of coffee. 'It would be my first real party at Belcarron. I think I'm feeling nervous already.'

While Evie and Blanche sat sewing in the drawing room, Victor limped out to the clifftop to watch the white sails of the yachts returning across the dark-blue waters of the bay. It was a perfect evening, cool, but filled with the special light that comes from the sea, the sort of evening Jack had sometimes talked about when they had been riding the pampas in the heat of the day. Victor moved to the cliff bench and sat down to rest his leg. Poor old Jack! Since his return to Belcarron, Victor had found his brother entering his mind more than at any time in the past. Because he should have been here instead of me, thought Victor, and, pushing back his yellow hair from his brow, stared again out to sea. Maybe that wasn't as true now as in the old days. Belcarron was also entering more into Victor's mind, holding him, as it had always held Jack and his mother.

Yet he did have a special feeling for the South American land his father had loved, the land of space and warmth and colour. He remembered Richard telling him when he was small of the excitement of riding to *rodeo*. Of the early mist clearing and the gauchos waiting for the sign of the circling *capataz*, the wave of the hand, the cry *'Vamonos!'* And then the horses leaping away with the gauchos making for the plain, the sun coming through, the dust rising, the gauchos' scarves flying, as they brought the cattle thundering to their appointed places. 'Victor, there is nothing like it,' his father had said, and then he had seen it for himself and been gripped by its magic. Just as Belcarron's different magic gripped him now. He had made the right decision, yes, one couldn't inhabit two worlds and one was no longer for him. But he couldn't help missing the one he had lost.

Chapter Forty-Five

The dinner party was arranged for the end of August, just a week or so before Rickie was due to go away to prep school. When she had finished writing her invitations, Evie helped his governess, Miss Talbot, a serious English girl, to sew on his name tapes, occasionally feeling her eyes stab with tears at the thought of his departure.

'I don't see why he has to go away to school,' she murmured, not looking at Miss Talbot, 'he's far too young.'

'Well, there's nowhere for him to go to school here,' Selina Talbot answered sensibly.

'But he could be educated at home. You could have stayed on.'

'Boys need to be with other boys, Mrs Wintour, and how would Rickie get on at public school, if he'd never been away from home before?'

'I don't see why he has to go to public school,' Evie answered.

Miss Talbot sighed and clipped off a thread, obviously deciding there was no point in continuing the conversation.

She would try not to worry, thought Evie. They were here, they were happy, it had all worked out well, and maybe Rickie would, after all, enjoy school. Victor said he had.

Tina and George arrived the day before the dinner, both looking well, less strained than in the time of the troubles when the plight of Ireland had added years to their brows. Tina had taken the plunge, rather later than most, and had had her hair bobbed. 'Of course George doesn't like it,' she told Evie.

'Men never do, but I've never regretted cutting mine.'

'Yes, but you suit it and I'm not sure I do. You don't think it makes my nose look bigger?'

'Of course not. You look lovely, and years younger.'

'Ah, if only I were!' Tina sighed. 'Maybe I'd have a baby. You have Rickie and Claire, Melissa has Tim Junior; I must admit, I sometimes feel envious.'

'You have your career and it's splendid.'

'Yes, but I'd like both. I always used to say that to George.'

'Tina, you talk as though it were too late, but you're only in your thirties!'

'But George is in his fifties, it would be too difficult for us to accept a child in our lives now.' Tina changed the subject. 'Shall we go up and sort out Mama's room?'

'So beautiful,' she murmured, walking to the open windows and looking out over the bay. 'Not as big as yours, Evie, but Mama never wanted to move. This was her room always.'

Evie joined her at the window. 'Loved this view, didn't she? But not those weekend cottages, of course. Still, Aunt Charlotte's happy with one, and things can't always stay the same, can they?'

'Any more than we can.' Tina turned to her sister-in-law. 'Are you happy here, Evie?'

'Yes, for the most part. There are things that I miss, naturally, but it's been such a godsend for Mama to have this place to come to.' Evie's eyes grew tragic. 'But I can't help feeling bad about Papa. I know he made terrible mistakes, let everybody down, but he must have suffered so much before he took his life, and now his name is never mentioned. It's as though he had never existed.'

'That will change, Evie. In time, your mother will get over the pain, she'll remember the good years. Then you'll be able to talk of your father again.'

'I hope so.'

'After all, something like that has already happened with Cousin Hester and Caitlin, hasn't it?'

'Yes, and I don't know how it could!' Evie cried passionately. 'After what Caitlin did to this family, I don't think she should ever have been forgiven!'

'Hester wrote to me. She told me Caitlin had been very

much affected by Mama's death and did not work again for the Republican Army after it happened.'

'I don't care, Cousin Hester should still not have taken her back. You surely won't forgive Caitlin yourself?'

'I don't know.' Tina moved to Alice's mahogany wardrobe and began to take out dresses. 'She also wrote to me, but I didn't reply. Do you really believe people can't change for the better, Evie?'

'Sometimes they can, I suppose.'

'I think Victor has changed.'

'And that's for the better?' Evie asked eagerly.

'Oh, yes, he's mellowed, hasn't he? Even shows signs of having a heart.'

'Because of the war. He told me once that if you'd been through the war, nothing could ever be the same again. Scoring points, being top dog, none of it mattered any more.'

'He's certainly changed. And so have you.'

'You mean, since I cut my hair?'

Tina smiled and did not elaborate, but she had not been thinking of Evie's hair. There had always been steel in Evie's character which none of them suspected. It had taken the family tragedy, her own baptism of fire, to change her, as the war had changed Victor. Now her newfound strength would be with her always.

They folded dresses and laid them on the bed. 'What shall we do with them?' Evie asked.

Tina, running her fingers down the dark-blue silk of one of Alice's favourite dinner gowns, said some should go to charity and the rest they would keep. There were trunks in the attic where they could be stored and it would be too sad to let them go to strangers.

'There's Mama's wedding dress, too – did you ever see it?'

'Her wedding dress?' Evie's eyes shone as Tina opened a chest and shook out the beautiful cream satin from its clouds of tissue paper. 'Oh, how lovely! See the tiny waist – imagine getting into that!'

'Yes, Mama was slim in those days and very tightly laced.' Tina carefully repacked the dress. 'Thank God we don't have to corset like that these days! Can't tell you what it can do to the female anatomy.' She looked around at her mother's dressing table and chest of drawers. 'There are all these photographs –'

'Victor as a little boy,' Evie said with a smile, 'and dear Jack. . .'

'Let's put them in a box,' Tina suggested, her voice thickening. 'We can sort them out later. What about these ornaments? Do you think your mother would like them to stay?'

Evie was taking a picture from the wall by Alice's bed and studying it. 'Who's this, Tina? It's not Bridie, is it?'

Tina came up and looked. 'That's Mena, Bridie's sister and Julio's mother.'

'Julio's mother? I don't think I've ever seen it before. How pretty she was, wasn't she? Do you know who painted her?'

'My grandmother. She was a tremedous painter, so Mama told me, painted everything and everybody. There are stacks of her things in the attic.'

'But your mother always kept this one by her bed,' Evie said softly. 'Do you want to take it, Tina?'

'No, it should go to Julio. If we put it with the rest in the attic, I'll send it some time. There, I think we've done all we can, Evie. You'll be having this room decorated, I suppose?'

'If you don't mind.'

'Of course not. Get some colour charts from Cork and let your mother choose, since it's to be her room.'

The two young women hesitated at the door, looking back at the room that had been Alice's, their arms filled with her clothes. Then Tina closed the door and they went up to the attic.

Charlotte and Bill had come over for tea from their weekend cottage and were sitting with Blanche, George and Victor on the lawn, where Tina and Evie joined them. Talk turned to the Morrys, due at Belcarron the next evening, of how Cavan had aged since Alice's death, of how things were at last looking up for the girls, with Daisy nursing at Oxford and *almost* engaged, and Moyra in London, following Tina's example and studying to be a doctor. Hugh, who was now virtually running Castle Morry, seemed to have recovered better than most from his wartime experiences and was said to have found the perfect girl in his fiancée, Penelope Inglis, whose family from Bantry was well known to the Wintours.

'What a relief those Morry girls have found something to do,' Charlotte remarked, accepting tea from Evie. 'There's a limit to the fun in arranging the flowers and visiting the sick.'

'You're thinking of poor Cecily, I suppose?' asked Tina. 'Actually, I believe there's talk of some curate, so it's fingers crossed for her. Oh, but it does annoy me when women still seem to think they have to marry to achieve anything!'

'We're not talking about achievement, darling,' George said lazily, 'only happiness.'

Tina paused in the act of biting into a cucumber sandwich and smiled. 'Maybe you have a point, George, but let's not argue.'

Rickie came running in, apologising for being late for tea, he had been busy with his caterpillars. 'Ugh!' Evie exclaimed, but looked fondly on her tall, leggy son, with his thatch of yellow hair now so like Victor's, but his mother's quiet gaze. 'Are you sure you washed your hands?'

'Of course, Mother. But what can I have to eat? I'm starving!'

As Rickie helped himself to the sandwiches, Bill asked whether he was looking forward to going to school. 'You're due off in a week or two, aren't you?'

'In one week and four days,' Rickie answered. 'Thank you, sir, I think I shall enjoy it.'

'Good for you! I never minded school, did you, Victor?'

'Best time of my life,' Victor said promptly, at which George grinned but said nothing.

'Rickie's not going to Victor's old prep school,' Evie put in quickly. 'That was in England and too far away. We've found a nice school in Cork which we think will do very well for him.'

'I'd have liked him to go to my old place,' Victor muttered, 'but I was overruled. Evie knows best.'

'Of course she does, Victor,' Blanche told him, 'mothers always do!'

'Oh, I'm sure you're right.' Victor reached for his stick and painfully rose to his feet. 'Anyone care for a bit of a stroll?'

'We're all far too comfortable,' Charlotte replied, but Tina, brushing crumbs from her skirt, said she would join him.

*

They moved slowly across the lawn and into the belt of trees they called their wood. It was understood that they would not be trying to scramble down the cliff to the beach. Victor's scrambling days were over.

'We cleared out Mama's room today,' Tina said as they progressed through the trees, enjoying the August warmth, the absence of wind, the shafts of sunlight striking through the branches.

'Suppose it had to be done. What's happened to the stuff?'

'Some we might give away, but most we've put in the attic.'

'I'm glad. Don't like to think of Mother's things going to strangers.'

They sat together on a new wooden bench. Since Victor's return, quite a number of seats and benches had unobtrusively appeared round the estate, attracting no comment, only understanding. Now Victor sat, his face creased with pain, and moved his leg several times to try to find its most acceptable position.

'I wish you'd let me prescribe a painkiller,' Tina said. 'There are new things coming out all the time, you know.'

'A fellow doesn't want to be drugged to the eyeballs.'

'It's not a question of being drugged. Why not use what there is to make life easier?'

He shrugged. 'I suppose I could have a word with old Robson, he looks after me.'

'I'll drop him a note myself.' Tina sat back, relaxing. 'Oh, you know, this is nice. I'm glad you came back, Victor.'

'You weren't so keen at one time.'

'That was before I knew it was Julio who was taking on the *estancia*.'

'I mean you weren't always so keen on me, personally.'

She turned surprised eyes on him. 'We always got on, didn't we?'

'Not in the way you and Jack got on.' Victor looked down at his well-polished shoes. 'I used to envy Jack, you know. I was the eldest, I was supposed to have everything, but Jack could charm the birds off the trees, just by being Jack. I never understood it.'

'Mama loved you just as much as she loved Jack, Victor, don't doubt that.'

'Did she? I was never sure.'

'You were the first-born, you were special. We always accepted it.'

He brightened. 'Tina, I have to tell you, there are a hell of a lot of things I regret. I mean, now that Jack's gone, I know I could have done so much more –'

'People always think that. Death is so final, there's nothing more we can do, ever, so we always think we haven't done enough.'

'I just wish he'd known I did care.' Victor drew a pattern with his stick in the soft earth. 'Don't see how he could have when I didn't know myself until he'd gone.'

'Don't think about it, Victor, you've suffered enough. It's time to look ahead. There's a new generation at Belcarron now.'

'That's true.' Victor struggled to his feet. 'Tina, it's good to have you here. Come whenever you can, and don't worry about buying one of those damn silly cottages, stay with us.'

'We only want it as a base for sailing. We'll still be coming round to see you, if you want us.'

As they retraced their steps, Tina spoke of Charlotte.

'It's funny, you know, but Mama said she'd told her once she was always jealous of Mama, yet it was Charlotte who had all the admirers, Mama was too quiet.'

'Are you saying I'm like Aunt Charlotte?' Victor asked coldly, but Tina laughed and took his arm.

'Not really. I'm the one most like her. We neither of us inherited the Wintour nose!'

'Good God, does it matter?'

'Ruined our lives. No, of course it didn't. Certainly not mine – I found other things to think about. But I suppose Mama and Charlotte might have got on better if Charlotte hadn't had a grievance.'

'Did she ever tell you why she had to leave Belcarron that time?' asked Victor, but Tina shook her head.

'I don't suppose it was much, do you? People got upset about such silly things in the old days.'

They came out from the trees to see the late-afternoon sunshine gilding the house, setting the windows ablaze, touching the newly tiled roof with such splendour that Tina gave a little cry.

'Oh, Victor, the house! How beautiful!'

'You can see where the money's been going. What with the roof and the new generator, we'll soon be drawing in our belts again.'

'My share's mainly gone to my project on poverty. It's criminal, you know, that the poor can't have medical treatment because they can't afford it. Something will have to be done.'

'I dare say,' Victor said, absently, 'but don't worry, I wasn't looking to you for contributions, I'm still solvent.' He laughed. 'If I run out, I can always call on Melissa!'

'Isn't it awful?' asked Tina, 'I keep forgetting her. She seems so absorbed into American life, she's hardly part of the family any more.'

'She'll come back to Belcarron one day,' said Victor. 'We all do.'

The tea party on the lawn had broken up. Millie, the parlourmaid, was clearing the table, while Charlotte and Bill strolled arm in arm towards the cliff, and Rickie pulled George around the side of the house.

'Probably wants him to go and see his caterpillars,' Tina said, with a smile. 'Oh, Victor – here's Claire!'

Blanche appeared at the glass door to the drawing room, holding Claire by the hand. The little girl was wearing a pink sun bonnet and a pink cotton pinafore over her dress and was trying to haul her grandmother towards a toy she could see lying in the grass.

'What is that?' asked Tina, screwing up her eyes in the sunlight.

'Just a painted top, used to be Mother's, I think. Rickie found it with a whole heap of stuff in the attic.'

'Ah, that's so nice,' Tina whispered, 'don't you think so, Victor? Each generation growing up and moving on and another following, all living here, using the same rooms, playing with the same toys.'

'You really want it all to last?' asked Victor. 'I thought you believed we shouldn't ever have been here.'

Before Tina could answer, Claire, who had spotted Victor, came running towards him, calling 'Daddy, Daddy!' Evie, who had joined Blanche, looked on, smiling.

'You'll notice I'm Daddy now?' asked Victor, stooping to kiss his daughter, who was entangling herself in his stick. 'Evie says no one uses "Papa" any more, and I suppose Evie knows!'

'Do I want it to last?' murmured Tina, fondling Claire's soft, red-gold hair. 'What a question! With my head, I agree, we shouldn't be here, should never have been here. With my heart, I'm just so glad we are. I used to have nightmares at one time, thinking I'd come back and find nothing here at all, and during the troubles, they got worse. I don't have them now, though. Oh, Claire, better not touch Daddy's stick!' Tina swept her niece into her arms and put her face against the child's smooth skin. 'Do you know you're a little Wintour? A Wintour of Belcarron? I don't see why it shouldn't last for ever, Victor, do you? We'll fit in to the new state. Why not?'

'Why not?' he repeated, as Evie came to him and took his arm.

'My dinner party tomorrow, Tina – I'm so worried. Who'd have thought, after all that's happened, I'd be worried about a dinner party?'

Chapter Forty-Six

Belcarron was waiting for its guests. All day, the maids had worked under Evie's direction, sweeping and cleaning, rubbing and polishing, and now the house preened itself in the evening light, knowing it was gracious and welcoming, not so shabby as it had once been, yet not too much changed.

Evie, powdering at her dressing table, was pleased. 'At least the house looks all right,' she called to Victor, 'now we only have to worry about the meal.'

'I don't know why you're worrying at all,' Victor replied, tying his black tie, feeling grateful he need no longer wear white tie and tails. 'The staff will get it right and if they don't, who cares? All the guests are old friends.'

'I shall care, it's my responsibility. Every hostess wants things to go well.' Evie studied her reflection and decided she didn't look too bad. Not beautiful, of course, but – she sought for the word – definite. A real person, at last, and as such, she need not mind being in charge. 'The problem is,' she told Victor, 'one always has to rely on other people. I know I can usually rely on Mrs Fahy, but then she has to rely on that old range. We really ought to think, you know, about having the kitchen modernised.'

'I think I'll go down to be ready to greet the guests,' Victor said hastily.

Tina was already on the staircase, standing at the long windows. Victor remembered that she was always ready first, never cared to spend too much time on her appearance, yet she was looking very attractive that evening, in a short, dark-red silk dress, with the Wintour pearls at her throat.

'Victor, how handsome you look!' she exclaimed as he joined her. 'You haven't changed a bit since your twenty-first.'

'Oh, I've changed,' he answered, watching the lights of the yachts bobbing through the dusk. He seemed subdued.

Even when Tina teasingly said, 'That's the wrong answer, you're supposed to say, "neither have you"', he did not smile. After a moment, however, he put his arm round her shoulder.

'Actually,' he told her, 'you're prettier now than you were then.'

'Victor, is that really a compliment?' Tina turned to look up into his face, feeling she was being oddly playful, wondering why, then realising she was trying to lighten his mood. It was a mistake; he was thinking, as she was, of Alice. She gazed out with him over the darkening bay. 'Mama's view,' she whispered. 'Do you sometimes feel her near, Victor?'

'Sometimes.' He glanced at his watch. 'I'd better go down.'

'I'll wait for George.'

As Victor made his painful way downstairs, Tina's thoughts stayed with her mother. This was where she had liked to stand, this was where she had died. It should have been a sad place, but Tina did not feel it so. If one believed in an afterlife at all, Alice must be happy in it, reunited with Richard and Jack. Of course, she had had to leave Belcarron. But did she sometimes return? Sensible and logical though she was, Tina sometimes felt her mother's spirit in the house, not as a ghost or a presence, just as someone remembered so well, she must still be part of the place she had left.

'Are you thinking of your mother?' George whispered, and Tina jumped as she swung round and found him beside her.

'George, you startled me. Yes, I was thinking of Mama. I sometimes feel her very close.'

'Not surprising. Her spirit fills the house.'

'You feel it, too?'

'It's a well-known belief that houses carry imprints of their previous owners.'

'Do you believe that?'

'I can't tell you why, but I think I do.'

Tina turned back to the window. 'I keep being reminded of Victor's twenty-first,' she murmured. 'I remember it so well.

Remember coming down these stairs with Melissa and Cecily, all dressed up, so excited about the ball. That was the first time you noticed me, wasn't it?'

'That's what you think.' George kissed her neck. 'I'd noticed you a long time before the ball.'

'We were all so happy then.'

'We're happy now.'

'Yes, but Mama has gone and Jack has gone, there's been the war and then all the troubles.'

'Let's go down,' said George, 'I think I hear a car.'

Cavan and Mavis Morry were the first to arrive, Cavan showing his customary pain at not seeing Alice, but concerned only for Mavis, who was looking very frail and needed his arm. When George, her cousin, bent his professional eye on her, she only smiled and moved to greet Evie, telling her how happy she was to be back at Belcarron.

'Such wonderful news about Hugh and Penny,' Evie murmured.

'Daisy's turn next,' put in Tina.

'I do hope so,' Mavis answered. 'But what do you think of Moyra following in your footsteps, Tina? You're her great idol now, you know!'

'Really? She must come to see me at the hospital, then, I'll show her some of my work.' As Mavis was borne away to talk to Blanche, Tina said in a low voice to George, 'Do you know, it only seems five minutes ago that Moyra was playing with dolls?'

'Darling, I'm afraid you're getting old,' George told her, with a grin.

Maybe I am, thought Tina; at least, I seem to be living in the past. As the doorbell rang and Kitty and Bernard Mountain arrived, followed by Lionel and Rosemary Pearce, she was more and more reminded of Victor's twenty-first, except that now the guests seemed so much older, so much more weary. It was a relief to see the youthful face of Penny Inglis smiling round the company, as Hugh made sure she knew everyone and her tall, stylish parents looked on.

'Young Penny will think me a frightful old hag to be a newlywed,' Charlotte whispered, but Tina squeezed her arm and told her she looked wonderful, which was true. Alice used to say that Charlotte never cared a row of pins for clothes when she was young, but as she had grown older she seemed to have found the knack of dressing well, declaring one must do something to make up for the wrinkles, and with her thin frame and unbobbed yellow hair, she always looked elegant. Clearly, Bill thought so. As he put her hand on his arm and led her into the drawing room, his sallow face was flushed with pride.

There was much talk of motors and routes and of how long everyone's journey had taken, until Penny remarked on the beauty of the room. 'I came here as a child,' she told Victor, 'but I'd quite forgotten how fine it is.'

'I used to come here as a boy myself,' Cavan murmured. 'The Wintours are our oldest friends.'

'I remember teasing Melissa,' Hugh said, laughing. 'How she used to hate me!'

'My angelic Hugh?' cried Penny. 'I don't believe it!'

'Please,' said Victor, 'take some champagne. This is a celebration.'

Another dinner party, another meeting of family and friends. The house had seen so many. Christenings, twenty-firsts, engagements, weddings. And funerals, though no one dwelled on funerals. Tonight the best silver was out again, glittering, the best crystal, shining, Blanche's exquisite rose centrepiece scented the air, as the wine went round and the courses were handed and it became wonderfully obvious that Mrs Fahy had won her battle with the range and Evie had no need to worry. Toasts were made, first to Charlotte and Bill on their marriage, then to Hugh and Penny on their engagement. Glasses were raised, Charlotte lowered her green eyes, Penny blushed, Bill and Hugh made short, witty speeches, everyone laughed. Then Victor stood to ask the guests to make the usual toast to absent friends and the departed; again people drank, then sat down, their faces subdued, until the mood mysteriously lightened and George cried, 'To the future!'

'To the future!' they echoed, and it seemed to them that it was good.

'We are never going to forget the Great War,' Victor said to his end of the table, 'and God knows how this new Irish state is going to work out, but we're at peace and that's something to be grateful for.'

'And on a lighter note, let's be grateful for something else,' Charlotte remarked, 'for the first time in living memory, Belcarron's roof does not leak!'

People smiled, but Tina said, 'Seriously, that's important. It means Belcarron can go on and on.'

'All thanks to you, Victor,' George commented.

'To Sofia and Julio,' Victor corrected. 'I should really have made a toast to them.'

'They count as absent friends,' said Tina.

'Shall you ever go back to Argentina, Victor?' Charlotte asked.

'Oh, I dare say. One day. I'd like Rickie to see the *estancia*.'

'I'm sure Julio will come back here,' Tina declared. 'So will Paul and Melissa and Cousin Hester. They'll all come back.'

'I came back,' said Charlotte.

'So did I,' said Victor.

'Do you think sometimes this place casts a spell?' asked Tina.

Before anyone could answer, Evie had begun to 'gather eyes', and the ladies rose en masse and made their way to the drawing room.

'Don't stay too long over the port,' Evie whispered to Victor, and he opened his blue eyes wide.

'Oh, come, Evie, this is a celebration, remember!'

'For us too, darling.'

Blanche, who was looking handsome in a dark-green, full-length dress that contrasted well with her still bright hair, took Evie's hand while Millie served the coffee. 'My dear, it's gone so well, I'm so proud of you,' she murmured.

'Thank you, but the staff did all the work. I must go down and let them know I appreciate everything.'

'Evie, you had to organise things. Whether things go wrong or right, it's the hostess's responsibility.' Blanche twisted a lace handkerchief between her ringed fingers. 'I used to think so much about my entertaining in BA. Maybe not enough about other things.'

'Mama, I know what you're trying to say, but you mustn't

blame yourself for what happened. You always supported Papa.'

Blanche shook her head. 'When Victor made that toast tonight to the departed, I felt a great wave of sorrow that I hadn't done more to help your father. I knew something was wrong, at the back of my mind I knew we shouldn't be spending the way we were, but Arthur was so desperate to do well, always trying to be like Edward, I just wanted to think he was successful. It was easier that way.'

'I really don't think you could have done anything, Mama.'

'After his death, I could have held up my head,' Blanche said, with sudden fierceness. 'I could have stood by him.'

'You were shocked, terribly shocked, we all were.'

'But I ran away, didn't I? I came here.'

Evie caught at her mother's hand. 'Oh, Mama, you don't regret coming here, do you? I thought it was what you wanted, I thought it was all the perfect solution –'

'No, of course I don't regret coming here, Evie, but I should have come to be with you, not to hide from my old life, I see that now.'

'Because you've had time to recover. Come, don't you see, Mama, you needed time?' Evie's eyes on her mother were gentle with understanding. 'We'll go back one day and you'll be able to see everyone, make it known how you feel, but now you must let yourself be happy here. We've been give a second chance, we must make the most of it.'

Blanche sighed and looked down at her untouched coffee. 'Evie, Victor always jokes that you know best, but, really, I think you do.'

Evie smiled and moved away, as Mavis came to talk to Blanche and compliment her on her beautiful flower arrangements.

'I always used to arrange the flowers in the old days,' Evie heard her mother say, 'in Buenos Aires, when my husband was alive.'

The men came in from the dining room; there was more coffee, more conversation, brandy for those who wanted it, and the evening pleasantly floated on, until people were in the hall again and goodbyes were being said. Cavan wordlessly shook Victor's hand, as George told Mavis he and Tina would be over next day to Castle Morry. The Mountains, the Pearces and the Inglises lined up to kiss cheeks, make their thanks, while Penny held Hugh's arm and said she hoped to see them all in October at her wedding.

'Your wedding,' Evie echoed, 'oh, that really will be something to look forward to! But poor Rickie will be at school, he won't be able to throw his rice.'

'So sorry,' Charlotte murmured, gliding up with Bill in tow, the last to leave, 'if I'd known he was so keen, I'd have willingly let him pelt the car. Ah, Evie, it's been lovely, we can't thank you enough.' Her gaze moved past Evie to the staircase. 'Seems so strange not to be collecting my candle and going up to my old room, though I suppose none of you needs candles now.'

Tina knew she was remembering Alice, not candles.

Bill put Charlotte's wrap around her shoulders, she waved her hand, then the door closed and the family was alone.

'Well done, Evie!' said Victor, stooping to kiss her cheek. 'I told you you had no need to worry.'

'Yes, I think it went off well – thanks to Mrs Fahy and the girls. Now, I must go and have a word.' Evie, flushed with success and relief, shooed Millie and Ginnie down the back stairs, telling them to do no more, they must simply go to bed, while Victor, yawning, asked if anyone would like a nightcap. Tina and Blanche declined and George, after a moment's hesitation, said, 'Better not, my head's going to be thick enough tomorrow as it is. Wonderful evening, though, Victor, one of the best.'

'Yes, it's been good to see people back at Belcarron. There were times, you know, when I thought we never would.'

'All behind us now, Victor.'

'I hope you're right.'

Evie came running from the back stairs. 'Ready to go up, Mama?'

'Oh, yes, my dear.' Blanche sighed. 'I've had such a lovely evening, but now I must confess, I'm a little tired.'

'I'm more than a little tired!' Evie kissed George and Tina. 'So nice to have you both here – Tina, shall we go and see

Bridie and Maisie tomorrow? I said I'd take the children.'

'I'd like that. Maybe there'll be time when we get back from Castle Morry.'

'Evie's mother certainly seems happy,' George observed, as Blanche and Evie made their way upstairs. 'Looks like you did the right thing, Victor, bringing her over.'

'Seems particularly happy tonight,' Victor answered. 'Maybe she's getting over Arthur at last.'

'Coming to terms with it,' Tina agreed. She caught George's hand. 'If you're really not going to have another whiskey, darling, shall we go up?'

Victor watched as his sister and her husband climbed the stairs, paused, as they reached the long window, then moved on. I'd better start on the locking-up, he thought. Takes me so damned long to do anything these days.

He made his rounds, checking the downstairs windows and doors, a chore that was not so necessary now but was something they still kept up, just in case. Of course, on the terrible evening when his mother had died, no one had broken in, they had simply knocked and been admitted; Victor's rage when he thought of it was as intense as ever. All was quiet when he looked out of the front door, except that the night wind was beginning to stir and a few fallen leaves were scattering. No need to worry now, though, about the roof, however strong the wind, and he smiled with satisfaction as he closed and bolted the great door and hooked on the chain. What a grand thing it was, then, to have a good, sound roof! Tina was right. Belcarron could go on and on. Provided it was allowed to, of course.

He returned to the staircase and, leaning on his stick, looked up the length of it. Seemed a long, long way up. Better get started. Yet, as he put out his hand to hold the banister, he stopped, pierced by the knife of memory. It was the night of his twenty-first birthday. His mother was standing beside him, here at the foot of the stairs, still beautiful, still youthful, her blue eyes on his. 'It's been a good day, hasn't it?' he heard her say, then felt her kiss on his cheek. It was so real, he could scarcely believe it was no longer 1907, he was no longer twenty-one, his mother was not beside him. He still seemed able to hear her voice; she was speaking of his father. He touched her hand, but then he was climbing the stairs, swiftly, easily, as he hadn't climbed them in years, not looking back. He hadn't known what to say to her, he had never known what to say.

'That's how it always was, Mama,' he whispered, 'I never could say what I wanted to say to you. But now you know, don't you, all those things I might have said? And you know I've come back to Belcarron?'

It eased him a little, to think that she did.

In the nursery at the top of the house, young Claire slept soundly, while her nursemaid slept in an adjoining room. Rickie, however, in his slice of a room across the landing, switched on his light and lay awake, worrying about his caterpillars. They needed masses of ragwort, or else groundsel, and who would collect it while he was away? He'd asked the maids, but they'd taken one look at the striped caterpillars and cried, Mother of God, they wouldn't have a thing to do with them, so they wouldn't! And Terry, who looked after his pony, said, sure he'd do it, if he had the time, which meant he probably would not. Miss Talbot might have helped him out, but she had already left, and he was certain the nursemaid would say she couldn't be leaving Claire, so it would have to be Mother, even though she wasn't keen, there simply wasn't anyone else. He couldn't ask his grandmama, Daddy had his bad leg, and the cinnabars must have their food or they would die. It really was too bad, having to go to school, he had far too much to do at Belcarron.

He knew it was very late, but he slipped out of bed to look again at his trunk in the corner. It had his initials on – ARW – they stood for Arthur Richard Wintour, but of course he'd be called Wintour at school. Mother had said he needn't stay if he didn't like it, but he was pretty sure all mothers said that and he couldn't see Daddy letting him leave. He would just have to stick it out and get to like it. All the grown-ups said they'd enjoyed school, so that's what they must have done.

Wish I hadn't got to try, thought Rickie sitting on his trunk.

Suddenly the door opened. It was his father.

'And what do you think you're doing?' he asked.

'I'm sorry, Daddy, I couldn't get to sleep, I've been worrying about my caterpillars.' Rickie hastily climbed back into bed as Victor limped across and sat beside him.

'What's the trouble, then?'

'Well, it's the feeding and looking after them and everything. No one wants to do it and I've got to go to school.'

Victor smoothed back his son's hair. 'Why didn't you ask me? I'll do it.'

'Would you?' Rickie's eyes shone. 'I never thought you'd –'

'I'd what?'

'Have the time.'

'I can still collect leaves, Rickie, even if I have got a damaged leg.'

'I know, I'm sorry. It's the ragwort they like, or else groundsel. I think they like ragwort best. Do you think you could find that?'

'I think so,' Victor answered, with a smile, 'and always remember, Rickie, if you want any help, ask me. Now, better try to go to sleep, it's very late.' Victor tucked in the sheets and stood looking down at his son, who had closed his eyes to please him. 'Not worrying too much about school, are you?' he asked awkwardly.

Rickie's eyes flew open. 'Not really. Except – well – Mother thinks I'm too young, but I'm not, am I? I mean, other boys go much earlier, don't they?'

Victor sat down on the bed again. 'In the ordinary way, you'd have gone when we first came back to Ireland,' he said carefully, 'but bad things were happening then, we didn't think it would be safe for you to go to Cork. All that's over now, though, and you'll be fine, I promise you. You won't be the only boy starting late.'

'That's all right, then.'

'And it's true, Rickie, you will get to like school. I don't say at the beginning – it'll all be strange and you might be homesick – but in the end you'll be happy. You'll make friends you'll keep all your life, and if you stayed here, you wouldn't have any friends, would you?'

'I've got lots of things to do, though.'

'You'll have lots of things to do at school, and the good thing is you won't be far from us, you won't have to cross the sea to England, so that'll make things easier, won't it?'

'Yes.' Rickie stared into space, folding the hem of his sheet between his fingers. 'Now that I know you're going to look after my cinnabars, I'm not really worried, Daddy.'

'That's the spirit.' Victor loosened his evening tie. 'And if anyone – you know – tries to play the fool, you stand up for yourself. Once they see you're willing to do that, they'll leave you alone.'

'Is that what you did?'

'Yes, that's what I did.' Victor stood up. 'Goodnight Rickie.'

'There'll always be plenty of groundsel, won't there, even if you can't find the ragwort?'

'Plenty. You leave it all to me, I promise I won't let your caterpillars starve. Now, go to sleep, or it'll be morning before you know it.'

'May I keep my light on?'

'If you like.' Victor grinned. 'Safer than a candle, eh?'

'Where have you been?' Evie asked sleepily when Victor lay down beside her, settling his leg with his usual effort.

'Talking to Rickie. Little devil was still awake.'

'He was asleep when I looked in!'

'Fooled you. He's been worrying about who's going to feed his caterpillars when he's away.'

'Those ghastly little striped things – I hope he's not thinking of asking me.'

'It's all right, I've volunteered.' Victor punched his pillows. 'I think I've put his mind at rest.'

'I wonder . . .' Evie stared into the darkness. 'He's not really worrying about his caterpillars, Victor, he's worrying about school.'

'We had a talk about that. He understands what's involved.'

'I still don't see why he has to go away. If we'd stayed in BA, he could have gone to day school.'

'Come on, darling – all mothers think like that. My mother was just the same, but I survived, didn't I?'

'And what about Jack?'

Victor hesitated. 'Jack survived, too.'

'Wasn't happy, though, was he? Sometimes, you know, I think Rickie is more like Jack than you, Victor.'

He lay quite still. 'I don't know if that's bad or good,' he said quietly.

'Oh, have I hurt you? I'm sorry, darling, I'm sorry.' She flung her arms round him. 'I wouldn't change you, Victor, for anyone in the world, I'm not trying to run you down! Jack was just more vulnerable, that's all, and I worry that Rickie might be too.'

'Everyone is vulnerable, Evie.'

'I know, I know.'

He gave a groan and held her close. 'But I wish I'd done more for Jack when I had the chance. Oh, I hope you're wrong, Evie, I hope Rickie isn't like him! He minded about so many things. I'll tell you what, though –' Victor raised himself on one elbow and looked into Evie's shadowy face – 'if Rickie really doesn't like school, he needn't stay, we'll find a tutor. How would that be?'

'I could be quite wrong. Rickie may not be like anyone, may be just like himself. And stronger than we think.'

'Like you,' Victor told her.

They lay together, too tired to make love, and listened to the wind outside as it gathered strength, knowing they were safe, they were secure. Belcarron held its Wintours close, as it held its secrets, held its ghosts, and across the dark cliffs and the darker sea, Rickie's light shone, like a tiny beacon.